THE COMANCHE CODE

A BELLE BANNON THRILLER (No. 2)

MIKE PACE

Where the author comes first...

FOUNDATIONS
BOOKS

Foundations Book Publishing

4209 Lakeland Drive, #398, Flowood, MS 39232
www.FoundationsBooks.net

The Comanche Code
A Belle Bannon Thriller
By Mike Pace

ISBN: 978-1-64583-101-3

Cover by Dawné Dominique Copyright 2022
Book Design: Laura Ranger
Book Formatting by Bella Roccaforte

Copyright 2023 Michael A. Pace

Published in the United States of America
Worldwide Electronic & Digital Rights
Worldwide English Language Print Rights

To Anne, of course

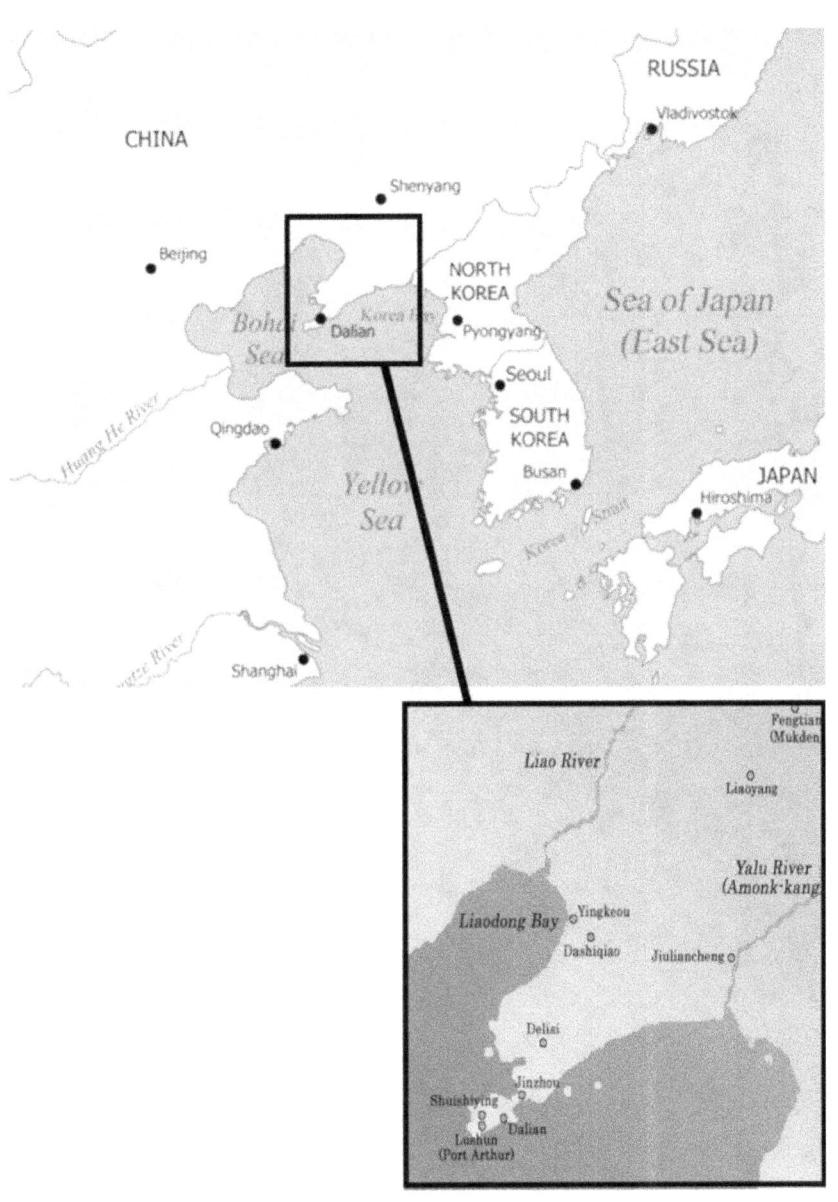

LÜSHUN (PORT ARTHUR), LIAODONG PENINSULA
NORTHEASTERN CHINA

Resting here until day breaks
And shadows fall and darkness disappears
Is Quanah Parker
Last chief of the Comanches

Grave inscription of Quanah Parker, c.1848-1911

"James, will you please put out the light?
**Last words of Theodore Roosevelt to his trusted valet, James
Amos, January 5, 1919**

CHAPTER 1

B elle Bannon was losing a stare-down with a dead buffalo when she heard the faint sound of breaking glass.

She sat on an uncomfortable museum bench in front of a display featuring a life-sized version of the iconic animal while she waited for her sister. Her ears pricked, listening for more tinkling glass.

Silence.

Past midnight. The Panhandle Plains Museum was deserted except for Jenny, Scout, and Belle. Scout, fully mended from the Sundance incident several months earlier, slept at her feet, and her sister was still back in the tiny intern's office, looking for a file needed to complete an American history term paper.

After fifteen minutes in any museum, the smell—dry, musty, like the things they displayed—gave Belle a headache. This museum was no exception, and her fifteen-minute deadline had passed five minutes earlier.

Probably my imagination. She returned to her quilting, whip-stitching pieces of black fabric arrowheads onto a cream background. Fortunately, quilting had a calming effect. Unfortunately, her relaxed mind felt free to wander about on its own, completely unrestrained by its owner. Its first stop was home, Park City, Utah, where the Sundance murder investigation had concluded. The images of those who died—some innocent, some pure evil—filled Belle's head. Next brain stop: Alonzo. She freely admitted she missed him. Her untethered brain then suddenly reversed direction, zooming back three years to the "Zagros incident"—*incident* being a typical military bullshit cover-your-ass term. The faces of the dead Marines flashed—

More breaking glass, this time unmistakable. No one other than two females and a big dog was supposed to be here. Belle stuffed the fabric, needle, and thread into her quilting pouch.

"*Resta qui,*" (Stay here.) She left her pouch on the bench and headed down the dimly lit main hallway toward the source of the sound.

Rounding the corner, she stepped into the Comanche Life room. *Light switch?* She rubbed her hand along the inside of the doorframe. No luck. The lights had been turned off when the museum closed hours ago, and the only illumination came from the faint security light filtering in from the main hall.

Something caught her eye in the far corner of the room under one of the display cases. Hard to tell in the low light, but it looked like broken glass. She took no more than a step or two toward the case when she felt movement behind her.

She turned a split second too late.

A pole slammed deep into her gut, doubling her over. A kick flashed toward her head. Gasping for breath, she managed to duck inside the kick arc and jam her heel down hard on the attacker's planted foot. He lost both his balance and the pole. That was all she needed. Belle sucked in a lungful of air and shot an angry elbow to his throat, knocking him back. He stumbled across the pale light beam from the hallway, struggling to—

A shoe scraped the floor behind her.

This time the pole butt smashed into her temple, knocking her to the floor. The world faded in and out like someone was playing with a dimmer switch to set a mood. Her mood set immediately at the pain-and-brain-fog level.

Both of the attackers were hovering over her now. *Are they Asian? Should've seen the second guy. Getting rusty.* Through her haze, she could barely make out what looked like a spear point aimed at her chest. She tried to roll away, but her body rudely ignored all directions from her scrambled brain.

The hovering spear point inched higher as the attacker readied a fatal downward thrust. The last moments before death. No time for profound thoughts on the meaning of life or musings about a heaven or a hell. Only an icy fear freezing over every cell of her body.

A blur of movement, then a guttural roar. Struggling to focus, Belle saw 150 pounds of pissed-off fly through the air, crashing into the spear holder.

Scout!

He pinned the taller attacker to the floor and sunk his teeth deep into the man's arm, shaking it furiously like a favorite toy. The man shrieked something like "*Qi si wo le . . .*"

Where was the other guy?

She fought to stay alert, but a heavy black curtain steadily descended, fully intent on blocking all attempts to retain consciousness.

CHAPTER 2

Belle's eyes fluttered open to a fuzzy image of Jenny's worried face before fading to black again.

"Belle. . .? Jenny's voice echoed as if she were calling from the other end of a long dark tunnel.

"Belle!"

Her typical museum headache—dull, manageable—had been overridden by the exploding-brain variety. She tried to lift her head and instantly triggered a shock down her spine.

"Lie still." A young male voice.

Sounded like good advice. More voices. Belle recalled her SERE training—survival, evasion, resistance, escape. *It's all in your mind, Marine, and who's in charge of your mind?* I am, sir! *Force yourself to focus on something else. Control your mind, control your pain.* Catchy phrase, Sarge, but truthfully, not a whole lot of help right now.

Gritting her teeth, she forced herself to sit up. The pounding in her head immediately ratcheted up to jackhammer level. "Shrimp?"

Jenny brought her face even with Belle's and offered a reassuring smile. "I'm fine."

"Scout?"

"He's fine, too. If it wasn't for him . . ."

"Yeah, I know."

Belle's vision mostly cleared, and she immediately felt crowded as EMTs crouched tight on each side of her. They poked and prodded, checked her eyes and her vitals. The short one, a kid who didn't look old enough to shave, offered his diagnosis: "Ms. Bannon, we think you've suffered a slight concussion."

No shit. "How about you pop me a few Tylenol, and we'll pronounce your job done here."

"You sure?"

"I'm good, thanks." She pushed herself up, and the pain subsided a bit. Scout emerged from behind Jenny and flashed a goofy dog smile.

A slim woman stepped forward, her strong features distorted with worry. Belle figured she was about her age. She wore jeans and a bright orange and magenta blouse that worked nicely with her bronze complexion.

"This is Nora Yates," Jenny explained. "She's the curator here."

"I came as soon as Jenny called," Nora said. She pushed her long black hair away from her face. "Ms. Bannon, I can't tell you how sorry I am this happened. The police just arrived, and they'll want to interview you if you're up to it."

"What did they take?"

"Thanks to you and your dog, the only thing that seems to be missing is Comanche Chief Quanah Parker's war lance."

———

Belle sat on an uncomfortable straight-back chair in Nora's cramped office with her quilting pouch in her lap. Books, boxes, and Western artifacts—an old split-seat McClellan saddle, a war bonnet, a Spencer carbine—littered the floor, leaving room for just one chair. From a shelf, a stuffed timber rattler coiled on a slab of bristlecone pine, its dead eyes fixated on Belle, ready to strike. The hairs on the back of her neck stiffened. She hated snakes, even dead ones.

An untethered, half-deflated "Happy Thirtieth!" silver foil balloon struggled to remain airborne in the corner above her hero dog. Nora sat at her small desk. A framed photo of a girl, maybe four or five years old, rested on the corner of the desk.

"Happy birthday." Belle was sure her voice didn't sound as festive as the comment warranted.

"A few days ago," Nora responded. "Thanks."

Nora offered, and Belle accepted, a third glass of water. She would've much preferred a beverage from the vodka family of clear liquids, but that would have to wait.

With no place for him to sit, a Canyon police detective, who'd introduced himself as Lopez, half-leaned, half-sat on the corner of Nora's desk, hovering over Belle. Short, middle-aged, with a heavy mustache, Lopez looked like he could shed fifty pounds and no one would notice. They were sitting in such tight quarters that she and Lopez had to interlace their knees. Belle wasn't happy about his shin being so close to her girl-space. He pulled out his iPad and made a few entries. Whatever happened to the battered pocket notebooks detectives always carried in the movies? Belle guessed they'd disappeared along with the crumpled raincoats.

"So, your full name's Belle Bannon?"

That was one question she felt she could answer with confidence. "Isabella. Although nobody calls me that unless they're pissed or really need my attention."

Lopez offered a half-smile and kept his eyes on the notepad. "And you think both guys were Asian?"

"With the low light and my blurry vision, I can't be sure," Belle replied carefully, "but yeah, I think so. I remember one was smaller than the other."

"Did either man say anything?"

"Not that I can remember at the moment."

"Anything else you can tell us about them?"

She maintained a deadpan expression. "The taller one should have a couple of puncture wounds in his arm."

Lopez allowed himself a slight grin. "What brings you to Canyon, Texas, Ms. Bannon?"

"I was here with clients. I'm a hunting guide for Peabody, a national outfitter working out of Park City. Heading back tomorrow."

"Peabody has a good reputation. Never heard of a female hunting guide."

She lowered her voice to a stage whisper. "We're taking over the world."

"Tell me about it. So, where were you shooting?"

"Bows, not guns."

"A female bow hunter, just like that girl in the *Hunger Games.* Catnip something or other."

"Right, just like Catnip." Belle suppressed a smirk. "My clients were hunting wild hog east of Amarillo. Afterward, I took my little sister to dinner. Jenny goes to school here at West Texas A&M. She interns at the museum and will be working here full-time when she graduates in the spring. On the way home, she wanted to stop by and pick up some paperwork. She parked me on a bench in the main hall while she did what she needed to do. Waiting there, that's when I heard the glass shatter."

Lopez entered Belle's contact information and stood to leave. "I'll check hospitals for a severe dog bite. Sure, we'll find them. Good news is, all they took was the lance, thanks to your dog." He glanced over at Scout sitting in the corner with his chest jutting out like he was waiting for someone to hang a medal around his neck. "What kind of dog is that anyway?"

"Part Newfoundland, part royal standard poodle."

Lopez grinned. "So does that make him a Newdle?" He laughed at his own joke.

That Lopez, what a cutup.

CHAPTER 3

The vodka diminished her headache. Belle was not new to concussions and in the past had been warned by doctors to avoid alcohol. She'd ignored them and found that a shot of vodka actually helped ease the pain. While a second round was tempting, she restrained herself. Alcohol also supposedly contributed to her other problem, and she was trying to cut back.

After Belle told Nora the only thing she needed was a drink, Nora and Jenny had insisted on introducing her to the Maroon Buffalo, a late-night restaurant only a few blocks from both Nora's home and Jenny's dorm. Named after the college's mascot, the restaurant was filled with a noisy bustle of college kids. A pleasant mix of beer and barbecue filled the air.

The town was in the midst of a warm spell for March, low 60s, so they'd decided to sit in the restaurant's enclosed outside garden to accommodate Super Dog, who at the moment happened to be curled up at Belle's feet sleeping off a late buffalo burger dinner. She wondered how many other schools celebrated victory on the field by eating their college mascot. *Wolverines? Wildcats? Rattlers? Don't think so. Maybe the Delaware Blue Hens.*

Belle shifted on the cracked Naugahyde chair cushions, which she assumed had once been maroon but now tended toward a muddy brown. They'd spent most of the time over dinner discussing the robbery and how, but for Scout, Belle would've been skewered like a carp on a spear.

"Anybody want another burger?" Belle asked. Both Nora and Jenny shook their heads.

"I still can't believe that more valuable pieces weren't stolen," Nora marveled.

"I'm sure the Canyon police will catch the thieves in short order," Jenny said.

Sitting across from Nora and her future employee, Belle was struck by how much they resembled each other. Jenny, who took after their Italian mother, could well have been Nora's younger sister. Same height, same long dark hair, dark eyes, and complexion. Nora had a slim figure, and Jenny normally did too, but at the moment her figure happened to be un-slim because she was eight months pregnant.

"Love your nails," Jenny said to Belle. "New color?"

Belle could tell by the twinkle in her sister's eye that she was teasing. Jenny couldn't overcome the idea that a tough Marine would fuss about her nails. "As a matter of fact, it is. Autumn Pear." Belle's run-in with the thieves had resulted in two chipped nails, and she'd taken an extra five minutes in the museum restroom to allow an application of the golden brown quick-dry polish to harden before they left.

"I like the color," Nora said.

Jenny changed the subject. "In addition to running the museum, Nora is one of the top Native American symbologists in the country."

Nora patted Jenny's hand. "She's just trying to butter up the boss."

Jenny giggled. "It's true."

"And what exactly is a Native American symbologist?"

Nora's eyes brightened. "Historically, many Native Americans believed not only every person, but every *thing* possesses a spirit, and they reflected this belief in how they communicated by employing symbols."

"Not really that different from other cultures," Jenny noted.

The perky young waitress reappeared. She wore tight maroon shorts and a tighter low-cut white T-shirt with the words, "Go Buffs!" emblazoned in maroon across her chest.

"Sure you don't want another round?" Nora asked.

"No thanks. Think I'll switch to coffee," Belle responded. Physicians routinely advised against a concussion sufferer consuming caffeine. No alcohol *and* no coffee? Right.

"Make that two," Nora said.

The waitress turned to Jenny.

"I'll pass."

The waitress left to fetch the coffee, and Jenny yawned. "I need to walk back to the apartment. It's already tomorrow in Seoul, and Cory might call."

Cory, her boyfriend and the father of her child, only had a short time left on his tour. An Army engineer, before Korea, he'd spent time in the sandbox but fortunately had stayed out of danger . . .

Ricky, Sean, Charles; Ricky, Sean, Charles . . .

Jenny's voice broke in. "You okay? Belle? You with us?"

Shit. She'd been more successful lately barring their images from her brain, but her guilt kept yanking open the damn door to ease entry. "Sorry. Still seeing a few stars."

"Promise me you'll go to a doctor first thing in the morning."

"I'm fine. Honest."

They all stood, and Jenny gave her big sister a hug. Belle planned to leave first thing in the morning and head home to Park City, so this was goodbye for a while.

Jenny embraced Nora. "Thanks so much for, you know, everything."

"You're welcome." The night air had chilled, and Nora broke the embrace. "Jenny, you're shivering."

"I'm okay, it's a short walk."

Nora unzipped her jacket—white, with a full multicolored headdress on the back along with the museum logo. "Here. You're pregnant and we can't have you catching a cold."

"Absolutely not. I said I'm fine."

Nora offered her hat. "Take them. From one mom to a soon-to-be mom."

Belle chimed in, "Do what she says, Shrimp. She's the boss."

Jenny accepted the jacket, zipped it up so it covered her baby bump, and pulled the hat down tight on her dark hair. "Thanks. I'll return them tomorrow." She turned to Belle. "So sorry about tonight. Please take care of yourself. You're my favorite sister."

"I'm your *only* sister."

Jenny smiled, offered a short wave, and left the restaurant.

The coffee arrived, and Belle noticed Nora took hers black. Belle was a heavy-cream-and-sugar gal herself. And the flavorings, she loved the flavorings. Her boss, Harlan, claimed drinking flavored coffee made her some kind of a girly-girl, but he'd never tasted marshmallow caramel crème.

"What a great kid," Nora said. "Everyone at the museum loves her."

Belle offered a warm smile. "It's very nice of you to not only give her a job but also grant her maternity leave right off the bat."

Nora waved her off. "Nothing to do with nice. Jenny's amazing, and the museum will be lucky to have her."

"She was a late surprise for our parents, so I'm almost ten years older. Sometimes she makes me feel like an antique."

"The enthusiasm of youth." Nora leaned back and heaved a melodramatic sigh. "They haven't experienced enough of life to become cynical yet. I have a young daughter, and her energy is both exhausting and stimulating."

Belle glanced at Nora's empty ring finger. "Husband?"

"Ex. You?"

"No husband. I came close to becoming engaged once, for about a minute and a half. Turned out he was a jerk. Funny how I didn't notice when we were dating."

Nora winced. "It happens more often than not. Anyone special now in your life?"

Belle immediately thought of Alonzo. While recuperating in Park City, he'd been approached by some slick government suit from DC about leaving the DEA and joining another federal law enforcement agency. Alonzo wasn't allowed to tell her anything more, but it sounded like secret agent bullshit. He hadn't said yes or no, but at the moment he was overseas on temporary assignment to see if he wanted to make the transfer permanent. Unfortunately, his abrupt departure had interrupted a relationship in the budding stage. "Nothing official."

"So, Jenny told me you're into quilting. How did that start?"

That was a question she didn't want to answer and hesitated longer than she should have. "When I left the Marines, I dealt with some readjustment issues, pretty common I've been told. One day you're a warrior trying to survive in a world of death and destruction and no rules. The next, you're expected to be a peaceful member of polite society. One of the therapies recommended was quilting. The theory is it takes your mind off other stuff." She figured part of her explanation was true, but only part. "I'm copying the designs of authentic Native American rugs. Working on a Navajo quilt at the moment."

"Never heard of that before. Does the therapy work?"

"Sometimes."

The waitress brought a bowl full of various flavoring packets. Belle combined drops from four of them into the coffee with the care and concentration of a research chemist and took a healthy sip. Her own medical opinion informed by experience concluded that the vodka-coffee combo therapy would significantly diminish what remained of her headache. "What's that lance worth?"

"I'll have to check the insurance appraisal, but my recollection is somewhere in the neighborhood of twenty thousand dollars. The longest-surviving of Quanah's seven wives, Topay Parker, donated it to the museum back in 1960."

"Maybe a private collector hired these guys to steal the lance," Belle hypothesized.

"Possible, I suppose. I can't see why the thieves would've focused first on the lance among all the Quanah pieces. Topay also contributed Quanah's headdress, which is much more valuable."

"What about descendants? With seven wives I assume there are a bunch of them, and like any barrel of humans, inside you'll find a few rotten apples. Maybe a member of the Quanah Parker family tree figured he was entitled to make some big bucks selling Grandpa's stuff. He hires these Asians to steal valuable artifacts, and they come away with just the lance because they're rudely interrupted by me."

"Anything's possible, but I've come to know many of the descendants over the years, and it's hard to believe any of them would be capable of burglarizing the museum and trying to kill you."

Belle suddenly remembered the nameplate on Nora's desk—Nora *Parker* Yates. The straight black hair, the razor-edged cheekbones. *Got it.* "You're a descendant of Quanah Parker."

She offered a half-smile. "He was my great-great-grandfather."

Bai Sun waited in the unmarked white rental van parked half a block from the museum. Fen had dressed the wound in his arm with a practiced hand, stopping the bleeding. In the field, Bai had suffered a few bullet wounds over the years, but for some reason the dog bite felt worse. Four Ibuprofen had barely quieted the throbbing pain. He had more powerful painkillers in his kit but couldn't take the chance the narcotics would dull his senses. At least for the next few hours, he needed to remain fully alert.

The original plan had been to take many artifacts from the museum, so attention wouldn't be focused on the lance. Mao had called earlier to confirm the lack of on-site security at the museum after hours. The retrieval of the artifacts should have been, as the Americans say, a piece of cake. He and Fen had been trained to expect the unexpected, and he blamed himself for not making sure the museum was empty. They managed to escape with the lance, but Mao was not pleased, particularly when he learned they'd been thwarted by a woman and a dog.

Mao had quickly adjusted the plan. The operation consisted of two parts: the lance first, then Nora Parker. The lance was now safely wrapped in the back of the van, but the woman was the key. She was the decoder.

Bai glanced at his partner. Short, with the body of a boy, her blank expression did not completely hide her concern. "Do not worry, the woman should emerge at any time." He struggled to hide his own impatience. The woman had to emerge from the restaurant soon. Her home was within walking distance, and they planned to take her when she turned onto Elmhurst, a much more secluded street than Fourth.

The only complication was the tall woman and her dog. If she drove

Yates home, they would have to wait until Yates entered her house. The night before, Fen had closely examined the exterior of Yates's home and reported no obvious signs of cameras or entry alarms. Still, a street extraction would be preferable.

He was hardly surprised that Fen displayed no emotion. Her tenure with MSS, the Chinese Ministry of State Security, extended five years longer than his own. They'd worked together several times before, and he'd never seen the woman smile. Or frown, for that matter. He had no idea how old she was, but he'd see her disarm, neutralize, and kill men much bigger, younger, and stronger. Her colleagues called her *Bishou*— dagger. She could fillet a salmon or a man with a surgeon's precision in the time it took to say hello. Despite her skills, after several unfortunate incidents resulting in an unnecessary accumulation of dead bodies, her superiors had deemed her too unstable for serious missions, and she'd been assigned to routine clerical duties. When he had approached her and explained both the opportunity and the risks of the operation, Fen Lao had jumped at the chance to join him.

"That her?" Fen pointed at a young woman emerging from the restaurant. She carried a baby in her arms.

Bai strained his eyes. The lighting was poor, the night overcast.

Fen's voice brightened. "She have a baby?"

"No, no baby. And too tall. Not her."

He'd heard rumors a while back of Fen giving birth to a stillborn child. She never mentioned it, and neither did he.

A few minutes later a lone figure wearing a white jacket with an Indian headdress on the back exited the restaurant and walked away from them down Fourth Street, all but disappearing in the dark.

Bai recognized the jacket and smiled. "That's her."

Strange. She didn't turn onto Elmhurst.

CHAPTER 4

J enny made her way down Fourth Street, her gait more of an amble given her advanced pregnancy. She couldn't recall a time when she'd been so happy. New baby coming, new job, new life with Cory. And she'd just spent time with the two most awesome people in the whole world.

Nora was amazing, and Jenny had looked up to Belle her entire life. Her sister was the toughest person she knew—male or female. Belle had inherited her dark blond hair, light coloring, and emerald-green eyes from their dad's Irish heritage. Her smooth skin used to drive Jenny crazy, especially during Jenny's early teen years when she had to lather on a bucket of concealer every morning to camouflage her latest overnight crop of zits. Belle had assured her that in a few years her face would clear, and, of course, Belle was right.

Almost six feet tall, muscular—Jenny once saw Belle do a six-rep bench press at 225 pounds—Belle had the kind of body that caught the eyes of many men. Not voluptuous, boobs-falling-out-of-your-dress hot. More like athletic, flat-belly hot. Jenny remembered attending Belle's ballet recitals when she was very young, and her big sister still retained the graceful movements of a dancer. When it came to her appearance Belle had only one obsession—her nails. Jenny smiled to herself. She loved teasing her older sister about the tough Marine showing off her latest mani-pedi.

When Jenny was a kid, Belle had called her a shrimp because of their age and size differences. The nickname stuck. Growing up, Jenny hated the name, but now both viewed it as a term of endear—*Ouch.* The baby kicked her hard. He—or she—wanted to be born.

She heard the rumble of a car engine and glanced over her shoulder. A white van pulled up beyond her and stopped under a broken streetlight. The passenger-side window rolled down. Probably a college parent in town, unfamiliar with the streets. Jenny bent to eye level. "Hi, can I—?" She froze.

The ugly black gun barrel pointed directly at her head.

Belle found herself enjoying Nora's company. A table card hawking the restaurant's "world-famous chocolate fudge cake" caught her eye.

"Interested in sharing a piece of fudge cake?" she asked conspiratorially.

Nora's eyes lit up just as her phone rang. "Sorry, I forgot to switch it to vibrate." She checked the screen. "It's Jenny." She tapped the green button and switched to speaker mode.

"Hi. Your sister and I were just about to share a dessert. Sure, you don't want to come back and—"

"Belle . . .? Is Belle still there?" Jenny asked, her breath ragged.

"You okay?" Belle asked, alarmed. "Is it the baby?"

Jenny's tearful voice came out in snatches between gasps. "I was walking home, and this van pulled up, and they had a gun . . . they thought I was Nora and—"

A male voice with a light Asian accent took over. "We will be in touch, Ms. Yates. Answer calls ending in seven. If you involve the police, she dies."

The call terminated. Belle continued to stare at the phone as if it had passed through a time warp from another world. Jenny? Shrimp? *My little sister?* Somewhere in her body a spigot opened up and poured battery acid into her stomach.

Nora tapped her phone so violently she almost knocked the phone from her hand.

Stress amped Belle's voice up a full octave. "What are you doing?"

"Calling 9-1-1."

Belle snatched the phone away. "No!" She forced herself to take a deep breath and lower her voice. "Not yet. If we do, and the kidnappers find out—"

"How are they going to find out? We have no choice. The police can trace the call."

"I said, no!" More deep breaths. "Sorry, but once the police or FBI are involved, it's out of our hands. We can't take a chance, not yet anyway. Jenny may be twenty-one, but she's still just a kid. And she's pregnant." Belle glanced down and saw her knuckles had turned white from squeezing the phone. She slowly relaxed her grip. "The reason he told us about a phone number ending in seven is from now on communication will be through an untraceable burner phone. He couldn't use the burner the first time or you likely wouldn't have answered. I'm sure after ending the call they removed the battery and SIM card in Jenny's phone."

Nora's brow furrowed. "They didn't say anything about money."

"Our parents are dead, and it's not like we have a trust fund sitting in a bank somewhere. Our uncle makes a decent living as a lawyer in Park City, but the family isn't what anyone would call wealthy. Jenny said they'd mistaken her for you. Unless you have a huge bank account, the timing can't be a coincidence. The kidnapping must have something to do with the lance. You're Quanah's ancestor and the museum curator."

Nora sprang up from the table, almost knocking over her chair. "Give me my damn phone. We need to call the FBI. Now!" Her outburst drew stares from those seated around them. Suddenly self-conscious, she slinked back down into her seat. Her eyes bore into Belle. She grabbed Belle's wrist and spoke in a harsh whisper. "We have to contact the FBI, Belle. They're the ones who handle kidnappings." She bit her lower lip, then snatched a napkin from the table and dabbed her eyes. "My God, the poor girl."

"After our parents died, Jenny was raised by my aunt and uncle. Before we do anything, I need to call Uncle Sal." She tapped her phone.

A few minutes later, Belle finished up the call as they walked to the parking lot. "Don't worry, I promise. Love you." She ended the call and reported to Nora.

"Sal and Aunt Helen are vacationing in Sicily, visiting relatives. Apparently, there's a nationwide labor strike. Airports are shut down. They're rushing out now to rent a car and drive to France or Switzerland, wherever they can find a plane ticket home."

"I could only hear your side of the conversation, but I take it they don't want us to go to the police."

"Aunt Helen was crying so hard I could barely understand her. She looks on Jenny as her own kid, and with the baby coming . . . well, you heard. They both made me promise we wouldn't call the police and take a chance on the kidnappers hurting Jenny and her child. Sal said to spend whatever was necessary to bring Jenny back safe."

Nora shook her head in frustration. "I don't understand. They knew immediately they'd abducted the wrong person. Jenny was pregnant for God's sake. Why didn't they just let her go?"

"Jenny must've seen their faces before they realized their mistake. If they released her their plan, whatever it is, would've dissolved. We need to know what the abductors want."

Nora let out a deep breath. "What they want is me."

"But we don't know why, other than a strong suspicion it has something to do with Quanah Parker. Sal and Helen adopted Jenny after my mom died. I feel I have to defer to their wishes. And frankly, I'm not sure I disagree with them."

Nora heaved a deep sigh. "I don't know, Belle . . ."

Belle's mind spun in all different directions. "Something else. Until we know more, we should think of your security and the security of your daughter."

"Sadie's spending the week with her dad in Lubbock. My ex is well-armed and is surrounded by lots of friends who are well-armed. She's very safe there." From the hesitation in her voice, Belle suspected Nora was trying to convince herself. "But I'll call him to make sure."

"Please don't tell him why you're worried. We can't take a chance of him contacting the police."

Nora paused, then nodded reluctantly. "Understood."

"And you should ask an armed male—colleague, boyfriend—to spend the night at your house."

"No boyfriend, and no male friend I could trust not to go to the authorities."

"Then maybe go out of town for a few days. Visit a friend or a family—"

"Absolutely not. I'm certainly not going to put any friend or relative in danger. Besides, I'm the one the kidnappers really wanted. I need to be close by."

"Then you can share my hotel room. There are two beds. We'll swing by your place first so you can pick up some clothes."

"I'll be fine in my own house."

Belle stopped and faced her. "Listen to me. These people are serious. They thought nothing of trying to kill me back at the museum. My sense is these aren't street thugs, and they'll probably call your number again. We both need to be there when the call comes in. If you were their target, you're going to be somehow involved in the next step."

Another long pause before Nora spoke. "Okay, but first stop back at the museum. I want to pick up my Quanah Parker files."

They climbed into Belle's Jeep Cherokee, and she drove out of the lot, struggling to focus on the road. Jenny was the only family she had left. She could not, she *would* not allow anything to happen to her. She bit her lip hard. No crying, not now. Now she needed to tamp down her emotions and focus, *focus*. A few tears escaped anyway.

"When I stop at home, I'll get my gun," Nora said. "You have a weapon?"

Belle always took a handgun with her on a hunt in case she needed to put a wounded animal down. She'd lost her S&W .44 mag Stealth during the Sundance incident and just bought a new one a few days before the hog hunt. "Yeah."

At that moment Belle wanted nothing more than the chance to use it.

Bai Sun headed north toward Amarillo.

From the back seat, Fen addressed him in their native tongue, and while her voice was soft, her words cut as deep as her famous dagger. "You were so sure."

"I saw Yates leave through the employee entrance yesterday," he responded, more defensively than he intended.

"Was she pregnant?"

Bai paused. He had already conceded extracting the wrong woman had been a mistake and didn't appreciate Fen reminding him of the fact. "I wasn't close enough to tell, but she was the same height, had the same hair color. Mao said she was Comanche; the description matched. And she wore the same jacket and hat."

The girl's voice cracked. "W-what do you want? Where are you taking me?"

Bai switched to English. "So long as no one does anything stupid, everything will turn out just fine." He realized he was speaking as much to himself as to her. He glanced in the rearview mirror and saw the girl slumped over next to Fen. "Would you like some water?" He took care to keep his voice soft so as not to further traumatize her. Not surprisingly, her eyes were red from crying. She nodded. "Fen, please give our guest some water."

Stone-faced, Fen reached down into a small cooler, withdrew an unopened bottle, and handed it to the girl sitting beside her. Jenny Bannon, not Nora Parker Yates. They had the lance but the wrong woman. He was not anxious to report to Mao, but the plan would not be aborted.

The payoff was too high.

CHAPTER 5

The Holiday Inn Express room was typical—clean, tight quarters, two twin beds, TV, small desk and smaller bathroom. The windows didn't open, and the noisy heating system had sucked the last drop of moisture from the already dry air. Between the beds, a crappy painting of the Palo Duro Canyon hung on buckskin-patterned wallpaper showing signs of wear, and the window offered a breathtaking view of the parking lot.

Almost 2:00 a.m. Belle couldn't believe it. Over the previous twenty-one hours, she'd finished up an exhausting hunt, driven her clients to the airport, taken six dressed hogs to the local food bank, hung out with Jenny, been attacked and knocked unconscious by two men intent on killing her, consumed pain pills and vodka, and been told by one of the attackers that he'd kidnapped Jenny and would murder her if Belle went to the cops. She was beyond exhausted, and the Holiday Inn bed tugged her hard like a powerful magnet. Yet her brain wires were dialed up to high voltage, and she knew she couldn't sleep.

Upon entering the hotel room, Nora had planted herself at the small desk and opened her laptop. She'd also brought along a file about two inches thick marked "Quanah Parker." Belle watched over Nora's shoulder as she examined several black and white photos of the war lance.

Why hadn't the kidnappers called? What did they want? And what did it have to do with a Comanche chief who'd died over a hundred years earlier? Jenny was tough, but she had to be scared to death, especially for the baby. *Oh my God, if anything happens*—Belle sucked in a deep breath and forced herself to tamp down her emotions. She was the one on the front line. She'd been there before coolly making decisions with the lives of ten young men at stake, but this was different. Jenny, Sal, Helen, everyone would be counting on her to make the right choices. *If I were them, would I rely on me? Not so sure.*

"Anything jump out at you?" Belle asked.

"You said you thought the kidnappers were Asian?"

"Yeah," Belle answered distractedly. "Although, when Scout was munching on the guy's arm, the man sounded like he was shouting in Spanish. *Qi sole*, something like that."

Nora's fingers flew across the keys. "Don't see anything in Spanish." She switched to a Japanese, then to a Chinese dictionary. "Could it have been *qi si wo le*?"

"Sounds right."

She read aloud from the screen. "A Chinese exclamation, like a person would make if he whacked his thumb with a hammer."

A touch of satisfaction crept into Belle's voice, and she glanced at Scout watching from the bed. "Or if a big spotted dog were ripping your arm out of its socket."

"They could've been Americans who just happened to be of Chinese descent, Nora offered."

"You're the expert. Was there a Chinese connection to Quanah Parker?"

"I have no earthly idea. Pockets of Chinese immigrants were scattered throughout the West at the end of the nineteenth century. They'd provided much of the labor to build the transcontinental railroad. When that work ended, some stayed in America, working mostly as domestics."

"Could they have been employed by Quanah after he surrendered?"

Nora's lips pursed. "Unlikely. Because he'd been born to a white mother, he was accepted into white society and later became a wealthy rancher. He never turned away a Comanche in need, and I'd be surprised if he employed any Chinese labor."

Belle's phone buzzed, and she glanced at the screen. An unfamiliar number ending in seven. Her pulse quickened. "It's them! Jenny must've given them my number." She put the phone on speaker mode and answered. "Hello?"

The same voice with the slight Asian accent. "The lance contains a code. The code leads to a jade box. Please tell Miss Yates to decipher the code and find the box."

"How can she decipher it?" Belle snarled. "You have the lance."

"I'm sure she has photos. Produce the jade box, and the girl will be exchanged. Fail and she dies."

Belle's attempts to smother her rage were largely unsuccessful. "What the hell are you talking about? What kind of code? Is Jenny all right? Put her on the phone! Now!"

The kidnapper's voice remained maddeningly calm. "Answer calls ending in three. If you contact Washington, the girl dies."

"Wait, wait—!" He was gone. Belle tried calling back, but no one answered. "*SHIIITT!*"

"If we contact the police right now, can't they trace the phone's location?" Nora asked.

Belle took two deep breaths. "Sal and Helen were adamant."

Nora softened her voice. "Belle, Jenny's legally an adult. Of course, the views of your aunt and uncle should be considered, but—"

"No 'buts'," Belle interrupted with a steely tone. "Sal and Helen may not have any legal control, but with Cory out of the country, they and I are the only family Jenny has. At least for the time being, I'm going to honor their wishes. Besides, until we know more, I'm not prepared to take any chances. Now, you got a better picture of this lance?"

Nora slipped a color close-up photo out of her file and handed it to Belle. "The weapon extends maybe eight feet, including the slim stiletto blade."

A banded beadwork design wrapped around the shaft, and red feathers protruded from the non-lethal end.

"Are those eagle feathers?" Belle asked.

"Turkey feathers dyed with sumac," Nora explained. She pointed to the center band. "I never noticed this before, but the center design band, the green one with the symbols, is different from the other two. Look how the red beads appear a shade darker compared to the two other bands."

"Which means what?"

"Quanah used the lance in battle going back to when he was a young man. The different shade of beads could well mean the original design was changed."

Belle brightened. "To include the code. Okay, you're the symbologist. What do the symbols mean?"

Nora leaned back and sighed. "If only it were that easy. Comanche symbology is not like our language, where the symbol, a combination of letters formed into words, equates to a specific meaning. A Comanche symbol can mean many, many things, and you really need to know the context."

"Jesus, we don't have time for context. Can't you figure it out? You're supposed to be the expert." Nora didn't respond. "Sorry, she's my little sister, and the idea that at this very moment someone could be doing God knows what to her—"

"No need to apologize. Remember, I was the target. Belle, I promise you I'll do whatever is necessary to bring her back safe. And I doubt they'll hurt her and lose their leverage if they want this jade box. By the way, did you notice he didn't give us a deadline?"

Belle replayed the short conversation with the kidnapper in her mind. She was right. On the other hand, the kidnapping and theft of Quanah's lance didn't appear to be the work of common criminals. The kidnappers weren't going to wait forever, and if they had to abort their efforts they'd leave no witnesses.

Over the next thirty minutes, Belle became quite familiar with every inch of the room—sitting, standing, fidgeting, pacing, standing again—while Nora closely examined the row of ten roughly drawn symbols beginning with a feather shape. The markings were hard to read, and she used a ruler to neatly reproduce them on a sheet of paper.

"Anything?"

Nora sighed in frustration. "More questions than answers. For example, this eagle feather is common throughout Native American lore representing strength, courage, and leadership. But here the feather is all white."

"So what?"

"Never seen that before. The feathers are always two-toned, and one of the colors is dark."

Some of the symbols were apparent even to Belle—an arrow, a four-legged animal. "Are those wavy lines water?"

"Probably. And the single arrow is a common symbol for peace. The triangle with two long lines on top could be an antelope head, and the four-legged animal might be a deer or a buffalo. The last symbol appears to be a moon, but I've always seen it pointing in the opposite direction."

"What about the third symbol, the U?"

"Flip it over so the points are aiming down, and we'd have a common symbol for war, but I've never seen this U before. And the box could be a number of things."

"The box is outlined in white on a field of green. The kidnappers are looking for a jade box. Jade's green." Belle knew her concern for Jenny was causing her to push Nora. She didn't care.

"Comanches didn't deal in jade, but maybe you're right."

Belle struggled to control her impatience. "So, what do the symbols say? A white feather, a buffalo, water, a peace arrow, a backward moon."

Nora closed her eyes and took a deep breath, then spoke very slowly.

"Don't you understand? These few symbols could mean a thousand things."

"Jesus, so what you're saying is you have no idea where the jade box is?"

Nora snapped back. "That's right, *Isabella,* that's what I'm saying. I-don't-know."

She tapped her pen on the small black dot and the vertical arrow. "I've never seen these before either." Her voice reflected her mostly successful attempt to gain control of her emotions.

Belle sought to follow her example and calmed her tone. "The arrow doesn't have feathers."

"It's not an arrow, it's a war lance. But again, I've never seen it positioned straight up that way. These other two lances pointing right are also confusing. A single lance pointing in that direction can mean protection—a warrior protecting his tribe, or even a tribe offering protection to an allied tribe—but two together like that? No. And that tiny black dot next to the box could simply be a beading flaw."

"Maybe the rectangle isn't the jade box," Belle offered.

"I suppose it could represent a structure of some kind."

"Yes! And the dot tells us the location of the jade box in relation to that structure." Belle felt a jolt of excitement. They were making progress.

"It's also possible that the symbols are original to Quanah. Sometimes tribal leaders would devise their own symbology for certain words or concepts that would only be understood by loyal family members."

Belle's excitement dissolved. "Are these markings found on his headdress or any other Quanah artifacts at the museum?"

Nora paused, trying to remember. "No, I don't think so. If I hadn't been told they contained a message, I would've assumed these were random symbols, decorations if you will. I'm sorry, Belle. As individual designs the symbols are impressive, the beadwork high quality. But I see no message, certainly no directions to a location where we would find a jade box. There's a decent chance the kidnappers were misinformed and made a mistake."

Belle did her best to suppress the rising panic threatening to consume her and quickly dialed the burner number. She didn't expect anyone to answer but hoped the call might roll to voicemail. No such luck. She tried tapping a long text message: *Hello. Nora Yates has tried her best, but she can't decode the symbols on the lance. We think you've been misinformed, and you definitely have a beef with whoever told you otherwise. But holding Jenny against her will cannot convert a line of beaded images into directions to your jade box. You need to release her. Jenny's a smart girl, a new-mother-to-be. She's not going to do anything that might put her child in danger. You made a mistake. It happens. Don't make a bad situation worse. Let her go. Walk away. Please.*

"Hopefully it will work," Nora said, but her tone belied her words.

"Problem is, even if they believe me, we have to assume Jenny's seen their faces." She swallowed hard. "There's no way they'll let her live." Saying those words out loud sent a wave of nausea washing through her stomach.

Nora checked her watch. "It's past 3:00 a.m. We both need to get some sleep."

"I can't sleep."

"Try. Neither of us will be able to help Jenny if our minds aren't sharp, and at the moment, my brain is moving quickly toward mush mode." She headed for the bathroom, and Belle reclined on the bed knowing she would be unable to sleep.

Belle knew Jenny was tough. She'd won all-league honors her junior year as a goaltender on A&M's field hockey team. She would fight like a pissed-off mama bear to protect herself and her baby. But she faced steep odds and would be expecting her big sister to save her.

The moment Belle's head hit the pillow she was out.

When Belle awoke, she realized she'd fallen asleep in her clothes. Fine if you're on patrol in the sandbox, but not so cool when spending the night at the Holiday Inn in Canyon, Texas. She checked her watch. Ten after seven. Damn.

Nora wore fresh white denim jeans and a brilliant turquoise scoop-necked top. She was on her phone. "I don't need a reason to make sure my daughter, *our* daughter is safe . . . Please just—" The person on the other end, most likely her ex, must've hung up. She remained quiet for a moment, staring at the phone, and then noticed Belle's eyes were open. "Good morning."

Belle sat up and swung her legs over the bed. "Morning. Your ex?"

Nora nodded. "He can't understand why I called to make sure Sadie's okay. Really can't blame him. I've never done it before."

Belle frowned. "Why didn't you wake me?"

"I was about to."

Belle smelled coffee and saw a large paper cup on the corner of the desk next to a handful of creamer packets. Definitely not from the vending machine. "That for me?" Nora nodded.

Scout curled up at Nora's feet. "I better go walk my dog."

"Already done. The hotel manager has a couple of beagles, and she parted with two cups of kibble. I mixed in a few bites of bacon. Hope that's okay."

Scout's ears perked up, and he looked up at Belle with a contented expression, then licked Nora's ankle. Belle knew that large amounts of fatty meats weren't good for dogs, but Scout was addicted to bacon, and a little bit was okay. Besides, the bag of dry dog food she'd brought for the hunting trip was now empty. "I'm sure he's fine. Thanks." Belle nodded toward Nora's computer. "Any progress?"

"Not really. I've been searching Native American symbology sites, including those of the most renowned experts in the field, but so far I've come up empty."

"The jade box must've been taken in one of Quanah's raids. It had to be small enough for him to carry away on horseback. Which means it could be hidden anywhere."

"The box itself would have no value to Quanah," Nora said. "He'd view it only as something to trade."

"Trade for what?"

"Guns and horses. During the 1870s, the Comanches were the most feared tribe in the West. As their leader, Quanah Parker was directly or indirectly responsible for ruthless murder, rape, torture, and pillage victimizing whites across the southern plains, especially the buffalo hunters who'd stripped the land clean of the herds that sustained the Comanches and defined their nomadic way of life."

Belle thought Nora's remarks came across as unusually smooth, as if she were giving a prepared lecture. On second thought, her role as curator probably put in her situations where she did exactly that.

Nora continued. "So, prior to his surrender, he needed guns and horses. After he surrendered, he required food and supplies for his people. If he ever actually possessed the box, it could be anywhere now."

Belle grabbed clean clothes from her duffel and shuffled into the bathroom. After an in-and-out shower, she emerged ten minutes later dressed in fresh underwear, a plain white T-shirt, and jeans. The pounding spray of hot water on her body had always seemed to jolt her mind from dead stop to fifth gear in a matter of seconds, and she entered the room speaking as if Nora had been party to her ruminations.

"We have to assume the kidnappers have good reason to believe Quanah didn't trade the box for food or guns, and that it remained in his possession or control. Why else would there be a secret code beaded onto the lance?"

Nora paused a second, caught off balance by the lack of ramp-up to the conversation. "It's unlikely the beading was added during the years he was still at war because of the risk the lance would be lost in the heat of battle. The museum didn't receive the lance until 1960. The weapon was Quanah's prized possession, and it's improbable Topay would've permitted anyone else to fool with it after Quanah died in 1911."

Belle mixed portions of three flavoring packets into the coffee and took a long sip. "So we focus on the thirty-six-year span between 1875 when he surrendered, and 1911, when he died. Did he live on the reservation during that period?"

"For the first years, yes. Then in 1890 he built what became known as the Star House and remained there for the last twenty-one years of his life. His descendants still gather at the house in Cache, Oklahoma, every couple of years, for a reunion of sorts. Quanah had seven wives and twenty children, so there are a bunch of descendants. I've gone to the reunion a number of times. The place is pretty impressive. Two stories, eight bedrooms, ten-foot ceilings. He entertained dignitaries—other chiefs like Geronimo, and even President Roosevelt—in that house. The four huge stars on the roof give the house its name. Quanah supposedly added the stars to proclaim he was the equivalent of a four-star general."

"Then while you're trying to figure out the code, let's go to Star House and look around. Hell, maybe Quanah hid the jade box in the vegetable garden." Nora shook her head. "What's wrong?"

"The house was built outside Fort Sill, Oklahoma. His daughter, Linda Parker Birdsong, stayed in the house after his death until 1957, when the Army was about to demolish it as part of the fort's expansion. She arranged for the house to be moved to Cache."

Belle anxiously tapped her phone. "Okay, looks like under a four-hour drive to Fort Sill. Let's go. On the way, we can come up with a reason for the army to let us dig around the original site. We tell them we're part of an archeological exploration. You can use your position as a museum curator. Tell them you're a descendent of—"

"We can't dig around the original site."

"Because . . .?"

"Because the original site's been paved over for a shopping center."

CHAPTER 6

A shroud of helplessness wrapped Belle tight like a straitjacket. When past challenges arose, she usually had a choice of multiple plans of action. The lack of any path forward felt suffocating. She had to move, get out of the stuffy hotel room. Maybe leaving Nora alone to work might help.

She walked Scout around the block to do his business, figuring the fresh air might help her come up with an idea, but she discovered her heartache for Jenny was blocking every attempt at logical thought. Jenny's whole life lay ahead of her—career, marriage, children—and these bastards threatened to strip all that away over a stupid jade box? Belle pictured a face-to-face with her captors. Her fists clenched, her forearms roped tight, and a thin wisp of white light slipped under the door to what a shrink had once explained was her "lizard brain," the part that controls the most primitive, non-rational part of the human mind. The light was intoxicating, like a powerful opiate allowing her to untether from everyone and everything around her. No rules. Only Belle and the object of her rage.

She took a deep breath. She needed to keep cool. *Jenny* needed her to keep cool.

You're the doorkeeper.

Her fists slowly unclenched, and the white light retreated. She crossed the parking lot and headed for the hotel entrance.

She noticed a black sedan, containing four occupants, parked in the far corner of the lot. Interesting, as there were plenty of spaces much closer to the entrance. The driver appeared to be Asian. Was the car there when she'd left twenty minutes earlier? Possible, but she didn't think so. She walked toward the sedan. Likely a group of A&M math professors waiting for a visiting colleague. Perfectly innocent.

The driver spotted her. Definitely Asian, but unlike her attackers, he was bald. He gunned the engine and sped out of the lot. She tried to catch the license plate, but the sedan moved too fast. Again, plenty of perfectly innocent explanations. She briefly considered attempting to follow the sedan in her Cherokee, but the chances of success were virtually nil, so she led Scout back to the hotel lobby.

She stopped at the continental buffet for a couple of egg sandwiches and two more coffees then walked to the elevator. Several complimentary *USA Today* newspapers were neatly stacked on a side table. The headline read: "Congressional Battle Looms in Washington."

Washington.

Nora hadn't moved—still glued to her laptop. Belle couldn't think of a reason to burden her with suspicions about the black sedan driven by a bald Asian. Nora needed to concentrate on decoding the symbols. Still, something the kidnapper said nagged at Belle.

"Washington."

Nora lifted her gaze, clearly mystified. "Excuse me?"

Belle set the food and coffee on a bedside table. "Don't you find it curious that the kidnapper warned us not to call Washington? He didn't mention the local cops, or even the FBI. He said 'Washington.'"

Nora tilted her head. "Good point."

"Any Quanah connections to Washington?"

"Absolutely. Once he surrendered and assimilated, Quanah traveled to Washington over twenty times, not only on behalf of Comanches, but all Native Americans. He'd learned English and turned out to be a natural spokesman."

"Big change from his past life."

"I know. He even became friends with the president. Quanah and five other Indian chiefs, including Geronimo, rode in Teddy Roosevelt's inaugural parade. The president met all of the chiefs prior to the parade, and he really hit it off with Quanah. Remember the photo hanging in the Comanche Room showing Teddy and Quanah posing together on horseback?"

"The only thing I remember about the Comanche Room," Belle said sharply, "is two Asians bent on turning me into a shish kebab."

"Roosevelt signed the photo, 'To my good friend, Quanah Parker, a true Rough Rider.' The president visited him here in the Panhandle, and they'd go wolf hunting together. Teddy was a regular guest at Star House."

Belle's eyebrows rose. "Could there be a connection between Roosevelt and the jade box?"

"No idea."

Belle's pacing quickened, and because of the size of the room, she found herself walking in circles. A fitting metaphor. "Okay, jade's a gemstone highly prized by the Chinese culture, right? You never hear about French jade, or Irish jade."

"And . . .?"

"The lance is stolen by Asians. They want a box made of a material traditionally associated with China, so that fits. Then we have this Washington reference."

"You're probably reading too much into the Washington comment," Nra said gently. "The FBI's headquartered in Washington, they could've simply meant don't call the FBI."

"Possible, but Teddy Roosevelt could be the Quanah-Washington link."

"You're really reaching, Belle. Roosevelt is only one of many options. Quanah interacted with numerous congressmen, agency personnel, and other lobbyists. If we keep layering assumptions on top of assumptions, we could end up miles away from an answer."

Belle focused again on Nora's drawing of the ten symbols beginning with the white eagle feather. She had an idea.

"You said the eagle feather represents strength and leadership. Like a chief?"

"Yes, why?"

"And it's white. A white leader. A president!"

Nora's face brightened. "And the president who had the strongest connection to Quanah was Roosevelt."

Belle was on a roll. "What happens if we limit our time window further to Roosevelt's term in office?"

Nora tapped a few keys and read from the screen. "Roosevelt was president from 1901 to 1909."

"So, if we find a connection among Quanah Parker, Teddy Roosevelt, and China that occurred between 1901 and 1909, you'd have the context you need to work the decode?"

She shook her head. "Belle—"

Belle pressed. "Is it possible?"

She sighed. "Possible? I suppose."

Belle knew she was caught up in her own enthusiasm, but she couldn't help it. "And with that three-point connection maybe we'd even be able to find the box ourselves! Without the lance symbols."

"A real long shot."

"Long shot's better than no shot."

For the next half hour, Nora researched Roosevelt, focusing on China and Quanah Parker. Her efforts revealed the president's interest in the Far East. But the articles almost exclusively dealt with Japan, and specifically Japan's war with Russia in 1904–05, with little linking the president to China.

Belle couldn't shake the ticking of the clock in her head. While the kidnappers hadn't given them a deadline, she knew they wouldn't wait forever. "Look, we don't have time to conduct research ourselves. Isn't there an expert on Roosevelt we can call? Maybe here at the university?"

Nora entered the search request. "Several American history professors at A&M, but nothing indicating they're Roosevelt scholars. How about Dr. Horatio Burke? The National Endowment for the Humanities created an endowed chair in Theodore Roosevelt Studies at Dickenson State University."

"And Dr. Burke's sitting in that chair?"

"Don't think there's a real chair."

Belle read over her shoulder. "I doubt if he's sitting anywhere. It says at the bottom of the entry he died last year."

Nora continued scrolling. "Roosevelt scholars are scattered all across the country. Dozens in his home state of New York, a bunch in California, none in Texas."

Belle pulled out her phone. "Start calling."

An hour of attempts to reach the Roosevelt experts by phone proved unsuccessful. They started with the Roosevelt Trust but were told the woman who could help them was on vacation in the Caribbean. The trust advised them to send an email, and they'd be happy to forward the message. To convey the urgency of the situation they would have to provide information that might trigger an immediate call to the FBI, something they couldn't allow to happen. Nora typed a short message emphasizing her connection to the museum and asked for a prompt response without including any details.

The rest of the experts were affiliated with colleges and universities. Since the spring term had ended, they'd scattered, and the schools wouldn't provide personal phone numbers. They left callback requests, but the chances of the professors receiving the messages and responding in a timely manner were slim.

Nora filled the time digging further into Native American symbology sites. Scout filled the time snoring on the bed. Belle filled the time quilting, her mind trying to connect Quanah Parker, Teddy Roosevelt, and China. Was there a connection, and if so, what did it have to do with a jade box?

Belle checked her cell every thirty seconds, but the phone didn't ring. Sitting for hours in a tree-stand waiting for a whitetail to peek through the brush called for patience. Sitting in a Holiday Inn waiting for a professor to call back while Jenny's life hung in the balance called for action. But what action? "I feel like we're spinning our wheels," she finally said.

"Maybe there's somebody in government who can educate us about a Roosevelt-Quanah-China connection," Nora suggested.

That gave Belle an idea. She tapped a number on her speed-dial.

"Who are you calling?"

"Ben Porter. We served in the Marines together, and now he works for the Defense Intelligence Agency."

Ben picked up after two rings. "Belle, been a while. To what do I owe the pleasure?"

Belle and Ben almost had a thing. After a bloody but successful mission, their squad was awarded a few days leave. They headed to Rome where they spent most of the night reminiscing and toasting those they'd lost. Lots of toasting. She stumbled back to her hotel room and was almost asleep when she heard a knock. She opened the door to see Ben, grinning from ear-to-ear, holding a bottle of Chianti. She invited him in, and one thing almost led to another. Almost. Belle knew he was married with kids, and though difficult at that moment, she'd adhered to an ironclad rule: no sleeping with married men. Later, Ben thanked her for her restraint, and they'd remained great friends ever since.

"I'm in a bit of a jam and need a favor." She spoke matter-of-factly as she knew how he would answer, and she was right.

"Name it." Ben's tone immediately turned serious.

Ben was a straight shooter, and she worried he might have a problem with keeping quiet about the kidnapping. "Before I do that, I need your word you'll keep what I tell you confidential."

"You got it."

She quickly summarized the previous night's events and explained their need for any information that might link Roosevelt, China, and Quanah Parker.

"You really need to go to the FBI."

"She's my little sister, Ben, and the kidnappers have convinced me they're deadly serious. There may well come a time when I change my mind, but for now there's too much we don't know. My aunt and uncle who raised her agree. So, do you know anyone in government who we can turn to?"

"I'm sure there are lots of experts here in the city, but I doubt if any will talk to you without knowing the reason. And if you give them the reason, they'll probably feel compelled to call the FBI and report the kidnapping." After a long pause, "There is someone."

"Great, give me his number."

"One of my old professors at Georgetown. Dr. Moons is a renowned Roosevelt scholar. I should warn you, she's suspicious by nature, and there's a good chance she won't talk to you over the phone, even with me vouching for you. She'll need to see you face-to-face. Hang on a second."

Before Belle could respond he put her on hold, and she filled Nora in on the conversation so far. Less than two minutes later he came back on the line.

"I checked and she's still in town."

"Don't suppose you can tap a few keys and find us her cell number? I'd like to at least try to talk to her by phone."

"Sorry. But I booked you both on a flight from Amarillo to Reagan through Dallas, leaving in ninety minutes."

"That's crazy, we're not flying—"

"I'll pick you up at the airport. Later." He hung up before she could speak.

Belle froze for a moment. Flying to Washington was crazy. On the other hand, if this professor could help bring Jenny home safely . . .

Scout's ears perked up. He knew something was going on. She'd have to leave him behind. Hopefully, the manager could find someone she could pay to walk and feed him. She turned to Nora.

"Okay, let's go."

Nora didn't move. "What are you talking about? Let's go where?"

"Haven't you always wanted to visit your nation's capital?

CHAPTER 7

Trailed by Nora, Belle exited the terminal at Reagan and found Ben leaning against a beige Buick in the no-parking zone. The car's special license plates carried certain privileges. African American, a few years older than Belle, tall, Ben Porter resembled Michael Jordan in his prime.

Belle smiled inwardly. Yeah, he looked like a young Michael Jordan, except Ben was a complete klutz—couldn't jump, slow as shit, couldn't catch a beach ball. Instead of sports, he'd joined the chess club in school and in his senior year took second place in the state finals. He decided to follow his father into the Marines and applied for Force Recon, the service's most elite unit. At first, he'd been rejected—in the eyes of the brass, a six-foot-six NBA clone didn't fit in with their concept of the ideal stealth reconnaissance fighter. Ben persisted, mind changed, and despite his lack of natural athleticism, he turned out to be one of the best the unit ever produced. He'd saved her ass on a number of occasions.

It had been a while, and she was glad to see him. They embraced, and she introduced him to Nora. The moment they pulled away from the airport, Belle anticipated the first words out of Ben's mouth. She was right.

"You really need to consider changing your mind about the FBI. They know how to handle kidnappings."

"Not yet. I figure if we can find this jade box, our hand will be strengthened in negotiating her release." She remembered the point of Quanah Parker's spear aimed at her chest. "I don't think there's any doubt the kidnappers will kill Jenny if we don't find the jade box."

"What time's our appointment with Professor Moon?" Nora asked.

"You're in luck," Ben replied. "She's heading home to Rochester this afternoon, but as a favor, she's squeezing you in before she leaves. You have an appointment with her two and a half hours from now at her office. A word of warning. Don't bullshit her, or she'll bite your head off."

"Thanks." Belle wasn't sure how she was going to manage talking to the professor without bending the truth a bit—the full truth would likely compel her to call the cops—but Belle would deal with that problem when the time came.

"I didn't know how long you'd be staying," Ben said, "but I reserved a room for you at the Georgetown Inn on Wisconsin Avenue, just in case you can't find a flight back tonight. It's pricey, but we have an account there, and I arranged for a substantial discount. You have time to check in, grab some lunch, and walk to campus."

Ben's expression turned sheepish, and Belle quickly realized why.

"Uh, you should know that Tyler's in town."

Belle's face froze in disbelief. "You have to be kidding me."

"Your ex-boyfriend?" Nora asked.

Belle wasn't happy. "He doesn't know I'm here, does he?"

Ben purposely maintained his focus on the road ahead. "We were having a cup of coffee, catching up, when you called."

"So, he knows where I'm going?"

"I didn't volunteer anything, and I doubt if he could hear your side of the conversation."

"But he heard everything you said."

Ben nodded.

Nora asked, "What am I missing here?"

"Nothing important." The last thing Belle wanted to do was talk about Tyler Cox.

Ben pulled into the traffic on the Fourteenth Street Bridge. "For what it's worth, he tells me he's changed."

"Great, good for him." Speaking of men in her life . . . "By the way, have you ever run across a DEA agent named Alonzo Longabaugh?"

"Nope, never heard of him. We don't really interact that often. Why do you ask?"

"Met him in Park City. Nice guy." Her nonchalant shrug fooled nobody.

Ben chuckled. "When Belle Bannon says 'nice guy,' that tells me he might be someone special."

Ben knew her too damn well. She changed the subject. "Maybe while we're meeting with the professor, you could use your unparalleled investigative skills to see if you can uncover any leads on Jenny's kidnappers."

After dropping off their stuff in the hotel room, they set out on foot for the Georgetown campus. Belle noticed the air was much heavier compared to the Texas Panhandle, and the looming rain clouds made it worse.

They found Prospect, a narrow street lined with pricey brick town-homes, and headed west toward the university. As they walked, a dark sedan slowed as it passed, then sped on ahead. Hard to tell for sure, but to Belle, the driver appeared Asian. Or he could've been Italian. Or a Norwegian with a tan.

With time to kill before their meeting, they decided to grab a quick bite and found a table outside the Peacock Cafe. The cafe offered a full sandwich menu and a variety of coffee "enhancements," so Belle overlooked the fact that their chairs were entirely too small to accommodate the average human ass.

"Are you sure he'll be okay?" Nora asked for the third time.

"Positive." She'd left Scout alone in the hotel room with plenty of food and water. For fifty bucks the manager himself had agreed to take him for a walk every four hours so he could do his business. The dog was in heaven—his own bed, plenty of sustenance, and the TV turned to his favorite channel, Comedy Central. He also liked ESPN and the Discovery Channel, but his favorite was CCTV. When Jon Stewart left, the dog had moped around for days.

The familiar chime from Belle's phone signaled a text. "Sal."

"Did he rent a car?" Nora asked.

"Says with the strike, all of the rental agencies are slammed. He's working on it."

"He and your aunt must be going through hell."

"Yeah." They weren't the only ones.

Belle noticed a bald Asian man sitting in a dark sedan parked across the street a few doors down. Could it be the same guy she'd seen in the parking lot at the Canyon Holiday Inn? Had he followed them to Washington? Unlikely, given the short amount of time that had passed. They'd sat toward the front on each leg of the trip, and Belle didn't remember any Asians walking past them on the plane. Unless the guy had access to private air travel, the chances were slim it was the same person. She noticed he wore sunglasses on a gray, overcast day. To look cool? Maybe. Maybe not.

"Don't look up but it's possible we're being watched."

From the little time she'd spent with her already, Belle knew Nora was not one to hide her emotions. Her eyes widened and her body tensed. She glanced toward the car, then caught herself and quickly twisted her head away to stare at the quite uninteresting trunk of an elm tree. "That's crazy. How could they know we're here? We can't assume every Asian male who crosses our path is her abductor."

Belle knew she was right, of course. Still, if even a small chance existed that the men in the black sedan were associated with the kidnappers, then a small chance existed that Jenny Bannon could be inside the trunk of that black car.

"Wait here." Belle pushed her toy chair away from the toy table.

"They're probably innocent people going about their day," Nora said. The nervous tone of her voice suggested she didn't completely believe her own words.

"No harm in checking."

"If it is them, they'll be armed."

Belle didn't care. She decided on the direct approach, not a particularly brilliant plan, but she didn't have time to develop a particularly brilliant plan. Fortunately, traffic was light. She crossed the street and reached the sedan. The driver sat up, surprised. She had to remind herself that the chances these men were affiliated with the kidnappers were remote, like rolling a two or twelve in street craps. The occupants in the car most likely were completely innocent. Four guys waiting for a pal, probably chatting about the latest gallery opening.

Then the driver's three buddies each reached his right hand inside his jacket and kept it there. Maybe they had an itch. Maybe not. Snake eyes.

The driver held up his palm signaling his pals to ice it. Belle wasn't in the mood for pleasantries.

"I'm Belle Bannon, Jenny's sister. Where is she?" Direct approach. The driver's response would tell her all she needed to know. He didn't respond. That told her all she needed to know. She focused her gaze as if she could see his eyes behind the shades. "We can't crack the code. We don't even think it *is* a code. Somebody gave you bad information. We haven't contacted the cops. If you return my sister now, I swear we'll not report the kidnapping. Everybody goes forward as if nothing happened. She's eight months pregnant for God's sake."

Again, he didn't respond.

Belle found that rude.

In the first hour of the first class of the first day of Recon training, the instructor recounted the importance of the surprise element going back through history to the most ancient military battles. It still applied today.

She reached both arms into the car, grabbed his lapels, and yanked his head and shoulders out through the window, pinning his arms tight against the window frame. In a flash, his pals had guns in their hands, but Baldy's body blocked their line of sight. She moved her face so close to his that she could smell his putrid lime cologne and whispered in his ear, making her point as simply as she could.

"If you've harmed her, I will spend every second of the rest of my life searching every rat hole in every corner of the world, if necessary, to find you," she hissed. "And when I find you, you will beg me to end your life."

Suddenly, she felt it. The white light slowly filtered under the door leading to her lizard brain.

No.

She had to focus, to breathe.

Not now.

She squeezed her eyes shut. *Breathe deep . . . deeper . . . slower . . . Hold control . . .*

Focus . . .

The light faded back.

She opened her eyes to see a hand extending out the back window. The hand held a gun. The gun was pointing at her head.

She wrenched Baldy's shoulders so hard he winced in pain. His body now acted as a shield. The gun didn't fire, and the hand pulled back. A glance in the side mirror told her why. A DC police car approached. No siren, routine patrol. She shoved Baldy back into the car. He immediately pushed the ignition, the car started, and he quickly pulled away into the traffic.

The sedan moved fast, but she was pretty sure she spotted a diplomatic plate. A diplomat would have access to private air travel. Made sense.

When Belle returned to the café, Nora was pissed.

"Jesus, Belle, they had guns. Are you crazy? Going off the rails is going to get both you and your sister killed."

Belle couldn't respond, because she was right. Going off the rails can get people killed.

Ricky, Sean, Charles . . .

They ate in silence. Well, to be accurate, Nora ate. Belle's encounter with Baldy had killed her appetite. She paid the bill, and they continued down Prospect toward campus.

Nora's voice softened. "I didn't mean to yell at you back there. I know you're doing what you think's best."

"No, you were right. I need to do a better job of controlling my temper."

"I couldn't believe you yanked the driver halfway out the car window. Pretty impressive. I remember reading a couple of years ago where the Marines decided to allow women in frontline combat. Were you in that group?"

"For a little while." Belle needed to change the subject and reached for her phone. "Better call Ben." He answered on the first ring. She told him about the encounter and described the car with the diplomatic plates. He said he'd check it out and warned them to be careful. Good advice. He asked about the lizard door. She told him she had everything under control.

She didn't think he believed her.

CHAPTER 8

Professor Amy Moon was a thin Korean-American woman in her mid-fifties wearing baggy jeans and a black turtleneck. She had close-cropped gray hair and flashed skeptical black eyes behind thick, blue-rimmed glasses. She cleared a stack of files from the second chair to allow them both to sit.

After introductions, Belle spoke first. "Thanks for seeing us on such short notice."

Dr. Moon spoke in a light, lilting voice, completely at odds with Ben's warning about her no-bullshit demeanor. "You're lucky to have Ben Porter as a friend. He told me Ms. Yates is affiliated with the Panhandle Plains Museum, and you both have an interest in T.R.'s connection to Quanah Parker."

Belle was glad to hear that was all Ben told her. "Correct." She glanced at a black-and-white photo of Roosevelt on the wall. The picture wasn't a formal pose; rather it showed him leaning back, laughing like he'd just heard a funny joke.

"Amazing man," Dr. Moon said, a soft reverent smile creasing her face. "One of my favorite photographs because it most accurately captures his larger-than-life personality. Here was a man whose family wealth ranks him among our richest presidents—he was worth more than $130 million—but he had little interest in money. He wanted to wring the last drop out of an active life, and he was most successful. Now, I'm sensing this is a matter of some urgency, and the reason for that urgency is not something you wish to share."

"That's right," Belle said cautiously.

"Okay, you've piqued my interest. How can I be of assistance?"

"It's not simply the Teddy Roosevelt-Quanah Parker connection," Belle began warily. "Through Nora, I've learned a little bit about that."

"Teddy had a great deal of respect for the Comanche chief and Quanah's past life fascinated him. As you probably know, the President was himself a writer, having authored over thirty books. And that doesn't include his journals and letters. On a number of occasions, he spent time with Quanah talking about the chief's early years."

Nora's eyes brightened. "And he took notes?"

"Exactly."

Belle glanced at a filing cabinet behind her desk. "Don't suppose—"

She smiled. "Unlike modern presidents, Ms. Bannon, there's no Teddy Roosevelt presidential library. Instead, his papers are scattered across many libraries, mostly university collections. They've been indexed and digitized. Your museum might well find them of interest, and if you leave your email address, I'll send along those documents dealing with Quanah Parker."

"But there's another factor," Belle said. "A third point of the triangle —China. What, if anything, could link Quanah, Roosevelt, and China?"

Before responding, Dr. Moon paused a moment as if caught off-guard by the question. "I know of nothing connecting Quanah Parker and China." She nodded toward Nora. "That would be more up your alley."

"What about Roosevelt and China?" Belle asked.

"That's different. Teddy was the first president of what would later be called the American century. In the early years, negative attitudes toward races other than Caucasian were widely accepted. Those attitudes not only involved Blacks but Asians, what the politicians then referred to as the 'yellow peril.'"

"Did Roosevelt support this Asian racism?"

"It's always dangerous to impose today's morality upon those who lived in different times, but yes, like many Americans back then, Teddy did harbor some anti-Black, anti-Asian beliefs. And yet his closest confidant was a Black man, his valet, James Amos, who went on to a distinguished career in the FBI after Roosevelt's death. He even wrote a book about his time with the President."

Belle pressed, "But again, what could possibly connect China to Quanah Parker?"

Nora interjected before Dr. Moon could respond. "Maybe the key is timing. Quanah rode in T.R.'s inaugural parade in 1905."

"March 4, to be exact," Dr. Moon added. "And then a month later he visited Quanah for a wolf hunt."

"Any diplomatic issues involving China during that time period?" Nora asked.

"If you call war a diplomatic issue," Dr. Moon chuckled. "Then yes. The Russo-Japanese War was unique because virtually none of the battles took place on Russian or Japanese soil."

Even Belle could see where she was heading. "The Russians and Japanese were fighting over China?"

"Not a very sexy war, Ms. Bannon. It all came down to warm water. Russia needed a warm water port with easy access to the Pacific. Port Arthur, at the tip of China's Liaodong Peninsula, fit the bill, so the Russians pressured China to grant them a long-term lease of the port. Japan was still smarting from being forced out of Korea by Russia. The friction between the two countries built up, and in February 1904, Japan severed relations with Russia. Three days later Admiral Togo Heihachiro sent ten warships to Port Arthur where they attacked the Russian navy. That started the war, and eleven months later, Port Arthur finally fell to the Japanese."

Belle was confused. "What about China? Port Arthur was inside its borders."

"China was officially neutral. Remember, back then China was very weak. Favoring one of the combatants over the other was a 'pick-your-poison' situation."

"And Roosevelt?"

Dr. Moon gestured toward the portrait. "Teddy, probably more than any other American leader of his time, believed that 'Manifest Destiny,' the idea that America had a moral imperative to expand throughout the continent, applied beyond our borders. He saw America as an emerging world power and pressed for expansion of American influence. But at the time his beliefs were in the distinct minority, and most Americans and elected politicians rejected them."

Nora said, "So he decided to insert himself as mediator."

"Correct, and the two parties agreed. On August 6, 1905, delegations from Russia and Japan arrived in Portsmouth, New Hampshire, to begin peace negotiations. Teddy managed the process from his home in Sagamore Hill on Long Island."

"But Japan won the battle of Port Arthur," Nora asked. "Didn't it have the upper hand?"

"Yes and no. Japan won the majority of the battles, yet its victories had not been clearly decisive. More important, it couldn't continue to maintain its armies and was heading for bankruptcy. But in the end, most would score the treaty as a Japanese victory. Between the two poisons, China preferred Japan because it showed more respect to Chinese citizens during the war. Roosevelt steered the negotiations toward Japan, and Japan was permitted to remain in control of Port Arthur."

"Why would Roosevelt favor Japan?" Belle asked.

The professor paused and glanced away for a moment before answering. "A rumor surfaces every now and then that China cut a secret deal with Teddy to tilt negotiations toward Japan and to protect Chinese interests. Curiously, after Teddy's death in 1919, his executor found a canceled check for fifty thousand dollars made out to an account in a Hong Kong bank controlled by China. That's about $1.5 million today. The reason for the check, what it paid for, and whether it connected to this rumored agreement was never discovered. Ten years later, China came to regret favoring Japan when Japan forced China to grant it a ninety-nine-year lease of the Liaodong Peninsula including Port Arthur. After Japan was defeated in World War II, Russia again took over the peninsula. The port wasn't returned to China until 1955."

Belle had never heard of the Liaodong Peninsula or Port Arthur. She wasn't interested in a further history lesson and wished the professor would get to the point. Was there a China-Roosevelt-Quanah connection or not?

"There's a record of Quanah visiting Speaker Cannon in Washington on behalf of Native American interests in late June of 1905, a little over a month before the Portsmouth negotiations began," Nora said. "Any evidence he met with Roosevelt around that time?"

Dr. Moon gave a confident nod. "If you review Teddy's journal where he recorded his interviews with Quanah, I believe you'll find a total of eight sessions, and if memory serves, one of those meetings took place in June 1905. The president intended to write a book based on these interviews, but sadly, he never got around to it. From all accounts, these meetings dealt exclusively with Quanah's biography; there's nothing in there about Teddy himself, and certainly nothing about China or the Russo-Japanese War." She glanced up at a wall clock. "I'm afraid I have another appointment so . . ."

Belle couldn't think of anything else to ask her. No connection linked Quanah Parker to China through President Roosevelt. Their flight and visit had been a waste of precious time. "Thanks again for seeing us on such short notice."

Dr. Moon rose and shook their hands. "I wish I could've been more helpful."

The sound of splattering raindrops drew her attention to the window. "Do you have an umbrella?"

"We traveled light," Nora responded.

She reached behind her desk and retrieved a large blue and gray Georgetown Hoyas umbrella. "Here. I've got a bunch of them in the closet. I'm not going to press you on the reason for your inquiry, but I sense it's a matter of some gravity. So, good luck."

———

Jin Choi and his men silently waited in the black sedan parked on Prospect Street, the staccato pinging from the heavy raindrops pelting the car hood the only sound. Since his confrontation with the tall blonde woman, he'd kept his expression and the tone of his voice free of emotion in front of his men, but inside he was fuming. Bannon had caused him to *diu lian,* lose face in front of his associates, something that had never occurred in his fifteen years with the organization. Fortunately, his opportunity to address the situation would occur very soon. His orders from Peng were to terminate Yates but kill the *gwai poh* only if necessary. He allowed himself a small smile.

He hoped it would be necessary.

CHAPTER 9

The deluge attacked them head-on, pelting the umbrella-like bullets from an M27, and the strong wind made holding the umbrella steady a continuing challenge. Black storm clouds hovered over them like a lid, turning day into night.

Because of the rain, Prospect Street appeared deserted—no people, no moving cars, no dogs, no cats. Even huddled together, they could barely shield their faces from the onslaught. Almost instantly their clothing soaked through to the skin.

Nora had to shout to be heard over the sound of the rain clattering onto every solid surface in its path. "Maybe we should duck into a doorway until the storm passes."

"We're wet anyway, let's keep going." The umbrella substantially limited Belle's ability to see ahead. She stumbled on the curb crossing 36th Street, but Nora grabbed her arm, and she regained her balance before falling.

"I had hoped we would've learned more from Professor Moon," Nora said. "The Russo-Japanese War seems like the only thing happening during our time window with any kind of Chinese connection."

"But no Quanah link to the war."

"We have to keep trying."

The kidnappers aren't going to wait long, Belle thought. "Question is, did they bring Jenny here? And what about the diplomatic plates? They would support a connection to a foreign country, and the most likely nation is China. Which also supports the theory that the kidnappers likely aren't Americans of Chinese ancestry."

They crossed 36th Street and passed the Georgetown graduate school building. Nora paused and pointed down a long narrow stone staircase. A plaque at the top read "The Exorcist Stairs."

"One of my favorite movies ever," she said. "Must've watched it ten times."

Belle had only seen *The Exorcist* once on TV as a kid, but she remembered the climactic scene where the priest tumbles down the five-story flight of stone stairs to his death. She recalled having nightmares for a week. They turned away and continued walking toward 35th Street.

"Could be the value—"

"What . . .?" Nora couldn't hear over the sound of the rain, now smashing into the pavement with the force of a fire hose.

Belle raised her voice almost to a shout. "Could be the value of the box is not only monetary but political."

"That might explain—" Nora shrieked as a black-gloved hand slid past Belle's face, grabbed Nora's head from behind, and jerked it back, exposing her throat.

Belle instinctively shot her forearm straight up to block what she knew would be the hand with the knife. Trapping the attacker's wrist tight against her body, she wrenched her torso, grabbed his wrist with both hands, and yanked down while jamming her knee into the small of his back.

He hit the wet pavement face up with a smack. The knife skidded away. In a split-second, she straddled him, her hands around his throat. She was pretty sure she'd seen him before in the backseat of Baldy's sedan. Chinese, thirties, close-cropped military haircut.

"Where is she?" He struggled to roll free, but while strong he wasn't that big, and Belle had little trouble pinning him down. The pounding rain splattered his face, forcing him to squint.

"Biaozi!" (Bitch!)

This jerk had just tried to slit Nora's throat and probably helped kidnap Jenny. The lizard door flew open, and the white light streamed into her brain. She welcomed it in and pounded his head twice hard against the pavement. The white light cut off the sound of Nora screaming and now engulfed Belle's every thought, every action.

She hauled him back to the Exorcist Steps. He was barely conscious and couldn't stand on his own. She bent her knees, and his upper torso flopped over her shoulder. She straightened fast and used the added energy to easily shove the man down the narrow stone stairway. They watched as his body bounced from one step to the next like a rag doll until it finally reached M Street far below. Belle's mind bathed in the intoxicating white light. Euphoria engulfed her.

Something was pulling on her arm. The white light slowly retreated behind the door.

"Belle. . .?"

That same voice.

"Isabella, the black car . . .!"

What black car . . .?

The last wisps of white light disappeared.

Nora's voice. "Run!"

Belle looked up. A black sedan was speeding toward them. Baldy's car. Two hands protruded from the windows. The rain muted the crack of the guns, but not the sound of the bullets pinging against the pavement at their feet. Belle grabbed Nora and dove behind the front of a parked Chevy Suburban where the engine block provided the best protection from incoming fire. Glass shattered as the next volley sprayed just above their heads. Nora screamed. The car stopped. All Baldy and his men had to do were climb out of the car, take a few steps, and shoot them point blank.

Belle heard the rain-muted sound of screeching tires. Another car zoomed toward the scene. More gunshots, but these weren't directed at them. She lifted her head just enough to peek over the Suburban's hood. Another black sedan coming up behind Baldy. Another arm reaching out the window. Baldy gunned his ride. The wheels spun on the wet pavement before achieving traction, propelling his sedan forward.

The second car stopped, allowing Belle a brief glimpse of the driver.

Not Asian. Electing not to give chase, the second car made a three-point turn and headed in the opposite direction.

Oblivious to the buckets of rain drenching them from head to toe, Belle and Nora stood completely bewildered.

Belle returned to the top of the Exorcist steps, and Nora followed. Down below on M Street another black sedan pulled up. Two men jumped out, transported the body of Nora's attacker to the back seat, and in a matter of seconds sped away. Couldn't be Baldy's car, not enough time.

What the hell was that?

Belle stepped out of the shower into the spacious bathroom and dried herself off, then slipped into a plush hotel robe. She'd expected the bathrobes at a pricey hotel like the Georgetown Inn to be top quality, and she wasn't disappointed. Upon arrival, they'd wrung their clothes as dry as they could in the tub, then asked housekeeping to toss them into the industrial dryer. She entered the bedroom where Nora sat at the desk in front of her laptop. She wore a matching bathrobe, and her hair was still damp. She sat on the corner of the bed and nodded toward the TV tuned to the local news channel. "Anything?"

Nora shook her head.

Belle couldn't believe it. "Bullets flying in the heart of Georgetown, and no one reported seeing a thing?"

"I still don't get it. Why would they want to kill the one person they're counting on to decode the lance? Makes no sense."

Belle had gone over it and over it in the shower with no real answers. "Maybe the kidnappers only intended to frighten you to amp up the pressure."

"If it hadn't been for you, that knife would've slit my throat. Not to mention they tried to mow us both down with bullets."

Good point. "The only thing I can think of is there could be two groups, both Chinese. And if I'm right and I really did see diplomatic plates, one may be working for the Chinese government. One group wants you alive to lead them to the jade box, the other wants you dead so you don't."

Nora's expression darkened. "What about the cavalry, the people who rescued us?"

Another question meeting a dead end in Belle's shower analysis. "No clue. When the car turned I saw the driver was a white male, definitely not Asian."

"But why didn't they stick around?"

Belle struggled to tamp down her feeling of helplessness. "I don't know, but I think at this point all we can do is keep working on the decode."

"While you were in the shower, Dr. Moon emailed Roosevelt's notes on his conversations with Quanah."

"Anything helpful?"

"I only had time to skim them quickly. Fascinating from a historical standpoint, but other than confirming the Quanah-Roosevelt connection I didn't see anything that would specifically help us with the code."

After a frustrated sigh, Belle asked, "So now what?"

"Crazy Alice."

Belle rolled her eyes. "Of course. Why didn't I think of that?"

"Sarcasm doesn't become you. There's this old Comanche woman, Crazy Alice. Met her once. She's been around a long time, and I've heard she's fluent in Comanche symbols, particularly the early stuff, so I want to pick her brain."

"If that's so, then why didn't you contact her earlier?" Belle snapped, then paused and took a deep breath. "Sorry."

"Alice Bluefeather runs a string of whores on the Boulevard in Amarillo and surrounds herself with very dangerous people. You have to catch her when she's relatively sober, and even then having a conversation is difficult. She'll say anything for a buck and is totally unreliable."

"Any better ideas?"

"Just that I'd like to know more about this jade box. If you were right and those were diplomatic tags on Baldy's car, then it's unlikely a Chinese diplomat would risk murdering a young woman on America's streets solely because of money. Which suggests the box must have some worth over and above the value of the jade itself. So, while you were in the shower I googled and found this gallery down on M Street that specializes in vintage Asian pieces. They're open till nine, and we're here anyway. As soon as our clothes come back, we could check out the gallery. There's a late flight back to Amarillo through Dallas I think we'll still be able to make. Assuming you think Scout will be okay."

Earlier Belle had called to check on her dog. The manager informed her that Scout not only was doing great, but hotel staff members continued to slip him leftover table scraps. "He's fine."

Nora's phone buzzed. She retrieved it from the bedside table and checked the screen.

"Everything okay?"

Nora read the short text. "I'd left another message for Buck, and he's confirming Sadie's fine, but pissed I'm asking."

"I assume Buck is"

"My ex. He's on the PBR tour and every May comes through Lubbock for the rodeo."

"Sounds like the perfect name for a bull rider."

"He lives in Albuquerque, but Lubbock's only an hour and a half from Canyon so the last couple of years I've let him pick up Sadie and take her down there for a few days. She stays with him and his girlfriend in their trailer. She loves it, he loves it. Gives them some father-daughter bonding time."

"Very civilized."

Buck Yates slipped the phone back into his pocket.

Kind of weird, Nora asking him if Sadie was okay. Why wouldn't she be okay?

He made his way up the ramp toward the chute and glanced at his watch. Ten minutes. The roar of the crowd signaled one of the guys was having a good ride. He thought again about Nora's message. Maybe he'd call her later and ask what's up. Probably just worried about a six-year-old girl dropped into a rodeo environment—lots of tough, foul-mouthed young men who drank too much and fought too much and chased too many women. He could understand that; he'd been one of those guys once. Hell, his stupid behavior cost him his marriage. He'd often wondered what would've happened if—

"You ready, Buck?" Willy was working the gate.

He tossed his phone to Willy, then wound the braided polypropylene rope tight through the fingers on his right gloved hand.

He rubbed rosin on the glove, climbed the wall of the chute, and lowered himself onto the bull. He was a big man, six feet two, 220 pounds, but he'd never had to spread his legs so wide on a mount. Donald D. Duck, at over 1500 pounds, was the largest bull he'd ever ridden, a huge mass of tightly packed muscles ready to explode, the nastiest bull in the pool.

He tightened his helmet. A year earlier Donna had stepped outside after telling him Sadie had something private to talk to him about. He'd grabbed a Coke and slumped down in the faded green upholstered chair. She'd crawled up into his lap and said—he remembered her words as if she'd said them minutes ago— "Daddy, I don't want you to die, so I think you should wear a helmet so those mean bulls don't step on your head and squoosh it." Ever since then—

Willy asked, "Ready, Buck?"

Buck nodded and flushed all thoughts from his brain except his clear intention to remain atop a raging bull for the next eight seconds.

The gate opened. The crowd roared. The bull shot out of the chute.

He only lasted three seconds.

An hour later he'd passed the first phase of the concussion protocol with the rodeo doctor. He'd need to stay away from riding for a few days until they checked again for lingering symptoms, but that was no big deal. He walked with a slight limp and carried his broken helmet in his left hand as he set out for the long trek to his trailer, parked in the corner of the event performers' lot. Every muscle ached, and even with the benefit of four Tylenol the pain from his sprained shoulder throbbed.

As he walked, his thoughts wandered to Nora's sudden concern for Sadie's safety. Mighty curious. His daughter had spent time with him from the beginning of the separation. While there had been bitterness and recriminations like most other marriage breakups, those had passed quickly due to his sobriety and Nora's gentle nature. Her last text said to be on the lookout for Chinese strangers. Weird. He could probably count the number of Asians he'd seen in Lubbock on one hand.

His head pounded as he limped to his trailer. But he was alive and not huddled up in a wheelchair with his brain scrambled, holding a drool cup under his chin. He couldn't wait to show his battered helmet to Sadie.

Because of her, Daddy's head didn't get squooshed.

CHAPTER 10

B elle finished dressing and plopped down on the edge of the bed toweling her hair. Nora, still in her robe, sat at the desk facing her computer but didn't appear focused on the screen. Belle sensed something was on her mind and had a pretty good idea what it was.

Nora rose from her chair and sat next to Belle on the bed, her eyes cast down. "I-I need to ask you about . . . about the man you threw down the steps."

"You mean the one who tried to slit your throat?"

"You saved my life. The way you handled that man, very impressive, especially for a—"

"Woman?"

She offered a half-smile. "Anyway, thank you."

"But . . ."

Nora hesitated for a long moment. "When you had him on the ground he was incapacitated, barely conscious. I told you to stop so we could maybe question him. But you completely ignored me, like . . . I don't know, you were in another world."

She lifted her head and held Belle's gaze, like she was trying to see the thoughts inside her brain, expecting an explanation.

Belle's first instinct was to tell her about the Zagros incident, about how she was responsible for the deaths of Ricky Cohen, Sean Zielinski, and Charles Washington. Fellow Marines. Brothers. But she didn't follow her first instinct, chickened out, and said nothing.

No one spoke for a few moments, then Nora took Belle's hand and whispered, "You don't owe me an explanation. And again, thank—"

A knock at the door. The maid with their clothes.

Nora opened the door. It wasn't the maid. Tyler Cox eased her aside and stepped into the room.

He flashed a smile that would make a used-car salesman proud. "Hello, Belle. Been a long time." He closed the door and stood silent for a moment before his smile edged toward a smirk.

He'd gained weight. Tyler had always been a big man—couple inches taller than Belle, white-blond hair, ruddy complexion, and a body that would put many professional athletes to shame. But he'd gone soft, even jowly, and now a paunch spilled over his belt. His pale skin showed the red blotches of a drinker who wouldn't or couldn't stop. His rheumy blue eyes roamed up and down the women's bodies, taking their time. Nora nervously cinched her robe tighter.

Belle leadened her voice. "What do you want?"

Another smarmy smile. "That's not a very friendly greeting, Belle. What happened to, 'Hi, Tyler, how are you?'"

"Hi, Tyler, how are you? What do you want?"

"I'll leave you two alone," Nora said, heading for the bathroom.

"No need for that," Belle said. "Tyler was just leaving."

Nora paid no attention, entered the bathroom, and closed the door.

Tyler took a step toward Belle, backing her up. He stopped and held up his hands, palms open. "Look, it's been a long time. I just wanted to see you, see how you were doing. There's no reason we can't be friends."

"Actually, there is, Tyler." She pointed to the left side of her jaw.

"I've said it a million times before, and I'll say it again. I'm so sorry." His words dripped with false sincerity. "I'll never be able to forgive myself. But I don't see a scar. The jaw looks great." Another head-to-toe once-over. "Everything looks great."

"Ben says you've changed. If so, I'm glad, I really am. But we're in the middle of something here, and I need you to leave."

His eyes flashed toward the bathroom, and his expression hardened. "Wait a second. Are you two—?"

"Get the hell out of my room, or I'll call security."

"You're a muff—?"

Belle pushed past him toward the phone. He grabbed her arm, jerking her back. She resisted for a moment, then augmented the force of his pull with all the strength she could muster. The result was a sharp elbow blasting deep into his mushy gut. He shouted out in pain and released his grip.

His voice came out in breathless rasps. "You . . . bitch—"

She spun behind him and locked her arms around his head in a move she'd practiced a hundred times in basic recon training. He struggled, but despite his size, she was able to easily control him. *Control.* She felt a mild sense of pride that the lizard door remained closed. What's the saying? Cool, calm, collected? A good sign.

She pushed him toward the door, where she faced a slight logistical problem. To open the door, she would have to release her grip, and Tyler was now flailing about like a fish on a line. A 250-pound fish. She thought of slamming his head against the door jamb, just enough to stun him, so she could free a hand, but she was trying to reduce violence in her life if possible. Fortunately, the door opened with an up-and-down lever, so she was able to use her hip to pull the lever down and open the door enough to insert her foot. Using her leg to open the door wider, she shoved him out into the hallway. She resisted the temptation to trip him—after all, there'd been a time when she'd shared a bed with the idiot. She pulled the door shut and checked the peephole. He stared back at her, knowing she was watching. She expected a finger, but instead, he smiled, blew her a kiss, and shuffled off.

It wasn't the gesture that bothered her. Rather, the look of venom in his eyes delivered a clear message—she hadn't seen the last of him.

Since Belle and Nora hadn't spent the night, the hotel only charged them half of the already discounted rate. Belle suspected the double discount wasn't their normal policy, but Ben's DIA connection made them minor VIPs. She thought of asking if they could keep the bathrobes but didn't want to push her luck. She was mildly surprised that Nora didn't quiz her about Tyler's visit. Her only comment had been, "Man trouble. I get it."

When they stepped outside, Ben was waiting, and he looked worried.

"I need to take you ladies to FBI headquarters."

So much for small talk. Belle wasn't pleased. "You promised to keep what I told you confidential."

"Don't worry," Ben rushed to reply, "I kept my word. But while you were meeting with Dr. Moon, I did some digging and discovered there's a secret ongoing investigation into a Chinese smuggling ring operating throughout the US. The ring's affiliated with one of the Hong Kong triad gangs. They steal high-end art and artifacts and use diplomatic channels to safely transport the items back to China where wealthy businessmen purchase them for exorbitant prices."

"So that could explain the diplomatic tags," Nora said.

"Exactly," Ben said ruefully. "The gang's called *Meili Yishu*, beautiful art. Yishu for short. A poetic name for a ruthless enterprise. So far there's been no evidence of murder or kidnapping involved, but the triad gangs are some of the most lethal criminal enterprises in history. I'm sure they wouldn't hesitate to do whatever was necessary. With one phone call, I can arrange a meeting now with the agent-in-charge of the Yishu task force."

When Belle hesitated, Nora spoke up. "If this Yishu gang is responsible, the FBI might already have an idea where the kidnappers could be holding Jenny."

Ben and Nora were right. But she couldn't ignore the image of herself lying on her back against the bare museum floor with a spear point hovering above her chest. If the kidnappers discovered they'd gone to the Feds, she was certain they'd kill Jenny. "Thanks, but right now I want to see if we can find this jade box ourselves, because at least then we'll have some bargaining power. Maybe after we find the box Sal will decide to let the FBI negotiators handle it."

Ben shrugged. "Suit yourself. I'll continue poking around to see if I can figure out who rescued you. Doubt it was the Fibbies."

Belle couldn't ignore Tyler's visit. "Tyler stopped by."

"How did it go?"

Belle spoke matter-of-factly. "Not so well for him."

"Shit. He begged me to tell him where you were staying. I told him but also said you were busy with something important. I didn't want to go into any detail for obvious reasons. He said he just wanted to say, 'Hi' and apologize again in person. It's very important to him that you know he's changed."

"He hasn't."

"I'm sorry, Belle."

"I know he's your friend."

"It's really weird," Ben mused. "On every other level, he seems even-keeled. But when you dumped him—"

"You need to tell him to stay away from me."

Ben nodded firmly. "Got it. And please, be very careful. If Yishu has Jenny, you're dealing with ruthless killers."

Good advice.

Her phone pinged. No name appeared on the screen, and no number with three as the last digit. A mistaken misdial? A scam caller from a New Delhi fellow named Fred? Or—she answered. "Hello?"

"Hi, Belle."

Alonzo. His baritone voice wasn't completely smooth, more like honey dotted with salted nuts, not unlike the man himself. She tried with limited success to suppress the smile she knew was creasing her face. She missed him and was happy to hear his voice. "How are you? Where are you?"

"Fine," he chuckled. "And Europe."

A former DEA agent, Alonzo had met Belle during the Sundance incident. They'd saved each other's asses and then connected emotionally, spiritually, and physically. He'd been recruited to some off-the-books government outfit and over the past month spent his time on secret agent stuff he couldn't talk about in places he also couldn't talk about. She knew that's why he said "Europe" instead of London or Rome or Paris.

"I came across a report from our, uh, group," Alonzo continued, "and was alarmed to see your name mentioned."

That surprised her. On the other hand, if Baldy was a Chinese diplomat misbehaving by trying to kill two American women . . . "I gather you can't discuss it over the phone."

"You gather correctly. He sounded apologetic. "But I'm now aware of your Georgetown run-in with someone who qualifies as a person of interest to us. You'll likely be contacted by one of my colleagues, Stella Alvarez, and you should know she's one of the good guys."

Belle wanted to confirm that the person of interest was Baldy and squeeze as much information out of Alonzo as he'd allow, but she figured doing so over the phone might not be the greatest idea. Besides, she didn't know if he was aware of Jenny's kidnapping, and she worried that talking about it to a former drug agent who now happened to be some kind of black ops dude might qualify as going to the cops in the eyes of the kidnappers. So, she held her tongue. "When might you be coming back to the States?"

"Because this person of interest happens to be in Texas at the moment, I'll be boarding a plane shortly for Dallas."

"I also happen to be in Texas at the moment. Outside Amarillo to be exact."

"Oh, really? What a coincidence." His tone suggested it was anything but.

"You know your new gig doesn't give you the automatic right to be a smartass."

"Point taken," he laughed. "Soon as I land, I'll find you."

"Good. Your person of interest is of very special interest to me at the moment."

"Understood. Stay safe. And Belle?"

"Yeah?"

"Looking forward to seeing you." He ended the call.

Me, too.

"Should I assume by your expression that Alonzo is your someone special?" Nora asked.

Belle didn't respond. Her smile gave the answer.

On the way to the Georgetown Vintage Jewelry and Antiques Shop Nora had asked a perfectly reasonable question wondering how Belle and Alonzo had met. Belle filled her in on the abridged version of what had occurred at the Sundance Film Festival. Nora's reaction had also been perfectly reasonable.

"I can't believe you're still alive."

Belle couldn't either.

The shop was located on M Street, tucked between a larger Urban Outfitters and a much larger Tommy Bahama. The store required patrons to ring a bell and be buzzed in. They rang, were buzzed, entered, and immediately sank deep into plush gray carpet surrounded by matching gray walls. Dimly lit except for the display cases, the store wasn't overly large. They appeared to be the only customers.

A conservatively dressed Asian woman, maybe mid-forties, wearing an expensive gray suit greeted them with a soft voice, a practiced smile, and an outstretched hand.

"Good afternoon. I'm Sarah. How might I be of service?"

They each took turns shaking her hand. Belle found herself lowering her voice to just above a whisper, as if they were standing in the viewing room of a funeral parlor. *Okay, not the greatest of metaphors under the circumstances.* "We understand you specialize in jade pieces."

Sarah bowed her head and waved toward the back of the store. "Of course. This way." They followed her to a long glass case holding various shades of jade encased in bracelets, necklaces, and rings. On one end of the display, Belle spotted three jewelry boxes. She noticed no prices were attached to any of the pieces.

"We're interested in a jade box," Nora said. "Which of these pieces is the oldest?"

Sarah reached under the case and produced a roll of dark gray felt. Belle looked around for a sign somewhere prohibiting any color other than gray. Sarah rolled the felt out on top of the case and smoothed it flat with the back of her hand. After unlocking the sliding glass door, she set the smallest box on top of the felt. The box looked to be about four inches square with pale green jade carvings on all six sides.

"This piece dates to shortly after the overthrow of the Qing Dynasty in the Xinhai revolution," she said with a reverence more suited for the

Holy Grail than a pretty green box. "It was used to hold jewelry, and as you can see the box is itself a marvelous gem."

In keeping with the understated surroundings, Belle tried to come up with an understated approach to learn the price but settled for, "How much does it cost?"

Sarah twitched but maintained her tone. "Seventy-five thousand dollars."

Belle nodded, saying nothing, as if she'd actually consider paying that price for a jewelry box if she had seventy-five grand lying around, which she didn't, and as if she wanted a jewelry box, which she didn't.

Nora asked, "When was the Qing Dynasty overthrown?"

"The revolution only lasted a few months and concluded in 1912. February, I believe."

Belle and Nora exchanged glances. Quanah Parker died in 1911, meaning if they were to stick to their assumptions, the jade piece the kidnappers were after likely came from the Qing Dynasty.

"We were interested in something from the late Qing Dynasty," Nora said.

A female voice spoke behind them. "Then you have exquisite taste."

They turned to see another Asian woman approach from the backroom as Sarah retreated. She wore a vivid yellow and orange flowered dress and stiletto-heeled shoes the color of celery. Maybe fifties, maybe thirties, hard to tell. Small, barely five feet. Long black hair, fire-engine-red lipstick. The owner, Belle surmised, and suffering from whatever behavioral disorder applied to someone who required people and things around her to fade away so she could stand out. Daisy in the dandelion patch disorder? Belle wouldn't be surprised if such a thing existed. She thought of her lizard door. There seemed to be a disorder for everything.

"I'm Eleanor Zhang, the owner. How may I be of service?" Very cool, very professional, very self-assured.

On the way to the store, they'd whipped up a story about an antique jade box, a family heirloom Belle knew had once belonged to her uncle, but she'd never seen. Poor Uncle Harry had lived in Washington before he'd recently gone to his just reward, and the jade box had disappeared. She was the executor and was trying to track it down.

"So, you're looking for your uncle's jade box and believe it dates to the late nineteenth or early twentieth century?" Belle nodded. Sarah looked to Nora. "Are you also a family member?"

"Only a friend."

"We understand you specialize in jade," Belle said, "and we thought we'd see if you might be aware of a jade box newly on the market."

"Do you have photos? Can you describe it?"

"Sorry, no. Only that it came from that period and is supposed to be valuable."

"What would a jade box from that era be worth?" Nora asked.

Eleanor replaced the $75,000 jewelry box in the case. If she was disappointed, she wasn't going to make a sale, she didn't show it. "That depends. The jade market today is going through the roof. Two years ago, this jewelry box would have sold for less than half the current asking price. Sotheby's Hong Kong recently sold a jade necklace at auction that once belonged to the American heiress Barbara Hutton for almost $28 million."

Belle wasn't interested in a necklace and had no idea who Barbara Hutton was. "What about a jade box?"

"The jewelry is what's driving the market. I can't think of any jade box that would fall anywhere near that price point, certainly none of which I'm aware that exceed a hundred thousand."

A hundred thousand bucks was a lot of money, Belle thought, but enough to justify a sophisticated burglary and kidnapping? Probably not.

"No exceptions?" Nora asked.

"None I know of unless your uncle Harry somehow came into possession of the Hudie Box." She pronounced it *Ooo-dee-eh*.

"What's that?" Belle asked.

"*Hudie* is the Chinese word for butterfly. Empress Dowager Tzu-Hsi ruled the Qing dynasty from 1861, when she was twenty-six, until her death in 1908. She was known to love butterflies. She commissioned her greatest artist to create two identical jewelry boxes, each depicting her image surrounded by butterflies. She insisted on using jade, considered the stone of heaven and believed to ward off evil. The artist selected only the finest Burmese jade, and the workmanship was stunning."

Eleanor walked behind the counter and retrieved a small laptop from under the case. After a few clicks of the keys, she spun the screen around so they could see. The picture showed a beautiful jade box. Carved into the lid was the image of a Chinese woman in a full ceremonial dress surrounded by butterflies.

"Looks larger than a jewelry box," Nora said.

"The Empress Dowager presumably possessed many fine jewelry pieces and required a larger container. The box measures about five inches by nine inches. As I said, two identical boxes were crafted. This one resides in a special chamber of China's National Museum in Beijing off Tiananmen Square. The photo doesn't come near to doing the piece justice. I've had the privilege of seeing the box in person. It is exquisite, the stone glows in even the softest light. Almost like it's alive."

Belle asked the obvious question. "And the other Hudie Box? Where might that be?"

A touch of impatience leaked into Eleanor's voice. "No one knows. A rumor persists that the second box was presented as a gift to another head of state, but during the Xinhai Revolution most of the country's diplomatic records were destroyed, and official inquiries over the years were not successful."

"Did those inquiries include the United States?" Belle asked.

"Yes. By law, your government must keep detailed records of diplomatic gifts, and the Hudie Box was never registered. I doubt very much if your uncle . . .?"

"Harry."

"Of course. I believe it extremely unlikely your Uncle Harry ever possessed the Hudie Box, and I'm not aware of any other jade box from that time period currently on the market." Her tone conveyed that their enjoyable time together was sadly coming to an end. She walked them to the door, and everyone shook hands.

Nora said, "Thank you for your time."

Belle had to ask. "Just out of curiosity, what would the Hudie Box be worth?"

"Very difficult to say. Because of its historical significance, I'd estimate somewhere around fifteen million dollars."

Fifteen million dollars could definitely justify kidnapping and murdering a young woman and her unborn child. Belle caught her breath as the impact of that thought hit her. She had one more question. She didn't expect an answer but wanted to see the woman's reaction. "By the way, have you ever heard of an organization called *Meili Yishu?*"

"No."

Belle looked for the slightest tell, anything that might indicate she was lying, but saw nothing. They thanked her and left the store.

Eleanor Zhang dialed the number, and the call was answered on the second ring. A young woman spoke in lightly accented English.

"Embassy of the People's Republic of China. How may I direct your call?"

"Connect me to the attaché for the Ministry of State Security."

CHAPTER 11

Despite a population of over 200,000 residents, Amarillo did not have a Chinatown district, someplace where Bai Sun could blend in.

He'd considered taking the girl to Dallas or even Houston, where the Bellaire Road area's Chinatown was one of the nation's largest. But Dallas was a five-hour drive from the Panhandle, and Houston even longer. Too far away from the vast plains and canyons where Quanah Parker had lived and roamed over a hundred years earlier. Bai had to assume the Comanche chief hid the box somewhere in his home territory. Once the Yates woman successfully deciphered the code, they would need to move quickly.

Before switching out the burner phones he'd read Bannon's text claiming Yates was unable to crack the code. He refused to believe it. Quanah Parker was an uneducated savage, hardly a sophisticated code writer. Bannon and Yates needed more motivation. He'd initially refrained from imposing a deadline, but his patience was waning. Once a deadline was set, he would need to abide by it and be prepared to accept the possibility that Yates, in the end, would be unsuccessful. If that happened, they would need to find another expert. The girl would die, but that didn't bother him. She was a tool, nothing more, and a tool that doesn't work ends up discarded.

Mao had arranged for them to "hole up"—a term Bai had learned from watching American Western movies—in a two-bedroom apartment two stories above a Chinese restaurant on Route 40. The restaurant's proprietor, a wizened little Chinese man who reminded Bai of a squirrel, was all too eager to accept a sizable supplement to his weekly income. He visited three times a day with a tray of food, although calling what he offered "food" was an exaggeration. The restaurant was located in the corner of a run-down strip mall that also contained a Vietnamese nail salon, a bail bondsman, and a pizza joint run by the squirrel's Italian wife. Bai had "suggested" to the squirrel that a double pepperoni might be nice for dinner.

Their hostage knocked from inside the locked second bedroom. Her pregnancy had become a nuisance; it seemed like she had to urinate almost every hour. He nodded to Fen who'd been sitting on the torn couch reading quietly. She stood, put her book down, and walked to the bedroom. After unlocking the door, she led the girl to the single bathroom and waited outside.

Bai noticed Fen again brushed the girl's belly with her hand as she passed. At first, he'd assumed the contact was an accident. But he soon realized the hand contact occurred every time Fen escorted the girl. He sighed. Not only did he have to deal with Yates and Bannon, but now he felt compelled to keep an eye on Fen. Were anything to happen to the girl, they'd lose all leverage.

He sank back onto the grimy blue recliner and rested his eyes. He and Fen shared the lumpy bed in the larger bedroom, and because of his sore shoulder he'd slept very little. Despite the painkillers, his arm continued to throb from the dog bite. He hoped he might have a chance someday to fire a bullet into the brain of the *mogui gou*, devil dog. Fen tossing and turning in her sleep hadn't helped. There'd been no thought of sex with his colleague, although he suspected if he'd asked Fen would've agreed. Not because she wanted to; she would simply consider it part of her job.

He still had faith in Yates, and perhaps extracting the wrong woman might actually have increased the chances of success because of Bannon.

To save her sister and the girl's unborn child, the tall *gwei poh* would continually push Yates to solve the puzzle.

He tapped his phone and reread Mao's U.S. intelligence dossier on Bannon: twenty-nine, six feet tall, 155 pounds, blond hair, green eyes. Born in Park City, Utah; moved to Pittsburgh when she was twelve. Ran into some trouble there and spent a year in juvenile detention. After her parents' deaths, her uncle moved her and her sister back to Park City. She spent a couple of years at the University of Utah, then joined the Marines and was in the first class of females assigned to front-line combat duty. Her outstanding performance qualified her for the elite Force Recon where she excelled, but she was discharged early due to an unspecified medical condition. She returned to Park City, finished up getting her degree, and taught high school English in Salt Lake City for several months. She left unexpectedly and took a job as a hunting guide for Peabody Outfitters. All in all, not a person to underestimate. Bannon's military training had already proven beneficial when she saved Yates' life in Georgetown. Mao had identified the attacker as Jin Choi, someone else not to underestimate.

The bathroom door opened, and the girl emerged, her face streaked with tears.

"Please, let me go. I won't tell anybody."

Her voice sounded weak, defeated. She bent over, her shoulders heaved, and she broke down in sobs. Fen led her back to her room.

"Wait. Bring her here." Bai stood and carefully unwrapped the lance resting on the battered coffee table. Fen dutifully led the girl to the table. The girl earlier told them she worked in the museum as an intern.

He pointed to the markings in the beadwork. "What do they mean?"

She barely glanced at the lance. "I don't know."

"Tell us the meaning, and we'll set you free."

This time the girl focused on the beadwork wrapping the lance. "I . . . I was only an intern."

His voice lowered, now guttural, menacing. "Look more closely."

She wiped away tears and, body shaking, bent close to the lance. "This could be a deer, or-or maybe a buffalo."

"A place. We're looking for a place, a location."

She stood up. "I told you, I don't know." The tears were flowing freely now.

He nodded to Fen, and she led the girl back toward her room. The girl resisted. Fen applied light pressure to a nerve bundle above the girl's elbow. She yelped in pain, then allowed Fen to escort her to the room.

As the door closed, the girl dropped to her knees and whimpered, "Please, let me go, I promise . . . my baby. . ." Fen locked the door.

Bai shook his head in disgust. Like most Americans, the girl was weak, pathetic. He didn't care about her baby. Across the globe, babies died every day. And he didn't care about her. He was tired. Tonight, he would suggest Fen sleep on the couch. He leaned back in the filthy chair and closed his eyes. Just a short nap until dinner arrived. As he dozed off, his mind filled with the image of a giant pepperoni pizza.

Jenny Bannon had a plan. The trips to the bathroom were legitimate. The baby—she now felt certain it was a boy—seemed to enjoy tap dancing on her bladder. But she'd also used her toilet visits to project a frightened, sniveling weakling to her captors. Not that she wasn't scared; she was. Particularly for her baby. And Fen touching her belly at every opportunity sent shivers down her spine. But she also wasn't a pathetic weakling.

She'd listened intently through the thin walls with the hope of learning something, even though they spoke in rapid-fire Chinese. There'd been two phone calls from someone called Mao, like Mao Tse-tung, the father of communist China. The calls were short, and the male captor spoke in English. She learned his name was Bai and the female, Fen. At least Bai seemed like a real human being. The woman came across as some kind of fembot. She hardly spoke, but Jenny harbored no doubt that the woman was lethal. One time, while Fen was escorting Jenny back to her room, Bai asked Fen into the kitchen. While they talked in whispers, he accidentally bumped a teakettle off the stovetop. Moving at light speed, so fast she seemed not to have moved at all, Fen shot her arm out behind Bai and caught the kettle before it hit the ground. Maybe she *was* a fembot. A *Fen*bot.

The shade over the single window in Jenny's room was drawn and taped shut. She'd been told if they found any evidence of her attempting to undo the tape, they would slice her baby from her body and burn it in front of her eyes. After observing Fen's dead eyes while Bai made the threat, she believed every word.

The bedroom window was nailed shut, but that wasn't the case for the small window over the filthy tub in the bathroom. During her first visit, she stood on the edge of the tub with the full intent of opening the window and shouting for help. But there were two problems. First, the window was painted shut, and second, the window faced the back of the strip mall. Beyond the narrow service lane three stories below, she could only see dense woods. Even if she could open it, there would be no one to hear her cries for help.

Nevertheless, on each bathroom visit she'd used her fingernails to try digging away the paint binding the window shut. Maybe she'd see someone emptying trash into the rusty green dumpster below, and who knows? If she could open the window she could scream for help.

On the last trip she'd attempted to raise the window and on the third try was successful. A quick peek revealed a narrow ledge below the window leading to the flat roof covering half of the strip mall, one story below. If she could crawl along the ledge without falling and make it to the roof, she could call for help. She'd closed the window carefully to avoid making any noise and returned to her whimpering act when she stepped outside the bathroom.

They'd fed her pizza, and she forced down the food only because of the baby. Asian food was one of her favorites, but the stuff they'd given her earlier had been nearly inedible.

Even with the shade taped over the window, the shade glowed a warm tan color during daylight. At night the single light near the green dumpster behind the building provided the only illumination and turned the shade a dirty gray. She knew Belle and Nora were doing everything humanly possible to find the jade box, but she was worried about Bai. On the second call with the mysterious Mao he'd said something to the effect of, "We'll make it clean." He could've meant any number of things, but Jenny had a feeling Bai was referring to disposing of her and the baby whether or not the jade box was found.

She heard a click, and the door opened. Fen entered with a face completely devoid of expression and closed the door behind her. She moved toward Jenny, forcing her against the bed. Fen's eyes didn't stray from Jenny's belly.

Jenny's eyes widened, and her voice caught in her throat. She rasped, "Please don't hurt my baby."

Without a word, Fen pushed her up against the bed, slid her hands down the top of Jenny's jeans, and rubbed her belly. Jenny froze, afraid the slightest move could trigger a violent reaction.

The baby kicked, surprising Fen. She pressed harder on the spot of the kick.

The door opened and Bai entered. He spoke in a soft voice to Fen. *"Qing likai."*

It sounded to Jenny like he was asking Fen to leave.

At first it appeared she didn't hear him, and she continued to probe the spot of the baby's kick. Then she stood to Jenny's side, wrapped one arm around Jenny's belly, and cooed, *"Wo de baobei."*

Jenny froze. She didn't need to understand the words. Fen's intentions were obvious. The Fenbot wanted Jenny's baby.

Fen finally followed Bai out the door. The door closed, and Jenny heard the familiar click of the lock. She breathed again.

She needed to make her move soon. Very soon.

CHAPTER 12

Belle had to force herself not to smash the accelerator to the floor as they pulled out of the airport parking lot and headed northwest along Amarillo Boulevard, looking for the cheap whores who hopefully would lead them to Crazy Alice. If this old Comanche woman could decode the lance, Belle would be able to negotiate for Jenny's release.

"Might want to slow down," Nora cautioned, as Belle zoomed through a yellow light.

Belle ignored her and only reduced her speed when they entered a neighborhood that would welcome being called seedy as an upgrade. Only a few streetlights remained lit, and the long shadows cast by the unsavory-looking characters parading down the boulevard jumped unevenly like spastic marionettes across abandoned storefronts and the occasional red neon sign spelling out "Bar" or "Sex Shop."

Belle prayed Crazy Alice would come through. They either had to decode the lance or somehow find the Hudie box on their own. On the plane ride back from D.C. they'd both skimmed Roosevelt's journal entries recounting his conversations with Quanah about the Comanche leader's life. While the president's retelling of Quanah's exploits was fascinating, they hadn't found anything so far that would help them locate the Hudie box without the benefit of the code. Was this Yishu gang a key?

"How would this Yishu gang know about the Hudie Box?" she asked.

"We have to presume Quanah received the box from Roosevelt," Nora said, "who in turn accepted it as a diplomatic gift from China. If, as Ben said, Yishu includes Chinese diplomats who smuggle the art back to China, it's fair to assume the gang could've learned about the gift from the Chinese government."

"And Baldy's tied to Yishu?" Belle offered.

"Who knows?" Nora's shoulders slumped. "Yishu could have nothing to do with it, and he represents the Chinese government. They simply want the jade box returned to take its place next to its twin in the National Museum."

The possibilities had been careening around in Belle's head like pinballs. None of them made sense. "There's one problem. Whether it's Yishu or the Chinese government, why would their agents try to kill you? You're the one person who supposedly can discover the box's location. Why not stand by and wait for us to find the box, then swoop in and recover it?"

"The kidnappers want me alive. The question is, who wants me dead? Who *doesn't* want the box recovered?"

"We're obviously missing something."

"And Jenny's caught in the middle."

Belle noticed that the strollers stopped to take notice as she drove by. They were used to cars moving at a slow cruise, and a speeding SUV signaled cops or bad guys with guns. She slowed just as her phone rang. She checked the screen. *Jenny!* "Hello, hello?"

"Belle. . .?"

Her voice automatically softened. "Are you okay, Shrimp? Have they hurt you?" She switched the phone to speaker mode.

"I'm . . . fine."

She sounded far from fine. Her voice was weak and quavering. Like she was struggling not to cry. Nauseating fear gripped Belle's stomach.

"Where are you?" A long pause, and they could hear a muffled voice in the background. "I . . . I'm not allowed to say. They want me to give you a message."

Jenny sounded frightened. Understandable. But more than that, it came across as pitiful. Belle's little sister was no wimp. Either the kidnappers had really hurt her, or she was purposely diminishing herself in front of her captors. "Jenny, listen to me—"

"They said to tell you if you haven't found the jade box in seventy-two hours, they'll . . ." She couldn't hold back any longer, and the tears made it impossible for her to continue. Then she said, "Bye-bye."

"Jenny, wait—"

"Bye-bye."

The now familiar voice took over. "If you miss the deadline, the girl and her unborn child will die. And it will not be an easy death."

Belle spoke through gritted teeth. "If anything happens—"

The line went dead. Belle's heart hammered furiously. Seventy-two hours, three days. Belle couldn't flush the kidnapper's voice from her mind. *It will not be an easy death.* And something else was nagging at her. She turned to Nora. "On the phone, right at the end, Jenny said, 'Bye-bye.' Then she repeated it. Did you think that was kind of weird?"

"I assumed she was simply saying good-bye."

"You're probably right, but it sounded fake, out of context. Like a flight attendant saying 'bye-bye' as you file past on the way off the plane. Maybe she was trying to tell us something." Angry and frustrated, Belle hit the gas. "Where the hell is this crazy woman?"

"Up in the next block on the left."

Belle spotted three prostitutes hanging out in front of a bar. With a red neon sign overhead reading "Danny's." Belle pulled to the curb and noticed the light was out on the capital M. Nora saw her reach for the Stealth.

"Wouldn't do that. They see you're armed, they'll shoot us both."

Belle wasn't sure who "they" were, but she heeded Nora's advice and slid the gun under the driver's seat out of sight. They moved away from the car quickly and headed down the cracked concrete stairs to the bar. An audience of eyes watched from the shadows, and Belle figured the odds the Cherokee would still be there when they returned were at best even money.

Manny's was little more than a dark, smoky, hole-in-the-wall—a wide hallway with a small bar along one side. Belle could see two doors at the far end of the room. One led to a restroom; no sign, but an emerging patron struggling with his fly gave it away. The faint odor of urine wafted all the way to the front of the bar.

Belle assumed they were heading to the second door, the one guarded by a huge white guy with a drooping mustache. He wore a gun in a Western holster and a bandolero across his chest. The bartender, a stubby man with squinty eyes and a greasy t-shirt, stared at them as if they'd just arrived from Jupiter. They squeezed past the dark figures hunched over the bar, careful not to touch the wall, and headed back to Pancho Villa.

The guard was even bigger up close, over 250 pounds. He reeked of garlic and after a moment Belle could see why. He was eating peeled garlic cloves like popcorn from a paper bag. She noticed his gun was a vintage Colt 45 with an inlaid pearl grip, right out of an old Western movie.

"We're here to see Alice," Nora said.

When he spoke, his voice was little more than a series of grunts. Spittle leaked out of his mouth and drizzled down his unshaven chin. "What about?"

"She knows me," Nora said. "Tell her Nora Yates is here to ask her advice on a personal matter."

He nodded in Belle's direction. She knew what he wanted. She assumed the position with her hands pressed against the slimy wall and her feet spread. Pancho ran his hands roughly over her body searching for weapons. He rubbed his groin against her butt and groped her breasts hard, then turned to Nora and leered. "Your turn."

"Sorry, pal, that's not going to happen," Belle said.

Nora said, "It's okay."

Belle could tell by the quaver in her voice that it wasn't okay. "Why don't we do this, pal? You take my friend in to see Alice while I wait out here. I'm sure a big tough guy like you can protect Ms. Bluefeather."

The guard pulled his gun and pressed it hard against Belle's forehead. "First, you're gonna lie down on the floor with your hands behind your head, bitch, then I'm gonna search your friend real thorough. No tellin' what she's hiding inside her pants."

They didn't have time for this bullshit. Belle raised her hands. He smiled. In a microsecond her right hand slapped the gun away. She stepped in flush with his body and used both hands to leverage the gun from his grip. He stopped smiling. She flipped the gun so she was holding the barrel and smashed the butt into his temple. He staggered, then slumped toward her. She dropped the gun and rammed her shoulder into his chest. His body slammed backward into the cheap door, busting it open.

Belle heard the scrape of bar stools behind her and quickly retrieved his gun. She turned, and while she didn't point the gun at them directly, the bar boys got the message and returned to their cheap beers.

They entered a small dark room that smelled of tobacco and bad whiskey. Nora closed the door behind them, and they stepped over Pancho's unconscious body on the way to an old woman sitting at a table. Two middle-aged Latina women stood before her dressed in eight-inch heels and what looked like blue-sequined underwear. From Belle's point of view, it appeared that both ladies might benefit from a larger size. None of the three seemed surprised by the somewhat dramatic entrance. The two Latinas shuffled past them without expression and stepped over Pancho as if he were a pile of dog shit. They left the room, presumably having been directed to return to duty.

Alice Bluefeather hardly looked the part of a pimp pushing cheap whores on Amarillo Boulevard—ash white hair in two uneven frizzy braids, hooded lids that covered her eyes but for a thin slit, furrowed skin that draped across her face. She wore a black western shirt complete with a red string tie, a full red print skirt, and black cowboy boots. An unfiltered cigarette dangled from the corner of nicotine-yellowed lips, and a bottle of whiskey rested next to a near-full glass on the table in front of her. The woman didn't flinch when they sat down without invitation. Belle set Pancho's fancy gun on the table next to the whiskey bottle.

"Hi, Alice," Nora said. "Remember me? Nora Yates from the museum down in Canyon?"

The old woman remained silent, frozen in place, and stared straight ahead.

"This is my friend, Belle."

Alice eyed Belle up and down. "You want work?" Her voice sounded like the first words of a drunk the morning after a long bender. She reached across the table and grabbed Belle's left boob, the second time she'd been groped in the last minute. Belle curtailed her reflex to snap the old woman's wrist in two, figuring they didn't want to start off on the wrong foot.

Alice grunted her approval. "I make you good money."

"Thanks, but I'll pass. And sorry about your enforcer. I'm sure he'll be fine."

Alice barely shrugged.

Nora tried a cheery approach. She smiled, opened her file, and showed Alice the close-up of the lance's center-band bead design. She kept her voice light. "We'd like to talk to you about symbols we found on Quanah's lance." Nora used her phone's flashlight feature to illuminate the photo. Alice didn't move.

Belle tried an un-cheery approach. "We'll be happy to pay you for your time and expertise."

"How much?"

Belle put a hundred-dollar bill on the table next to an overflowing ashtray. Alice scratched the hundred one time with a long yellow fingernail, like a blackjack player asking the dealer for another card. Belle laid a second hundred on top of the first. Alice stuffed the bills into her shirt pocket and pushed Nora's phone light away. Using two hands to hold one of the photos so close to her eyes it touched her nose, she grunted, then set the photo back on the table and drained half her whiskey glass in one swallow.

Nora directed Alice to the close-up of the new beadwork in the center of the lance. "This is newer, added after the original. You can tell by the color." Alice studied the photo again, then nodded her agreement. "We need to know what these symbols mean."

Alice jabbed her fingernail at the second symbol. "Antelope. Quahadis."

"Quanah's band of warriors was known as the Quahadis," Nora

explained. "Means antelope."

Alice's heavy brow furrowed, and she pointed to the first symbol. "White eagle feather. Never see before."

Belle jumped in. "We think it refers to Quanah's friend, Teddy Roosevelt."

"What about the rest?" Nora asked. "We're looking for a place."

Alice pointed to one of the outer bands. Nora examined the spot closely.

"What is it?" Belle asked.

Alice responded, "Bird."

"Sorry, I don't see a bird," Belle responded.

Nora aimed her light revealing a single yellow bead and a single black bead next to each other. She grimaced. "Damn, I should've spotted it."

"Spotted what?"

"It's a Kiskadee. A yellow and black bird indigenous to the Panhandle. When tribes battled each other, as in any war a need exists to transmit messages. To avoid secret information falling into enemy hands, the tribes used a *bah-has-tkih*. The word is actually Navajo but over time was adopted by most tribes. It roughly translates to a code key. The Kiskadee was the symbol used to convey that what appeared on the surface was a diversion. The message could only be learned through translation using a *bah-has-tkih* held by the friendly tribe member."

"You mean like a code book where tree means horse and horse means cow?"

"Only not a book. Usually, an article of clothing—moccasins, headband, bracelet, belt. And of course, the *bah-has-tkih* would change regularly to keep the code secure."

"Could this *bah-ha-tkih* be something already in the museum's collection?" Belle asked hopefully.

"Unfortunately, no."

Belle's heart sank. "But Quanah created this code over a hundred years ago. The chances of the *bah-has-tkih* still being in existence has to be near zero." Neither Nora nor Alice spoke, their silence affirming Belle's worst fears. Her nausea ratcheted up.

They weren't going to meet the deadline.

CHAPTER 13

Nora watched through the windshield as Belle walked past the gas pump holding her phone high in the air, searching for a good signal. She'd tried calling her uncle in Italy, but the cell reception was bad.

They were both exhausted. Nora had offered to drive down to Canyon, but Belle declined. Since they'd left Alice Bluefeather, Belle had remained virtually silent. Eyes straight ahead, her hands squeezing the steering wheel in a death grip, afraid she'd never see her sister alive again. Nora couldn't help but feel guilty. She was the kidnapper's target, not Jenny.

She'd asked Belle about texting the kidnappers and offering to exchange herself for Jenny. After all, she was the one they originally wanted. She was no hero and had no death wish. Being curator at the museum was her dream job. She was in excellent health and planned to live a long fulfilling life where she could watch Sadie grow to full womanhood. And she assumed that at some point down the road a special person would enter her life.

Belle said they had a much better chance to save Jenny and the baby if Nora were not confined in the kidnapper's grasp. She knew Belle was right, but the guilt still engulfed her. She could not allow—she *would* not allow—Jenny's baby to die because of her.

As soon as they'd left the bar Belle had repeatedly tried calling and texting the kidnappers on Jenny's phone to beg for more time, but no one answered. Without the *bah-has-tkih*, deciphering the symbols on the lance would be impossible. There were a thousand places Quanah could've hidden the jade box and a thousand places his wife, Chony, could've left the *bah-has-tkih*. Why did Quanah elect to leave the code on this particular lance? No doubt he had owned many similar weapons in his lifetime. The file showed that Quanah's last wife, Topay, warned the curator to take special care of the lance as it had been a gift from Quanah's father.

She lowered the window and breathed in the warm night air. The image of her famous ancestor filled her mind. She pictured Quanah, not as a wealthy rancher or political advocate, but as a young man. Twenty, maybe twenty-one. 1869. Blue eyes framed by high cheekbones and bronze skin. A young man entering his prime. She remembered Roosevelt's notes transmitted from Dr. Moon describing Quanah's account of a battle with a band of buffalo hunters. She pulled out her phone, found the download, and began to read . . .

———

A posse of thirty angry men from the settlements near San Antonio, armed with their dreaded buffalo rifles, caught up to the band. The battle was short-lived as the Comanches' weapons were no match. The band prepared to retreat.

Quanah did not want to fall back. He'd stolen the horses, killing no one, and he had no interest in giving them up. But he followed Tahaka as the leader led the band single file up a narrow trail winding through the foothills. He rode at the end of the line. A sharp bend in the path ahead gave Quanah an idea. He veered off the trail into the high brush where he was hidden from sight.

The posse approached a short time later, and Quanah watched through tight foliage as the whites passed by single file. Quanah saw a long gap at the end of the line followed by two stragglers. He slid out his numu titsi wai, war lance, from its thick buffalo-hide scabbard. The lance had been a gift from his father. Made from the Bois D'Arc tree found in the Red River valley, the wood was extremely hard, perfect for bows, war clubs, and lances. When his mother had been captured thirty-three years earlier, Cynthia Ann Parker had known nothing of Comanche beadwork; now she was considered among the best beaders in the tribe. She decorated the lance with blue and russet beaded bands, and tufts of red turkey feathers attached at the end. He'd never used the lance, saving it for a special time. The whites following them carried the big guns; they were buffalo hunters, his sworn enemy. It was time to bathe the lance in blood.

"Aieeee!" He dug his heels into his pony's flanks and burst through the underbrush, startling the two men. With surprise on his side, he was able to thrust the lance into the soft belly of one of the whites before the man could pull his weapon. The man rolled off his horse without making a sound.

He turned to the second man who had already pulled his sidearm from its holster. In the close quarters Quanah had no room to turn the lance around in time. He smashed the butt-end of the lance into the man's chest just as he pulled the trigger. The bullet whizzed by Quanah's head, close enough for him to feel the puff of air as it passed his ear. Another thrust into the man's chest; his horse reared up and he tumbled off. The rider hit hard, and his revolver went flying into the underbrush.

Quanah slid off his pony, stood over the defenseless man, and held the tip of his lance at the rider's throat. The gunshot would alert the other whites. He needed to hurry. Quanah glanced at the saddle where the .50 caliber buffalo rifle protruded from its scabbard. He saw fear in the man's eyes. Without a second thought, Quanah thrust down, slicing through the white man's neck, nearly severing his head.

He withdrew the lance and held it high above his head—his father's gift, his mother's handiwork, and now newly adorned with white man's blood. He would value the weapon until he took his last breath and the Great Spirit called him home.

Nora looked up from her phone, now fully alert. Quanah's story raised a question they'd never asked. The lance meant the world to him, but why did he choose it to preserve the code? He could've simply written the symbols on a sheet of paper and sealed it in an envelope. Her mind churned. Of course. The lance not only bore the symbols, it was actually a required piece of the decode. Like if the directions for building something were written on a special wrench needed to tighten unique bolts.

She felt confident now that the lance represented in the series of images was the actual lance upon which the symbols were beaded.

She pulled out her notes and studied the symbols.

Belle started up the Cherokee and pulled out of the station onto the nearly deserted highway. Nora had explained her theory that Quanah's lance was itself part of the code. Made sense. But without the *bah-has-tkih* they were still spinning their wheels.

Nora put away her notes and sighed, the frustration evident in her voice. "We're stuck. We have no choice. We need to call the FBI."

The connection had been bad on Sal's end, but enough of her uncle's words got through to let Belle know Sal and Helen had finally hired a car and were driving north to find air service back to the States. The final message was most clear: no police.

Nora shook her head. "I'm not coming up with any alternatives."

"Not all of the symbols are false," Belle opined. "The antelope is legitimate, the white feather. And the green square has to mean the jade box. Is there a way to work backward to recreate this *bah-has-tkih*? It's a common code-breaking technique."

"And code-breaking comes in handy when spotting up a wall-hanger?" Nora retorted.

Belle smiled at Nora's slang for a large buck. "You're a hunter."

"I'm three-quarters Comanche and live in Texas," Nora deadpanned. "So, answer my question. How do you know about code-breaking?"

Belle hedged. "Took a course in the Marines."

"Why'd you leave?"

Belle paused for a moment. "It was time." She could tell Nora wanted to press further, but fortunately she didn't.

"A *bah-has-tkih* doesn't lend itself to 'working backward,'" Nora explained. "It's not something where if you know an F is an E you go through a message and turn all Fs into Es. Besides, we have no idea if the *bah-has-tkih* still exists, or, even if it does, where it's located. So, we're back to trying to find the jade box without breaking the code."

Belle didn't hide her frustration. "And how are we going to do that?"

"I may have an idea. Remember Professor Moon told us Roosevelt's closest confident was—"

The bullet smashed the side-view mirror, spraying broken glass into Nora's lap.

"Get down!" Belle's pulse jacked up past redline as she roughly pushed Nora's head down toward the console.

In the side-view mirror a dark sedan accelerated toward them in the passing lane. *Baldy.* Belle pressed down hard on the gas pedal and weaved the Cherokee back and forth.

Bullets pinged into the back cargo door. If they hit a rear tire the car would spin out and crash into the ditches lining the road. She withdrew her Stealth from the holster wedged next to the seat. Good news, as a revolver the weapon wouldn't jam; bad news, it held only six rounds.

Despite her speed the sedan gained, shrinking the distance between the two vehicles. From the corner of her eye Belle saw a hand reach out from the sedan's passenger window. Nora unbuckled her seatbelt and hunched her body down into the footwell. A second later the Cherokee's backseat window shattered.

Belle glanced down at her. "Where's your gun?" she demanded.

"Packed away!"

Belle handed her the Stealth. "Crawl into the back seat and fire two shots." The extra ammo was packed deep inside the duffel far back in the cargo section. If Nora tried to retrieve it, she'd be exposed. "We need to make the six rounds count."

Nora slid between the bucket seats and huddled on the back floor.

After quickly brushing away the glass shards, she stretched out prone on the bench seat.

Belle weaved back and forth, trying to avoid giving Baldy's crew a clear shot, but the sedan was too fast. "Coming up on us . . . Now!"

Nora rose to her knees, held the revolver steady in a two-hand grip, and fired twice.

Belle glanced in the mirror and saw the sedan's passenger-side window explode in a hail of glass. The car swerved left then spun out and stopped when one of the back wheels caught in the soft grassy gully edging the road. Ahead was a deserted straightaway. Belle jammed the pedal to the floor, and the Cherokee shot forward, soon nudging over ninety. In the rearview mirror she could make out two men spill from the sedan and struggle to push the car back onto the road.

"They still coming?" Nora's position flat on the floor muffled her voice.

Belle checked the mirror. The sedan was back on the road. "Yeah. Get ready."

Nora rose up with the Stealth and positioned herself to fire when the sedan came alongside.

Except the sedan didn't come alongside. A long gun protruded from the back passenger seat.

"Down!"

A split second later the rear window shattered. Nora screamed.

"You okay?"

Nora's voice shook. "I-I think so."

Belle felt a sharp pain in the back of her neck and yanked out a spear of glass painted red with her blood.

The next shot fired through the now open rear window, through the passenger headrest, and smacked into the dashboard. Belle scrunched down as low as she could in the seat while still being able to see the road. She checked the side mirror. The sedan had fallen back out of their range behind the Cherokee and were firing a long gun that solved any range problems. That Baldy was a clever little shit.

Rule one in survival training was use any advantage you have no matter how small. Except she didn't have—Wait, yes, she did. Four-wheel drive.

She took two deep breaths both to calm herself and to project a confidence that she definitely didn't feel. "When I slow down, they'll be on our ass. Fire two more shots."

"Slow down?" Nora cried. "Are you crazy?"

"Probably." She tapped the brakes, and the sedan rushed up fast. At the same moment, Nora fired twice through the back window. The sedan swerved.

Nora whooped, "Think I got the guy in the passenger seat!"

"Hang on!"

Belle slowed more, then cut hard right. The rear wheels fishtailed, but somehow the car didn't flip. They flew over the narrow gulley, landing hard on the barren terrain. She goosed the pedal, and the four wheels spun out. The area had been recently deluged with a spring downpour, and the earth was soft and muddy. After what seemed like an eternity, the tires gained purchase. The SUV jumped forward into the darkness. She had to focus her eyes on the land ahead and couldn't spare a moment to check on their pursuers. "You see them?"

Nora shifted her position to get a better view. "They're backing up . . ."

"What?"

"I can't tell for sure, but—*shit*. It looks like they found a turn-off. Probably an abandoned dirt road. They honeycomb this whole area."

Belle risked a glance in the rearview. The lights of the sedan headed toward them, but the car wasn't moving as fast as they were. She maneuvered the Cherokee around some sagebrush and turned southwest. In the far distance, a few lights from cars moved west on what had to be Route 60. If they could make it there, they'd be safe. She doubted Baldy would risk a gunfight on such a heavily traveled highway. The space between the two vehicles was expanding wider and wider. She felt confident now they'd make the highway and safety.

"Belle!" Nora pointed to a gorge ahead—a deep arroyo, maybe ten feet wide—like a mythical giant had gouged across the road with a mythical hoe.

"Shit."

"Can't we go around?" Nora pleaded.

"Too soft even for four-wheel-drive. We're sure to get stuck." The road approaching the gorge elevated somewhat. *Was it possible?*

Nora glanced behind her. "Belle . . .?"

"No choice. We're going to jump."

"What? Have you ever done that before?"

A bullet slammed into the back hatch. Then three more rounds pinged into the engine compartment.

The car stopped. The engine died.

"Belle!" Nora shrieked.

She tried the ignition. The engine started right up, but the car wouldn't move forward. She glanced over her shoulder. The sedan's headlights were moving closer.

"Must've hit the transmission." She tried reverse and the car moved smoothly.

"We can only go backward?"

Belle backed in a half circle, so the rear of the Cherokee pointed toward the gorge.

Nora's eyes widened. "You can't jump now!"

"Didn't you ever see *Fast and Furious*?"

"I don't remember Vin Diesel driving backward!"

Two more bullets pinged into the Cherokee's hood. She had no choice. "Hold on!" She floored the accelerator.

The Cherokee moved closer to the gorge, and Belle realized the expanse was much wider than she'd originally believed—closer to twenty feet. The incline of the road as it approached the washout would serve as a ramp, and the vehicle's front weight, now in back, would help the car's lighter rear end lift easier as it led over the ditch. But the slower speed would significantly reduce their chances of clearing the gully. Another shot smacked into the Cherokee's hood. Her heart raced, and her breathing alternated between rapid-fire and dead stop.

She jammed her foot to the floor. The engine's whine and Nora's screams melded together as they whipped backward. She felt the car begin to elevate, and in a few seconds they were airborne.

An instant later she knew they weren't going to make it.

The Cherokee crashed down hard, rattling every bone in her body.

Nora yelped. The back wheels had cleared the gully, spinning on dirt and gravel seeking purchase, but the vehicle's front end dangled backward over the edge. The smoke and stench of burning rubber filled the car.

"We're stuck!" Nora shouted.

"Jump into the back seat to add weight!" Belle ordered.

Nora crawled forward into the back seat. "Here they come!"

Belle crushed her foot to the floor and hoped the torque generated by the reverse gear would be strong enough to drag the front end out of the ditch. She tried easing off the accelerator. For a moment the back wheels continued to spin, then—movement. She reduced the gas even more and this time the rear wheels gripped the gravel surface. She felt them being pulled forward—actually, backward. The front wheels hit the edge of the ditch, gripped, and rolled up.

Nora raised her arms in celebration. "Yes!"

Belle floored the gas pedal and the Cherokee moved back down the road. She glanced back; they'd now moved beyond the range of Baldy's long gun.

"Think they'll jump?" Nora asked.

"Don't know." She glanced down at the speedometer—barely forty miles per hour. "But if they make it over, we're finished."

Jin slowed the sedan as it approached the ditch.

His man in the front seat was seriously wounded, unlikely to survive. The shooter in the back said, "Sir, I'm not sure this car can make it."

Jin was livid. "They jumped it going backward, so you are telling me we cannot do the same when we have the ability to generate twice the approach speed?" He angrily floored the gas pedal and the sedan accelerated. Airborne for a moment, it crashed into the far side of the gorge, landing hood up at a seventy-degree angle.

"Is everything all right, sir?" asked the shooter.

Jin's words dripped with sarcasm. "Let us consider. I'm strapped into a car positioned as if it is being readied for a space launch. Judging by the noise I heard at impact, we have broken an axle. Does that sound like everything's all right to you?"

Jin took a deep breath and struggled to rein in his anger. He could not permit himself to again lose face in front of a subordinate. *Qi si wo le!*

CHAPTER 14

Water rolled down Peng Xiao's short legs as he stepped from the pool. He slipped into a lush robe held out for him and settled into a lounge chair to await the call.

A servant approached, carrying a silver tray containing a tall glass of sparkling water. Peng waved him off. The servant bowed and exited the indoor facility. Next to the door hung a photograph of Mao Tse-tung meeting Soviet General Secretary Nikita Khrushchev in 1958; it had been taken right there, inside the pool building.

The facility was located on the western side of Zhongnanhai, the Chinese seat of government. As President of the People's Republic of China, Peng had access to the pool facility whenever he desired. His additional roles as General Secretary of the Communist Party, General Secretary of the Central Committee, and Chairman of the Central Military Commission made him the Paramount Leader of China.

He elected to take the call here rather than in any of his offices because the pool building was easier to sweep for listening devices. No one could know about or hear his upcoming conversation. His leadership was in trouble. Li Fong was coalescing a political coup. Already he heard Li was only one or two votes shy of ousting him as Secretary of the Party.

Li was a hothead. Young, brash, but admittedly a much better speaker than Peng. Li itched for a military confrontation over America's heavy naval presence in the South China Sea. Currently, both America's Third and Seventh Fleet patrolled the waters. Li brushed aside any reservations expressed by others of the worldwide disaster that would occur were China and America to escalate such a military confrontation to a nuclear level. Li argued that neither side would use nuclear weapons because to do so would mean mutual destruction. He presented a scenario of an all-out conventional war where China's superior military strength would prevail.

Peng had to admit the young man sounded convincing. And a significant segment of the population, bristling with pride and energy based on China's new role as a world leader, seemed itching for a fight. They considered the South China Sea—the area of the western Pacific bordered by China, Vietnam, Taiwan, Cambodia, the Philippines, Indonesia, Malaysia, and Singapore—to be China's backyard and deeply resented America's robust military presence. It was no accident that the most popular song in his country at the moment, performed by a young rapper, was entitled, "China Will Make America Call Us Daddy."

Having just celebrated his seventieth birthday, Peng had the benefit of wisdom only age could confer. He knew a military confrontation with America would be disastrous. Which is why he'd tasked Jin to take out the Yates woman.

His phone vibrated. Jin. He made the connection and listened. When Jin concluded his report, Peng ended the call without saying a word.

Jin had failed to kill her but assured Peng he would soon be successful. Jin was fiercely loyal to him, but if Jin failed, the contents of the Hudie Box could come to light. The act of Peng's great-great-great-grandmother would doom his presidency, and his nation likely would be catapulted into war. Peng sighed deeply and headed for the dressing room.

At least for the moment he had a country to run.

CHAPTER 15

Baldy hadn't followed them. Belle figured he didn't clear the arroyo and would be tied up for hours finding his way back to civilization.

They reached the highway and flagged down a pickup heading east. The driver gladly offered to drop them off in Canyon. They loaded all the gear from the Cherokee into the back of his truck. Before pulling away, the driver, a rawboned cowboy of few words with a silver handlebar mustache, mumbled barely loud enough to hear. "Couldn't help but notice your truck's pointin' backward."

Belle elected not to respond.

His eyes caught the bullet holes. "You need the cops?"

She politely declined. He nodded and barely spoke until they reached Canyon where he dropped them off at a Shell station with a tow truck and a tow truck driver named Larry.

Belle gave Larry the location of the Cherokee and told him the car would need a new transmission and bodywork. A lot of bodywork. Larry agreed to rent her a fifteen-year-old green Chevy Tahoe to use until the Cherokee was fixed. Apparently, some guy driving through from Denver left it for repair, and when he saw the bill said, "Keep it."

Belle told Larry he might notice a few bullet holes in the Cherokee but not to worry. They'd been target shooting fueled by a few too many longnecks. Belle got the strong impression he didn't believe her, but also that he didn't care.

They arrived back at the Holiday Inn really late or really early, depending on your point of view.

Nora stretched and yawned. "There's nothing we can do until daylight. You and Scout are both welcome to come back to my place. The bed in my guestroom is probably more comfortable, and my coffee is definitely better."

Belle accepted her kind offer. She picked up Scout, paid the bill, and they headed over to Nora's two-bedroom rancher. Belle was counting on Baldy being reluctant to mount a frontal attack on a suburban street, and if he tried to enter surreptitiously, they had a fail-safe alarm system in the form of a black-and-white Newdle. Belle asked Nora to wake her at six.

Nora was right about the bed. Very comfortable. Belle rolled out and checked her watch on the way to the bathroom, awakened by the aroma of strong coffee and fried bacon. Almost 8:15 a.m. Damn. She dressed quickly and found Nora sitting at the kitchen table with Scout curled up at her feet. She was reading a book and feeding him bits of bacon from her plate.

"You were supposed to wake me," Belle scolded.

"We're not going to find Jenny if you're so sleep-deprived you can't think."

"What about you?"

She ignored the question and nodded toward the stove. "Bacon, eggs, and coffee."

"Thanks." Belle found a plate on the counter and helped herself to breakfast.

Nora spoke without looking up. "Scout's been walked and fed. I went to the store. Your fancy creamer's in the fridge."

Not knowing for certain how to take her words, Belle thought she should probably be mildly offended. But when she opened the refrigerator door to find a container of chocolate almond fudge coffee creamer, all thoughts of offense evaporated. Nirvana.

"Thanks." Scout didn't even bother to glance up at the sound of Belle's voice. "Looks like you found a friend for life."

"Yeah. By the way, why'd you decide to name him Scout?"

"My dad loved watching old black and white reruns of the *Lone Ranger,* and he made me a fan. Tonto's pinto horse was named Scout. You know, he'd say 'Get-um up, Scout.'"

"'*Get-'em up?'* Do you realize how racially insensitive that is?"

"Uh, the actor who said it was Jay Silverheels, a full-blooded Indian," Belle pronounced with authority. She could see Nora's temperature rise and was a bit surprised.

"He was only half Mohawk, and his real name was Harold Smith. '*Get 'em up,* Scout?' Really?"

Feeling a touch guilty, Belle hastily changed the subject and gestured toward the book. "You've been busy."

"Couldn't sleep, so I visited the all-night university library."

Belle sat opposite her and expected Scout to park at her feet. Instead, he gave her a look roughly interpreted as, "She feeds me bacon, not that dry kibble crap." Right on cue, Nora reached down and dropped another bacon bit into his mouth.

"So, our little adventure last night wasn't sufficient stimulation and you felt compelled to take out a library book?"

"Professor Moon told us one of Roosevelt's closest confidants was his valet, James Amos."

Belle got it. "And he wrote a book."

She held up a slim volume so Belle could read the title. *Theodore Roosevelt: Hero to his Valet.* "Published in 1927. I couldn't download it from Amazon, but a number of copies can be found in libraries across the country."

"Including West Texas A&M. Find anything?"

"The short answer is no. I'm trying to connect the dots. Eleanor Zhang told us the second Hudie Box was rumored to have been presented to a head of state. Roosevelt was president when the Hudie Boxes were crafted, so it's reasonable to assume he was the recipient. And we're already working on the assumption the white feather on the

lance represents Roosevelt. The strongest Chinese connection to
Roosevelt is the Russo-Japanese war, a war that was resolved in 1905,
during the time the president and Quanah were hanging out. Remember, China had an interest in persuading Roosevelt to protect its interests during peace negotiations between Russia and Japan."

"Bribing the ref."

Nora's deep sigh conveyed her disappointment. "Problem is, there's
very little reference to the war in Amos's book. And we can't forget the
dots are nothing more than educated guesses."

"Assumptions on top of assumptions."

"Right. The box just as easily could've been the heirloom of a
rancher or his wife, and Quanah snatched it during a raid."

"Then why would Quanah have bothered to conceal its existence
and identify its location only by a code beaded onto his war lance?"
Belle argued.

"Fair question."

"Also, how would Yishu know about it? Baldy's involvement is key.
His diplomatic connection is the most reasonable evidence to support
the theory the box was a diplomatic gift, whether he's working for the
gang or his own government."

"Point taken," Nora responded. "But we're still only playing the
odds." She handed Belle the book.

Belle barely tasted her breakfast as she skimmed through it. Nora
was right. Nothing helpful. Belle didn't hide her frustration. "If James
Amos really was one of Roosevelt's closest confidants, we have to
assume he knew about the box. But no official record of the gift exists."

Nora cleared their dishes and carried them to the sink. "So, if
Roosevelt received the jade box, he did so off the books." She hesitated,
and her expression changed to that glazed look of someone whose mind
is working overtime. "I've written a couple of books."

"Impressive."

"Not really. They were short, little more than historical essays
published by the university press. The point is, I learned that the
published book, particularly a historical work targeted to a general
audience, contains only a small percentage of the author's raw
research."

Belle saw where she was heading. "So, you think Amos probably knew about the jade box but decided not to write about it?"

"A reasonable assumption, yes."

"How does that help us?"

"He may have told someone, a friend, a wife, a close family member."

"And the story of the jade box, and perhaps its location, became part of family lore passed down through the generations? Major long shot."

Nora opened the book to the title page where an inscription hand-written in ink read: *To the Cornette Library, Best wishes, Vera Amos, FBI (ret.) (granddaughter of James Amos.)* "So, what do you think?"

The clock was ticking, and they were nowhere. "Long shot's better than no shot."

Contacting the FBI revealed that Agent Vera Amos's last assignment had been the Denver field office. The personnel department there wouldn't provide Vera's current address. Hardly surprising.

A Google and Facebook search found four women living in the metro area named Vera Amos, and their images revealed two were white, two were African American. One of the African American women looked to be in her early twenties, while the other was shown holding a pink orchid in one hand and a purple championship ribbon in the other. The caption read: "Vera Amos wins first place in Denver Flower Show orchid category." Unfortunately, the woman appeared to be in her early sixties, too young to be James's granddaughter. Still, no date was visible on the photo, so it could've been taken years earlier.

Nora's fingers tapped the keyboard searching for garden clubs in the Denver metro area.

She clicked on the website of the one that sponsored the annual Denver Flower Show, found the number, and dialed from her cell phone. Her call was answered on the first ring.

She switched to bright, cheery mode. "Hi there. This is Nora Smith from the *Sacramento Bee*, and we're doing a story on garden clubs in the Rocky Mountain States and . . . Yes, Smith. Anyway, everyone knows about the Denver Flower Show, and I wanted to see if I could set up an appointment to interview your president . . . Probably next week. We'll feature it in the Sunday edition because that's our largest readership . . . Yes, next Tuesday would be perfect. We'd also be interested in interviewing some of your longtime members. We understand you have a former FBI agent who was active for many years . . . Vera Amos, that's right. That's the name we have. I understand she's a lovely woman."

Nora glanced Belle's way. At least they had the right Vera Amos. Was she still alive, and would the woman on the other end of the call provide Vera's number? Nora put the phone on speaker. "Would you happen to have a contact number?"

A long pause. *Come on, come on.* The woman's voice came over the speaker. "Sorry, I had to look her up in the directory. Vera's an emeritus member due to her many years of contributions. 303-555-6437. What time will you be arriving Tuesday, Ms. Smith?"

"Let me firm that up and get back to you." Nora said goodbye and immediately called the number. After four rings the call rolled over to voicemail.

Belle whispered, "Leave a message."

They couldn't be completely candid with Vera for fear of triggering an FBI inquiry, so Nora said she was curator of the Panhandle Plains Museum and was working with her co-author on a book about Roosevelt and Quanah Parker. Nora explained her interest in any relevant information Vera had that might've been handed down from her grandfather.

Vera called back within minutes, and Nora put the call on speaker. After introductions she relayed their story.

Vera responded, "I'm sorry, but I know of no family lore relating to James's time as Roosevelt's valet other than that found in his little book."

They were about to thank her for her time and say their good-byes when Vera added, "But I do have his research notes up in the attic."

They needed to handle this carefully, and Belle struggled to speak calmly, avoiding any display of enthusiasm. "That's interesting. We'd love to review them."

"I suppose that would be okay," Vera responded hesitantly. "Give me your address, and I'll mail them down to you. But first I need your word that if you use any of his research, James will receive proper credit in your book."

Big problem, Belle thought. There had no time for mail—snail, Fed Ex, carrier pigeon, or otherwise. She eyelocked with Nora, sending the silent message.

The message was received. "Of course," Nora said, "he'll receive all appropriate credit. But we're already behind our publisher's deadline. I wonder if we might fly up to take a look?"

Vera's tone took on an edge. "Uh, when were you thinking?"

Nora glanced Belle's way. "Well, let's see. How about today?"

Vera didn't respond. After a few seconds of silence Belle feared she might've ended the call. Finally, she spoke.

"If you want to go to the trouble," she said carefully, "you're welcome. I'll be home all day."

Nora arranged with an intern to watch Scout, and they headed back to the Amarillo airport. The short-term parking garage was full, so Belle dropped Nora off at the terminal and drove to the long-term parking facility. Every floor was packed, and she had to drive to the roof level for a parking space. After parking, she walked along the wall toward the stairs.

The sound of screeching tires stopped her in her tracks. A red blur flashed across the corner of her eye. A moment later a red convertible sped straight for the empty space next to the Tahoe, driven by a man with white-blond hair. She didn't need to see the driver's face to identify him. *Tyler.*

She heard the squeal of tires as he slammed on the brakes. The tires screeched, and the car spun toward her out of control. She had no time to dodge left or right. In a nanosecond she'd be crushed against the wall like a bug on a windshield.

She jumped up.

But not high enough.

The car smashed into the wall, its grill pinning her right ankle. She screamed out in pain, certain that her ankle had been crushed to a bloody pulp. She glanced down. The ankle was caught in the space between two vertical grill bars and appeared intact. She looked around. The upper parking level was deserted.

Tyler, wide-eyed and clearly shaken, jumped out of the car. "Oh, my God. Belle, are you okay?"

"Just back the damn car up!"

"Really sorry." He hurried back to the car. "Going a little too—" And then he stopped and slowly turned. His expression changed, like someone had flicked a switch. There it was, his smarmy smile. "Whoa, look at Wonder Woman, squirming like a fish on a pike."

Belle's left leg was free and resting on top of the lateral part of the bumper. She tried using it to lever up her leg. No luck. "Back up the damn car!" She could see his eyes were red, and she knew it wasn't from spring pollen. He was high on something—drugs, booze, maybe both.

He folded his arms. "I meant what I said back in D.C., Belle. You look fantastic. So, are you and that cute little brunette an item?"

"How did you find me?"

"I'll always know where you are," he answered with a smug smile.

She had a plane to catch and a sister to rescue. She didn't have time for Cox's bullshit. But she knew him well enough to understand the more she antagonized him, the worse off she'd be.

She forced a softened tone. "Tyler, I apologize for gutting you back in the hotel. When you grabbed me, my training automatically kicked in. Ben speaks very highly of you and tells me you have a great job."

"Not that great. Private security for rich assholes. But the pay's okay, and the company has all of the latest locator tools."

Which was how he'd tracked her. Cell phones, air travel records, hotel registers, social media. Everything and everybody's wired. Too easy.

"I must admit, Belle, I never figured you for a lesbian. In fact, if I recall you seemed to really enjoy normal sex. You know, the kind between a man and a woman."

Jesus, what did I ever see in this jerk? "Tyler, please listen. You remember me talking about my little sister, Jenny?"

"Yeah, you showed me her picture once,' he responded with a leer. "I remember she has a great rack."

Belle closed her eyes and gritted her teeth. The lizard door in the back of her brain cracked open and a wisp of white light leaked through. *Hold, control.* She focused hard on the door, visualizing it, and mentally shoved it closed. "Jenny's in trouble. Nora and I—she's Jenny's boss, not my lover—we need to board a plane in thirty minutes to help save her."

He stepped toward her, not changing his expression. His face reminded her of one of those smooth white Halloween masks worn by villains in slasher movies. Eyes that don't blink, no facial muscle movement. She noticed him clenching and unclenching his right fist. *Shit.* She wiggled her ankle. It hurt like hell, but she was pretty sure it wasn't broken. She tugged again but couldn't pull it loose. Tyler Cox was in complete control.

He took a step closer, not hearing a word she'd said. "Don't worry, I'm not going to hurt you bad. You know I would never do that. Just mess up that pretty face a little bit. You have to admit, there need to be consequences for what you did to me at the hotel."

"We both know that has nothing to do with your anger."

His smirk disappeared, and he lowered his eyes. "You should've told me, Belle. You had no right."

"A miscarriage. A miscarriage, Tyler, not an abortion, as I've told you a million times."

"Bullshit. You didn't want the kid, *my* kid, because it would've derailed your quest to be famous as the first Marine woman in frontline combat."

How was she going to reason with an idiot high on drugs? "That's simply not true. You know me well enough to understand that fame is the last thing I want."

"We were having a boy, weren't we?"

"Jesus."

"Weren't we?"

"I don't know. I was only seven weeks in. Now, please, back up the car. I promise I'll meet you for dinner anyplace anytime to talk about it. We were barely out of our teens, and—"

His right shoulder twitched, and she raised her left arm to block the punch. The arm absorbed most of the blow, but his fist skimmed across and collided with her mouth. He was inside her arc now. She locked her left arm around his right and yanked him hard toward her. She curled her fist, save for her protruding knuckled forefinger in the classic Ipon-ken Shoken technique, and struck him hard in the temple. If she'd had more room to extend the strike he would've been on the ground, but due to the lack of leverage he only staggered back and dropped to one knee.

He grimaced, shook his head to clear it, then rose to his feet, grabbing the car handle to regain his balance. His eyes burned into her. Tyler Cox, the young man she knew, had disappeared and in his stead was a delusional monster. He slid around to the back of the car and unlocked the trunk. She knew what he was after.

I was so stupid. I should've let him hit me. He might've gone away after one punch to teach me a lesson.

She frantically wiggled her foot back and forth, trying to pull free, but the foot stuck. He fumbled around in the trunk for a few seconds before retrieving a tire iron. Because she'd been about to board a plane, her gun remained stowed in the car. His promise not to hurt her bad was out the window.

"Tyler don't do this," she pleaded. "Your career, your whole life will vanish, and you'll spend the rest of your life in prison. It's not worth it. *I'm* not worth it."

His expressionless mask was off now, and his face dripped with blind rage, leaving no doubt as to his intentions. At that moment he didn't care about his career, his life, prison.

Nothing in the world mattered to him other than planting that tire iron deep in her skull. *What did I ever see in this psycho?* She knew the answer. She was young, stupid, and horny. Old story.

She furiously wiggled her foot, this time more left and right. She felt her shoe loosen. Tyler retreated a few steps. She figured to maximize force he was going to come from the back of the car and swing as hard as he could at her head. If she tried to block the iron, the force of his swing would easily break her arm and make the next blow—the fatal blow? — a piece of cake.

"I loved you so much. And you murdered my son. Maybe, *maybe* I could've forgiven you. But then you dumped me. Tossed me aside like yesterday's garbage." His eyes completely lost focus. Any last wisps of reason had evaporated.

"I'm sorry, Tyler. I—"

"Remember what I said back in Pendleton? If I can't have you—"

Her foot pulled loose from the shoe, and she braced it on top of the front bumper. He covered the distance between them in two giant leaps while at the same time sweeping the tire iron back behind his shoulder.

She sprang high toward him, inside his swing arc, caught the iron under her armpit, and locked her arm around his bicep. Using her whole body, she twisted hard, freeing the iron and sending him sprawling. She snatched the iron from the pavement, stood over him, and raised it high in the air. "Don't move."

They both heard the sound of a car engine. She glanced quickly over her shoulder as the nose of a vehicle moved up the ramp to the roof level. She pressed the point of the iron into his throat. "Leave me alone. Go live your life. If you persist in stalking me, I'll kill you."

She tossed the tire iron over the wall, retrieved her shoe, and hobbled toward the stairwell door. She paused and glanced over her shoulder to make sure Tyler wasn't following her. Still on his back, he hadn't moved. Staring at the sky, he wiped tears from his eyes. Her body shivered. *Shit, what was that?* For a chapter of her life—a very thin chapter—Tyler Cox had meant something to her. And then she thought of the baby ... She gasped then bit her lip, angry at herself for feeling anything other than revulsion for a man who a minute earlier had tried to kill her.

She opened the door and headed down the stairs to catch the terminal bus.

CHAPTER 16

Belle pulled out her quilting pouch to pass the time on the uncrowded flight to Denver.

"What will it look like when you're finished?" Nora asked.

"Hopefully, a Navajo rug with a wheat-colored background and a black and gold arrowhead border. I have one hanging in my house back in Park City. This is for the daughter of a friend."

"Maybe you could do a Comanche rug next. Red was the dominant color. Speaking of red, how's your lip?"

"Fine."

While waiting at the gate, Belle had used ice from a concession stand wrapped in a handful of napkins to stop the blood and reduce the swelling. She'd told Nora she tripped in the garage, lightly twisted her ankle, and bruised her lip when she hit the floor. No use raising her stress levels any higher. Belle's own stress, while elevated, fortunately hadn't reached lizard-door level. She was both curious and pleased that her lizard door hadn't flung open during the confrontation with Tyler. After all, he'd been about to plant a tire iron inside her brain. The only thing she could figure was that she'd once had feelings for the jerk.

Nora returned to her laptop. Belle needed to clear her head, so she continued sewing, hoping to occupy her mind with something other than Jenny's plight. Her plan worked for only about a half hour. Then the image of a photo on her mom's piano flashed in her head. The picture showed Belle as a nine-year-old holding her newborn sister in her arms. Over the years, Jenny had always looked up to her. Belle was her protector, yet now she felt so helpless. She set her quilting aside. She had to press Sal much harder. The Fibbies were professionals; she and Nora were rank amateurs. She would love to hear Alonzo's opinion. Before boarding, she'd tried to call him, but either he was still in the air on the way to Texas, or the number he'd given her no longer worked. But he was now an official secret agent. He'd find her.

"Done quilting?" Nora asked.

"Mind wandering."

Nora inclined her seat back. "Try to sleep."

"Can't."

"Then read a book."

"Don't have one."

She handed Belle her laptop. "Check out Roosevelt's journal notes on his interviews with Quanah. It reads like a modern-day thriller." She closed her eyes.

Belle opened up one of the files sent by Professor Moon. Roosevelt's notes were handwritten but not hard to read.

October 10, 1871. Most of the Comanches had surrendered and resided on the reservation, but the Quahadis led by Quanah remained at large. Colonel Ranald Mackenzie took on the job of finding, capturing, and if need be, killing Quanah's band. Mackenzie led 600 men and twenty-five Tonkawa scouts armed with Colt revolvers and Spencer carbines into Blanco Canyon searching for Comanches. That night they camped, confident they were safe. Throughout the Indian campaign, with few exceptions, the hostiles always avoided soldiers unless trapped with no escape.

Quanah's tactic was to use surprise and force the horse soldiers off their mounts. In the middle of the night the peace of the camp was shockingly disrupted by war cries and cowbells. Soldiers looked up to see mounted Comanches decked out in war paint crash through their camp. Mackenzie's own tent was run over, and horses were cut loose including Mackenzie's own prized gray.

The raid left sixty-six soldiers without a mount, and these men had to be sent back to the supply camp. Mackenzie was furious and, with the remainder of his men, rode off to Blanco Canyon searching for Quanah Parker.

A detachment from Mackenzie's force happened upon a small band of Comanches leading stolen horses through a narrow passage. Eager to exact revenge for the embarrassing camp raid, the attachment charged the Indians, chasing them through the passage into a box canyon. Only there did they realize Quanah had set a trap, and they'd taken the bait. The band of Comanches turned on them. They looked behind to see Quanah and the rest of his warriors had sealed off a retreat. They were trapped. They heard a high-pitched keening sound from above. Comanche women peering down from the canyon rim cheered on their men like they were witnessing a sporting event.

The battle was fierce, and Quanah, decked out in black war paint and a bear-claw necklace, killed a number of soldiers at close range. To Quanah, the soldiers were defending the buffalo hunters and deserved to die. A full massacre was only averted when the Tonkawa appeared, sending Quanah and his men riding up narrow trails, climbing the canyon walls to safety.

Roosevelt's account of Quanah's display of passion, honor, and courage impressed Belle. Quanah intended to exact justice no matter how overwhelming the odds were. He selected his war lance, a treasured gift from his father, as the location for the Hudie Box symbols. Could Quanah's passionate hatred for the buffalo hunters itself be a clue to the jade box's location?

Her thoughts were interrupted by the pilot's voice coming over the loudspeaker, advising passengers to prepare for landing.

On the way to the Avis counter Belle's phone chimed. A text from Ben Porter. No message, only a link to the Washington Post website. She tapped the link, and the Post's headline filled the screen: "FBI Arrests 38 in Chinese Smuggling Ring." She showed the headline to Nora, and right on cue the phone rang. Ben.

"Did you see my text?" he asked anxiously.

"Yeah, but I haven't had a chance to read the story."

"I just got off the phone with the Yishu task force AIC. You could tell he was excited. Apparently, they've been targeting the gang for almost a year."

Belle struggled to keep her voice even. "Anything about Jenny?"

"Sorry, Belle. I talked to him generally without referencing your situation, and he was pretty adamant that they never saw even the slightest evidence of kidnapping. Murder, yes. But kidnapping would involve loved ones and add an element of unpredictability they didn't want and didn't need. The investigation also identified a number of Yishu members with diplomatic creds, including a couple stationed at the Chinese embassy here in Washington. But I seriously doubt they were the ones who assaulted Nora in Georgetown."

"Shit."

"My feelings exactly. I'll keep digging. Where are you?"

"In Denver, trying to track down information from a descendent of Roosevelt's valet, a man named James Amos. Amos was known as the president's closest confidant, and he wrote a book about his personal experiences with Roosevelt. We're hoping Amos knew something about the Hudie Box and might've passed that information down through the family."

"Sounds like a long shot. But then again, a long shot's—"

"Yeah, we know," she snapped. After a deep sigh, "Sorry."

"No problem. One more thing. I called Tyler to unload on him for his behavior in the hotel room. He's not at work. I was told he decided to take a few days off for a personal matter. He's not answering his cell. Now, that personal matter could be any number of things, but—"

"Tyler tried to bury a tire iron in my skull at the airport parking garage." She was surprised by the calmness of her own voice.

Nora stopped in her tracks. "What?"

"Jesus, are you okay?" Ben asked.

"Yeah. And so is he. I remember one time when we were together, after more than a few drinks, he told me if I ever left him, he'd make sure no one else could have me. I assumed he was simply telling me how much I meant to him in his typical ham-handed way. Now I know I should've taken him literally."

"I can call the Amarillo police," he offered, his voice dark with anger. "Have them track him down."

"No. I don't have time to deal with Tyler's bullshit right now."

"Suit yourself. But promise me you'll be careful."

"Always." She ended the call.

Nora continued looking straight ahead as they walked. "For what it's worth, I knew your bloody lip didn't come from tripping. As I said, when it comes to man trouble, I get it. But for the life of me I don't understand how you would date a guy like that."

"Tyler is a very bright, very clever man," Belle explained wearily. You'd think someone with his temper would've manifested it throughout his life. But his background, going back to his youth, was very normal. I've met his family, and they couldn't be sweeter. He's been successful throughout his entire life, which probably contributed to the problem. He never experienced failure. When he didn't make the cut to join Force Recon, I think he was stunned. That was the first time he'd failed. He holds me responsible for both failures, and honestly believes that I got the Recon spot meant for him because I'm a woman."

She hesitated before going any further. She'd only known Nora Yates for a few days, and under normal circumstances she'd never confide very personal matters to someone she hardly knew. But the circumstances they found themselves in were about as far away from normal as one could get. And Belle trusted her.

Her voice softened. "But what really sent him over the edge was I got pregnant with his child, and two months into the pregnancy I miscarried. Heartbreaking. But Tyler believed—still believes—that I intentionally aborted the child because it could interfere with my military career. He began hitting the booze and the drugs hard and lost all semblance of reason. He's dangerous and unpredictable."

Nora didn't speak for a few long moments, deep in thought. Finally, she sighed and held Belle's gaze, her voice steady. "Okay, I understand why you didn't volunteer any of this information. And on most levels, your personal life is none of my business. But going forward, if we're going to rescue Jenny, we need to trust each other without question."

Belle nodded. She was right.

They easily found their way to Vera Amos's house with help from the trusty GPS lady, and forty minutes after leaving the Denver airport, Belle parked the rental in front of a well-kept red brick Victorian in Denver's Curtis Park neighborhood. "This is it."

They made their way up a concrete walkway past several small flower gardens on the way to the front porch, but before they could knock, the door opened, and a tall African American woman appeared. Her white hair was cut to a tight Afro, and she wore jeans and a blue blouse. She had to be well into her eighties but looked fifteen years younger. Only slightly stooped now, Belle could tell that in her prime, Agent Vera Amos was not someone to mess with.

"Ms. Yates and Ms. Bannon, I presume."

Her voice was strong for a woman her age. They shook hands, and Belle offered her most charming smile. "Thanks for seeing us."

"I knew you were both lying,' she said matter-of-factly, "but my curiosity got the best of me. Come on in."

Belle figured her most charming smile needed work.

Belle and Nora followed Vera Amos down a narrow hallway wallpapered in a bright floral design to a small room. Pink and white orchids lined up in pots on the room's two windowsills.

Nora took in the sunny space. "What a lovely sitting room."

Belle figured almost all rooms in a house were for sitting, but she kept her thoughts to herself.

"Thank you," Vera responded warily. "Have a seat."

Nora selected a straight-back mahogany chair with an upholstered flora print seat, and Belle settled into a very comfortable pale blue armchair next to the orchids. Maybe calling it a sitting room was as good a description as any.

Nora got right to the point. "Ms. Amos, we're here—"

Vera gestured for her to stop then glanced from one to the other. "You wouldn't have flown up here with such urgency if you were simply concerned about researching a book. I'll be ninety years old in September, plenty of time to develop a pretty accurate bullshit meter, and your story is pushing the needle deep into the red zone."

Belle quickly confirmed her original impression that Vera was not someone to mess with.

"Now, who wants to be the first to tell me why the hell you're really here?"

Belle glanced at Nora who nodded her agreement, then turned back to Vera. "If we tell you, you might feel duty bound to take action, and an innocent young woman, my younger sister, Jenny, will likely die along with her unborn child." She could see her answer had surprised her host.

Vera clearly wasn't expecting that answer, and she paused for a moment before speaking. "I see. And if I do help you?"

"There's a deadline. It's possible your assistance might increase our chances to save her."

Vera stood and walked to a window. After dipping her fingers in a bowl of water resting on a nearby table, she sprinkled droplets onto the bark nuggets in the flowerpots. Belle could see she wasn't really focused on the posies. She turned, held Belle's gaze, and spoke with a calm authority.

"Ms. Bannon, it's been over twenty-five years since I was an agent for the FBI, and as you know, my grandfather had a stellar career in the Bureau."

"I understand he was the first African American agent."

"I'm not diminishing his role as a trailblazer, but his legacy in the bureau meant much more to him. He helped bring Murder, Incorporated, and a Nazi spy ring to justice, just to name a few. My point is, if I believe it's in the interest of justice to help you, I will. If not, I won't. So let's take this one step at a time. What is it you want?"

Nora jumped in. "We're looking for a box, a jade box. It could be a valuable Chinese artifact."

"Okay, it's pretty obvious your sister's been kidnapped," Vera said impatiently, "and you need the box to exchange for Jenny. You understand that the FBI has a great deal of experience handling kidnappings."

"We're aware of that," Belle responded. Vera raised an eyebrow in a go-on gesture, but Belle remained silent.

Vera returned to her seat and let out a breath. "Again, what is it you want of me?"

Belle's words spilled out. "We could be way off base, but given the ticking clock, we had to make several assumptions. First, that the box was a gift to Roosevelt, presumably either directly or indirectly a gift from China. Second, the gift took place sometime between his inaugural parade in March of 1905 and the death of Quanah Parker in 1911. And third, the box somehow found its way into Quanah's possession."

"Quanah Parker, the Apache Indian?"

Nora corrected her. "Comanche."

Belle continued. "Your grandfather was one of Roosevelt's most trusted confidants, so we were hoping his book might've shed some light on the jade box and its connection to Roosevelt, China, and Quanah."

"Because you're looking to find a clue to its whereabouts."

"Yes," Belle continued, "but unfortunately James's book didn't mention Quanah or the jade box, so we thought there could've been information discovered during his research, but not used in the book, something that might've been passed down orally to his family. And then on the phone you mentioned his research notes."

Vera's eyes narrowed. "And why should I trust you with James's work product? I don't know you, and, frankly, your story sounds more like a Netflix thriller than real life."

Belle couldn't criticize Vera's skepticism; she would've felt the same way. Sitting forward in the chair, Belle eyelocked with the former agent. "I understand, but ask yourself, what would be our motive? It's not like James's notes have any monetary value. Our parents are dead, and I'm the only family Jenny has right now that can do anything to rescue her. The chances those research notes have any value to our ability to save her are slim, and yes, we might be grasping at straws. But at the moment your grandfather's notes are the only straw available to grasp."

Vera Amos cast her eyes down and remained still for several moments. Finally, she stood. "Excuse me, please."

She left the room and in less than a minute returned carrying a battered tan leather valise covered in a thick layer of dust and smelling of nesting critters. Belle thought she could make out the raised brass initials JA on one side just below the grip.

"After you called, I dug this out of the attic. Passed down from my father. I looked through the contents, but I'm afraid there's nothing earth-shattering inside, only James's research notes and early drafts of the book. I don't remember anything about Quanah Parker." She set the valise down in front of Belle. "Please don't make me regret my decision."

Nora drove to the Denver airport while Belle hastily examined the contents of the valise. Unfortunately, Vera was right—it contained mostly early drafts of the book manuscript. Belle found several letters from Amos's publisher along with maybe twenty-five pages of the author's handwritten notes. Since they'd already checked out the contents of the book itself, she focused on the research notes. They were difficult to read which was hardly surprising since Amos wrote them for his own purposes only. She found plenty of information about the Roosevelt family, but nothing about China or Quanah Parker or a jade box. The James Amos search had been a complete bust. More important, a waste of half a day.

Her phone rang. Ben. She put it on speaker mode.

He didn't bother with a greeting. "I think I may have found the cavalry."

"I'm listening."

"I have this friend, Steve, who works at State. He's not allowed to tell me much, but apparently they've been monitoring increased activity among MSS agents in-country."

"What's MSS?" Nora asked.

"Sorry. Spend time in Washington and you quickly learn to speak Alphabet Soup. MSS is the Chinese Ministry of State Security, China's CIA. There's this rumored secret ops unit on our side that may have interacted with MSS agents recently here in the District."

"Interacted? Sounds like a lady's tea rather than a bloody gunfight on a city street with Chinese secret agents," Belle said.

Ben laughed. "You're right. Laurie got on my ass the other day when I referred to Danny's Little League teammates as assets. Point is, if there really is this black ops unit, and if they're the ones who have been watching over you, that's a net positive." He paused for a second, and they heard muffled voices in the background. His voice lowered. "Have to run. Good luck."

A hard landing jostled Belle awake as they touched down back in Amarillo. The plane taxied to a stop, and the chime dinged permission to stand and gather their stuff. She dragged the valise out of the overhead bin, but the raised JA initials snagged on the bin clasp.

Click.

Nora and Belle both spoke in unison. "Did you hear that?"

Belle loosened the valise from the snag and balanced it on the seat arm. Ignoring all of the passengers pushing and crowding into them, she opened the valise and discovered the lining on one side had popped open revealing a secret compartment. She reached into the compartment and withdrew a single letter-size envelope almost two inches thick.

Scrawled across the face of the envelope in faded black letters was a single word: "Confidential."

CHAPTER 17

When they stepped off the elevator at the roof level of the parking garage, Belle's eyes instantly turned to the wall where she'd almost had her skull crushed in a losing battle with a tire iron. She was a bit surprised to see the old Tahoe intact. "I half expected we'd have to be dealing with slashed tires or a broken windshield."

Nora put a comforting hand on her shoulder. "Hopefully, he heeded your message to stay away."

Storm clouds loomed. Their pace across the lot quickened, eager to review the contents of James Amos's secret envelope. The Tahoe was one of only a few cars parked on the top level, and they appeared to be alone. A loud roar soared overhead as another jet took off, so close Belle felt if she stretched high enough, she could touch the undercarriage. Distracted by the sight and sound, several long seconds passed before she heard Nora's muffled scream.

Belle turned to see a tall, skinny Chinese man holding a silenced automatic to Nora's temple. Standing next to him was Belle's old pal, Baldy. Another one of his men drove a black sedan out of a parking space and pulled close, ready to take off.

How did Baldy find us? Belle wondered.

The man took a few steps toward Belle and reached out his hand. It took her a second to realize he wanted James Amos's valise.

She quickly offered the briefcase. "Sure, here. Just let her go."

He took the valise and stepped back. "You have become quite an irritant, Ms. Bannon." The man's voice was softer and higher than she expected. Almost feminine.

"I'm not sure what's going on, but an innocent young woman is being held hostage, and if we don't find this damn box they'll kill her. I say 'they' because I'm pretty sure now that the kidnappers play for a different team than you do."

"We do not have your sister, Ms. Bannon," he confirmed.

"Nora can help find the box. The one with the butterflies, right?"

He didn't answer, but she could tell from his silent expression that they were all looking for the same thing. "Instead of stopping her, why not help? Once the box is located, maybe you can pay the kidnappers a few million then return the box to your museum or your president's mantel or wherever the hell you want. I'm sure you guys have lots of resources. Jenny's running out of time. Instead of hurting Nora, help us."

"You do not understand, Ms. Bannon. The Hudie Box must *never* be found. And we do not intend to hurt Ms. Yates." He nodded toward the skinny man holding the gun to Nora's head. "We merely intend to end her life as painlessly as possible."

"Let me guess. As the only witness, I win the next bullet."

Belle measured the distance in her mind. No way could she reach the skinny man's gun hand in time. But she could reach Nora.

"I don't expect you to believe this, but I'm very sorry, Ms. Yates," Jin nodded to the gunman.

Belle leaped toward Nora and knocked her hard to the pavement just as the gun discharged. She sprang up to see the gun now trained on her head.

Thwitt.

The skinny man yelped and grabbed his thigh; blood poured through his fingers.

Thwitt, thwitt, thwitt . . .

She looked up to see a gun with a silencer protruding from the rear passenger window of a dark sedan on the other side of the lot. Baldy dropped the valise and used two hands to steady his gun and return fire. She scanned the pavement searching for Skinny's weapon, but guessed it slid under the Tahoe. With Baldy momentarily distracted, she coiled her body, about to spring forward and tackle him to the pavement, but he and his sidekick sprinted away to the black sedan and tumbled inside. The car took off before the doors even closed.

Nora crawled to her feet. Her forehead was bleeding.

"You've been wounded!"

"I'm fine." Nora touched her forehead. "Scraped it when you tackled me. Thanks, by the way."

Almost killed twice in one day. Belle decided never to park on the roof level again.

A moment later the cavalry drove over and stopped. Belle and Nora watched in curious fascination as the driver, a big blond dude, stepped out. He wore a dark suit, white shirt, subdued tie. Maybe forty, Belle's height, his suit jacket strained across a muscular frame. Belle was almost certain he was the same guy who'd rescued them in Georgetown.

A stocky woman emerged from the passenger seat. Short with frizzy black hair, a pretty face, and soft brown eyes. She wore a black suit, white blouse, and rubber-soled shoes.

And then someone else emerged from the back seat of the car. Alonzo Longabaugh. At the sight of Belle, his smile reached his ears, and he jogged toward her. They embraced, and Belle didn't care that it lasted longer than the typical platonic great-to-see-you-again hug. "You were the shooter."

"Yeah. Didn't want to kill him. Just shoo him away."

Alonzo was an inch or two taller than Belle in stocking feet. Dark blond hair, the long, sinewy muscled body of a sprinter, and a two-day growth of beard. He wore a light jacket, jeans, a denim shirt, and scuffed boots, and resembled old photos of his ancestor, Henry Alonzo Longabaugh, aka the Sundance Kid. His eyes, the color of a blue gas flame, brightened at the sight of her. Belle had missed those eyes and that smile. And the rest of his body parts.

"This is Stella Alvarez and Steve Kelly," Alonzo said.

Belle introduced Nora; handshakes all around.

"So, you all are secret agents?" Nora inquired with a twinkle in her eye.

Kelly didn't respond, instead asking, "You guys hungry?"

The women followed Alonzo, Stella, and Kelly to a roadside honky-tonk off Interstate 27 south of Amarillo. Ronny's Roundup was just what Belle expected when they parked out front under a neon sign advertising "Cold Beer, Hot Music." Jam-packed, loud, dimly lit, lots of cowboy hats, and the smell of beer in the air. Crowded into the far corner, a female singer spilling out of her low-cut, red-checked blouse fronted a four-piece country band that attempted to make up for talent with volume.

The only table available was positioned next to the dance floor. The five of them crowded around the table and ordered beers and food. The menu was quite limited—barbeque chicken, buffalo chili, and buffalo burgers. Belle wondered if they'd run out of cows in Texas.

Kelly tapped his feet to the music. "Song was written by John Rich, who came from these parts. He writes a lot of Jason Aldean stuff, too."

"I take it you're not 'from these parts.'" Belle surmised.

"Lexington, Kentucky, home of the world champion Kentucky Wildcats."

Up close now, Belle could see Kelly's blue tie was patterned with images of the university's Wildcat logo. Obviously, a big fan. "Okay, first, thanks for saving our ass. Again." She focused on Stella and Kelly. "You guys came to the rescue in Georgetown, right?"

Stella nodded. "Steve's our immediate supervisor. He and I were in the car following the shooters."

"Why didn't you stop?" Nora asked.

"We didn't want our fingerprints anywhere near a gunfight on Prospect Street," Steve replied.

"Ben Porter told me about you," Belle said.

Kelly seemed surprised. "He did? Ben's good people. I swear if they ever make a movie about Michael Jordan, Ben should get the part. Except he can't jump worth shit."

Belle grinned. "Or shoot or catch."

"What exactly is the name of your organization?" Nora asked. No one spoke. "I see."

"Sorry," Kelly said. "Don't mean to suggest our group is some cloak and dagger outfit straight out of a cheap spy novel with a hokey name."

"Uh, but we do have a hokey name," Alonzo said.

"Very hokey," Stella added.

Kelly shook his head and raised his palms skyward in an "I give up" gesture. "You can see the respect I get."

Nora joined a round of polite but thin laughter; Belle didn't. She focused on Kelly, since he was the boss. "Who are you and why are you here?"

Kelly handed her a credentials wallet. She flipped it open and held it so Nora could also read his full name, Steven Randolph Kelly, along with his photo and the seal of the Department of State, Bureau of Intelligence and Research—INR.

"So, your hokey squad works for this INR?" Nora asked.

Kelly took a long sip of beer and nodded. "The INR is older than the CIA. It's an arm of the State Department that performs many intelligence research tasks and is a member of the nation's overall intelligence team."

The waitress brought three longneck Buds, and a club soda for Stella. The agent's eyes continually scanned the room. A professional.

"Why have I never heard of the INR?" Nora inquired.

Belle guessed she knew the answer to that. "Because they want to remain under the radar. No movies, no TV shows about secret agents from INR. That way it's easier for them to operate both inside and outside our borders. Like an FBI-CIA combo meal."

Silence from Kelly, Stella, and Alonzo signaled that no additional information was forthcoming about who they were. Belle pressed. "Okay for now. How about the 'why' question?"

"We've been monitoring a fellow named Jin Choi," Kelly said, all business. "Jin's a Chinese MSS operative in the States. He teaches a course in Chinese history and culture at George Washington University and has been in America a long time. He's attached to the Chinese embassy in Washington. Near flawless English, very lethal. Choi is very close to China's president Peng. We're convinced Choi's the key to leading us to deeply embedded sleeper cells in our country, especially in the DC area. Outside of his cover teaching at GW, he's kept his visibility low, and we were surprised when he surfaced. We've been monitoring him as closely as we can and were able to disrupt the two attempts to take you both out. Although our sense is his principal target is Ms. Yates."

"I have yet to hear why this Jin guy's trying to kill us," Nora said sharply.

"And how did they find us?" Belle added.

The waitress brought their food order and left, but nobody seemed hungry at the moment.

Kelly held out a hand, palm upward. "Let me see your phones."

He checked out Belle's first, and his thumbs danced across the screen.

"It's ironic," Stella said. "If the government issued an order requiring everyone to embed a tracking chip under their skin so the feds could know where they were at all times, there would be a revolt. Yet we've all given the government the same thing voluntarily by carrying around cell phones."

Nora raised her brows. "Never thought of it that way, but you're right."

Kelly set Belle's phone aside. "You're clean." He examined Nora's phone and after only a few seconds, nodded. "Here it is. Garden-variety tracer. I'm disabling it." He tapped the screen a few more times, then returned their phones.

Nora's eyes narrowed. "When could they have gained access to my phone?"

"Where do you usually keep it?" Kelly asked.

"Mostly in my back pocket," Nora replied. "If I'm carrying a purse, I'll put it in there."

Stella smiled. "We women who keep our phones in our back jeans pocket are the easiest. It's child's play to pick up that phone. Has there been an instance lately when someone returned your phone to you?"

"No." Nora paused, then winced. "Well, yes. At the grocery store. I didn't even notice it missing. Then this redheaded man came up to me and said he'd seen it fall out when I bent down to check out something on the lower shelf."

"But he wasn't Chinese," Belle said.

Kelly smiled coldly. "MSS has substantial resources. They regularly pay American Caucasians to assist them in their activities."

"And you know where we are because you're following Jin," Belle concluded.

Kelly nodded.

"If they were that close, why not try to kill her then?" Belle asked.

"Too many witnesses," Kelly replied easily.

Alonzo said, "You both have asked why Jin and his men are trying to kill you."

"Under the circumstances I assume you'll agree it's a fair question," Belle said.

Kelly held her gaze. "Frankly, Ms. Bannon, that's our question for you."

Belle eyelocked with Nora. How much do they tell them? Belle trusted Alonzo but she didn't know the other two. Although Kelly had saved their lives on two occasions, he had a duty to do his job, and she couldn't take a chance on him feeling he had an obligation to go to the FBI.

Belle broke her gaze and faced Kelly. "Here's the thing. We don't know the answer to the 'why' question for sure, but we know it's related to an ongoing situation. Problem is, if we give you the details, you'll be compelled to take action, report it to the FBI, and if the bad guys find out—and my sense is they're pretty perceptive—my sister, Jenny Bannon, will be killed."

Kelly took another long drink of beer. "Okay, first you should know the FBI is no friend of mine. They've already screwed up three of my cases. The targets ran back and hid behind diplomatic immunity, and months of effort to find key sleeper cells went up in smoke."

"Forgive me for being blunt," Nora said, "but why the hell don't you just arrest Jin Choi?"

"We've been following Jin for five months. He's a key player, a liaison between the embassy and the sleepers. If we bring him in, we lose the opportunity to uncover them."

"But Jin must know you're on to him," Belle said.

Kelly smirked. "Jin doesn't lack for self-confidence. He views our pursuit as a kind of game. He believes he can do his job and still stay two steps ahead of the stupid Americans."

Alonzo, who'd been mostly silent, finally spoke. "I trust Belle and I think we should give her a little space."

Belle's gaze brushed Alonzo's long enough to convey her thanks.

Kelly paused for a moment. "Okay, here's what I'll do. You tell me what's going on, and I promise we'll take no official action for twenty-four hours. After that you'll need to report to the FBI, or I will."

"We need a couple more days."

Kelly paused for a few moments, then nodded his assent.

Nora took over, explaining everything they'd done from the moment of the burglary up through their visit to Vera Amos and their review of James Amos's writing notes.

"And?"

Belle jumped in. "We came up empty."

Nora must've picked up on Belle's signal, as she didn't mention the confidential envelope hidden in Amos's valise. Belle wanted to know what was in that envelope before deciding to turn it over.

"Here's what's curious," Belle said. "We originally thought Baldy—Jin—might've been part of the Yishu gang, the one the FBI just arrested. Then we believed he was working for his government to recover a national treasure. Yet now, in the parking garage right before you saved the day, Jin said, 'The Hudie Box must never be found.'"

"I agree," Kelly said. "Makes no sense."

"Any theories?" Alonzo asked.

"Haven't had time to think about it," Kelly replied. "When I get a chance, I'll call back to Washington and run this Hudie Box through our databases," Kelly said. "But the most important thing now is recovering your sister safe and unharmed. I'll get a copy of the police report for the museum burglary. Anything you've thought of since then that's not in the report? A further description of the kidnappers? Anything, no matter how small?"

"No. Think I told them everything. The detective's name is Lopez.

He's not aware of the kidnapping so if you contact him, please keep it that way."

"I told you we'd give you a little time, and we will. But if you're smart you won't hold me to my promise."

"What could the FBI do at this point?" Nora asked.

"How did the kidnappers contact you?" Stella asked.

"First, through Jenny's phone," Belle replied. "Then they switched to burners. We tried calling back. Most of the time we heard no connection and no voicemail rollover, but I think a text might've gone through."

"If you were able to send a text, it's possible the Fibbies could provide a general idea of the phone's location at that point in time. But if they're regularly switching out burners, it's unlikely a trace could be undertaken."

"But they could try," Nora said. "And why can't you guys at least try? You're spooks tied into the whole intelligence apparatus."

"Because questions will be asked, questions you don't want me to answer. I told you I'm not particularly a fan of the FBI, but the truth is they are very good at dealing with kidnappings and have much more experience than we do."

"One more thing," Belle said. "It's probably nothing, but when Jenny was on the phone alerting us to the kidnappers' deadline, at the end she said, 'Bye-bye' twice. It just seemed weird. She sounded scared to death and —" Belle observed Stella's expression perk up. "What?"

Kelly's expression hardened. "A notorious MSS agent named Bai Sun has been off the grid for a couple of weeks."

"So, it's possible Jenny was trying to tell you Bai Sun is the kidnapper," Alonzo said.

Made sense to Belle. "There were two men at the museum."

"Could the second person have been a woman?" Stella asked.

Belle remembered the other attacker was small in stature. "Yeah, I guess so. Why?"

"Bai Sun is known to sometimes team up with an agent named Fen Lao, and she's also off the grid."

"Fen Lao's a psycho," Kelly said. "They call her *Bishou* which means dagger. Supposedly she can slice a man into a hundred pieces before he knows he's dead."

Nora visibly shuddered.

"But the three of them—Jin, Bai, and Fen—can't be working together," Belle added.

Kelly nodded. "Based on Jin's message to you at the airport, probably not."

"Makes no sense," Belle said. "Bai wants us to find the Hudie Box, and Jin wants to make sure we don't find it."

"America's not the only country with crazy politics," Alonzo said. "Who knows what internal Chinese politics might be at play here? The important thing is returning Jenny to safety."

"Soon as I leave, I'll make some calls and see if we have an LKL for Bai and Fen," Kelly said.

"LKL?" Nora inquired.

"Sorry. Last known location. Look, I'm not going to sugarcoat this. You both need to know these are dangerous people. Jin, Bai, Fen, all three of them."

Kelly's pocket buzzed, and he checked his phone screen. He pulled out his phone and checked the screen. "Afraid we have to go," he said, "but I'll be in touch. Please be careful. Jin obviously wants Nora dead, and I don't think he likes you very much either, Belle. We'll try to keep tabs on him, but he's a slippery little shit, so don't count on us to save you."

Belle held his gaze. "Understood."

All rose and shook hands. Belle noticed that Alonzo made sure his shake of Belle's hand was businesslike. "Thanks again for saving our asses," Nora said.

"Twice," Belle added.

"You're welcome," Kelly replied. "One last thing. In addition to Jin Choi being a formidable adversary, MSS has clusters of operatives in every state, mostly American mercenaries. With one phone call he can gather a couple dozen men to his side. You underestimate him at your peril." Kelly took his untouched burger plate from the table. "Maybe I can get them to wrap this. See you guys soon." He handed Belle a business card. "Call me if you change your mind about going to the Bureau.

I can get you to the right people very fast." He weaved his way through the crowded dance floor, stopped at the bar to pick up a to-go box, then left.

Alonzo lingered. Did Belle want to kiss him? Hell, yeah. But not the time or place.

He took her hand. "I'm really sorry you have to go through this. You potentially have two of China's top agents roaming around out there, and you both are number one on their dance card. I realize you're not going to follow my advice, but please be careful."

"I'm always careful."

"You know how to reach me." He squeezed her hand and turned to leave.

"You forgot your burger."

"Give it to Scout. Tell him it's from me." One last smile, then he headed for the door.

Belle felt a small pang of disappointment as he disappeared out the door, which pissed her off. Belle Bannon didn't do pangs.

"I can see why you're attracted to him," Nora said. "Are those blue eyes for real?"

"Yeah, but now one hundred percent of my attention has to be focused on Jenny."

"You could've told him privately about the confidential envelope in Amos's valise," Nora offered.

"I trust him with my life, but I didn't want to put him on the spot before we know what's in it." She opened the valise and pulled out the envelope, but quickly realized the venue offered insufficient light to read it. They could've used their phone flashlights, but the noise from the bar made it difficult to concentrate. "Let's get out of here. We can read the documents back at your place." Nora nodded, and Belle replaced the envelope back inside the valise.

The singer started in on the up-tempo song, "I'm Here for the Party," and even more couples began to dance, bumping into tables ringing the dance floor.

Belle signaled the waitress, and she quickly brought the check along with a couple of plastic boxes for the burgers. They deposited the food in the containers, and Belle dropped two twenties on the table.

A big, flushed-faced, bearded guy wearing a cowboy hat and western shirt was dancing up a storm so close to Nora she couldn't push her chair back to leave. Couple inches taller than Belle, probably a hundred pounds heavier.

Belle reached up and tapped the guy on his shoulder. "Excuse me, the lady needs to get up."

The fellow, who clearly had been over-served, flashed a grin to a buddy lounging at a nearby table. Instead of moving back, he stepped closer and shook his ass in Nora's face, much to the delight of his dancing partner, a heavily made-up bleached blonde whose tight jeans made it impossible for her to bend. The last thing Belle wanted was any trouble, so she pulled a ten from her pocket and offered it to the guy.

"Here you go, big fella," she said in a friendly voice. "Have a cold one on me. Just give my friend a little room. By the way, you're a helluva dancer. Ever think about going on one of those TV dance shows?"

"Your friend?" He smirked. He gave me the head-to-toe once over. "Is she a special friend?"

Walk away, walk away . . .

He then snatched the ten and glanced back at blondie and his buddy with a "watch this" expression. "Be happy to give your squaw bitch room." Before Belle could react, he shoved Nora hard to the floor in front of the buddy. "Now she has lots of room."

The buddy—short, skinny, black cowboy hat, and a florid face shaped into a stupid grin—stood up from the table and bent down to Nora.

"Here, let me help you up." He lifted Nora to her feet, and in the process roughly groped her breasts. Nora spun hard and jammed a flying elbow in his throat. He bent over, clutching his neck, gagging. Nora stepped back, then spun again, this time firing her foot into the groper's head with a move that would make any MMA fan proud. The blow knocked him to the floor, stunned.

Belle won the battle to control her temper. She grabbed Nora's hand. "Let's get out of here."

"You bitch!" The big cowboy roared.

Belle sucked in a breath as her internal struggle to keep the lizard door shut intensified. She tugged Nora toward the exit. "C'mon."

The cowboy reached back to punch Nora.

The lizard door crashed open. White light flooded Belle's brain.

She leaped onto his back and locked her arms around his neck in the classic chokehold position. A few seconds later he collapsed to the floor and rolled onto his back, semi-conscious.

She straddled him, wrapped her hands around his throat, and watched as his lips made odd kissing motions.

"Belle?"

"He can't breathe!" Blondie shrieked.

Belle crushed an Ipon-ken fist to his temple, and he immediately blacked out. She didn't care, as she fully intended to pound his fat face into a bloody pulp.

She felt a bunch of hands grab her from behind, but in a blind fury she fought them off. Then in her head she heard the voice of her friend, Carrie, from home. *You're the doorkeeper, Belle. You're in control . . .* This time she listened.

She softened the pressure. More hands joined in and pulled her off the jerk.

Nora's face was inches from hers. "Belle! *Isabella!*"

The white light drifted back behind the door.

"Belle!" Nora gasped. "Oh, my God."

CHAPTER 18

Belle found Nora's silence deafening as they drove through the streets of Canyon.

Luckily, Belle had been pulled off the cowboy. Because the bar was located in the upper west side of Texas rather than the Upper West Side of New York City, the unwritten cowboy code had been invoked. The operative rule being, if some jerk assaults you or your companion, you have a right to beat the shit out of him. Particularly if you're a woman. Though technically cleared by the code, Belle didn't like the way the assailants' pals were eyeing them, so they'd grabbed the valise and their to-go bags and got the hell out of there.

Nora stared out the passenger-side window, not shifting in her seat, for the entire trip. She was pissed. *She has every right to be. Damn.* Since the Sundance incident Belle had kept the lizard door closed. Then the Exorcist Steps, then Ronnie's Roundup. Why now? Maybe the stress of Jenny's kidnapping. Maybe the frustration of feeling so helpless. Maybe . . . *who the hell knows?*

She pulled into Nora's driveway. Nora exited the car quickly without a word and headed for her door. Belle stepped out, cast her eyes down, and spoke barely above a whisper. "If you want me to leave, just send out my dog; we'll be on our way back to the Holiday Inn. I'll go over the stuff in the envelope and call—"

"No. I want you to stay here." Nora spoke without inflection.

"Nora..."

She turned her back and entered the house, leaving the door open. Belle grabbed the valise and followed her inside.

Before she'd even closed the door, Scout jumped into her arms, almost knocking her over.

She scratched him behind his ears. "Good to see you, too, buddy." Together they walked into the kitchen. Nora had already scraped the leftover burgers into his dog bowl, and he quickly abandoned Belle for ground buffalo. At that moment Scout was a very happy dog. At that moment he was the only happy mammal in the room.

Nora opened the refrigerator. "Want a beer or glass of wine?" Again, the monotone.

"Beer's fine." Belle set the valise down on one of the kitchen chairs and set herself down in another. Nora brought two beers, handed Belle one, and sat across from her.

After a long sip, Nora studied the label on the bottle, picking at the edges while she spoke. "I'll be honest with you, Belle. There are so many conflicting thoughts colliding inside my head right now that I feel like my brain's about to explode. The man was an ass. He knocked me to the floor without provocation and used a racial slur. I fired the first blow, putting him down. When you came to my rescue it appeared you were way overmatched—a female taking on a man much bigger and stronger. A large part of me was proud you prevailed." She took a deep breath. "But he was already unconscious. We won. Time to get out of Dodge. Instead, you almost killed him. If three guys hadn't pulled you off, you *would've* killed him. Does an explanation even exist?"

Belle paused a few seconds before answering her question. "Yes."

"But you are reluctant to provide such explanation," Nora accused.

Now Belle took a turn studying the beer label.

"Buck Yates was a good man," Nora said. "*Is* a good man. But he had a mean streak that came out when he'd been drinking. And he drank a lot. Part of the culture, I guess. Looking back, I think the booze started out as a painkiller. You have no idea the level of injuries those large-stock riders suffer on a routine basis. Some could handle the drink, some couldn't. Buck couldn't. He only hit me twice. After the first time, I gave him one more chance. The second time came only a few weeks after that. I was holding Sadie in my arms, and the blow knocked me over a table. She wasn't hurt, but she could've been. An hour later when he was sleeping it off, I walked out."

Without thinking, Belle responded defensively. "I saw what you did to that jerk who groped you."

"You're right, I can take care of myself. I carry a Comanche warrior's blood in my veins. But I always try to remain in control, and I wasn't going to allow Sadie to see her mom and dad in a physical brawl. That was four years ago. I found this great job at the museum, and to his credit Buck didn't beg me to come back. I think he was scared he might hurt Sadie, too."

"And now?"

"I have sole custody, but we keep in regular touch. I really want Sadie to have a father in her life. He's off the booze, been off it for several years, and has a girlfriend. I met her once; she's very nice and loves Sadie." Nora took a deep breath. "Sorry, didn't mean to tell you my life story, but you need to understand. I will not allow myself or my daughter to be around a violent person who can't maintain control. Never again, man or woman."

Neither of them spoke for what seemed like forever. Her comments unfortunately sounded all too familiar, closely mirroring words said to Belle by a close friend during the Sundance incident. If she was going to save Jenny, she needed Nora's help. She sighed deeply. "Have you ever heard of IED?"

"Yes, of course. Improvised Explosive Device. Small homemade bombs used by terrorists in the Middle East. Responsible for many American deaths."

"Actually there are similarities, but the acronym also stands for Intermittent Explosive Disorder. It's used to describe a behavioral disorder where a series of stimuli trigger disproportionate, uncontrolled rage in a person. Rage that usually continues unabated unless and until stopped by an outside force. Some people call it the Incredible Hulk disease."

"And you're telling me you have this IED?"

"For the most part I'm able to control it, but yes, I suffer from IED."

"How did you learn you had it?" Nora asked carefully.

"I was born and spent my early years in Park City, but when I was a teenager, my dad moved us to Pittsburgh. We lived in a tough neighborhood, and I ran with a rough crowd. This kid was trying to force his way into my pants, and I hurt him pretty bad. Almost killed him. The judge didn't buy my self-defense argument, and I served a little time in juvie. A shrink there, she's the one who diagnosed me."

Nora's face pinched in a sympathetic frown. "I'm sorry, must've been tough. Have you ever . . . you know . . .?"

"Killed someone during an episode?" Belle offered.

"You don't have to tell me."

"The answer's yes. I spent two years in Marine Force Recon."

"What's that?"

Belle rotated the beer bottle absently between her fingers. "Like the Navy SEALS or the Army Special Forces. Its motto is *Celer, Silens, Mortalis.* Swift, silent, deadly. That pretty much sums up its mission. We capture enemy combatants and interrogate them. I was one of only two women in the unit."

"What happened?" Nora asked, almost in a whisper.

She'd confided the story recently to her friend in Park City, so the words came easy. "We were operating in the Zagros Mountains north of Mosul. The week before he was to ship home for good, one of my best friends in the unit was blown to pieces by a bomb in the marketplace. We caught the man who planted the bomb. The C.O. ordered us to make sure this narrow mountain pass was safe from an ambush before he sent three platoons through the next day. We needed the prisoner to tell us where his fellow rats were positioned so we could clean them out that night. The prisoner was tied up in a tent at our makeshift camp. I'd drawn guard duty and was alone with him before questioning was to begin. The prisoner spoke broken English. I remember his words as if he were in this room with us now. He said, 'I hear they serve your friend as hamburger tonight for dinner.'"

Nora blanched. "He was baiting you."

"I maintained restraint, but he'd hidden a knife up his ass and attacked me. During the struggle I got the upper hand. My IED tripped in, and I turned into Incredible Hulk mode. The disorder's tied to the so-called limbic or lizard brain, the oldest part of the brain, the one responsible for primitive survival. There's this light—sounds weird I know—I see this white light in my head and it completely takes over, blocking all normal controls. I was on him in a second, beating his face to purple mush. When they finally pulled me off, he was dead."

"My God," Nora breathed.

"The C.O. was livid and threatened a court-martial, but my platoon mates stood up for their sister, and the C.O. decided he needed my gun—I was the best marksman in the unit—if we were going to try to find the hostiles and clean them out. I led seven men up into the rocky terrain bordering the pass. Thanks to me, we had no intelligence concerning their specific whereabouts, and we walked into an ambush. Three of my men—my friends, my brothers—were killed. If I hadn't strangled Ahmed, we would've likely learned the location of the hostiles, and three good men would still be alive today."

"Likely, but not certainly. Look, I'm sorry, I really am. Did they follow through with the court-martial?"

Belle chuckled without humor. "No. The brass was afraid a court-martial would present too great an opportunity for dirty laundry to be aired, and the politics of court-martialing one of the first women assigned to front-line combat didn't fit their PR narrative. But they needed to get me out of there, because they couldn't take a chance on my condition putting my fellow Marines in danger again. And they were absolutely right. So, they gave me an early medical discharge. I returned to Park and became a hunting guide." Belle sipped her beer. "I figure not too many people I could hurt out in the wilderness."

"Isn't it kind of rare for a hunting guide to be female?"

"Our numbers are growing every year, but, yeah, it's still unusual. I found that the shock disappears quickly, and I receive more than my share of repeat customers."

"No problem getting a gun permit?"

"The Marines kept my record clean. What happens in the sandbox stays in the sandbox.' Besides, I live in Utah, not L.A."

Nora offered a weak smile, then shifted uncomfortably in her chair. "Are you on medication?"

Belle sighed, and a touch of weariness infected her voice. "When first diagnosed, they put me on Lithium, but it made me feel like a zombie. I'd weaned my way off it and hadn't experienced any incidents until recently."

Nora nodded slowly. "Thanks for telling me." Her features softened, like a burden had been lifted from her shoulders, and rested her hand on Belle's. "And again, thank you for defending me."

Belle held her gaze, offered a weak smile, and nodded. A moment passed with both of them frozen in place. Nora slowly removed her hand from Belle's and slid James Amos's yellowed confidential envelope from the dusty valise, resting it on the table between them. A faded address label on the envelope bore the name, James Amos. The envelope was postmarked September 10, 1926, and the return address showed it came from his publisher.

The envelope had been opened cleanly with a letter opener. Belle pulled out a stack of papers bound with a brittle rubber band that nearly disintegrated as she set the documents on the table. A quick thumb-through revealed handwritten notes—some neat and orderly, some hurriedly entered on scratch paper—as well as typed manuscript pages with faded pencil edits. She focused on the top sheet, notes written in now pale-purple ink on yellowed lined paper. On the top line someone, likely Amos himself, had written, "Maybe include."

"It's dated February 15, 1909," Belle said.

"Back then the president was sworn in the first week of March, so Amos made these notes during Teddy's last couple of weeks in office." She pulled a chair next to Belle, and they both read to themselves.

T.R. just back from meeting with Taft. Not happy. Taft was one of T.R.'s best friends and promised many current cabinet members would be retained. Especially Garfield at Commerce. T.R. told me Taft not keeping promise, belittled Garfield. T.R. mad. He also told me Taft about Liaodong Agreement. Taft said not interested, didn't want to see it. Said T.R.'s ideas on global influence, navy build-up, would lead to war.

Advised T.R. to burn it. I think president's feelings were hurt. Told me to keep LA in safe at Sagamore.

Nora stood, retrieved her laptop from the kitchen counter, then returned to her seat. Belle watched as she googled "Liaodong Agreement." There were plenty of entries about the Liaodong Peninsula on China's eastern coast. As they'd learned from Professor Moon, the peninsula and its jewel, Port Arthur, had passed back and forth between Japan and Russia for over a century until the mid-fifties when China regained control for good. Articles described Port Arthur, now called Lüshun, as China's most important naval, submarine and military base and the home of its most advanced naval vessels including China's nuclear attack submarine fleet. But Nora found nothing linking the peninsula or Lüshun, to any agreement between China and Roosevelt.

Belle turned to the next page of notes dated July 30, 1913.

Sag. Hill. T.R. told me about meeting with Wilson this a.m. Didn't go well. T.R. told Wils. about LA. Wils angry, accused T.R. of being imperialist. Made fun of Big Stick diplomacy. Said best hope for country was neutrality. Wils told T.R. to destroy LA. I asked what to do. He pounded fist on table, shaking lamp. Said "keep it until somebody running this country grows a set of balls."

Belle could see Amos's notes weren't in order as the next page was dated eight years earlier. She skimmed it. "These pages appear to be part of a draft insert for his book. The writing's better. Listen to this. Dated June 22, 1905. 'Sagamore. Three guests this morning. China Ambassador Chen, Moody, and, later, Quanah Parker.'" I nodded to the laptop. "See who Moody is."

It only took a moment for her to find the answer. "William Henry

Moody, Roosevelt's attorney general. A year and a half after Amos wrote that note Roosevelt nominated him to the Supreme Court."

Belle continued reading aloud. "Moody drafted a secret agreement between U.S. and China where Pres. agrees to help China in NH.'"

"NH must mean New Hampshire," Nora said. "Remember, Portsmouth was the location of the Russo-Japanese War peace negotiations."

"And since the war took place on Chinese soil, China would want a friend in those negotiations protecting its ass. So Teddy agrees to look out for China's interests in the negotiations, and in return receives this Liaodong Agreement, an agreement the two presidents who succeeded him wanted no part of."

"What's in the agreement?"

Belle read the next pages. "These look like an actual proposed manuscript insert that was rejected." They both read Amos's rejected manuscript pages to themselves.

We were in the President's study, just the three of us—T.R., Ambassador Ling Chen, and me. T.R. set down his bathtub—Ted, Jr. had called his huge white porcelain coffee mug "the bathtub" several years earlier, and it hadn't taken long for the whole Roosevelt clan to adopt the name. The president rolled forward in the leather-backed cane rocker, his full attention focused on Chen. He watched with satisfaction as Chen signed four original copies of the agreement.

Chen offered the pen to the president. The four copies lay neatly side-by-side on T.R.'s desk. Each paragraph was written in both English and Chinese. T.R. had already gone over the document with Mr. Moody. Fortunately, Moody was fluent in Mandarin and confirmed both versions were identical. After signing all copies, T.R. pulled a caramel-leather check portfolio from the top drawer of his desk, wrote a check, and handed it to Chen.

Chen told T.R. America was fortunate to have a president with sufficient personal wealth to provide the financial consideration for the agreement and hoped someday he would be repaid. T.R. replied that he didn't care whether he was reimbursed. Chen took the check and two copies of the agreement. T.R. gave me one copy to put in his office safe. T.R. walked Chen to the porch to see him off. Chen offered the president a parting gift, a green jade box covered with a female figure surrounded by butterflies. After Chen left, T.R. inserted the second copy of the agreement inside the jade box and left it on his desk.

He told me the agreement must remain secret until the time was right. An isolationist mood pervaded Washington, and the agreement would not be well received.

After Chen left, I immediately escorted the president to the north porch where his second guest awaited. Quanah Parker, once one of the most feared hostiles in the country, was now an advocate for Indian rights. T.R. had met Quanah at the inauguration, and they quickly formed a special bond. The Comanche was an imposing figure— tall, barrel-chested like the president himself, skin the color of burnished bronze, braided coal-black hair, and piercing blue eyes. Quanah was visiting Washington and asked if he could come up to Sagamore and meet about an Indian rights bill now held up in Congress.

They sat in the gray rockers overlooking the bay. T.R. was a frenetic man, but I never saw him more relaxed than that day sitting with Quanah. After offering Quanah advice and assistance, T.R. asked if he could continue his interviews about Quanah's earlier life. Quanah surmised T.R. was doing research for another book and he was right. That day Quanah told T.R. all about the second battle of Adobe Walls. Both T.R. and I hung on every word, spellbound. Quanah was a master storyteller.

Later, T.R. pulled me aside, said he had a bully idea, and asked me to bring him the jade box. He had great faith in his ability to judge a man quickly, and he trusted Quanah Parker. Called him a real Rough Rider. The president gave Quanah the jade box containing the second copy of the Liaodong Agreement for safe-keeping.

Belle leaned back in her chair. "So that's it. Finally, the connection. Roosevelt cut some secret deal with China. In return for protecting China during the Portsmouth treaty negotiations, he received something he believed was beneficial to the United States, something to do with the Liaodong Peninsula."

Nora's brow furrowed. "But this agreement couldn't have been an official treaty or Teddy would've needed congressional ratification."

"If it wasn't ratified, would it be enforceable?"

"Probably," she said. "If a president fears he won't get Congressional approval, he can structure an agreement as something other than a treaty. Back in 2015, for example, President Obama entered into a binding long-term nuclear arms agreement with Iran without Congressional approval. But Congress or a subsequent president could probably undo it, which is what President Trump tried to do."

"That's why you can't find any evidence of it. Roosevelt was worried if the agreement surfaced, it would've been undone by his successors."

"So, he kept one copy at the summer White House in Sagamore Hill and gave the second copy to Quanah for safe keeping, waiting for a more hospitable political climate."

Belle rose from the table, and her face brightened as the revelation hit her. "It's not the box itself Bai is after; it's the secret agreement inside."

"The kidnappers want to find this Liaodong Agreement," Nora added, "while China wants the agreement to remain lost."

Belle paced back and forth in the small kitchen. "But why? What did China and Teddy Roosevelt agree to back in 1905 that would justify China now unleashing Jin Choi to keep the agreement from surfacing?"

"Whatever it was," Nora continued, "its importance justified China authorizing whatever means necessary to recover the agreement, including murdering innocent American citizens."

Belle felt like they'd finally found their way to the secret door, and behind that door was the key that would free her sister. But that door remained locked. "What the hell was in that agreement?"

CHAPTER 19

Buck Yates smiled to himself as he watched Donna Kalinski crouch down and embrace his daughter.

Donna couldn't have been more different from Nora. In contrast to his former wife's slim build and dark coloring, Donna was a fair-skinned blonde with a little extra meat on her bones. But they shared one thing in common—both loved Sadie Parker Yates. He knew in Sadie's eyes Donna would never take Nora's place, but Sadie also had feelings for Donna. Donna had been dropping hints about starting a family after they got hitched, and while at first he wasn't overly enthusiastic, he'd begun to warm to the idea. Donna had even drawn Sadie into her little conspiracy; his daughter had told him at least three times in the last few days how much she wanted a little brother.

Donna kissed Sadie on the forehead, then stood and embraced him. "Sure you two are going to be okay?"

Buck grinned. "Somehow I managed to barely survive before you entered my life."

She patted his butt. "Barely survive is about right."

Buck opened the trailer door and the three of them stepped down to the narrow grassy strip on the edge of the parking lot. They walked Donna to her Honda parked nearby. Donna was driving back to Albuquerque to care for her sister who'd taken a turn for the worse after a year of fighting stage-four breast cancer.

Buck said, "Call when you get there and give Becky my love."

"Will do. I'll be back in three days." She looked down at Sadie. "You take care of your daddy, 'cause without a woman around he might just melt into a puddle." Sadie giggled and gave her a last squeeze. Donna opened her car door and paused for a moment. "That white van over there at the far end of the lot."

Buck turned and noticed the van. "What about it?"

She answered with a touch of suspicion in her voice. "I seen it earlier. Been there for hours with just the driver inside. "

"Probably waiting for someone to come out after the show," Buck said dismissively.

"Maybe," Donna responded, not completely convinced. "But there are a lot closer places to wait."

"Don't worry, I think I can take care of myself."

She gave him another kiss then slid into the Honda. They both waved as she drove away.

Buck led Sadie back into the trailer and closed the door. He glanced out the window at the white van sitting alone off in the distance and thought about Nora's warning to be on the lookout for a Chinese stranger. He couldn't make out the driver's features, but the man looked small, like a kid. Probably waiting for a friend and fell asleep. He turned his attention back to his daughter. "Who wants ice cream?"

"Me."

Buck wrapped his huge, scarred hands around Sadie's waist and tossed her high in the air. "I didn't hear you, so let me ask again. Who wants ice cream?"

Sadie waved both hands in the air. "Me! Me!"

He caught her and pulled her close. She slipped her slender arms around his thick neck. "I love you Daddy, and I'll always be your number one girl."

Buck Yates couldn't remember the last time he cried, but he was almost moved to tears as he carried Sadie Parker Yates to the small fridge for chocolate ice cream.

He completely forgot about the white van.

CHAPTER 20

Belle heard the *ping* and read Sal's text out loud.

"Isabella, Helen, and I beg you not to go to the authorities yet. The FBI has been generally successful in abductions where the kidnapper is an estranged parent, the situation in a majority of the cases. However, that success rate doesn't apply when the kidnappers are strangers. We can't take the chance, at least until we know more. Please keep trying to find out what they want and give it to them. Please. Still doing our level best to return ASAP. We'll never be able to repay you. Love, S."

Nora brought over two more beers from the fridge. Scout, sated with Ronny's Roundup burgers, curled up at Belle's feet. She was sure Nora could read the frustration on her face.

"Don't your uncle and aunt understand we have no leads?" Nora fumed. "That we've hit a brick wall?"

"I don't have kids," Belle answered, grasping for a diplomatic tone. "What would you say if instead of Jenny Sadie had been kidnapped?" Instantly realizing her response was insensitive, she followed up. "Sorry."

Nora plopped down in the chair. "That's okay. And you're right. I'd probably feel the same as them."

They needed to get back to work. There were a few other notes in James Amos's folder, but none that related to Quanah Parker or the Liaodong Agreement. The remaining material consisted of two additional rejected draft chapters for his book. The first was titled, "My Trip to Oklahoma with the President." Nora was a faster reader, so she passed pages to Belle when she finished. Nothing much of note. Amos told of accompanying the president to Quanah's home. Interesting, but nothing helpful. Then Belle saw Nora's body stiffen.

"You have to read this."

> Quanah walked to the other side of the room where a war lance leaned in the corner. I heard him tell the president, "When I die, I know not what will happen to this house, so I have instructed Chony to take green box to new location."
>
> He picked up the lance and rolled it in his fingers until what appeared to be new beadwork appeared. "Chony show location on lance. Only Chony, not other wives, know new location. I tell you where it will be buried." He looked at me. "But not you."
>
> Quanah then pulled the president aside, out of my earshot, and told him the new location.
>
> I am certain the president would've told me where Quanah planned to hide the jade box if I'd asked, but I never asked. Didn't feel it was my place to do so.
>
> Now, of course, I wish I had.

Belle looked up from the pages. "Says here Teddy's trip to visit Quanah took place in the fall of 1910. At that point Quanah, one of his wives, Chony, and Teddy were the only three people who knew the future site where the Hudie Box would be buried. James Amos never knew."

"Quanah died a few months later in February 1911," Nora said in a somber voice.

Belle shook her head. "But Teddy lived eight more years. With Quanah's death, why wouldn't he have recovered the box?"

"He knew the burial location, so maybe it wasn't a big concern.

Besides, he had the other copy of the agreement in his safe at Sagamore Hill."

"At some point that copy must've disappeared."

Nora slid the pages between them so they could read at the same time. The chapter was entitled, "The Last Days." Unlike the chapter covering Amos's trip to Oklahoma with Roosevelt, this one contained margin notes, probably made by the editor. Actually, the notes consisted of just two words: "Keep" and "No." Glancing over the pages, Belle recalled seeing a number of the "keep" paragraphs in the final book.

Nora pointed halfway down the page.

At the time, I resided in the city. On January 4th I received a call from Mrs. Roosevelt asking if I would return to Sagamore to help the president. I agreed on the spot and arrived that evening, shocked to see how much the president had declined. His face reflected a weariness I hadn't previously witnessed, even during his most trying days in office. I bathed and dressed him and at his request seated him in a chair so he could look out over Long Island Sound. He particularly wanted to see Center Island where he'd played as a boy. The president sat in that chair even in darkness, and I think in his mind he was replaying the wonderful memories from his youth.

The next day while the president slept upstairs, at Mrs. Roosevelt's request I attempted to organize the president's study. The colonel was notoriously sloppy and often forgetful, relying on his wife and me to locate books he'd been reading or articles he'd been writing. I found several items that I believed should be secured in the corner safe. As I approached the safe, a Chinese servant appeared with a cup of tea. He was a new hire and I was embarrassed that I'd forgotten his name.

"At Mrs. Roosevelt's request, sir."

"Thank you. That is very kind of her. Please set it on the desk."

While the servant dealt with the tea, I entered the combination and opened the safe. When I'd deposited the documents and closed the safe, I turned and was mildly surprised to see the Chinese servant still there. Actually standing close behind me.

He asked, "Will there be anything else, sir?"

I told him no; he bowed slightly and left the study.

That night I removed the president's robe and lifted him into bed about eight p.m. He asked me to sit with him. I agreed to his request, then rested by the fire while he dozed in fits and starts. At about eleven p.m. Mrs. Roosevelt came in to give him a goodnight kiss. Just after she left, the president said, "James, I've been going over unfinished business in my mind, and I thought about the agreement in the safe. You remember, the one I executed with Ambassador Chen back in '05 concerning the Liaodong Peninsula?"

"Yes, sir, I recall."

"If anything happens to me, I want you to give the agreement to Henry Lodge."

"Of course, sir."

"And we should recover the second copy, the one I gave Quanah. Remind me tomorrow to tell you how to find it. Now, James, will you please put out the light?"

I turned out the lamp on the small dresser then continued to rest by the fire while he slept. At about 4 a.m. I could hear him struggling to breathe. I left to summon the nurse, but when we returned, he'd stopped breathing completely. Dr. Faller was called and formally pronounced the president dead from an embolism.

All of my time during the following two days was consumed with the funeral, a modest affair in compliance with the wishes of the president and the family—a short prayer service at Sagamore, then a funeral at a church in Oyster Bay where only 500 people were permitted to attend, then burial at a nearby cemetery. Mrs. Roosevelt did not attend the funeral or the burial, electing to grieve at Sagamore.

The next day, January 9, I was gathering my things at Sagamore, ready to return to New York and my job at the Burns Detective Agency, when I remembered the president's request that I deliver the Liaodong Agreement to Senator Lodge. I opened the safe and pulled out the envelope. Something was wrong, it felt too light. I opened the envelope. Empty.

I immediately thought of the Chinese servant. He'd been in a position to observe the combination when I opened the safe. I hurried to the kitchen and learned the man had disappeared four days earlier, the same day he saw me open the safe.

Fortunately, I knew another copy existed. Quanah Parker had died eight years earlier. I contacted his wife, Tonarcy, and learned that Chony, the only wife who knew the location of the jade box containing the agreement and the one who had beaded a code onto Quanah's war lance leading to the location, had died in 1913. I asked Tonarcy to decipher the code, but she couldn't without something called a bah-has-tkih. *At my request, she asked Quanah's other surviving wives, but they also were unable to read the code.*

Unless the lance is deciphered, the Liaodong Agreement will be lost to history.

Belle sat back, her head spinning. "If we assume, as Amos did, that China sent an agent to pose as a servant and steal the agreement, it follows that they wanted to walk away from a deal they'd signed only fourteen years earlier."

Nora's fingers flew over the laptop keyboard. "Looks like China was ruled by warring factions in 1919. Whatever Ambassador Chen agreed to in '05, those warlords didn't like it."

"When the Chinese agent successfully stole the agreement from Roosevelt's safe, they figured they were home free."

"According to Amos, the Chinese knew there were two copies."

Belle straightened up again, planting her elbows on her knees and steepling her fingers. "Agreed, but when the second copy didn't surface, they must've assumed it had disappeared and decided to let sleeping dogs lie. The question is, why has this all resurfaced now, a hundred years later?"

"I don't know, but I do know we have to try and find the *bah-has-tkih.*" Nora skimmed Amos's last chapter. "The reference to all of Quanah's wives has given me an idea."

Belle watched as Nora typed a username and password onto a screen headed "QPD."

"What's QPD?"

"Quanah Parker descendants," Nora answered absently. "With so many wives, there are now hundreds of us. Back in 2011, a fellow named Gwynne wrote a book about Quanah called *Empire of the Summer Moon*. It became a bestseller and a finalist for the Pulitzer. The book caused a flurry of activity, people scouring their family tree for a Quanah connection. More people joined the descendant ranks, and efforts to do a better job of organizing the descendants took hold. Thus, the website. Anyone can view the main site, but you have to be a verified descendant to access the 'descendants only' page."

"And that helps us how?" Belle groused.

"We now know from Amos's file that of Quanah's seven wives, Chony was the one who beaded the code onto the lance, and she was the only person other than Quanah and Roosevelt who was aware of the new location. Chony must've been the one who created the *bah-has-tkih*."

Belle figured she knew where she was heading. "You said the *bah-has-tkih* was usually embedded in an article of clothing—a belt, moccasin, whatever. Is it possible Chony passed down through her family information relating to this *bah-has-tkih*, or the item itself? Maybe even the actual location of the jade box?"

"I'm saying two things." She ticked them off her fingers as she continued. "First, it's possible, unlikely but possible; and second, we have no better ideas."

Belle couldn't argue with her logic. "But as I recall, Chony died over a hundred years ago leaving three or four generations of descendants."

Nora opened the page reserved for blood relatives, then typed "Chony" in the search box. A genealogy chart appeared. "Looks like she had three children with Quanah, two males and a female. One of the boys died at the age of nineteen. The girl made it to thirty-seven." She ran her finger along the graph on the screen. "But her youngest boy lived into his mid-seventies. Seven kids from three wives, all of whom have passed. Lots of grandchildren and a lot more great-grandchildren."

Belle checked the list of Chony Parker descendants aged younger than ninety. "There has to be seventy of them presumably still living. What do we do, try to call them all? And that assumes we can locate them."

"You told me once we have to play the odds. The first-born son had special prominence in Comanche culture. So we focus on the first male offspring of Chony, then *his* first offspring, down the line."

Belle dragged her finger in a zigzag motion down the screen. "If we discount first-born female children it looks like there's only one contemporary first-born male of a first-born male of a first-born male. Neville Parker. You know him?"

Nora brightened. "No, but I think I met his younger brother, Cordero, once at the annual Parker family gathering. If I'm not mistaken, Cord's the sheriff of Gracie, Texas."

"Neville's the first-born son. He's the one we have to find. Any ideas?"

Nora thought for a moment. "Olivia."

CHAPTER 21

"Go fish."

Buck Yates frowned, eliciting a giggle from his daughter. "You sure you have no kings?"

Sadie shook her head with a flourish. "Nope. Go fish."

Buck exaggerated a sigh, selected the top card from the stack, and slipped it between two other cards in his hand. "Little girls are supposed to be nice to their old daddies." She giggled again, then studied her hand intensely.

He'd taught her the game the last time they'd been together, and playing Go Fish on the trailer's rickety fold-down table had become a new before-bed ritual. Face washed, teeth brushed, PJs on, then Go Fish.

Because of the concussion protocol he wasn't allowed to ride again for three more days. In the past the forced vacation would've driven him crazy, but he actually enjoyed spending the downtime with his daughter. He smiled to himself. Maybe he was getting old. Happens to everyone. Very few bull riders still on the circuit were older than forty. The skill level remained; the problem was the healing time.

Sadie asked, "Do you have any . . . aces?"

Buck pulled two aces from his hand and passed them across to his daughter. She squealed with delight and laid down the remaining cards in her hand.

"I win!" She raised both hands in the air, triumphant.

An exaggerated frown. Oh, no, not again." She giggled. "Come here and give me a goodnight hug."

Sadie jumped down from her seat and crawled into his lap. She wrapped her arms around his neck and kissed him on the lips. "I love you, Daddy."

"I love you, too, sweetheart." Buck knew someday his daughter would become an eye-rolling, pouty teenager who wouldn't want to be seen in public with her daddy. That was okay. He'd enjoy the moment now with their official go-to-bed exchange. "Now go hit the sack, Jack."

"My name's not Jack."

"Go jump in bed, Ned."

She shouted, "My name's not Ned! It's Sadie Parker Yates."

"And who's Sadie Parker Yates?"

"Your best girl in the whole world!"

"You're right! Now, off to bed, young lady."

She scampered off to the back of the trailer and its only bed, paused, turned, blew her daddy a final kiss, and closed the door.

Four hours later, Buck slept restlessly on the small couch. A tapping at the trailer door awakened him. Who the hell was that? The guys knew better than to come by at this hour when Sadie was visiting. He tossed aside the blanket, staggered over to the window, and looked outside. The white van—had to be the same one they'd seen earlier—was now parked directly in front of his trailer. A small Asian woman stood at his door. She knocked again. What the hell was this? He thought about Nora's warning to be on the lookout for a dangerous Asian. He could see this woman was unarmed, and her tiny stature posed no threat.

He opened the door. "Yes? Can I help?—"

A blur of movement caught the corner of his eye. A millisecond later he felt blinding pain between his eyes, then fell back and crumpled to the floor.

Holy shit, the bitch just kicked me in the head!

She entered and closed the door. Still stunned, he crawled to his feet, swaying to find his balance. The woman was very small, probably weighed little more than a hundred pounds. She must've come to the wrong trailer.

He puffed out his chest and lowered his voice. "Who the hell are you?"

She didn't respond and showed no expression, like she was some kind of robot.

He took a deep breath and tamped down his anger. "Here's the deal, lady. You obviously have the wrong guy. Now you smacked me pretty good, and I have a right to act in self-defense. But I don't hit women, so I'm willing to let this pass so long as you—"

Suddenly she had a knife in her hand. *Jesus, where the hell did that come from?* Okay, this bitch was some kind of nutcase. He'd toss her out of his trailer, then call the local cops. He didn't want her hurting anyone else.

Buck took one step forward and grabbed for her. She wasn't there. Somehow, she'd slipped behind him. What the hell was this? *Some kind of ninja kung-fu bullshit?* Fine. She assaulted him and threatened him with a knife. He had a right to retaliate so long as he didn't hurt her too—

She zipped past him before he had time to react. He felt something dripping into his palm and looked down. She'd nicked his arm with her knife. He laughed.

"That all you got, lady? Cause in my business—"

She was flush up against him, then beyond arm's length in the blink of an eye. He felt a sting along his hip and looked down. She'd cut him again. Okay, no more bullshit. He charged her. She rolled on the floor under him. He felt instant pain in both his ankles.

Christ! She'd sliced through both his Achilles tendons. He stumbled to the floor.

"Who are you? What the hell do you want?" He rolled up to his knees, the intense pain from his ankles now registering. The woman was obviously crazy, and he needed to make sure she didn't know Sadie was asleep in the back room. Fortunately, the door was closed. She stood next to him now. He swept his muscular arm hard across her ankles, but her legs weren't there. *Where the hell—?* He felt the knife slice rapid-fire in what seemed like a hundred different directions across his back. His once-white t-shirt turned solid red. Blood, *his blood*, dripped onto the cheap shag carpet.

He tried to stand, but the moment he raised up he saw a flash of movement, then felt a stab of pain on the side of his head. Something flopped onto the floor. His ear! *Oh, my God, the bitch just cut off my—* He balled up his fist and swung as hard as he could at her face. She pulled back with the ease of a champion boxer. Another flash, another sting, this one across his forehead. Blood flowed into his eyes, making it difficult to see.

He stumbled around on his knees swinging wildly but connected only with air. *Who was she? What did she want? Was he going to die? Was he dying?* Oh, God, he still had another forty or fifty years left. He couldn't die, he needed to see Sadie grow up and get married and have a family. He loved his granddaddy, and he wanted to be a granddaddy someday. And Donna . . . he needed to marry Donna.

He felt something penetrating his right eye socket. He tried to muffle his scream with only partial success. He couldn't see.

The woman was behind him now and he felt the knife puncture his kidney. Funny, this time he hardly felt the blade. Somehow, he was staring at the ceiling with his left eye. How did he end up on his back?

"Daddy?"

Oh my God, Sadie.

She was on her knees, bending over him. What would happen to her? Donna was gone, and no one would likely bother to check on the trailer for a couple of days.

"Please don't hurt her." He heard what he thought was his voice, but it sounded all gurgly, like someone else. Like how it sometimes sounded in a dream.

Wait, that's it! Of course, this is a dream. A nightmare. The mother of all nightmares. He relaxed and thought of his daughter's arms wrapped around his neck.

Time to hit the sack, Jack.

He allowed the blackness to descend and engulf him. He would wake up in the morning and everything would be just fine.

CHAPTER 22

The horizon ahead turned from iron gray to a dirty orange as dawn broke behind Belle. Driving west on Route 60 toward the New Mexico border, the dull light revealed splotches of dry scrub brush covering wide expanses of empty plain—a dreary, near-monochromatic landscape of desert tans and browns as far as the eye could see. Not what anyone would include on a list of the most scenic interstates in America.

They'd grabbed a few hours of sleep, and at 6:15 Nora phoned Olivia Parker, the woman responsible for the QPD website. Olivia wasn't happy they'd called at such an early hour, but when Nora told her of the importance, she'd promised to get back to Nora quickly.

Ten minutes later she'd called and reported that Neville was born, raised, and still resided in Clovis, New Mexico, an hour and a half west of Canyon. She confirmed Neville, now in his fifties, was a descendant of Chony, but couldn't offer an address or phone number and didn't know his profession.

Fifteen minutes after that they were on the road provisioned with a few energy bars and two giant travel cups of coffee. Scout remained at Nora's place, comfortably curled up on the kitchen rug with ample food and water nearby. On the way, she'd called her intern to make certain his bathroom needs would be covered.

The monotony of the scenery allowed Belle's mind to drift, finally landing on the talks between Quanah and Teddy Roosevelt. Ten miles later that thinking resulted in a new theory.

"Quanah had Chony bead the symbols on his war lance, something very important to him. He originally hid the Hudie Box under the floor-boards of his house, again a place with great meaning as it symbolized an important stage in his life—his assimilation into white society and poli-tics. So, when he decided to move the box, wouldn't it stand to reason he'd select a place that meant something special to him and not a random location? Maybe a battle where he won a great victory?"

"Makes sense," Nora responded. "Problem is, before he surren-dered, he'd roamed over hundreds of square miles throughout the southwest and engaged in many battles not only with soldiers and buffalo hunters, but other tribes as well. A small skirmish with opposing factions of his own tribe could've meant more to him than his defeat of Mackenzie at Blanco Canyon. And that even assumes he chose a battle site. He could've buried the box at the location where one of his many children was born. But you raise a good point, something we should keep in mind if we have to choose from several leads to follow." She pointed to a sign indicating the exit for the town of Farwell. "Maybe another fifteen or twenty minutes."

"Then what?" The online white pages for Clovis listed five Neville Parkets. Who knew Neville was such a popular name? Two included phone numbers, three were unlisted—no phone or address. Nora had called the two numbers and struck out. One guy was a college student and the other a ninety-year-old in a nursing home.

"Clovis isn't that big, maybe thirty thousand residents," Nora said. "If Neville was raised there, went to school there, I'm hoping somebody in town might know him."

After another twenty minutes of beige monotony, they passed a sand-colored sign welcoming them to Clovis: "Community for Family." A smaller sign off to the side read: "The Biggest Little Music City in the Whole World." Belle drove along a wide expanse of railroad tracks, turned onto Grand Avenue, and found a place to park a half block from the Peggy Sue Diner.

"A diner's as good a place as any to start," Belle said. "Hungry?"

Nora nodded. "The place looks like it's been here for a while."

They entered to see that the diner was half full. Sliding onto round, backless stools with red vinyl tops, they rested their elbows on the old-fashioned, speckled, white Formica counter. The waitress approached them immediately. Maybe late sixties, bottle-blonde hair wrapped tight in a bun on top of her head. And black frame glasses. Belle noticed all of the wait staff wore the same glasses. Apparently, the populace of Clovis, New Mexico, had a serious vision problem.

The waitress—her name tag read "Janelle"—offered each of them a laminated two-sided menu. "Howdy, folks. Can I get you something to drink to start you off?"

Janelle had a raspy cigarette voice and a smile that came across as genuine. They both ordered greasy eggs, greasy bacon, and buttered toast. The menu didn't specifically use the word "greasy," but Belle read between the lines. She figured the best approach was to establish a little rapport with Janelle before asking about Neville. Baby steps. "What's with the glasses?"

She pointed over her head to a black-and-white photo taking up most of the wall showing Buddy Holly wearing his iconic black frame glasses. Of course. "Peggy Sue" was one of the early rocker's most popular hits. "So, was Buddy Holly from Clovis?"

Janelle shook her head. "Lubbock, but he recorded a bunch of his early music at the Petty Studio over on West Center."

The light went on in Belle's head. "Including 'Peggy Sue.'"

"Bright girl." Her smile conveyed her sarcasm was all in fun. Belle thought they were connecting a little bit.

Nora dispensed with baby steps. "We're looking for a man named Neville Parker. Would you happen to know him?"

Her face didn't harden, but it did take on a more serious expression. "Might I ask what you want with Neville?"

Okay, what do you do here? Long story, short story, made-up story, or no story? Belle was about to come up with a passable pitch when Nora showed Janelle her museum ID, and flashed a restrained, professional smile.

"My name's Nora Parker Yates, and I work for the Panhandle Plains Museum. I'm also a distant cousin of Neville. The museum displays a number of Parker family heirlooms, and we wanted to see if Neville might have information that could help us provide background for some of these pieces."

Brilliant because it was true. Well, kind of true.

Janelle nodded, accepting Nora's explanation, then checked her watch. "Neville works as a guide over at the Rock & Roll Museum, but they're not open yet so you have time to eat. The Peggy Sue breakfast is the best in the west."

Belle had no reason to challenge the claim that the Peggy Sue breakfast was the best in the west, but she'd hardly tasted hers. Her mind raced with thoughts of Jenny and the ticking clock.

They stood outside the Norman & Vi Petty Rock & Roll Museum. A bright red awning shaped like an elf hat sliced in half hung over the double doors. A piano-key motif wrapped around the bottom of the awning, and an over-sized Stratocaster electric guitar was attached to the front.

They entered and spotted a slim man, maybe mid-fifties, leading a small group of tourists past display cases featuring photos and artifacts from Buddy Holly, Waylon Jennings and the rest of a long list of early rock and country artists who'd received their start in Clovis. Gray streaks began at the tour guide's temples and feathered back into his close-cropped jet-black hair. Had to be Neville. Not only did he wear the stupid Buddy Holly glasses, so did each of the tourists. They must've passed them out when the tour started.

Belle's first instinct was to burst through the tourists, grab him by the shoulders, and ask him about the *bah-has-tikh*, but she restrained herself. They followed along, hoping the tour was nearing its end. Neville's deep baritone easily projected to everyone in the small group.

". . . and Buddy originally titled the song that would become Peggy Sue, Cindy Lou after his niece, but changed it to the name of his drummer's girlfriend. Here are several photos showing the back of the studio where Norman and Vi built a little apartment so Buddy and the Crickets could stay and record whenever they wanted. In this apartment, Vi installed one of the very first microwave ovens. And this was back in the mid-fifties, folks." A few of the tourists *ooohed* their approval.

Each of the following ten minutes ratcheted Belle's impatience a notch tighter. *C'mon. C'mon! Buddy Holly, microwaves, very interesting, I'm sure. But time to bring the tour to a close.*

Finally, Neville stopped, thanked the group for their attention, and invited them to peruse the gift shop. "And feel free to keep your Buddy Holly glasses, folks. Just don't try to use them to read or you'll go cross-eyed." Neville told the little joke as if he'd just thought of it instead of it being the standard send-off he probably delivered three times a day. The tourists laughed then dispersed. Neville seemed to notice Belle and Nora didn't laugh and hadn't dispersed. He probably also noticed they weren't wearing Buddy Holly glasses.

Belle spoke first. "Neville Parker?"

He stiffened, probably taking her for a cop or a process server.

Nora stepped in front of Belle and extended her hand. "I'm Nora Parker Yates from the Panhandle Plains Museum, and I wondered if we might take a few minutes of your time."

Without a word, Neville led them to the front of the museum where they sat in a replica of a fifties malt shop booth. Belle wasn't really sure what a malt was, but apparently they were real popular back in the fifties. The booth featured fire-engine-red vinyl seats, a gold-flecked Formica table, and a small jukebox playing only the hits produced by Norman and Vi Petty.

Neville sat across from them, dead silent.

Okay, how do we play this? Belle decided to try Nora's approach of mixing the truth with a dash of omission and a sprinkling of exaggeration. "Mr. Parker, as Nora told you, she's from the Panhandle Museum over in Canyon. I happened to be visiting her a couple of days ago when the museum was burglarized. The thieves stole Quanah Parker's lance.

They've contacted Nora and told her they will return the lance unharmed if she would decipher a line of symbols on the lance, symbols the thieves believe is a code of some kind. We've come to believe the only way for her to do what the thieves ask is to locate a *bah-has-tkih,* a Comanche codebook if you will."

Neville stared at her blankly, and Belle couldn't read whether he was buying her story. She went on, "The museum desperately wants the lance returned. We now understand that your ancestor, Chony Parker, was the one who beaded the symbols, so we're checking with her descendants to see if they might've inherited something—a headband, bracelet, belt, or some other item—that might contain this *bah-has-tkih.* Do you by any chance own any family heirloom passed down from Chony, something that could be this codebreaker?"

Neville didn't speak. Belle couldn't really blame him since her pitch was full of holes like: What did the thieves want? What was her relationship to the event? Maybe they were the thieves. Why weren't the police here instead of—?

Neville's skeptical gaze stopped her train of thought, and he answered an unasked question. "Yes."

Belle didn't have time for games. "Excuse me?"

"You're not excused because your story is total bullshit."

Okay, *total bullshit* was a bit harsh.

He turned to Nora. "I've been to your museum. It owns and displays many items linked to Quanah that are much more valuable than this lance." He took her hand in both of his and eye-locked with her, like a palm reader. After a couple of beats he said, "I sense you are a good person with a pure heart. Tell me why you need this *bah-has-tkih.*"

To Nora's credit, she didn't look away. "To save a life."

He nodded, glanced Belle's way with open disdain then returned his undivided attention to Nora. "There are several of Chony's personal items that were passed down to me and my little brother, including a couple of beaded buckskin bracelets."

Belle was about to ask if he still had the bracelets but, given her credibility status, she wisely held her tongue.

Nora couldn't keep the excitement from her voice. "And these bracelets still exist?"

"Cord has one of the bracelets. I gave the other to my daughter, Lizzie. She loves it, thinks it brings her luck. Wears it all the time. Now that you mention it, the bracelet does have an interesting bead design that I've never seen before."

Belle couldn't hold back any longer. "Can we talk to her?" The maddening ticking from the clock in her head pumped louder, and her resolve hardened. *I don't care what you say, we're going to find her, and we're going to talk to her, and we're going to find and talk to her now.*

"Sure." Neville offered a cold smile. "But you'll have to drive to Carlsbad first."

A middle-aged Chinese man wearing granny glasses stepped into Neville Parker's tiny office in the back of the Norman & Vi Petty Rock & Roll Museum, locked the door behind him, and pointed his silenced gun at Neville sitting behind his desk.

Neville's eyes widened, and his whole body shook. "W-what do you want?" He stood and pointed toward the door. "The cash register's at the front entrance, but there's not much—"

"Sit. Where did Yates and Bannon go?"

Neville gulped and took his seat. "I don't know who—"

In one long stride the stranger stood next to Neville, jammed the barrel hard against his temple, and sighed. He had no patience for amateurs. "Two choices. Live or die."

Neville's voice quavered. "I-I don't know these people. Were they tourists?"

A mixture of intense training along with years of experience had invested the stranger with the ability to tell when even the most accomplished liars were being untruthful. And this man was the farthest thing from an accomplished liar. But why would he try to protect two strangers whom he'd just met? Wait, did he just glance at a photo on his desk? A young woman. Probably a daughter. He took a chance.

"Don't worry, no harm will come to your daughter."

"H-how did you know?"

The stranger didn't respond.

"What do you want with them?"

Enough. "If you don't tell me, I will kill your daughter."

Neville responded instantly. "Okay, okay, please don't hurt her. Carlsbad. The caverns. Lizzie works there as a ranger. Yates and Bannon want to see her bracelet, an heirloom from Quanah Parker. That's it."

The Chinese stranger pulled out his burner to notify Choi. Now, what to do with Neville Parker? Their standing orders were to avoid injury to innocent Americans unless absolutely necessary. But he could think of no way to keep this man reliably quiet. He was certain no one had seen him enter and he didn't spot any security cameras outside the building. Parker was alone in the museum.

"Sorry."

"Wait! I told you what you—!"

Pfft.

Blood spurted out all over a stack of photos of a skinny white guy in black glasses holding a guitar.

Replacing the phone in its cradle on his wide mahogany desk, Chinese President Peng Xiao swiveled his chair to face the large burnt orange monochromatic painting of *Changcheng,* the Great Wall. Over the years, he had found that the painting opened his mind and allowed his thoughts to focus.

Jin Choi had just reported the identity of the man who was responsible for kidnapping the American girl, the man intent on recovering the Hudie Box and its contents. Bai Sun, one of his country's most important assets, had gone rogue. Peng had heard of Bai, and the file's description of the agent as competent, experienced, and loyal was consistent with Peng's recollection. Jin considered Bai a friend. Something had turned him. But what?

Was Bai working for Li Fong? On one level, it made sense. If the Liaodong Agreement came to light, the embarrassment to Peng visited upon him by his famous ancestor would be more than enough to sway those party members courted by Li, and Peng would lose the presidency. In fact, the heavy loss of face before the Chinese people would probably compel Peng to resign on his own. Worse, with the hothead Li in charge his country would almost certainly trigger a bloody war with America.

Jin had to find Bai and his *fafeng* crazy partner, Fen Lao, and kill them. Jin also needed to kill the Yates woman and, if necessary, her lethal friend. Bai, Fen, and Yates. To be safe all three needed to be eliminated.

Jin had been unsuccessful in locating Bai, but now reported Yates and Bannon were heading to a cave in southwestern United States. Jin was on his way to the cavern and expressed confidence Yates would be terminated. Without her expertise Bai was highly unlikely to find the Hudie Box, and Jin would have more time to locate the traitor. Peng wished he could be there to fire a bullet into Bai's brain himself.

Yates was different, and her death would not bring pleasure to Peng. She was an innocent young woman.

He'd instructed Jin to make her death as clean and painless as possible.

CHAPTER 23

After driving almost three hours, Belle and Nora finally reached the eastern end of the Guadalupe Mountain range.

To Belle, the Guadalupes had nothing in common with the stunning Wasatch Mountain vistas back home. Instead of majestic pines and snow-covered peaks, the Guadalupes offered non-majestic views of brown dirt, sagebrush, dry grass, scraggly cactus, and every now and then a gnarly juniper. She found it hard to believe that hundreds of feet below them, a whole underground world of interlocking caves extended over a hundred miles.

A short time later she drove through the entrance to the Carlsbad Caverns National Park, then along a winding road to the visitor parking lot. Before getting out of the car, she called to check on Scout. Nora's intern had taken him over to her sorority house to hang out, and the girls of Chi Omega were treating him like a king. The big fella always had a way with women.

They followed several tourists into a single-story, tan building where they found a well-lit visitors' center with a small restaurant, restrooms, and a bank of elevators.

Her phone dinged. A text from Ben: *Brass called me on carpet. Shut down my access to intel systems. In two days I'll have to tell them about*

Jenny or I lose my job. Sorry, Belle. Let me know when she's safe. Good luck. (BTW, still nothing from Tyler. Be careful.)

"Shit," Belle mumbled.

Nora asked, "What's up?"

"Ben Porter's superiors found out he'd been helping us," Belle groaned. "He's now out of the loop. Somehow, he arranged for a two-day reprieve. After that, he'll be duty-bound to tell them about the kidnapping."

Nora's expression hardened. "If we haven't found her in two days, we'll have to go to the FBI ourselves, no matter what your uncle says." She paused for a moment and shifted her posture. "Again, Jenny's an adult, and I'm sorry, but we need to do what we think is best for her. I know up to now you've agreed with your aunt and uncle, but time's running out and—"

Belle's eyes shot fire at Nora. "Jesus, don't you think I know time's running out!" She took a deep breath. "Sorry."

Neither spoke for a long moment.

Sick with worry, Belle didn't want to argue. She made a decision. "Okay, how about this? If Lizzie doesn't have the *bah-has-tkih*, we call the Feds."

"Deal," Nora replied.

They made their way to a short line in front of the information desk. After offering assistance to a family of four and a thin Asian man in granny glasses, a young blonde woman with a wide friendly smile greeted them. "May I help you?" she asked. In her crisp khaki park ranger uniform she looked like a grown-up Girl Scout about to pitch them on the merits of Thin Mints and Peanut Butter Patties.

"We're looking for Lizzie Parker," Belle said. "I understand she's a ranger here." Belle didn't think it possible, but the young woman's smile widened further.

"Oh, Lizzie. Everybody loves Lizzie."

Sweet, very sweet, but all Belle cared about was her damn bracelet.

The ranger flipped through a list of names on a clipboard. "Lizzie's off today, taking photos for her Chandelier book."

Nora wrinkled her brow. "She's writing a book about lighting fixtures?"

The ranger chuckled. "No, no. Chandelier's a cave. A number of the decorative limestone formations inside look like lace chandeliers, so that's how it came by its name. The cave was discovered by accident fifteen years ago, and over the last year we've been working on preparing Chandelier for public viewing. Should be open in a couple of months."

Belle didn't care when it would open. She needed to find this cave and Lizzie and her bracelet as soon as possible. "How far's the cave?"

"Not far," The ranger assured them. I'll give you directions. But it's Saturday and the work crew leaves early. She'll leave with them, so if you want to catch her, you'll need to hurry."

The ranger's directions to Chandelier were straightforward: drive along a narrow dirt road until it ends, then hike up the hill. The road terminated at a clearing that someday soon would probably be paved over for a parking lot. Most of the space now served as a construction staging area and contained rebar, lumber, and empty pallets stacked in piles.

Belle saw three parked vehicles—two older pickup trucks, each with a Dallas Cowboys sticker on its bumper and a twelve-gauge hanging across the back of the cab, and a newer pickup that had just been washed. Although the ranger said the cave would be well-lit, to be safe she stuck her big boy flashlight in the cargo pocket of her pants. The chances of Jin appearing at this remote spot were virtually nil, especially since Steve Kelly had disabled the tracer on Nora's phone. But *virtually* can get still you killed, so she also loaded the Stealth and tucked it into her belt under her shirt.

To say the landscape was barren would be charitable. Scrub brush and low-growing vegetation struggled to survive in the parched soil. Not a tree in sight. They hiked up the steep, rocky trail. Halfway up, they encountered two construction workers heading down to the parking lot —a beefy guy with a bushy red mustache, lugging a heavy roll of conduit over his shoulder and a thick, hard-faced woman, who looked like she could take out the redhead in two rounds of three, carrying a pickaxe.

"Sorry, ladies," the woman said in a deep drawl. "This is a construction site. No visitors."

"We're looking for Lizzie Parker," Nora said. "We work for her publisher. She's expecting us."

The second worker jerked his beefy thumb over his shoulder. "She's just finishing packing up her photo stuff. Wait here."

"You bet," Belle responded in as cheerful a tone as she could muster.

The workers headed down the path to the lot. The moment they drove off, Belle and Nora continued climbing until they could see a formation ahead that appeared like someone had taken a thick sheet of ugly rock, folded it over several times, then poked a hole in it. A generator to power both lights and tools hummed off to the side. The entrance itself was very narrow, nothing like Carlsbad, and looked like a giant gopher hole. Without pausing, they walked past a neatly printed sign reading: DANGER. HARD HAT AREA, AUTHORIZED PERSONNEL ONLY.

At the edge of the pit, they saw a steep escalator still under construction. A temporary wooden staircase next to it led down into the cavern. Belle could understand why the Park Service would want to develop the cave for public access; unlike those visiting Carlsbad, a tourist exploring Chandelier would enjoy a much more realistic sense of what a true caver experiences.

Belle's phone pinged.

"Sal?" Nora asked.

Belle blanched as she read the text, then looked up. "Aunt Helen suffered a mild heart attack on the drive north. She's at a hospital in La Spezia. I'm sure it's from the stress of Jenny's kidnapping. She's going to be fine, but they'll be there for a few days. He's trusting me to get Jenny back safely."

"I'm so sorry."

Belle dropped her gaze and shook her head. "I can't believe it. Aunt Helen had experienced a heart attack two years earlier, but since then there's been no problems. It's just . . . I don't know. She's 5000 miles away, and I feel a little helpless that I can't do something. For many years Helen filled the shoes of a mother to Jenny and me."

"The best thing you can do for your aunt is save Jenny."

Belle knew Nora was right. After a long pause, she took a deep breath and sent back a text with her love and encouragement.

Focus, I need to focus. She returned her attention to the escalater.

"Maybe we should wait up here," Nora said, a note of hesitancy in her voice.

Belle could tell Nora was anxious about descending into the hole. "You wait. I'll find her and hopefully bring up the bracelet for you to examine."

"I'm not letting you go down there alone." Nora forced a smile. Who's going to protect you if something happens?"

"You sure?"

"You go, I go."

Another ping. This time, Alonzo. Belle momentarily brightened.

Where r u?

She responded: *Carlsbad. Looking for bah-ha-tkih.*

His final text: *Jin could be nearby. Pls be careful.*

Good advice. Belle checked to make sure her gun was fully loaded, then hurried down the stairs, maintaining her handrail grip to keep from falling in the dim light. Nora wasn't keeping up. "I can slow down if you want."

Nora flapped her hand toward the darkness below. "Go, go."

They moved down through the narrow hole that reminded Belle of the Earth's anus. Not that she'd ever actually observed the Earth's anus, but if it had one, this hole would definitely resemble it.

Belle noticed the generator cable running alongside them, intertwining with the temporary railing posts. At its narrowest circumference, she thought if she stretched, she could almost touch the cave walls. Light from far below helped illuminate the stairway, as there were no lights on the stairs themselves. From the top the descent appeared steep but short. Once they descended below the surface, she observed the lights far below and realized how much deeper they still had to go.

After descending over ten stories they finally reached the bottom. The portable lights showed what the space would look like once the work was completed and opened to the public. Belle judged the entrance room to be about seven feet high, maybe twenty, twenty-five feet square. Clearly the end result would be nowhere near the scale of the Carlsbad entrance. A quick scan of the space confirmed Lizzie was not there. The only exit from the reception area appeared to be a narrow passage in the rock, less than three feet at its widest. A faint glow of light filtered in from the other side.

Belle took a step into the passage and called out, "Hello?" Nothing. She tried again, this time a little louder. "Hello? Lizzie?" She was about to shout a third time when she heard a young female voice.

"Coming!"

A minute later the shadow of a figure moved toward them.

"Jeez, Bev, I just needed a few more minutes, and by the way, your voice sounds—" She stopped abruptly at the sight of Belle. "You're not Bev." The passage was only fifteen feet long; she was at one end, Nora and Belle were at the other. They hesitated to move closer for fear of spooking her.

"Hi, Lizzie. I'm Belle Bannon, and my friend here is Nora Yates. Your father told us where to find you." She paused, expecting a response, but Lizzie remained silent, so Belle continued. "Your dad said he gave you a bracelet. Buckskin, rawhide, not sure, but it contained a beaded design and is a family heirloom from Chony Parker."

Lizzie was backlit, so Belle couldn't make out her features very well, but putting herself in Lizzie's place, Belle assumed the young woman was confused and wary.

Nora raised her hand in a "we come in peace" gesture. "Lizzie, I'm Nora. I'm curator at the Panhandle Plains Museum. I know our suddenly showing up here of all places must be disconcerting. We only need a few minutes of your time, and the reason we came down here instead of waiting topside is that a life's at stake and every minute counts."

Silence. Then, "I've been to that museum. A Georgia O'Keefe painting is on display there. What's its title?"

Without hesitating, Nora replied, "Red Landscape."

A beat. "Grab a couple of brain buckets on the shelf there and come on back."

CHAPTER 24

Belle noticed Nora's hands shaking as she slipped on the helmet and buckled the chinstrap. "You can stay here while I talk to her," she said kindly.

"I'm coming," Nora insisted. "If she's wearing the bracelet, I'll take some quick pictures, and we can leave."

"I can take a picture."

Nora's eyes widened, and her head pivoted back and forth, taking in the surrounding rock walls. "I said I was coming," she said, her voice slightly shaking.

Belle guessed that Nora suffered from claustrophobia. Pretty common. Even Alonzo had it. But to Nora's credit, she followed Belle into the narrow passage. The teardrop-shaped opening was widest at the bottom. Belle reached back for her hand, but after only two steps the passage narrowed to the point where they had to turn sideways to move forward. The walls at their head level narrowed further. Nora stopped.

"Crouch down where the passage widens," Belle suggested.

Nora crowded into her back. "Just move." She took a deep breath and held it.

They wriggled forward, and less than a minute later, they emerged from the narrow passageway into a huge chamber. Lizzie Parker stood in the middle of the space, folding a tripod. A backpack, a white flash umbrella, and several camera bags rested at her feet. Two small camera lights aimed straight up to a ceiling forty or fifty feet overhead. The breadth of the space extended beyond the point where light faded to black.

Nora glanced above her. "I can't believe we're over a hundred feet underground."

"Don't think about it. We'll be back on top soon."

Lizzie Parker looked to be mid-twenties, barely five feet, willowy. Belle could see the family resemblance to Neville. Dark hair pulled back in a ponytail, dark eyes, mahogany complexion. She wore jeans, a white t-shirt, gloves, and rubber-soled boots. Belle couldn't tell for sure, but she thought she spotted a brown bracelet wrapped around the girl's left wrist.

"Don't mean to be rude," Lizzie said, "but I was expected to be out of here twenty minutes ago. If my boss finds out I broke the rules, he's going to be a very unhappy camper."

The young woman didn't know them from Adam, so Belle figured a little small talk wouldn't hurt. "No problem. I understand you're writing a book about this place."

"More showing than telling." Lizzie returned to packing her bags. "The cave was only discovered fifteen years ago, and cavers are still mapping it. Already a hundred twenty-seven miles have been discovered, and there's more to go."

"Wow. That's like the distance between Lubbock and Amarillo," Nora said.

"I know, crazy," Lizzie replied. "Chandelier's actually bigger and deeper than Carlsbad, although no one's discovered a chamber as large as Carlsbad's Big Room yet. We've found speleothems down here never seen anywhere else in the world. Several books cover the discovery and exploration of the cave, and while they included a few photos, none focus exclusively on describing the breathtaking beauty of the place." She pointed above their heads. "For example, you'll never see anything like that in Carlsbad. Or anywhere else for that matter."

They looked up and spotted a twenty-foot-high stalactite formation that resembled a giant chandelier completely covered in pure white snow.

"So that's where the cave got its name," Nora said.

"Selenite," Lizzie explained. "A rare transparent crystalline form of gypsum."

Lizzie panned her helmet light around the chamber, and Belle could understand her enthusiasm. The white crystalline formations created the feeling that they stood in the middle of a virgin forest after a heavy snowstorm. She resolved to return to Chandelier when she could appreciate it more. Depending on Lizzie's answer to her next question.

"Any snakes down here?"

"Doubt it. About a month ago I spotted a couple of black-tails."

"Rattlers?"

"They hibernate in the caves and feed on bats," she said casually. "But this late in the spring they'll most likely be gone."

Most likely?

"Now, what's all this about my bracelet?" Lizzie zipped a camera bag closed, then held up her wrist so they both could see it. Belle could make out a beaded design, but Nora would have to study it much more closely to identify the symbols.

Belle took the lead. "A few days ago, a burglary occurred at Nora's museum. The thieves stole Quanah Parker's war lance. They later called and said they would return the lance if Nora could decode a series of symbols beaded into the lance by Chony Parker. We discovered that to interpret the code, a separate code key was needed."

"A *Bah-has-tkih.*"

Belle didn't hide her surprise. "That's right."

Lizzie offered a quick smile. "Don't act so stunned. I'm part Comanche."

"Of course. Anyway, we figured Chony might've passed down this *bah-has-tkih* to her children and grandchildren. We found your father, he confirmed the bracelet's existence and told us where to find you. The thieves gave us a deadline. That's the reason for the rush." Belle thought her story was improving, but she wasn't sure Lizzie bought it. She was right.

Lizzie swung the backpack onto her shoulders. "Okay, here's the thing. I think you're lying. Well, maybe that's too strong a word. More like shading the truth. I also sense you're both good people, so I'm guessing there's something at play here more important than the return of a museum artifact."

Time was ticking away. Belle was about to rip the bracelet off the girl's wrist when Nora placed a restraining hand on her arm.

"What Belle just told you is accurate, but you're right, there is more to the—"

The *crack* of the gunshot echoed across the chamber.

"Down!" Belle spun around. The limestone formations offered plenty of opportunities for cover.

The Chinese man with the granny glasses who'd been ahead of them in line at the Carlsbad information desk emerged from the narrow passageway brandishing a gun.

Behind him, two more Chinese men stepped into the chamber, one of whom was her old pal, Baldy Jin. Belle fired a single shot at Granny Glasses, but missed.

Just then they heard a dull clicking sound from above. Bats, thousands of them, rattled by the gunshots, shifted back and forth as one across the ceiling. A few broke away from the rest and flew across the center of the chamber, flitting in all directions like giant insects.

Lizzie lay flat on her stomach behind a thick stalagmite. Eyes wide, shaking, fear etched across every inch of her face. "W-who are those men?" she rasped through gulps of air. "I don't understand. What's going on? I should never have trusted—" She ducked her head as more shots pinged into the rock in front of them. "Oh, my God—"

"How far to the next exit?" Belle whispered.

"There *is* no next exit," she hissed. "The way we came in is the only way out."

More shots, then another *crack* overhead. They glanced up to see a large chunk of the chandelier formation break apart. Lizzie screamed, and Belle stretched out her arms in an attempt to cover the heads of both Nora and Lizzie with only partial success. Shards of white rock showered down on them, stinging their exposed skin.

"Turn out your headlamps," Belle instructed. "They're using the lights as targets." She switched off the lamp on her helmet; Nora and

Lizzie did the same. The gunfire stopped as the entire chamber went black. *Now what?* For almost a minute, no one moved, no one spoke.

The total blackness was like a thick, living creature needing neither light nor breath. Belle imagined that if she reached out, she could actually rub it.

They heard shuffling and scraping, and a moment later powerful flashlight beams panned around the chamber.

Now Jin and his gang were the targets.

Belle would only allow herself one shot; she couldn't waste any more ammunition. Resting the barrel of the Stealth on a flat rock in front of her, she sighted the nearest light, took a deep breath, exhaled slowly, and squeezed the trigger. The light went out. An instant later they heard a yelp and what sounded like a falling body. One down, two to go.

Belle whispered across to Nora and Lizzie. "Four cartridges left. They'll continue to engage us until I run out of ammo. They don't know for sure how much I have left, but our fire has only come from one gun. Since I didn't unleash multiple shots, they'll assume I'm using a revolver rather than a thirteen-mag automatic. And it's unlikely I'd have brought extra ammo without any indication I would need it. Once I'm out of bullets we're sitting ducks. The bad guys can waltz in here and pick us off one by one."

She could hear both anger and fear in Lizzie's voice. "I don't understand. Who are they? What do they want? Who are *you*?"

Belle ignored her questions because at this point the answers made no difference to their chances of survival. Besides, she had her own question. *How did Jin find us?* Nora's address was no secret, and she figured he could've possibly followed them all the way from Canyon. Or maybe they'd put a tracer on the Tahoe. If they happened to get out of there alive, she'd check.

Nora turned to Lizzie. "I assume you have no radio that we could use to call for help."

Lizzie used the back of her hand to wipe away the tears trickling down her cheek. "Radio?" she responded, incredulous. "Why would I need a radio? The signal wouldn't reach outside the cave anyway. Cell phones won't work either." She sniffed. "Oh, my God."

Belle squeezed her shoulder. "Lizzie, listen to me. You're going to be okay, but we need to move back deeper into the cave. We have one advantage they don't. You. You know your way; they've never been here before."

More gunshots smacked into the surrounding rock formations, trying to tempt them to waste more ammo. If Jin and his men left the passageway and moved toward them, Belle would try to pick off another one. Otherwise, she wasn't firing. Then the flashlight beam moved to her left. A chance to take another one out. She couldn't pass it up. Again, she used the flat rock to steady the gun, sighted to the spot of light, and fired. The light went out, but this time they heard no cry of pain. *Damn. I bet they set a flashlight on a rock thinking I'd be stupid enough to shoot at it, and they were right.* Three bullets left.

If they stayed in place playing the game of shoot-the-light, the good guys were going to lose.

Belle crawled over to Lizzie and Nora. "Don't talk. Lizzie, we need you to lead us out of the chamber. Can you do that?"

Lizzie's shoulders heaved, and she struggled to mute her sobs. "I don't want to die."

Nora put her arm around the young woman and whispered into her ear. "You're not going to die, but we need you to be strong. You may not be in uniform, but you're a ranger. And these evil men are not only threatening our lives, they're defiling the cave. Lead us out of here, Lizzie. You can do it. We'll follow you."

Nora's speech must've struck a chord because Lizzie wiped her eyes with her sleeve and nodded.

The attackers turned on two lights: a lantern emitting wide, diffused light that only converted the blackness to dark gray shadows; and a narrow bright beam flashlight that panned back and forth across the cavern. Lizzie rose to a crouch behind the stalagmite cover and froze. She waited for the sharp beam to pass by, then whispered, "This way." She moved out, and they followed close behind toward a far corner of the room, zigzagging from one rock formation to another. Twice the sharp light beam momentarily caught them in its sights, drawing fire. Luckily, no one was hit.

Finally, they reached what in the dark shadows appeared to be a solid wall of limestone. They heard the sound of movement behind them, and Belle could tell from the narrowing of the light beam that the Chinese were coming. She considered firing another round to slow them down but decided to hold off until she had a clear shot.

The delineation between black and gray was almost non-existent. Unable to see, Lizzie trailed her hand across the wall, looking for the chamber exit. A moment later, the light beam caught her dead-on. She froze like a mime on a darkened stage bathed in a bright spotlight. Belle yanked her down an instant before a fusillade of bullets raked across the wall where she'd been standing. The attackers no longer needed to hesitate, and Belle could hear them moving quickly toward the three women. In a few moments the situation was going to move from bad to really, really worse.

Belle needed to spend one more bullet. With no time to steady the gun on a rock, she pointed the Stealth at the light and fired. She missed both the light and whoever was holding the light, but the shot had the desired effect of slowing them down. Lizzie suddenly moved quickly, changing direction.

"Lizzie . . .?"

She whispered, "there's a second exit to the next chamber, one they'll never find." She moved farther along the wall then disappeared.

Nora whispered, "Where'd she go?"

They heard something scratching a rock once, twice, three times and followed the sound, sliding along the chamber wall. Belle felt a hand reach out seemingly from the wall itself and grab her shoulder. Lizzie pulled her close. Nora, holding on to the back of Belle's shirt, followed into a tight squeeze. Lizzie slipped off her backpack and held it in her arms to more easily navigate a series of sharp-angled turns.

Nora whispered, "I can't breathe."

Belle squeezed her hand and gently tugged her forward. In a few minutes they were through to the next chamber.

Lizzie turned on her helmet light. "Because of the angled passage, they can't see the light, but we should keep our voices down just in case."

Nora and Belle switched on their helmet lights. Both were stunned to see they were standing on the edge of what looked like a giant white living room with an underground lake maybe two hundred feet across, covering the entire floor like a translucent rug. The ceiling here was low, only seven or eight feet, and the air smelled acidic, like vinegar or bad wine.

"It's called Wayne's Lake," Lizzie said, "named after Wayne Cook, the guy who discovered it. We must cross the lake to reach the Enchanted Forest entrance. We can hide there until those awful men give up and leave."

"Why can't we just wait here?" Nora asked.

"Even though the guano deposits are light, with the low ceiling the air becomes dangerously toxic after twenty or thirty minutes."

Belle shined her light down into the water, so crystal clear she could see to the bottom. "Looks like it's only a couple of feet deep so we can wade across."

"The purity of the water makes it seem shallow," Lizzie said, "but the lake's over fifty feet deep, so we'll swim." She unzipped the backpack and pulled out two yellow nylon zipper bags. "Put your clothes in here." In response to their puzzled expressions, Lizzie pointed to a handmade sign next to the lake: "No clothes in the water. Keep it pure."

Lizzie unzipped her jeans. "No matter how dire our situation, this lake has remained pure for a million years, and we're not going to be the ones to muddy it with the dirt and bacteria from our clothes. I realize we also have bacteria on our skin, but the clothes are much worse. So no skin, no go. You can tell your friends you skinny-dipped in probably the purest lake in the world." She undressed quickly. Nora and Belle paused only a moment before stripping off their clothes and securing them along with Belle's gun in the waterproof bags.

Lizzie explained, "Wayne Cook recorded the temperature as sixty-seven degrees Fahrenheit, but it might seem a lot colder because of the humidity." She entered the water without hesitation and began swimming. Nora took Belle's hand, and together they approached the water. Nora dipped her foot in then jumped back, almost knocking Belle over.

"It's freezing."

Maneuvering in cold water had been part of Belle's Recon training, and she didn't hesitate to step into the lake. Nora followed, and their bodies quickly adjusted to the temperature. The water was so clean, she couldn't believe they were three of only a handful of people in the history of the world who'd ever seen, much less been immersed in it.

Belle lowered her body until only her head remained above the surface. For a few unexpected moments the almost transcendent caress of the ancient lake water around her body blotted out the world around her. A momentary pang of guilt for allowing the indescribable experience to intrude on her rescue mission quickly dissolved. She shuddered, not from the chill, but rather from the almost spiritual feeling of the liquid welcoming her. Becoming her. Never particularly religious, she closed her eyes and allowed her body to float to the surface.

"Belle?"

A rebirth?

"Belle?"

A baptism?

"Belle!"

Belle opened her eyes and saw Nora waving to her from almost halfway across the lake. She returned the wave, then luxuriated in a slow glide across the crystalline waters, not wanting the experience to end.

Lizzie used a modified sidestroke so she could hold a light above the water. Belle followed the light, and after a while she'd reached the other side where Nora and Lizzie waited.

As she climbed out of the water, she couldn't shake the feeling that her immersion in Wayne's Lake meant something more than simply a possible path to safety.

"What took you so long?" Nora asked, a bit perturbed.

"Sorry," Belle mumbled.

After quickly dressing, they trailed Lizzie into a short passageway. She turned off her light; Nora and Belle did the same and followed Lizzie only by sound. Belle glanced over her shoulder for a last glimpse of the lake, but it had quickly faded into the darkness.

In a few minutes the walls of the passage slipped away, and Belle could tell they were in the next chamber, enveloped by a thick, suffocating cloak of absolute black.

CHAPTER 25

The girl said her name was Sadie Parker Yates, and Jenny quickly realized the child was Nora's daughter. She didn't know much about Nora's personal life. None of her business. But she knew Nora's ex-husband was a rodeo star named Buck Yates. Obviously, Sadie had been kidnapped to put added pressure on Nora. From the beginning, Jenny had believed Bai and Fen were bad people, but now she knew for sure. Kidnapping a little girl, that was pure evil.

The Fenbot had pushed Sadie into the bedroom a few minutes earlier without saying a word. The child appeared to be in shock and repeatedly told Jenny that someone needed to help her daddy. Jenny tried to console her with a promise that she'd find a doctor for her daddy as soon as they were released. In truth, she suspected Buck Yates was beyond help.

Now the need to escape intensified. Jenny was responsible not only for her unborn baby, but also for Nora's little girl. She supposed Bai might allow them to live, but the chances were slim.

The night before, she'd called through the door asking for a bathroom break. Bai informed her she was to knock, not speak. Later she knocked just to see how they'd respond. Fen unlocked the door and escorted her to the bathroom. Unfortunately, the woman didn't appear tired or sleepy and was fully dressed. Major weird.

They'd taken her phone and watch, but Jenny guessed the time was past midnight. Maybe two in the morning? She knocked on her door. About thirty seconds later she heard shuffling sounds, then the tinny rattle of the lock. The door opened and Fen stood there fully clothed in her standard black outfit. Jenny couldn't be certain in the low light, but dark blotches streaked across the woman's t-shirt. Just shadows? Blood? Buck Yates' blood? *My God, poor Sadie.*

Time for the tiny pitiful voice. She lowered her head and eyes, fully submissive. "Sorry, we both have to pee." She squeezed her thighs together for effect.

Fen stepped aside. Jenny took Sadie's hand and they passed through the doorway. She made a point of hurrying to the bathroom as though they really had to go. The moment they entered she closed the door behind them and slapped the toilet seat down hard enough for Fen to hear outside the door. On her earlier visits she'd intentionally stayed on the toilet a long time. Hopefully her kidnappers were conditioned to expect she'd be a while, especially now that Sadie also needed to use the facilities.

Jenny whispered, "We're going to sneak away so we can help your daddy, okay?" The girl nodded. "But we have to be real quiet so the bad people don't hear us." Another nod. Jenny crawled into the tub and pushed up the window sash. *Creak.* She froze. *Did Fenbot hear that?* No time to worry now. Once through the window she would stand on the ledge below the sill and help Sadie through.

She realized she hadn't given any thought to how she was going to exit through the window. Because of the height she couldn't slip through leading with her feet; she'd have to exit headfirst. But then how was she going to land on the ledge and avoid tumbling to the pavement far below? Maybe she should close the window, take Sadie back to their room, and just hope Belle and Nora found the stupid box in time.

The baby kicked her hard. A sign. No, the time was now. She pushed the window up as far as it could go. She balanced precariously on the narrow tub edge directly under the window, turned her back, and reached through, grabbing the frame from the outside. Bending her knees, she pushed herself up, headfirst through the opening. Now seated in the window frame, facing inward, she scooted her hips back, then dragged her left leg across the sill and dropped it hoping to find purchase on the ledge. Nothing but air. The ledge was too far below the window. *Shit.* She grabbed onto the frame as tightly as she could and pulled her right leg through. Dangling from the window, she allowed her grip to slide down the frame, catching splinters in her left hand from the old wood. She twisted her body the best she could so her baby bump wouldn't impede her descent. In a few moments she felt her toes touch the ledge. *Yes!*

She took a second to catch her breath, then reached up for Sadie. The girl poked her head out, and Jenny could see the fear on her face. She whispered, "It's okay, honey. Climb up, roll over on your tummy, and drop your feet out. I'll catch you." Sadie hesitated, and Jenny didn't blame her. "We have to help your daddy."

The sound of scraping, then Sadie struggled up into the window frame.

Jenny did her best to hide her fear beneath an encouraging voice. "Good girl! Now over on your tummy—" Jenny reached up and grasped Sadie's tiny waist. "I've got you, you can let go."

Sadie released her grasp and fell into Jenny's arms. The sudden force of the drop almost teetered them both over the ledge, but Jenny shifted her weight tight against the building, regained her balance, and pulled the girl down safely.

She took Sadie's hand and they shuffled carefully along the narrow ledge toward the flat roof, a maneuver made even more harrowing by her hippo girth. Any moment now she expected Fen to poke her head out the window, but so far so good. After what seemed like an eternity, she reached the flat roof and dropped five feet to the gritty surface, landing on her hands and knees. She risked a quick glance over her shoulder, certain she'd see the Fenbot leaning out the bathroom window with a gun in her hand. Still clear. Sadie dropped easily into her arms.

Jenny's hands bled from the window splinters and cuts from the sharp gravel covering the rooftop, but she barely noticed. Bending low, she hurried across the roof to the front of the structure. The restaurants were closed and the parking lot empty. Across the street the gas station was also closed. She returned to the back of the building where a thick expanse of trees extended as far as she could see. Wait, were those tiny flickers of light moving through the trees? Her imagination, or a road? Headlights meant cars. If they could make it there, she could flag down a car and use the driver's cell phone to call for help. But first they had to get down. Scanning the area quickly, she spotted a ladder in the back corner, and they hurried toward it.

The ladder was rusty, loose, and squeaky. Maneuvering her ungainly body to the first step without falling was a challenge. "Let me go first, honey." Twenty feet, one step at a time.

Her baby belly made descending the vertical ladder difficult. She momentarily thought of the rust and grime penetrating into and infecting the cuts on her hand. Tomorrow's problem. Sadie began to climb down after her and seemed more at ease navigating the ladder.

A voice from above pierced the night quiet. *"Go se!"* Shit!

Jenny looked up to see Fen reaching out the window, pointing a gun at her. She couldn't tell for sure, but the gun had a tube attached to the barrel. She'd seen enough TV to assume the tube was a silencer.

Pffft.

A bullet pinged off the flat roof above her. She descended faster and shouted up to Sadie. "Hurry!"

Bai appeared in the window and pushed away Fenbot's gun hand. *Guess he didn't want to kill his hostages too early.* Fen dropped to the ledge like a jungle cat, then easily glided across to the roof. *How did she do that so quickly?*

Jenny's feet touched the concrete drive, and in a moment, Sadie was beside her. Holding her protruding belly with one arm and Sadie's hand with the other, she lumbered as fast as she could into the thick trees.

Now what? She tried with only partial success to control her breathing. Fenbot was a professional and no doubt an excellent tracker. At ground level she could no longer see the lights, so they ran through the trees in a direction away from the restaurants. She wrapped an arm around Sadie, trying to protect her from the thick brambles that raked her own limbs and the scratchy vines slapping her face.

This was crazy. She'd never elude Fen. Probably the best thing to do was give up. After all, Bai had kept Fen from shooting them. She and Sadie were no use to them—*Ouch!* The baby kicked her again.

They would keep moving. Maybe they would find help on the other side of the trees. Assuming they made it that far. The thick woods reminded her of the fairy tales her mother and big sister used to read to her as a kid. She shuddered.

Jenny squeezed Sadie's hand tighter and led her into the dark place where wolves and witches roamed.

CHAPTER 26

The darkness was so thick now that Belle imagined she could actually feel its weight on her shoulders. "Where are we?"

"Enchanted Forest," Lizzie responded. "Two entrances from this chamber to the next—Queen's Throne. About twenty yards to the right is the main entrance, the one they'll probably take."

Belle had an idea. "Nora, you stay here and follow Lizzie."

"Where are you going?" Lizzie asked.

"I'll take the main entrance and wait for them," Belle replied. "I only have one cartridge left. Jin's the leader. If I can knock him off, my guess is his buddy will get the hell out of here."

Nora leaned up against me. "I'm going with you."

"No, you'll be safer with Lizzie."

Lizzie added, "Nora and I can slip through this chest compressor and then meet up with you—"

Nora's cracking voice interrupted. "Chest compressor?"

"Tell her," Belle said with a sigh.

"Caver slang," Lizzie said with a strained lightness. "No big deal. It means there's a long squeeze so tight you'll need to exhale to make it through. But again, it's really not that—"

"No way." Nora remained frozen in place. Lizzie took her hand. "Come on, the opening's a lot bigger than it looks."

"Belle. . .?"

No time for debate. "In the Marines we learned the best way to fight claustrophobia is to bite your lip or dig your nails into your legs. Pain punctures fear. You'll be fine. And look, you may hear gunshots. Whatever happens, keep going. Locate a place to hide. I'll find you. Go."

"Stay tight as you move along the trail through Queen's Throne," Lizzie instructed Belle. "A few yards to the right of the path, in the middle of the chamber, is a deep pit."

"How deep?" Belle asked warily.

"We named it Lucifer because it drops all the way to Hell. It's marked by a round, cream-colored mound that looks like the head of a penis."

"Got it. Stay away from Lucifer and the penis." She hurried off before Nora had a chance to follow.

Nora bit her lip hard, breaking the flesh. The pain didn't puncture her fear. Instead, she now felt pain *and* fear. But she still followed Lizzie into the squeeze. The opening wasn't too bad, but then she faced a flat space less than a foot wide extending for maybe ten feet. No way.

Lizzie whispered from the other side. "You can do it. If you move fast, it'll be over in seconds. Like ripping off a Band-aid. Be brave."

Be brave. Nora wondered if her Comanche ancestors ever suffered from claustrophobia when hiding from soldiers in a tight box canyon. She made a mental note to research that when she returned to the museum. *Might make an interesting article—*

Lizzie's harsh whisper rattled Nora from her musings. "Hurry . . .!"

The words of a Comanche dance chant entered Nora's mind. Words of calm, of inner peace. *"Hey ya hey yo, Ya hey e. Hey ya hey yo, Ya hey e. Hey ya hey yo, Ya hey e."* She took a deep breath, exhaled, and inched forward. The flat rock touched her nose and the back of her head. She couldn't breathe. Her palms dripped cold perspiration. *"Hey ya hey yo,*

Ya hey e." She turned her head, and the guano-covered rock scraped the side of her forehead. Tears streamed down her face.

"Good, good," Lizzie urged. "You're already halfway through."

The rocky space sandwiched her tighter. She stopped, frozen. The toxic odor from the bat shit filled her lungs. She couldn't move.

"Come on, you got this." Lizzie's voice sounded a bit closer.

An image of Sadie's face, the one with the Halloween cat whiskers, filled Nora's mind. At least Sadie had her father. Buck was no saint, but he loved their daughter and would take care of her. *Oh, my God, oh, my God, oh my—*

Lizzie barked. "Move."

She coughed. *Cough, coffin. Funny.* She half-heartedly wiggled her hips forward. *"Hey ya hey yo, Ya hey e."*

Another sharp whisper, "Again."

She wiggled her hips again, this time with more force, and moved a little farther. The flat rock now pressed hard against her chest. *Good thing she didn't have big boobs.* She exhaled. *Chest compressor.* She wiggled as hard as she could while forcing herself not to inhale and . . .

She was through. She took a deep breath, her shoulders heaved, and she fought back tears.

Lizzie gave her a quick hug, then slipped a flashlight under her own t-shirt, effectively muting the light. "Good job."

Nora's heart slammed around her ribcage. "Where are we?"

"Queen's Throne," Lizzie answered with a sweeping gesture. "But the unofficial name is the Bat Cave. The ceiling's covered with them, so try not to touch anything because it's probably covered in a foot of bat shit. You can actually get histoplasmosis from breathing airborne spores."

Nora didn't know what histoplasmosis was, but it didn't sound good. She continued to follow Lizzie who was guided only by her experience and the light under her shirt.

Maybe five minutes later, Lizzie stopped and stepped sideways into a tight space between two sheets of rock less than two feet apart.

"Come on in," Lizzie urged. "No one will find us here."

Nora hesitated. She could feel a trickle of cold perspiration drizzling down her spine, but she took a deep breath and followed Lizzie into the gap. Lizzie doused her shirt light, and the heavy blackness instantly wrapped itself around both women.

Nora wondered how long they'd have to wait for Belle. And how would Belle find them? She forced herself to take another deep breath and try to think of pleasant things. Sadie. She smiled, remembering her daughter's first day of kindergarten. She knew Sadie had been frightened when Nora walked away for the first time. She could see the little girl's face crinkle up, ready to cry and run after her. But she didn't. She was brave and simply offered a tiny wave, then turned to follow her new teacher into the school. How proud she was of her daughter that day. Now she herself needed to be brave.

Like Sadie.

For Sadie.

Then she heard a click behind her ear.

Lizzie pulled her light out from under her shirt and turned it on.

Nora found herself looking up into the business end of a gun barrel.

And behind the gun the grinning face of a Chinese man wearing granny glasses.

Belle cautiously moved along the main path through Queen's Throne, the only illumination coming from the muted light under her shirt. She noticed a few small, isolated shadows flitting around the cavern. Bats, no doubt. She assumed Nora and Lizzie were safely hiding behind one of the many rock formations scattered in the far reaches of the chamber, away from the main path.

With only one cartridge left, she couldn't win a shootout with Jin and his buddy. Her only chance was to ambush Jin.

The passageway into Queen's Throne was comparatively wide, and as soon as she entered the chamber she moved left, looking for a formation to hide behind and wait for Jin and his sidekick. The room smelled like bat shit, and she could hear the faint clicking sounds coming from the ceiling.

Then she heard Nora's voice off to the right of the main path.

A flashlight flicked on, and Belle ducked behind a guano-covered formation that looked like a person sitting on a rock. Twenty-five yards ahead Nora and Lizzie knelt in front of Jin and his pal. *Shit!*

Granny Glasses pointed a light at the two women. Jin aimed a gun. Belle could hear the fear in Nora's voice as she faced Jin.

"There's very little chance anyone can decode the symbols on the lance," Nora pleaded. "Whatever you're looking for will remain buried forever. Isn't that what you want?" She put her arm around Lizzie's shoulders. "And Lizzie has nothing to do with it. She had no idea who we were before we came here."

Lizzie appeared bewildered, and who could blame her? A few hours earlier she was a happy, optimistic young woman simply living her life. Now that life was going to be snuffed out before it hardly began because of something she knew nothing about.

Nora reached down and pulled the buckskin bracelet from Lizzie's wrist. "This is what we were searching for. It's possible, *possible,* the symbols beaded on this bracelet may help decipher the symbols on the lance, but Lizzie was unaware of the bracelet's possible significance. Please, you have to let her go. The best way you can guarantee whatever you're looking for will never fall into the wrong hands is to find it yourself. If you release us, maybe with the bracelet I'll get lucky and decode the lance. If so, we can all go and unearth the Hudie Box together. We lure Bai Sun to the site, he releases Jenny, then you can fight it out with him. You get the box, we get Jenny. No innocent dies. All we want is Jenny released unharmed. But we have to move now. The deadline's approaching."

Jin took the bracelet and tossed it aside without a glance. "Not an unreasonable argument, Ms. Yates. But as I see it the best way to absolutely guarantee the location of the . . . item . . . will never be discovered is, sadly, to take your life. He turned to Lizzie. "And you, Ms. Parker, turned up at the wrong place at the wrong time. Because you will be a witness to Ms. Yates's demise, something that could cause my country certain embarrassment, you have become what you Americans call collateral damage. This grieves me, for we do not take an innocent life indiscriminately."

Every muscle in Belle's body iced. She heard clicking and sensed movement overhead. The bats were probably about to exit the cave for their nightly hunt.

She sensed a flapping directly overhead. A wing lightly brushed across her face. She slapped at the creature and jerked her head away.

Her movement didn't go unnoticed.

Jin and his man instantly pivoted and opened fire. As she ducked down behind the limestone formation Belle fired her last bullet at Jin, just missing.

The sharp crack of gunfire triggered a huge swarm of screeching bats, descending down upon all of them like a throbbing black blanket.

Nora and Lizzie scurried off, doing their best to cover their heads with their arms. Granny Glasses dropped the flashlight while he and Jin each used their free hand to swat the bats away and their gun hand to fire at them. The more shots they fired, the more agitated the bats became. The cave's echo effect amplified both the gunfire and the bat screeching to a near-deafening level. The fallen flashlight now provided the only light, and it pointed toward Jin. Belle couldn't spot the two women, a good sign.

Belle moved quickly from the cover of one formation to another until she almost reached Jin and his sidekick. The bats surrounded her, but she did her best to ignore them. She wanted Granny Glasses's gun. He moved closer to her new hiding place. When he turned his back, she stepped out and crashed her jungle flashlight down hard on his skull. She heard it crack and figured he was no longer a threat. The gun dropped. Belle scooped it up.

Jin was occupied with the screeching bats and took a few seconds to realize he was alone, standing in the spotlight, an easy target. Belle pulled the trigger. *Click, click.*

She dove back behind a rock just as Jin fired, and the only things that saved her were the lack of light and the swarming bats. While Jin took a few moments to retrieve the flashlight, Belle scurried away from the main path and wound her way up through the maze of limestone formations. She didn't know how many rounds Jin had left, but she was hoping he was close to empty.

Jin yelped and Belle saw a bat hanging off the back of his shirt, screeching and nipping behind his ear. He frantically reached over his shoulder to swat it away, but the bat held on tight. He dashed to a short limestone tower near the chamber entrance and rubbed hard against it like a bear scratching its back against a tree trunk. The bat dropped off, but the main swarm, intent on returning to the surface to feed, engulfed him.

Jin hunched over and stumbled toward the entrance to escape. He didn't realize he was following the same path as the bats. At the entrance he turned in frustration and randomly fired back into the cave until his magazine was spent, then disappeared.

Belle heard a scream.

"Belle!" Nora's voice.

"Jin's gone," Belle said with relief. "Turn on your light."

"Lizzie's been hit!"

Immediately a bright beam of light appeared on the far side of the chamber. With her heart in her mouth, Belle rushed toward it and found Nora and Lizzie crouched behind a thick limestone formation that looked like a cream-colored chair ornately decorated in white and gold. The Queen's Throne. Lizzie's shirt was off. Her shoulder and bra were covered in blood.

Belle switched to soldier mode—all business. "Where were you hit?"

Lizzie grimaced. "Shoulder."

Nora fished through Lizzie's backpack and found a small first aid kit. "We were well behind cover, but his last shot ricocheted off a rock and hit her."

Belle used Lizzie's crumpled shirt to wipe away the blood around her left shoulder. Seeing a clean graze, she breathed a sigh of relief and offered an assuring smile. "You're going to be fine." She found a small bottle of antiseptic in the kit. "This will sting a bit."

"Just do it."

Belle poured the antiseptic onto the wound. Lizzie gritted her teeth but didn't cry out.

Belle quickly dressed the wound, and Nora tore open two packets containing Tylenol. She handed them to Lizzie along with a half-full water bottle. Lizzie gulped down the pills, and Belle helped her to her feet.

"You okay?" Belle asked. *Stupid question.* Lizzie smiled weakly and flashed her left thumb. "Then what do you say we get the hell out of here?"

Belle used Lizzie's bloody shirt to fashion a sling. Nora slipped the girl's backpack over her own shoulder, and Belle wrapped Lizzie's right arm around her neck.

Almost all of the bats had departed the chamber, and with the benefit of Belle's flashlight they were able to make their way down to the main path much faster.

Belle stopped. "Wait, the bracelet."

Nora scanned the stone floor with the flashlight until they spotted the bracelet crumpled up half-hidden behind a rock. She scooped it up, and they moved toward the entrance.

When they passed Granny Glasses's body Belle paused. A dead body meant more questions, and more questions meant more wasted time. She spotted the penis rock off to the left and slipped Lizzie's arm off her shoulder.

"Wait here." She dragged his body off the path to Lucifer's Pit. Somehow the man's glasses had remained on his face making him look like a gentle college professor. She didn't feel guilty about his death. The man had been intent on killing them. But as she stared into his dead eyes, she wondered about his backstory. *Was he married? Children? What did he do for fun? Was he funny, boring? Did he—?* She stopped herself. Was her transcendent immersive experience in Wayne's Lake making her soft?

She sighed. Now wasn't the time for soft. She rolled the body over the pit's edge, and watched Granny Glasses fall into Hell.

Then she heard an explosion.

CHAPTER 27

Jenny's torn t-shirt was streaked in blood from fighting her way through sharp brambles in the dark woods.

She'd tried hard to shield Sadie, and the best she could tell, except for a light scratch on one arm, the little girl was okay. She knew Fen was close behind them. She never heard the woman—she just knew. Jenny's mind flashed to an image of herself in a cheesy horror flick—the clueless heroine running through the dark woods with a deranged guy in a scary mask waving a bloody machete over his head chasing her. Except the horror movie heroine was never pregnant. Not very sexy for the obligatory shower scene.

She started out moving in a roughly perpendicular direction from the pale restaurant parking lot lights, but before long the trees and underbrush became so dense the lights disappeared, and now she moved solely on instinct. Suddenly, a thick tree branch appeared directly in front of her, and she bumped her head hard. *Ouch!* She veered left, gently tugging Sadie behind her. Was this the right direction? What if, somehow, she'd turned around in a circle and now headed back to the restaurant?

"Are we going to find a car?" Sadie asked. "The mean lady who hurt Daddy, she drove me here in a white car so I think we need a car."

Jenny forced an uneven calm to her voice. "Yes, honey, we're going to find a car."

A few more yards, then Jenny yelped as she slammed into another tree. She t turned right, crashing into a prickly bush. She instinctively wrapped her arms around Sadie to protect her and felt a sharp thorn gash her face. *This is crazy.* Her head pounded, and tears mixed with the blood on her cheeks.

Sadie looked up at her, so innocent. "Did you get an ouchie?"

"Yes, sweetie, I got an ouchie," she whispered. "But it doesn't hurt. Do you have any ouchies?"

Before the girl responded, Jenny squeezed her shoulder. "Shhh." She thought she heard a twig break behind them. Sadie heard it, too, and they both froze. Another tiny crack, this one closer. *Fen.* A part of her wanted to stop, let the Fenbot find them and take them back. Wouldn't that be best for Sadie? For the baby? Out here she was moving blind and already had tripped and fallen twice. She could do serious damage to the baby. All she had to do was call out and—

Sadie nudged her and pointed off to the right. Was that a flicker of light ahead? Probably her imagination. No, a light again, this time a touch brighter. Had they gone in a big circle? Was she seeing the light from the restaurant? She decided to move forward. If Fen found them first, Jenny would surrender quietly.

She continued fighting her way, bouncing from tree to tree in the dark, keeping Sadie safely behind her. As they moved closer, the light became more distinct and seemed to move slowly from left to right, then right to left. Headlights from cars traveling in opposite directions?

She whispered, "I think it's a road, we need to hurry." With renewed energy she plowed through the underbrush and reached the tree line. Up ahead across a grassy swale an unpaved road appeared. Maybe a service road of some kind. A car approached.

They hurried across the swale, and Sadie shot ahead. Holding her belly with both arms, Jenny stumbled forward following Sadie, who'd already reached the edge of the road. They both waved their arms in the air at what turned out to be an old pickup truck that might've been white fifteen years earlier. She glanced over her shoulder just as Fen emerged from the treeline.

The truck stopped, and she could see it contained only the driver. A woman, middle-aged, reached over and manually lowered the window. Friendly face, friendly voice.

"Goodness gracious, what in God's name are you two doing out here? And you being pregnant and all?"

Jenny again checked behind her, but Fen had disappeared back into the woods. "Do you have a phone? I need to call the police! Someone's trying to kill us!"

The woman appeared incredulous. "What? Yes, of course. Get in, both of you." She fished through her purse and retrieved a cell phone. Jenny quickly opened the door. Sadie climbed in and Jenny slid in after her. When the door opened the interior light came on. "I'm Lucy and . . . my God, honey, you're covered in blood." She found a crumpled box of tissues in the passenger footwell and dropped it in Jenny's lap. "We need to get you to a hospital."

"Thanks, they're just scratches," Jenny responded dismissively with a wave of her hand. "I really need to talk to the police."

"You got it." Her phone was an older flip-cover model. She opened the cover. "This guy who's after you and your daughter, none of my beeswax, but I'm guessing a boyfriend gone bad. Unfortunately, I see it all the time."

Suddenly they heard the sound of a gunshot. "Holy shit, he's shootin' at us. Both of you, get down in the footwell!"

Holding the phone in one hand, the woman attempted a U-turn, but the road wasn't wide enough. Jenny couldn't see from her crouched position, but she felt both of the passenger-side wheels dip down into the swale. She held Sadie as tight as she could. The truck will get stuck, Jenny thought. Or worse, flip over. She heard the rear wheel spinning in the soft soil, then almost miraculously it found purchase, and they were back on the road heading in the opposite direction.

"You both okay?"

"Yeah."

Sadie only nodded.

Jenny watched Lucy drive with one hand while she spoke into the phone.

"My emergency? My emergency is, I got me a pregnant young

woman and her daughter hiding in the footwell of my truck, and some crazy-assed boyfriend's shooting at them. She says—What's your name, sweetie?"

"Jenny Bannon." Her words spilled out. "We were kidnapped, and we've been held hostage upstairs of the Peking Express Restaurant, and—"

"Says her name's Jenny Bannon. Says she was kidnapped and held hostage above that Chinese restaurant off 40 . . . Her head's bleeding but she says they're just scratches . . . Okay, meet you there." Lucy closed the phone and dropped it into her purse. "They're sending a squad car and ambulance to the restaurant. We're supposed to meet them there. Although my guess is your boyfriend will be long gone. You can sit up now."

The access road intersected with a paved road, and before long they approached the strip mall parking lot.

Lucy said, "Doesn't look like the cops are here yet. I say we wait over there until they arrive." She gestured to a gas station across the street. Although the station was closed, the area around the pumps was well-lit. "Better safe than sorry." She made a left turn into the empty station and parked off to the side in the shadows. "If the bad guys are still home, no use parking under the lights like a sitting duck."

Jenny could hardly believe they'd actually escaped. The nightmare would end. She needed to contact Belle. "Could I borrow your phone? I need to tell my sister I'm safe."

"Be my guest."

Lucy handed her the phone, and Jenny dialed Belle's number. Just as she was about to tap the "call" button, she heard a scratching on the window by her ear. She twisted her head to see a gun barrel pointed at her face. The man holding the gun appeared to be Chinese, but it wasn't Bai. An arm snaked across her belly. She looked down to see Lucy reach across and roll down the window.

The strange man said, "*Zuò dé hao*, good job, Lucia." He spoke into a phone held to his ear. "We have them."

Lucy patted her on the knee. "So, how did you girls like my pizza?"

CHAPTER 28

Belle and Nora followed Lizzie back toward the cave entrance where they'd heard the explosion. Belle knew Lizzie must be hurting, but the adrenaline had kicked in. She wanted out of the cave as much as they did.

They passed the spot where Belle had shot the first man. She didn't see a body and suspected Jin had carried his fallen comrade away with him. Jin didn't want any questions asked either.

They entered Enchanted Forest and Lizzie stopped short. Her eyes widened and she pointed ahead to the connecting passageway between Enchanted Forest and Chandelier. The explosion had blocked the passageway with huge chunks of rock. *Jin.* Presumably, if he'd been successful he would've dropped their bodies into Lucifer's Pit and planted explosives that would significantly delay entrance into the string of chambers where DNA or other forensic evidence of the murder of three women might be found. On his way out of the cave, he'd pushed the button.

Even in the dim light Belle could see the blood drain from Nora's face.

Nora turned to Lizzie, not bothering to conceal her skyrocketing panic. "Y-You said this was the only way out?"

Lizzie nodded.

Nora could barely get the words out of her mouth. "Oh, my God. We're sealed in."

Belle tried lifting one of the boulders blocking the exit, but it didn't budge. No way were they going to dig themselves out.

Nora's voice quavered. "The workmen. When they see what happened, they can dig us out. They have equipment and—"

Lizzie interrupted her. "Thirty hours. Tomorrow's Sunday, and they won't return until Monday morning. Over thirty hours from now. They'll see my truck in the lot and know I'm still inside. The underground lakes here contain the purest water in the world. I think there are a few energy bars in my pack so we won't starve. We can wait till they come."

"No we can't," Belle said. She figured Lizzie deserved to know what was going on. Most of it anyway. "You heard Nora tell Jin that my little sister's life is at stake. Jin knows if he keeps Nora on ice until the deadline passes, Bai will kill Jenny, the motivation for Nora to decode the lance will have dissipated, and Jin can have the time he needs to find and take out Bai and his associate, Fen."

Lizzie's only response was her bewildered expression.

"We need to get out of here now," Nora said, struggling to keep the panic from her voice. "There must be a way."

They heard the now-familiar sound of clicking and gazed up to see the bats swirling overhead.

"They're stuck, too," Lizzie said.

Nora pointed to a corner of the chamber ceiling where the bat blanket was thickest. "They seem to be bunching up there."

Lizzie's face brightened. "They've found an exit."

In a few minutes, almost all of the bats had disappeared. Belle anxiously scanned the chamber walls, fueled by the hope, however slim, that a second exit could exist. "How can we get up there?"

"Just because a tiny bat can squeeze through doesn't mean we can," Nora said in frustration.

"We have to at least check it out," Belle pressed.

Lizzie pulled out her map and spread it on a flat rock formation. "Look here. The cave zigzags vertically up and down, but Enchanted

Forest is at the top of a zig. We're probably only sixty feet below ground. Maybe even less."

The bats disappeared at a point in the ceiling maybe forty feet overhead. Belle noticed the chamber wall closest to the opening consisted of uneven ridges, some as wide as two feet, most much narrower. "We use those ridges as steps to climb to the top. Let's go."

The climb turned out to be easier than they expected, and before long they balanced on a two-foot-wide ledge directly below a narrow gash in the rocky ceiling that reminded Belle of a crooked smile. *Is the cave laughing at us?*

"We need someone to check it out, see if the opening's big enough," Belle said.

"I'll do it," said Lizzie. "I'm the smallest."

"No way. You only have one working arm."

"If you can boost me up there, I can crawl inside with my right arm. Cavers routinely find themselves in squeezes where we can only use one arm. No big deal. Let's go, we're wasting time."

Belle formed her hands into a stirrup and boosted Lizzie up into the gash. The young caver slid her upper body through the gash easily, and once her shoulders were high enough she used her right hand to shine the flashlight inside the opening.

"There's a small shelf up here," she said. A few moments later they could hear the excitement in her voice. "And I think I can see stars! There's one squeeze, but it's not too bad. After that I think we can make it."

Lizzie tried to use her right elbow to leverage herself up all the way inside. Though she was using her good arm, her face grimaced in pain. She slid back down, her foot returning to Belle's hand stirrup.

"I'm lowering you to the ledge," Belle said. "Maybe I can—"

"No!" She took a deep breath. "I can do it."

Before Belle could respond, Lizzie screamed, "*Aaagh!*" and again tried leveraging up on her right elbow. This time she made it. "Yes! Nora's next."

"Why don't you guys go ahead and bring help?" Nora said weakly. "I can wait—"

Before she could object Belle grabbed Nora around her hips and lifted her up to the opening.

"Belle . . ."

Lizzie reached down with her right arm and helped pull Nora up and through. Belle rolled onto the balls of her feet, crouched, and jumped. On the second try she was able to grab hold and chin herself to the point where she could first swing one elbow, then roll her whole body up onto the shelf. The squeeze wasn't too bad, and even Nora, who continued to chant something Belle couldn't understand, made it through without complaint.

They spent the next twenty minutes crawling up a natural chimney, then popped to the surface under a graying sky and a handful of stars.

The three women rolled onto their backs on the rocky surface for a long moment and caught their breath, each of them, in her own way, coming to terms with the amazing fact that they were all still alive.

Nora and Belle sat in the Tahoe outside the Carlsbad Medical Center. After emerging from the cave, Belle had hiked three miles back to the Chandelier cave entrance and retrieved the SUV, then returned to pick up Nora and Lizzie.

The drive to Carlsbad—the town, not the cave—had taken about thirty minutes. Lizzie's bullet wound would require a police report. During the drive they'd asked her to keep them out of it if she could. They couldn't afford to waste another minute getting bogged down with the local authorities. She agreed and came up with a story blaming a deranged eco-terrorist. Apparently a fringe group of ultra-environmentalists who opposed any disturbance of Mother Nature had been active in the area and already had posted a string of messages on social media condemning the National Park's opening of Chandelier. Lizzie would say a single crazy found her alone down there, shouted some anti-government bullshit, then shot her and blew up the entrance. No, she couldn't recognize him, and yes, she wouldn't allow herself to be alone in the cave in the future.

Lizzie told Nora they could keep the bracelet until they found

Jenny. Hopefully, her story would hold up. At least for the next forty-eight hours.

Nora and Belle were exhausted. They'd cleaned up the best they could in the hospital restroom, then returned to the Tahoe. A cursory check resulted in the discovery of a tracer under the front fender. That's how Jin had found them. Belle tossed it into a trash can, and Nora finally felt comfortable enough to turn on the Tahoe's overhead light and carefully examine Lizzie's bracelet.

The blue and white beaded design contained five neatly formed symbols.

"Recognize them?" Belle asked.

Nora was so engrossed with the bracelet that she didn't respond. She opened her folder and compared the bracelet to the photos of the symbols on Quanah's lance.

Belle didn't press any further and headed back to Canyon, feeling excitement rising inside her. They'd found the missing piece of the puzzle. Nora would be able to use the *bah-has-tkih* to decode the lance. Eight o'clock. They'd find the jade box in time. Jenny would be saved.

An hour later, Nora tossed the bracelet onto the ledge above the dashboard in frustration. Belle had watched her produce several pages of handwritten notes and drawings, most of which were scribbled over. Belle hadn't said a word since they left the hospital and didn't even turn on the radio because she didn't want to disturb Nora's work. Finally, she couldn't wait any longer. "So?"

Nora sighed and closed her eyes. "So, it's not working."

"What do you mean it's—?"

"Christ, didn't you hear me, I said it's not working!" Her voice softened and she struggled to hold back the tears. "I'm almost certain the bracelet is part of the *bah-has-tkih,* but something's still missing."

Belle's phone rang, and she checked the screen. Ben. She put the phone on speaker.

Ben's tone was gratingly cheerful. "I assume since you answered the phone that you're both still alive."

"Not funny," Belle snarled.

"Sorry. Look, I don't have access to DIA files, but a simple google search revealed something that might be of interest. You told me you were checking out Roosevelt's valet, James Amos, and he wrote a book."

"That's right," Belle answered. "We gained access to his notes, and they confirmed that Teddy received the Hudie Box from the Chinese Ambassador in June of 1905. The president entered into a secret agreement with China. One copy of that agreement was later stolen, but Teddy had inserted the second copy into the Hudie Box and given it to Quanah Parker for safekeeping. Teddy died before revealing to Amos where Quanah had buried the box."

"What was in the agreement?"

"We don't know," Belle answered, "and Amos didn't say, but he called it the Liaodong Agreement."

"Okay, it's all starting to knit together," Ben said eagerly. "Here's what I found. Back in the mid-fifties, Amos's publisher was absorbed into a larger publishing company, which in turn was purchased by a California media conglomerate in 1974."

"And . . .?"

"Two months ago, that corporation was acquired by one of the largest companies in China."

Nora's brow shot up. "Some evidence of Amos's notes and drafts must've survived in the bowels of the original publishing company," Nora said.

"So presumably someone in the Chinese parent company found copies of his notes," Belle said, "and passed on the information to the Chinese government." Ben was right. It did all fit.

"But the government wasn't overly concerned," Nora provided, "because no one knew where Quanah buried the jade box," Nora said.

"Still, all governments leak," Ben countered, "and there's no reason to think China is any different."

Nora spoke faster as the pieces fell in place. "The story of Quanah and the Hudie Box leaks. Bai Sun and Fen Lao learn about the contents of the box and believe the Liaodong Agreement has value."

Belle continued the theory. "So maybe Bai figures he can extort big bucks from his home country to keep the document hidden. Bai and Fen kidnap the young woman they think will lead them to it."

Nora tapped her chest. "Me. Except they snatched the wrong person. The Chinese government discovers what the kidnappers are up to and have a 'holy shit' moment. For reasons we don't yet understand, they can't allow the box to be found and the Liaodong Agreement to surface."

Belle shook her head in frustration. "And Jenny's caught in the middle."

"Give me the word, and I'll call the Fibbies," Ben said. "Good luck."

He hung up, and Belle turned to Nora. "So is the bracelet the *bah-has-tkih* or not?"

Nora studied the bracelet, her eyes momentarily glazed in thought. "I think so, part of it. The design style's the same. Take, for example, the arrows, the second and fifth symbols. Comanche symbology uses both three-feathered arrows and four-feathered arrows interchangeably. The arrows in both the bracelet and the lance used three-feathered arrows, but they're pointing in different directions, which is unusual. The first symbol—five short vertical lines—and the third symbol—two points with a horizontal line drawn through them—I've never seen before. I did recognize the fourth symbol; it denoted a white soldier. I've tried to view the symbols in different combinations but it doesn't work. As I said, I feel like the bracelet is part of the code key, but something's still missing."

Belle picked up the bracelet and rolled it through her fingers. She had an idea. "The bracelet has half the number of symbols as the lance. Remember, Neville said there were two bracelets."

Nora perked up. "That's right. His brother, Cord, received the second one."

Belle's heart accelerated. "So is it possible—?"

"Yes!" Nora crowd, grinning. "Chony Parker could've made the *bah-has-tkih* in two parts. Two bracelets meant to be worn by two trusted family members or by the same person on each arm."

Belle reached for her phone to google the phone number of the Gracie, Texas Sheriff's office.

"Too late to call," Nora said.

"Sheriffs don't work nine-to-five; the office has to be open twenty-four seven."

She found the number and dialed, then put the phone on speaker mode. After five rings a high-pitched sleepy male voice answered.

"Gracie Sheriff's office. How may I help you?"

"Sheriff Cordero Parker please."

"Sheriff Parker will be in tomorrow morning at eight. What's the nature of the problem?"

Nature of the problem? *Nature of the problem?*

"Ma'am . . . ?"

Belle tapped the screen, ending the call.

Nora said, "We can grab a few hours of sleep and call him in the morning, or . . ."

If Cord Parker had the second bracelet, and if he was willing to share it with two strangers who refused to tell him why they needed it—two giant *ifs*—Belle wanted them to be there in person so Nora could check it out immediately.

Belle tapped the map app. "How the hell do we get to Gracie, Texas?"

CHAPTER 29

Nora's intern couldn't spend the night, and dogs weren't allowed in the dorms, so they had to swing by Canyon to pick up Scout.

When they entered Nora's kitchen, the temptation to crash for a few hours overwhelmed them. But every minute counted, so they grabbed a bag of chips, some dog treats for Scout, and a couple of coffees for the road. The phone's GPS said the trip would take three and a half hours to Gracie.

Belle called, left a message for Alonzo summarizing what had happened in Carlsbad, and told him where they were heading. No immediate response, so she assumed he was off-grid for the moment. They turned up the radio to stay awake, but it didn't work. They tried conversation. Nora talked about her daughter; Belle talked about Jenny. Nora talked about her job; Belle talked about hers. They listened to a few tunes on the radio.

"Tell me about Tyler," Nora said. "You must've seen signs of his erratic behavior."

Belle sighed, and her eyes glazed as her mind flashed back to that warm evening on the San Diego beach. "We were both going through Basic Recon training at Pendleton. He was tall, good-looking. As one of only two women surrounded by testosterone-soaked men, I could've had anyone I wanted. But Tyler was smart. He played hard to get. I was stupid and fell for it. He was so jealous, and when he didn't make the cut and I did, anger fueled that jealousy. One night he thought I was flirting with some grunt at a Tiki bar. We argued, and he sucker-punched me. I went down hard with what turned out to be a broken jaw. A ring he wore sliced my face along the jawline like a steak knife. A moment after it happened, he was on his knees in tears, begging my forgiveness. Cops were called, but I didn't press charges. That was it. Routine military romance over. Except for him it wasn't."

"Think he'll bother you again?"

Her mind changed channels from the sandy beach to the gritty concrete floor of the airport parking garage—Tyler on his back and her standing over him with a tire iron. She remembered his face didn't show fear. Instead, his eyes gleamed, almost like he'd welcome a tire iron smashing into his skull. She shuddered. "I hope not."

After listening to a few more songs from a country-and-western station, Belle heard Nora's tiny snores melding with Scout's not-so-tiny snores, leaving her multi-flavored coffee as the only thing keeping her from driving into a ditch.

She glanced in the rearview mirror periodically, looking for a tail, but in the dark all she could make out were headlights. She stopped for gas outside Chillicothe and watched passing traffic from the pump. Mostly pickups, SUVs, and compacts, but she did notice a couple of dark sedans passing by. Hardly surprising. Even at the late hour there had to be thousands of roomy sedans out on the roads. After all, they were in Texas.

A little while later she drove past a sign welcoming them to Gracie, "The Absolutely Positively Friendliest Town in Texas!" Population 3867.

The sheriff's office was connected to the town hall, a one-story redbrick building in the center of Main Street. A single patrol car was parked out front. Maybe Cord Parker had come in early. Or maybe he'd been called out of bed on a police emergency and returned to his office. Or maybe she was grasping at straws. But the damn clock was ticking, so she decided to check it out. After parking next to the patrol car, she left the two sleeping beauties in the Tahoe and entered.

Opening the door caused a bell to ding somewhere overhead, and a few moments later a door behind a counter opened. A slight, sleepy-eyed young man wearing a sheriff's uniform shuffled out.

"I'm Deputy Sheriff Tisdale. Can I help you?" If Barney Fife had a grandson, his name would be Deputy Sheriff Tisdale. His voice even squeaked. Belle figured he was the one who'd answered the phone when she'd called earlier.

She was too tired to fake cheerfulness. "I'm looking for Sheriff Parker."

"He don't come on duty until eight tomorrow. But I'm his deputy." The kid puffed out his chest.

"Need to talk to him on a personal matter. Don't suppose you can tell me where he lives? It's important."

"Against the rules," the deputy responded with an air of authority. "You know, national security."

"Of course." Somehow, she didn't think Gracie, Texas, was high on the list of terrorist targets, but she held her tongue. Eight o'clock. Part of her said she should push the kid, tell him about a life-or-death situation and to wake the sheriff now. The other part of her said that doing so would guarantee a call to the FBI. The other other part of her said, get some sleep or you'll be useless tomorrow. "Driving in, I saw a motel on the west side of town. That the only accommodations?"

"Yep, Gracie's Rest is it unless you want to drive fifty miles down to Elbert. They got a new Quality Inn down there."

"I'm sure Gracie's Rest will be fine. I'll be back at eight."

The door to the motel office was locked. Hardly surprising given the late hour, or early hour, depending on your perspective. Belle rang the buzzer, waited, rang it again. She could see an inner door open, and a heavyset woman with curlers in her hair wearing a tattered cloth robe emerged from what Belle guessed were her own sleeping quarters. She fumbled around on the desk behind a counter until she found her glasses, then shuffled across the scuffed brown linoleum to open the door.

"Come on in, sweetie." Her voice was rough from sleep.

Belle forced a weary smile. "Sorry to show up so late. You have a room?"

"Sure do. Sixty-nine bucks, plus you get a five-dollar-off coupon for breakfast at Gracie's Table." Belle assumed Gracie's Table was the diner. The woman squinted over Belle's shoulder, trying to see in the dark. "You got someone with you."

"Yeah, I was hoping for a room with two beds."

The woman's curlers bobbed as she nodded. "Got that."

"I also have a dog."

"Me, too. He's welcome so long as he don't shit on the carpet."

Belle chuckled. "Housebroken."

She shuffled around the counter and rattled through a drawer before pulling out a single key attached to a red saucer-sized plastic circle marked with a big white six. "Room six, last one on the end."

Belle told her they would be leaving early and paid in advance, then drove the Tahoe down the row of rooms to the last unit before the property ended in a copse of trees. She found both of their guns and stuck them in her belt. Didn't want to leave them in the car, just in case.

She woke Nora and helped her sleepwalk into the room. The beds were positioned to the immediate left, and the bathroom to the left of the beds. Directly across from the beds a single window looked out toward the trees in the back of the building. Scout followed them through the door and immediately leaped up onto a bed. Belle set the guns on the night table and helped Nora to the other bed. Less than half awake, Nora kicked off her shoes, removed her jeans and blouse, and slipped under the covers. The moment her head hit the pillow she was out. The room smelled slightly of mildew, so Belle cracked the window.

She figured she'd better bring in some clothes from the Tahoe. And some food for the dog. She left a table light on and the door slightly ajar so she wouldn't have to use her red lollipop key to re-enter.

Outside, the night was still. No moon, and the stars had disappeared behind a cloud cover. The only light in the motel parking lot came from a lamppost up near the office. Darkness shrouded the Tahoe as she opened the cargo door. She'd turned off the automatic interior light as a security precaution and now could hardly see anything, with the only light coming from the motel room window. After pulling out her hunting bow and leaning it against the car, she was able to reach the duffel. No use dragging the whole thing inside. Just needed her toiletry bag, a change of underwear, t-shirt, and socks. She set the duffel on the pavement and unzipped it partway. Hard to believe the day had started with Peggy Sue's best breakfast in the West. Seemed like days had passed instead of less than twenty-four hours. She was beyond exhausted.

A set of headlights turned into the parking lot and moved toward her. Probably another late-arriving motel guest. Except the car didn't stop at the office. The driver doused the headlights and slowed. The adrenaline pumped through her. She was awake now. *Shit, he's searching for the Tahoe, and dumbass me parks it right in front of our motel unit— green flag on four wheels shouting, "Here we are!"* How the hell did Jin find them, unless he followed from Canyon? Or maybe all the way from New Mexico.

She hoped the darkness would prevent them from seeing her close the cargo door. No flurry of bullets headed her way, so she presumed they didn't know she was watching. The black sedan pulled two spaces over from the Tahoe, and the driver window rolled down. Baldy—Jin. He had something in his hand, and Belle figured it wasn't a Twinkie. Because of the way the motel room door opened, he would have a point-blank shot at anyone coming out of the unit.

She heard a soft click. The passenger door opened, and a short chubby guy stepped out. She could just make out his head above the sedan roof. He didn't attempt to enter the room. They probably figured she was in there and, with the light on, fully awake. He turned right to circle the building. They were going to catch Belle and Nora in a cross-fire—Chubby through the window and Jin through the front door. Belle figured Chubby took the long way around so his shadow wouldn't pass in front of the window where they assumed she was sitting with a gun in her lap. If she shouted to warn Nora, Jin would be through the door firing before she could notch her bow.

But what about Scout? If he sensed someone lurking by the back window he would bark, triggering a shootout with only one side holding a gun. She had to get to the back window without being seen before Chubby arrived. She grabbed her bow and hugged the shadows. With Jin's attention focused in front of him, she was able to make it to the corner undetected.

She moved as fast as she could, rounding the next corner to arrive outside the back window before Chubby turned the corner from the other side of the building. She could see Scout was already off the bed, sitting inside on the other side of the window. Belle could observe Nora sleeping soundly. For a moment she thought of trying to wake her, but feared she'd have to shout too loudly.

She kept her voice low, barely above a whisper. *"Scendi. Silenzio."* (Down, Silent.) Wonder Dog did as he was told.

She hurried back to the corner of the building and turned out of sight a moment before Chubby rounded the corner from the other side. He didn't see her. She watched as he approached the window, crouched over.

She nocked an aluminum-jacketed two-blade carbon arrow from the quiver into the chip on the Hoyt bow, then lined up the tiny sight-hole on the bowstring with the sight-pin on the bow. Chubby was less than twenty feet away. An easy target to hit, but she needed a kill shot to drop the Asian in his tracks before he could warn Jin.

Chubby stood and took aim through the window. She only had one shot. To increase her odds, she needed him to face her.

She whispered, "Hey, Chubby."

He turned, a look of shock on his face. She loosened the arrow. With a soft whoosh, the two-blade shot through his right eye, sliced through his brain, and emerged out the back of his skull, freezing his finger before it could pull the trigger. He dropped with barely a sound.

She retrieved his gun and returned to the dark parking lot. Jin's attention was focused forward, and she was able to circle around the Tahoe to the back of his sedan without being seen or heard. One big step, then she pressed the barrel of Chubby's gun through the open window hard against his temple.

"Evening, Baldy." He looked up in shock.

She stripped the gun from his hand. "So nice of you to stop by."

Jenny wrapped her arms around the sleeping child and spooned up behind her, pulling the girl close.

There were no sheets or blankets, only a thin mattress covered with assorted stains, the sources of which she didn't want to think about. The chilly air in the room prompted her to wrap Nora's jacket around Sadie in an attempt to keep her warm. She envied Sadie's ability to sleep, an advantage of childhood. When an adult tells you everything's going to be all right, you believe her. Jenny had done her best to soothe the girl after their failed escape, rubbing her back, stroking her hair. But only Jenny's words of assurance had allowed Sadie to finally fall asleep.

What would happen now? At first, Jenny feared she would be punished for her escape attempt, and she had the strong impression that if Fen had her way they both would be dead. But Bai had protected them; without his hostages he'd lose his leverage. That awful woman, Lucy or Lucia, had even brought up an extra pizza just for the two of them. Jenny couldn't believe she'd fallen for the deception. The whole thing about returning to the restaurant to wait for the police? With the benefit of hindsight, Jenny realized a normal person would've driven them immediately to a hospital and met the police there.

She heard the key in the lock and instinctively shrank back against the cheap headboard. They'd already eaten, and she hadn't asked to go to the bathroom. Maybe Belle found the box. *Please, God, let that be the case.* The door opened, Fen stepped inside and closed the door behind her. Bai had been the one who'd done all the talking, and the Fenbot's appearance now alone was not a good sign.

The Chinese woman stood motionless inside the door. The single light outside near the dumpster barely filtered through the closed blind, and in the dim gray she looked like a wax figure, not moving, not speaking. Jenny was taken aback with how small she was, hardly more than a hundred pounds. Flat-chested, wearing black jeans and a loose-fitting black t-shirt, she more resembled a boy than a full-grown woman. Fen stared at her with unfocused eyes, and even in the dim light Jenny felt pretty sure the woman had yet to blink. How could she remain so still?

The last thing Jenny wanted to do was provoke her. Maybe a friendly greeting.

"Uh, hi."

Fen didn't respond.

Jenny whimpered, "W-what do you want?"

Again, no response.

Fen moved toward her like a ghost gliding on air and stopped at the side of the bed. She stared down at Jenny's belly, her face completely devoid of expression. Slowly she slipped her left hand under Jenny's t-shirt, then under the elastic panel of her maternity jeans. Jenny stiffened at the woman's cold touch. Should she push her hand away? Maybe scream for help? Bai already demonstrated he didn't want any harm to come to her until he found the jade box. But Bai was probably sleeping and would take a few minutes to arrive. What if screaming for help set off the Fenbot? Despite Fen's slight build, Jenny had no illusions about who was in control. Fen's hand slid over her skin. To Jenny it felt like a viper slithering across her belly, ready to strike at her slightest movement.

The baby kicked, and Jenny flinched. Startled, Fen snapped her hand away as if she'd touched a hot stove. Yet her expression remained unchanged. She replaced her hand and felt the child inside Jenny's womb move again. The woman pressed harder, then traced her fingers around the spots where the baby's feet had kicked. Fortunately, Sadie remained asleep, oblivious to the strange visitor.

Suddenly, Fen had a dagger in her right hand.

Where did the knife come from? Under her shirt? Jenny hadn't even seen a blur of hand movement. "Please . . ."

Fen laid the flat side of the blade on Jenny's bare belly. *Oh my God, she's going to cut open my womb.* Jenny was about to scream for help when Fen moved her left hand to Sadie's throat, encircling, not squeezing. The little girl didn't wake, but the message was clear. Call for help and the child dies.

Jenny's entire body shook as Fen slowly slid the flat end of the blade across her stomach. Another kick. Fen rested the blade over the spot of the kick and held it still, applying light pressure like a doctor with a stethoscope. The woman froze as if caught in a stop-action photograph.

But for a tiny twitch in her left eye, she showed no expression. Jenny couldn't breathe.

Then in a flash the knife disappeared, and a moment later the Fenbot was gone.

Jenny couldn't hold back the tears and buried her face in the filthy pillow.

Belle, wherever you are, please hurry.

CHAPTER 30

J in lay face down on the worn motel room carpet.

Nora stood above him, her gun pointed at his head. Maybe because of exhaustion the lizard door in Belle's brain never opened, and she remained strangely detached as she wrapped adhesive tape from her first aid kit around Jin's wrists.

Scout watched from the bed, never shifting his gaze from the man on the floor. Belle knew it had been difficult for him to stay down and silent when Chubby had been lurking just a few feet away, and she was proud of him.

Jin's expression remained passive—he was a pro, and no doubt had been trained to resist interrogation. Belle wanted some answers; he knew she wanted some answers.

First a little show-and-tell. Belle grabbed Jin's wrists and lifted him to his feet; he winced from the sharp pain caused by the pressure on his shoulder joints. She didn't worry too much about the man's discomfort because, not to put too fine a point on it, the asshole had repeatedly tried to murder Nora.

She pushed him to the window and shoved his head outside where, with the benefit of the room light, he could see his dearly departed colleague sprawled on the ground. Not a pretty sight. A glistening white gelatinous substance dripped from the arrow shaft.

"Too bad about your pal. But then again, death came quickly. You can take some comfort—he didn't suffer." She watched Jin's face. He did a good job of not reacting. But not a perfect job. Point made.

She jerked him back and pushed him toward the bathroom. Nora had slipped her jeans back on and was finishing up buttoning her blouse. "Jin and I are going to have a conversation in the bathroom. You'll want to remain out here."

Nora took a full step forward and kicked Jin hard in the balls. He screamed and doubled over, dropping to the floor.

"As a young warrior my great-grandfather competed with other young men to see who could torture a captured enemy the longest while still keeping him alive. Quanah always won." She eyelocked with Belle. "I am Comanche. This piece of dog shit has tried to kill me. I will not only observe, I will participate in the questioning."

Persuasive young lady.

They dragged him into the bathroom and dropped him into the tub face up. His legs sprawled over one end of the tub, and his bound wrists behind his back elevated his hips so his head was lower than his feet. Scout sat in the corner and watched intently.

"Pillow," Belle said, sounding like a surgeon asking for a scalpel.

Nora retrieved two pillows from the bedroom and jammed them under Jin's hips, making the tilt steeper from his feet down to his head. Jin's eyes widened; he knew what was coming.

Dr. Belle ordered, "Plastic wastebasket liner. Adhesive tape. Towel."

In a few moments trusty Nurse Nora returned with all items. Belle ripped the liner apart, so she had a flat piece of plastic, and taped the plastic over Jin's mouth. With the extra tape she bound his legs together to keep them from flailing. After soaking the towel in water from the spigot, she laid it over his face.

Nora handed her a plastic cup from the sink. She removed the cellophane covering and filled the cup with water from the spigot. Belle assumed Jin had received the same level of SERE training she'd received, so she poked her index finger into his solar plexus to see if he would try to time his breathing to the doses. With her other hand she slowly poured the water over his face. The plan was to fill the sinuses, throat, and mouth with water. The lungs remained clear so he wouldn't asphyxiate, but his entire upper respiratory system from sinuses to trachea would fill with water, triggering the survival instinct in the brain. The brain believed he was drowning even though he wasn't.

With her index finger she felt Jin trying to time his breathing and doing a good job of it. He'd obviously trained for this, but the average Marine lasted fifteen seconds. She'd made it to twenty-five seconds her first time before tapping out. By her third try, she'd lasted to just under three minutes. Jin might do better than that, but they had all night and he knew it. Belle interrupted the timing of the water doses to throw off Jin's attempted breathing manipulation. It worked. He bucked up and down, and with his feet bound he looked like a Chinese merman reeled onto the deck of a fishing boat. He made gurgling sounds, trying to speak. After fifteen more seconds she stopped and removed the towel. His eyes found Belle's, and he nodded.

She pulled the plastic off his mouth and propped him up against the side of the tub. He leaned over and vomited, most of it spewing onto his wet clothing. Nora spoke before Belle could open her mouth.

"Why are you trying to kill us?"

The act of speaking triggered a massive coughing fit and another vomit spew. "Just you." His voice was weak, raspy. He looked at me. "Her only if necessary."

She asked again. "Why?"

He spoke with nearly flawless English. "We can't take the chance you will lead Bai to the Hudie Box. It must not be found."

Belle's turn. "All because of the Liaodong Agreement?"

He nodded.

Her frustration spilled out. "Again, why? What's in that agreement?"

He hesitated, then followed her eyes to the harmless looking plastic cup of water sitting on the toilet seat. As a professional he knew when to fold his hand. If Belle had offered death as an alternative to talking, he might've chosen it in a selfless act of patriotism. But simulated drowning, over and over and over—no, that was too much.

He spoke now with a weak smirk on his face. "The United States of

America effectively owns the most important nuclear submarine base in China and doesn't even know it."

Both women stiffened, stunned and confused by Jin's words.

Belle spoke first. "What the fuck are you talking—?"

Nora interrupted. "Lüshun, Naval Base."

Jin tried to straighten up in the tub without success. Belle removed the pillow and helped him to a sitting position. The enhanced-interrogation phase had passed.

"Port Arthur back then," Jin continued. "Roosevelt had all of the leverage. My country was going to be carved up with Russia and Japan battling over who would get what pieces. Empress Tzu-Hsi was desperate. Among America, Russia, and Japan, America was the least of three evils. Tzu-Hsi knew the Portsmouth negotiations would result in either Japan or Russia controlling the port, and Roosevelt couldn't prevent that. But she was looking to the future and believed if America someday controlled the port, China would never again have to worry about her belligerent neighbors taking over."

The adrenaline had drained away so maybe Belle's lack of sleep is what prevented her from wrapping her brain around Jin's words. "You're telling us China sold Port Arthur and what is now the Lüshun Naval Base to the United States?"

"Leased. A ninety-nine-year lease to begin when China regained control of the peninsula. Roosevelt wrote a personal check for fifty thousand U.S. dollars, about $1.5 million today, a one-time payment for the long-term lease of Port Arthur and the Liaodong Peninsula. Roosevelt was a very wealthy man and believed the money was well spent. Your naval facility in Norfolk, Virginia, is the largest naval base in the world, home to your Atlantic fleet. Hundreds of ships and planes. Think what would happen if China showed proof it owned Norfolk."

Having been to the overwhelming "show of power" that was Norfolk, Belle saw his point. She tried to recall what Professor Moon had told them about Port Arthur and how its control had "ping-ponged" back and forth between Russia and Japan. "China didn't recover the peninsula until the '50s."

"April 16, 1955," Jin supplied.

"So ninety-nine years," Nora said slowly, "would mean the United

States, if it exercised its rights, could control the base and the peninsula until 2054," Nora said.

"Worse," Jin said. "The lease has an automatic renewal provision giving your country the right to renew for a second ninety-nine-year term by paying what today would be another million dollars. The practical effect is full ownership."

"And you only discovered this now?" Belle demanded, gaping.

"My country has been fully aware of the Roosevelt agreement and knew from 1955 forward that under the contract America completely controlled the port and the peninsula. But we had . . . 'acquired' Roosevelt's copy and believed no one else was aware of the deal. We learned that American politics of the day discouraged Roosevelt from making the deal public, and we understood that no legal obligation compelled the president to reveal it. We also knew the parties involved had signed a second copy of the lease, but it never surfaced, and we assumed the contract had been lost forever."

Belle jumped ahead. "Then you learned about James Amos's notes when the assets of the corporation that published his book were acquired by a Chinese company."

"Just a few weeks ago," Jin said, nodding ruefully. "An employee going through the archives found the editorial notes about Quanah Parker. My government had little concern. The Hudie Box had not appeared in all the intervening years, and no reason existed to believe it would ever be found."

"Then Quanah's lance was stolen," Belle growled, "and my sister kidnapped."

Jin's expression changed to unrestrained scorn. "Bai Sun. A traitor who will die a painful death. Like me, Bai spent more time in the States than in our home country. We went to university together here. We were colleagues, friends."

Nora asked, "He was a member of MSS?" Jin nodded.

Belle understood the connection now. "So, through MSS he learns of the Quanah code and the Hudie Box."

Another cursory nod from Jin. "He found out about it because *he* was the one assigned to investigate the discovery of Amos's notes."

"So, instead of reporting back to headquarters, he sees an opportunity to go rogue, find the Hudie Box, and extort his mother country for a few million bucks," Nora concluded.

Jin scoffed. "Bai and his *sha bi* bitch would not betray their country for a few million dollars. With our naval facilities worth many billions, my country would be willing to pay hundreds of millions, maybe even a billion dollars in ransom to keep the agreement from falling into American hands."

Belle had an obvious question. "But even if the United States recovered the contract, wouldn't China just tell our government to pound sand?"

Jin paused before answering. "The concept of *mian zi*, face, is difficult for Americans to grasp. For four thousand years, the culture of my country has emphasized bringing honor to the group, not embarrassing the group or any individual in the group. *Mei you min zi*, he has no face, is one of the most devastating insults one can hurl at another person."

Belle remembered Steve Kelly telling them Jin taught Chinese culture at George Washington University, and she found herself feeling as though she were sitting in a lecture hall. Jin was a walking contradiction—a highly educated college professor and a lethal killer. But she didn't care how smoothly he spoke; he'd repeatedly tried to murder Nora. There would need to be consequences.

"With the benefit of hindsight," Jin continued, "the Liaodong Agreement was ill-advised, but it nevertheless was—is—a binding contract. If my government attempted to ignore it, the loss of face with over a billion Chinese people would be unthinkable and unacceptable. The fact that America owned a critical Chinese military installation would also embarrass the Chinese people and, in turn, their government."

Nora was as incredulous as Belle was. "Are you saying China would simply step aside and allow the United States to take over Lüshun's nuclear sub-base along with the whole Liaodong Peninsula? I'm sorry, but that sounds difficult to believe."

"My country would go to great pains to persuade America not to exercise its rights," Jin explained wearily. "We'd offer to pay back the purchase price to either your government or the Roosevelt family or both, plus a sizeable buy-out bonus, probably in the hundreds of millions. We'd offer to cancel a significant portion of the debt America owes us. But if the United States refused a buyout and persisted in asserting its leasehold rights, China would be forced to relocate all of its sensitive military equipment—ships, submarines, weapon systems, military research facilities, and all of the support structures and personnel, a daunting task. My country could not simply ignore the agreement and, as you say, tell the United States to pound sand. They could not lose face."

Belle's voice dripped with disgust. "So, the easiest solution was to make sure the second copy—the Quanah copy—never surfaced. And if a few lives were lost in the process, that was a cheap price to pay."

"Very cheap under the circumstances." Jin paused, as if deciding how much more to say. "There is another much more sinister outcome you should contemplate. As is the case with your country, China is not without its extremist elements. President Peng is a direct descendent of Tzu-His who made the deal with Roosevelt. Were the agreement to surface, the effect on Peng would be more than simply losing face. Peng's hold on the presidency is already tenuous. There are internal forces right now gathering the political assets to challenge Peng."

"I guess America isn't the only place where politicians play dirty," Nora said.

Jin's voice, mostly calm, even matter-of-fact up to this point, took on a darker tone. "If the agreement were made public, Peng would be deposed, and these extremist elements would take over. The young leaders of this group are anxious to assert China's military might, power that in many ways exceeds that of your country. They would find any excuse to engage in war with America over the western Pacific and the South China Sea in particular."

Nora said what Belle was thinking. "That's crazy. A nuclear war would destroy both countries, not to mention most of the inhabitable world as we know it."

"These radical elements reason that the idea of mutually assured destruction would prevent both sides from going nuclear, and they believe China's superior conventional land and air forces would prevail. They acknowledge that America still has the upper hand at sea, but brag that our new *Dúshé* Viper missile would effectively neutralize that advantage."

Belle couldn't believe it. "That's insane."

"Agreed. But we both know of similar groups in America, including members deep inside both your Congress and current administration, who view my country as a threat to America's economic and military status in the world. They could easily use any Chinese opposition to America's rights under the Liaodong Agreement as an excuse to justify a military response."

"So, these opposing elements, as you call them, they're the ones behind Bai Sun?" Nora asked.

Jin's expression turned cold. "No. At the moment Peng's opponents are unaware of the agreement. Bai is on his own. His motivation is nothing more than greed. But if he is successful, because of their position in the government, Peng's opponents would have to be involved in authorizing the ransom payment to Bai in return for the agreement. I was ordered to make sure Bai is not successful."

"But why not work with us?" Nora asked. "If you helped us find the Hudie box, Jenny would be saved. You could burn the agreement. A win-win."

"A fair question, Ms. Yates," Jin replied with a solemn nod. "The simple truth is, killing you was the easiest and fastest way to assure that the agreement remained lost. Over time, Bai could probably find another expert to help him, but that person would be starting from scratch. We feel confident we'd find Bai before he was ultimately successful. I assume you will take my life, and I am fully prepared for that. But you must understand, my country will not stop until any possibility of the agreement surfacing is eliminated. And, frankly, it also is in your country's best interest as well. War between our nations would be catastrophic."

"There's just one problem," Belle said. "If the agreement doesn't surface, my little sister will die."

Jin sighed. "I understand your feelings, Ms. Bannon. I have children of my own, and the thought of harm coming to them is unthinkable. But war would result in millions of children dying on both sides, likely including your sister. Including my children. You also should know that while I have failed, there are others, many others who are here in America to make sure that contract remains buried. They will kill both of you without hesitation or remorse."

Jin sighed and looked away. He'd told them everything and was prepared to die. Nora and Belle locked eyes with the same unspoken question. Now what? They left Jin bound up in the tub and returned to the bedroom to talk. He wasn't going anywhere.

Belle's mind was approaching pudding territory, but fortunately Nora did a passable job listing options. "We can kill him. We can call Kelly. We can call the local cops. We can leave him bound up here at the motel."

Belle knew the last option was a loser. When the owner arrived in the morning and found a wet Asian tied up and gagged in her bathtub she'd release Jin, then call the cops. An APB would go out for a green Tahoe with two women and a spotted dog. That left three options. "If we call the local sheriff, we'll have to deal with Barney Fife Junior, and there will be lots of questions we don't have time to stick around and answer. I could put a bullet in his head. He deserves it and expects it. The good soldier. But . . ." She couldn't bring herself to do it and shook her head. "Sorry."

"I agree," Belle said with a grimace. "Finding a dead body in the bathtub would ratchet up the attention a hundredfold and trigger a manhunt for the killers. Us. That leaves Kelly."

But they didn't know where he was. Even if he happened to be in the area and arrived right away, she'd not get any sleep before connecting up with Cordero Parker at eight. If Kelly couldn't arrive till morning, they still had the issue of what to do with Jin in the meantime. "Let's lock Jin and his sidekick in the trunk of his car for a few hours so we can both get some sleep. I'll call Kelly in the morning, and he can come deal with it."

"Morning's a lot closer than you think," Nora warned.

"My point exactly."

Nora and Belle dragged Chubby around to the dark sedan. After breaking off the portion of the arrow shaft protruding from his head, they rolled his body into the trunk first. After dragging Jin out of the tub they gagged him, carried him outside, and dropped him on top of his colleague. Just before slamming the lid shut, Jin held Belle's gaze with a mix of resignation and determination. He nodded. Out of respect? Maybe. She slammed the trunk shut and carried the keys back inside.

They were beyond exhausted, and after the bathtub experience, neither was in the mood for anything but sleep. Gracie's Rest motel didn't feature 800-count single-ply sheets, but the bed still felt wonderful, and both fell asleep instantly.

It seemed like only a few minutes had passed when Belle's phone alarm went off. Thirty groggy seconds later she realized she was alone. No woman or spotted dog in sight. She sat up and rubbed her eyes. Nora had probably taken Scout out for his morning business. The door opened and they both entered. Nora didn't look happy.

"What's wrong?" Belle asked, instantly alarmed.

"Jin's gone."

CHAPTER 31

Belle, still dressed in nothing but her bra and panties, stood silently on the curb with Nora on one side and Scout on the other, staring down at the empty parking spot. Anyone observing might've thought they were watching a worm race.

Nora said, "The yellow T."

"Yeah."

All newer cars now featured a glow-in-the-dark yellow pull handle shaped like the letter T on the inside of the trunk lid. You pulled the T, the trunk opened. A child safety thing was mandated after a few kids crawled into car trunks, closed the latch, and suffocated. They both had been so sleep-deprived that neither had thought to disable the T-pull. Belle theorized that Jin must've opened the trunk, probably by pulling the yellow T with his teeth, rolled out, cut the tape on something nearby, and retrieved a second set of keys from one of those magnetic cases you attached under the fender as a back-up in case you locked yourself out.

Jin was back on the loose. No doubt he would gather up reinforcements and come for them again. Jin's explanation crystallized the extremely high level of resolve both he and his men possessed. Which, in the end meant one thing.

We have to find that damn green box fast.

They stopped at Gracie's Table for coffee and used the motel discount coupon towards a couple of breakfast sandwiches along with an order of bacon to mix with the kibble Belle kept in the car for Scout. At a quarter to eight they pulled into a parking spot behind the Gracie, Texas Sheriff's Office. She hoped the sheriff might arrive early. Scout had already consumed the kibble and bacon, but Belle still had a few bites of her egg sandwich left. She was a much more polite eater than her dog.

"Wonder who Gracie was," she asked Nora.

"No idea."

They noticed two parked patrol cars, so maybe their luck had changed. Belle rolled down the windows and left Scout in the Tahoe with her sandwich leftovers. The morning air was cool, and he would be fine. They entered to find Barney Junior twirling in his desk chair behind the counter. Startled by their entrance, he put his foot down and yelped when the spinning chair smacked his ankle against the counter support.

"You okay?" Belle asked.

Barney shot to his feet, knocking over the still-twirling chair. "Fine." His voice sounded even squeakier.

"We're here to see Sheriff Parker."

Before the deputy could respond the door behind the counter opened. Nora had shown Belle online photos of Quanah Parker. The man standing in the doorway was Quanah Parker without the braids. Late thirties, about six feet tall, barrel-chested, thick, muscular arms, large hands, dark skin, high cheekbones, and piercing Wedgewood-blue eyes that at the moment were sizing them up.

"Can I help you?" he asked. Not particularly friendly, not particularly unfriendly.

Nora stepped forward and extended her hand. "*Maruawe*" (Hello.) "Nora Yates. We met at the Quanah descendants gathering last year."

His expression softened. "*Unha hakai nuusuka?*" How are you? He shook her hand. "I remember. So, what brings you to Gracie, Texas?"

"This is my friend, Belle Bannon. We'd like to talk to you." Her tone projected an element of urgency.

"Ms. Bannon." Businesslike.

"Belle." She shook his offered hand, and they followed him back to his office. She closed the door behind them. The sheriff raised an eyebrow but said nothing.

The office was much larger than she expected. He waved them to two ladder-back pine chairs and took his seat behind a cluttered desk centered between a Texas flag and an American flag. Belle immediately noticed one wall covered with hunting photos showing Cord Parker posing over his kill—elk, bear, deer, wild hog, and mountain lion. In one picture he stood in knee-deep snow, smiling from ear to ear, next to a huge dead griz. She tried her hand again at preliminary small talk and gestured toward the photo. "Alaska?"

"Denali."

"Impressive. Looks about eight feet."

"Seven and a half, but close enough."

The bear's coloring was unusual, almost blond. "Berry bear?" Grizzlies that roamed in higher elevations actively fed on berries, and for some reason their coats lightened considerably.

Cord flashed his bright white teeth. "Yeah, we were looking for bighorn, but that fellow crossed our path. Now his head's hanging over my mantel, and I say hello to him every morning when I leave for the day. I assume you hunt."

"Guide for Peabody."

Cord raised an eyebrow. "Good outfitter. So, a woman hunting guide. That's a new one."

"We're taking over the world."

He laughed. "No doubt about that."

"Got to ask you. Who was Gracie?"

"Gracie Kane. Ran a whorehouse on the site of the motel. Lot of crazy shit went down out there over the years before Gail bought it."

Belle thought of Chubby with an arrow through his brain and Jin in the bathtub. Still a lot of crazy shit going down out there.

Nora wiggled in her seat, and, seeing she was anxious to move on, Belle gave her a nod.

"Cord, we're here about Chony Parker," Nora said.

"My great-great-grandmother." Cord's expression clearly conveyed his surprise at Nora's words.

Nora sat forward in her chair. "We spoke to your brother, Neville. He told us you have a bracelet passed down from Chony, a companion of the one he gave to his daughter, Lizzie. We believe that the two bracelets in combination may form a *bah-has-tkih*. We would like to examine the bracelet."

Cord leaned back in his chair and steepled his hands. "What's this about?"

Belle exchanged glances with Nora. How much should they tell him? As an officer of the law, he had a duty to take action if a crime had been committed. But they were running out of time, and she had a good feeling about the man. So, she took a chance and told him almost everything, leaving out only a description of the Hudie Box's contents.

When she finished, Cord turned away from us, stared at the wall, not saying a word for what seemed like hours, but was probably less than thirty seconds. Belle couldn't blame him; she'd given him a lot to think about. Finally, he twisted back and fixed his gaze on her.

"It would take a while to list all of the criminal offenses that have occurred if your story is true. Starting with the kidnapping and ending with you firing an arrow through the brain of a man with a gun outside your window in my town. No doubt your actions here and in Washington were clear cases of self-defense, but I'm obligated to investigate the death of the man at the window since it occurred within my jurisdiction. Speaking of jurisdiction, your story also obligates me to contact the FBI, the D.C. police, the State Department, the National Park Service, and probably a bunch of other government agencies."

Belle's heart sank. They were going to be held for questioning while the sheriff investigated Chubby's death. Bai's deadline would pass. Jenny would die.

A knock at the door. Barney opened it and escorted in one Alonzo Longabaugh, secret agent. Belle's face brightened.

Alonzo flashed a smile, introduced himself, and gave Cord his card. "Sheriff, I apologize for coming in after the show started."

Cord checked out the card. "Agent Longabaugh, I would ask what brings you to my sleepy little corner of Texas, but Ms. Bannon has just described a series of events that are . . . unique and involve a number of potential offenses."

"I understand. The problem is, at the moment two things are in play —a threat to national security, and the life of a young woman who happens to be eight months pregnant. Time is critical. We've given Ms. Bannon and Ms. Yates a short leash to resolve the matter on their own with off-book assistance from us so as not to trigger the kidnappers harming the young woman, were the FBI to jump in."

"Cord, can you at least tell us whether you have the bracelet?" Nora asked.

The police chief didn't respond to either Alonzo or Nora, and no one interrupted his silence. Finally, he spoke. "Ms. Bannon, the body of the man you say you killed is gone, so I have no real evidence of a crime committed in Gracie except for your crazy story."

Belle wasn't sure, but she thought he didn't consider her story crazy at all.

Cord locked eyes with Nora and spoke in deadpan. "Maybe tomorrow I'll get around to checking out the motel."

Okay, Belle really liked this guy.

Cord turned to Nora. "The answer to your question about the bracelet is yes and no."

Belle couldn't keep the excitement from her voice. "You mean, you have it?"

"Had. My wife got into drugs pretty deep. Mostly meth but also heroin and pills. Six months ago, she ran off with some jerk. Took my truck, my flat-screen, and cleaned out my bank account. She always fancied the bracelet. Never saw it after that, so I assumed she stole that, too."

"Where is she?" Belle asked.

"No idea."

Alonzo pulled out his phone. "What's your wife's name?"

"Sheila. Sheila O'Malley Parker."

Alonzo punched a number into his phone. The call was answered on the first ring. "Steve, we need to find someone. Fast. Her name is Sheila O'Malley Parker. Up until about six months ago she lived in

Gracie, Texas." After a momentary pause, Alonzo turned to Cord. "I need her phone number, her Social, and the numbers of any credit cards she might be using."

Cord fumbled around in his desk and found the Social Security and credit card information. "Don't know her new phone number, or even if she has one. I tried to call the old phone to locate her, but she must've ditched it."

"Give me the old number," Alonzo said. Cord did so and Alonzo passed it on to Kelly, then told him, "I'll wait."

"Can he really find someone that quickly?" Nora asked.

"Spooks can gain access to pretty much any information they want," Cord replied. Alonzo elected not to comment. "Sheila probably had to provide her old phone number to qualify for a new one."

Three minutes later, Alonzo thanked Kelly and ended the call. "She's a stripper at a bar," Alonzo said.

"What's the name of the bar?" Cord asked.

"According to Kelly, the name of the bar is 'Bar.'"

Nora didn't hide her frustration. "Where is this bar?"

"Uncertain."

"Kelly doesn't know where the bar is?" Belle asked incredulously.

"As I said, Uncertain. Uncertain, Texas."

CHAPTER 32

P eng Yuen offered a restrained smile and a bowed head as the other members of the party's central committee stood to toast him.

Li Fong lifted his glass of *baijiu*. The others around the table followed, and all spoke in unison with the honoring toast, "*Wo jing ni yi bei.*"

Peng drank a sip and took inventory of the men standing supposedly in his honor. The *wáng bā dàn* son of a bitch Li had picked up another vote, the man directly opposite Peng, the one with the widest smile.

The vote would come soon. If Jin failed and the Liaodong Agreement surfaced, certifying America's effective ownership of the Lüshun Nuclear Naval Base and the Peninsula, Peng would be deposed. He and his family would suffer extreme embarrassment, loss of face for the actions of his ancestor. But he could handle that. What shook him to his core was the very real possibility that with Li in charge, his country would instigate a war with America. Only minutes earlier, Li had expounded on how China's conventional military capabilities now exceeded those of the Americans, and repeated decades-old rhetoric about how the American presence in the western Pacific was an insult to every citizen in the country. Li and his followers lived in a gauzy dream of someday returning to the Zhenguan era of the Tang Dynasty and again ruling the world. They were fools.

The members took their seats and re-engaged in small talk among themselves.

Peng's private cell phone remained quiet in his pocket. He waited anxiously to feel the familiar vibration on his thigh, alerting him to a message from Jin that the Hudie Box was now safe from discovery. Jin's earlier report had been more than troubling. After the shootout in the cave, he reported that he'd tracked the two women to a motel in a small Texas town. There he'd lost a man and been captured by the two women. Peng's admiration for the women grew, especially the former Marine. To thwart one of China's most skilled agents was impressive.

Under interrogation Jin had revealed the contents of the Hudie Box to Bannon and Yates. Peng wasn't surprised by the lack of shame in Jin's voice. An experienced interrogator can extract information from even the bravest of captives. That Bannon and Yates knew of the Liaodong Agreement, while not particularly helpful, was of little real moment. Without the document itself, America could make no claim.

Fortunately, Jin had escaped. Before driving off, Jin was able to again attach a special tracer to the American's vehicle, behind the tailpipe so it would be extremely difficult to detect. The device, newly developed by MSS, could filter conversation through the vehicle, engine, and road noise, convert it to text, and transmit the text message to Jin's phone. Jin would be able to follow the Americans and know what they were saying.

After considerable thought, Peng had modified his orders. If possible, killing Yates was the first choice. But if Jin believed finding the Hudie Box was imminent, he was to wait for the Americans to recover the document, then take it. That way Peng could be absolutely certain the agreement would never surface in the future.

Peng liked America and had visited a number of times. He especially loved traveling to China's consulate in Houston. He enjoyed watching old American Western movies, and the Consulate General had given him several tours of the state where cowboys and Indians used to roam. The governor even presented him with a Stetson hat.

Now another battle brewed on the Texas plains. A battle that China had to win. For China's sake. For America's sake.

For the world's sake.

CHAPTER 33

Despite her struggle to keep from flooring the gas pedal, Belle had still exceeded the speed limit by no less than twenty miles per hour for the entire trip so far.

"Might want to slow down a bit," Alonzo said casually from the passenger seat. "Don't want to get pulled over."

"Haven't been stopped yet."

Alonzo cracked half a smile but didn't respond, and neither Nora nor Scout offered an opinion from the Tahoe's back seat.

Cord had considered joining the band, but he didn't want to leave his deputy in charge while he drove far out of his jurisdiction on what was essentially a personal matter.

Belle caught herself glancing at her nails. *Why did I do that? Because Alonzo was sitting next to me?* The polish was scraped and chipped from slugging bad guys and climbing around in caves. They looked horrible. *Stop it, you're acting like an idiot.* Here she was trying to save her sister from kidnappers by trying to find a hundred-year-old contract that could trigger a catastrophic war with China, and she was worried about her chipped nails.

"Uncertain is a funny name for a town," Nora opined.

"The town's located on the shore of Caddo Lake in the Texas

Bayou, a stone's throw from the Louisiana border," Alonzo said. "The name came from surveyors who were uncertain whether they were in Texas or Louisiana. The economy's almost exclusively tied to the lake—fishing, hunting, camping, swamp tours."

"How did you know that? Secret agent shit?" Belle asked.

"I googled it."

His blue-flame eyes actually twinkled.

A couple hours later they pulled into a truck stop to gas up, use the facilities, and grab food to go. Only a few other travelers were inside, and they found ready-made sandwiches from the cold case, including an extra one to mix in Scout's kibble. Nora and Alonzo walked to the back of a short line for coffee orders. Belle didn't need to leave instructions about her flavoring needs. She'd already seen her only choice was white powdered creamer from a cardboard shaker and either sugar or pink packets. *Ugh.* She headed down the narrow hall, passed a door marked "Stallions," and after two turns found one marked "Fillies" next to a fire exit.

"Hello, Belle."

She froze. *Tyler?* She turned around to see her ex-boyfriend displaying his customary smirk and holding a gun with a silencer screwed into the barrel. *Impossible. How did he know—?*

"Go." Tyler gestured toward the exterior door.

She needed him to move close enough for her to attempt a disarm. Maybe if she resisted, he'd be stupid enough to prod her with the weapon. He'd come inside her arc and that would be all she needed. "I'm not moving."

But Tyler was not a stupid man. "You think I'll come close so you can disarm me. Ain't gonna happen. You go through that door, or I'll pull the trigger."

Belle asked herself a simple question: Despite what he felt she'd done to him, could Tyler Cox actually shoot her? She looked into his bloodshot eyes. He was definitely hopped up on something. Yeah, she could easily see him pulling the trigger and then maybe turning the gun on himself. *Shit.* She needed time for Nora and Alonzo to come looking for her.

"Sure. No problem." She opened the door, and for a second considered slamming it hard back against him as she stepped outside. But he'd closed fast and hovered directly behind her for a moment as they crossed the threshold then quickly paused to allow safe separation.

Belle found herself in an isolated area behind the building blocked off from customer parking. Not a place the management would want potential visitors to see—a couple of old truck cabs on cinder blocks, a junk pile of rusting car and truck parts, old tires scattered across broken concrete. Deserted.

Tyler waved the gun toward a narrow space between the two abandoned trucks. "Over there."

The clock in her head ticked louder. She didn't have time for this bullshit. "What are you going to do Tyler? Shoot me? Your whole life would be ruined. You would—"

"My whole life's already ruined!" he screamed. "I lost my job. You told them about our little disagreement at the parking garage, didn't you?"

Little disagreement? "No, I swear I said nothing." She suspected Tyler's drug habit was the reason for his firing, but she kept her opinion to herself. She needed to stall till help arrived. "How did you find me?"

Tyler's face twisted his default smirk. "I put a tracer under the front fender of your car at the Amarillo airport."

Belle realized what she thought was the Chinese tracer actually belonged to Tyler. Which left open the question: How did *Jin* know where they were? Two tracers? Something to deal with later as at the moment she needed to devote her full attention to a disturbed man with a gun in his hand who felt he had nothing to lose. "You followed us to Carlsbad?"

"Nah. I figured you and your gal pal were doing a bit of sightseeing," Tyler sneered. "Sweet. Then you obviously ditched the tracer. I assumed you'd return to Canyon soon, although I didn't expect it to be that soon. I tracked you to Gracie, then followed you here. So the blond dude, he's your new boyfriend? What's the lovely Nora think about that?"

"Tyler, listen to me. I care about you, I really do. But you're messed up with the drugs and the booze. If you let me go, I give you my word I'll meet you in a few days and do everything I can to find you help."

"No one can help me." *God, were those tears on his face?* "I . . . I loved you so much." And then . . ." The gun shook for a moment in his hand. "And then, when I was the most vulnerable, you abandoned me. And took my son from me."

"Tyler—"

"Down on your knees!" Tyler snarled.

"Please, let's talk. I'm sure—"

"Do it!"

Shit. She inched closer to him as she knelt, keeping her toes bent so she could—

The fire door crashed open, and the tall frame of Alonzo Longabaugh filled the doorway. In a split second his gun was in his hand. "Drop it."

Tyler turned slowly, holding his hands away from his body, but retaining his gun. Belle sprang to her feet and snatched the weapon. He didn't seem frightened or agitated in any way.

Tyler grinned. "So, you're the new boyfriend."

Alonzo's gaze didn't even flicker toward Belle. "Shut up. Turn around, spread your legs, and put your hands on the wall."

Nora appeared behind Alonzo. "What's going—?"

Alonzo's eyes burned into Tyler, and the guy visibly flinched. "This snake was about to fire a bullet into Belle's brain."

Nora's jaw dropped. "Jesus."

The clock ticked not only louder but faster. Arresting Tyler Cox for attempted murder would involve calling in the local cops and take up the rest of the day. "Alonzo, we don't have time to deal with him."

"She's right," Nora said.

"If I let him go, he'll try again."

Tyler chimed in. "Tough decision."

Alonzo growled, "Shut up."

"Oooh, you're really tough with a gun in your hand."

Alonzo handed his gun to Belle. "Okay, asshole. You're real tough when picking on defenseless women. Take your best shot."

She'd never been called a defenseless woman before, but she let it slide.

Tyler was bigger, heavier, and crazier than Alonzo Longabaugh. He'd had hand-to-hand combat training taught by the country's best. She held Tyler's gun firmly in her grip, ready to shoot the big son of a bitch if he hurt Alonzo.

Tyler took a giant step toward Alonzo. She figured he was going to fake a roundhouse swing, expect Alonzo to attempt a block, then duck inside for a devastating uppercut. She'd seen him do it before in a few bar fights back at Pendleton. She was about to warn Alonzo, but things moved too fast.

Tyler faked his roundhouse, but instead of Alonzo attempting a block, he dropped to his knees, interlocked his right leg between Tyler's two legs, locked his arm around Tyler's calf, and leaned back hard. Tyler tripped forward, smacking headfirst onto the grimy pavement. Alonzo leaped on top of him in a flash, but Tyler was very strong and bucked him off. As Tyler rose to his feet, Alonzo kicked him in the head, snapping Tyler's head back. Tyler crumpled to his knees, defenseless. Alonzo scissored another foot to his face, splitting open his nose and knocking him out cold.

As someone who took pride in being able to take care of herself, Belle wasn't used to a couple of guys fighting over her. Did she enjoy it? Of course not. Well, maybe a little. Especially since the Sundance Kid won.

Alonzo stood and caught his breath.

Nora asked, "Now what?"

"Help me drag him to the truck."

Alonzo and Belle pulled Tyler across the pavement to one of the rusty trucks sitting on cinder blocks. Nora opened the squeaky door to the cab, and Alonzo shoved him inside. He pulled a plastic tie from a pocket and cuffed Tyler's hands behind his back. After gagging him with an oily rag he found on the floor, Alonzo pushed Tyler down into the footwell. Belle found a rusty chain in the junk pile, threaded it through the cuffs, wrapped it around his feet, and secured the chain to the brake pedal. Alonzo and Belle walked away.

Good riddance.

Then she stopped.

For reasons she couldn't fully explain, she was worried that with Tyler's newly shaped nose he might only be able to breathe through his mouth, and she wasn't interested in the idiot suffocating to death. *Wayne's Lake?* Maybe. She had never been accused of being a bleeding heart, but now her feelings of compassion were clashing with the tough-girl personality that had marked her entire life. The conflict felt more than a little uncomfortable.

She returned to the truck and leaped up on the cab step to check on him. Tyler stirred, and his eyes opened. He struggled to breathe. For a moment he seemed disoriented. Understandable under the circumstances. He spotted her and tried unsuccessfully to speak through the gag. She reached down and pulled the rag from his mouth. His expression turned venomous.

"You bitch." He struggled against his restraints.

She felt Alonzo now behind her.

"You have no idea what I'm going to do to both of you when I find you again. And then I'm going to track down your little sister, the one with the sweet tits, and—"

Alonzo nudged her aside and crashed his fist down hard against Tyler's jaw, knocking him out.

She tossed the gag aside, and they closed the truck door leaving Tyler Cox unconscious, bleeding, breathing, and tied down so no one could see him.

"I'll call the locals later, tell them he was drunk, got aggressive, and I had to cuff him," Alonzo said. "I doubt Tyler will want to press charges, seeing as how he's guilty of attempted murder."

If Tyler showed up again in her life down the road, Belle wasn't sure how she would deal with him. No time to think about it. Right now, every minute was precious.

She tossed Tyler's gun into the junk pile, and they returned to the Tahoe. She found Tyler's tracer under the front fender and tossed it. They jumped into the car, and she drove off before Alonzo and Nora had completely closed the car doors.

They needed to get to Uncertain, Texas. Yesterday.

Just shy of four hours later they passed a green sign welcoming them to Uncertain and listing the population as 94. Below the welcome a second sign proudly proclaimed: *"Location of the 1968 Film, Curse of the Swamp Creature."*

Belle drove down Mossy Brake Drive, and it didn't take them long to find the bar, a ramshackled wood-slatted structure with the word Bar painted in what was once red paint dripping across the uneven gray wood. Next door was a lodge with a long porch sagging so much the few chairs and rockers leaned close to the tipping point. The lodge, according to a tired sign hanging unevenly from the porch roof, was called *Lodge*. Belle was quickly coming to the conclusion that the inhabitants of Uncertain, Texas, lacked a threshold level of imagination.

They parked, left Scout in the car, and entered the bar. The inside was as dark as Belle expected, with a worn bar and a worn bartender off to the left. A few men dressed for fishing and hunting nursed beers at a couple of the eight or ten tables directly in front of them. The room was L-shaped and from around the corner they could hear Garth Brooks bragging about his friends in low places, interrupted by a few catcalls. A waitress approached, with a tired face suggesting she was probably much younger than she appeared. She wore blue jeans and an orange t-shirt with the phrase *Gals Ain't Uncertain in Uncertain, Texas!* printed in red sparkles across her chest.

"Y'all want a table, or you sittin' at the bar?"

"We're looking for Sheila," Alonzo said.

"You a cop?"

Alonzo flashed his creds so fast the waitress couldn't have had time to read them, but the fact he had creds at all left the desired impression.

The waitress sighed and shook her head. "What's she gone and done now?"

"She may be a witness to a robbery," Belle said. Which was kind of true seeing as how Sheila stole Cord's truck and TV.

The waitress nodded her head toward Garth. They wound their way through the tables and turned the corner. Maybe eight or ten more tables, these half-filled with grizzled men focused on a tiny stage in the corner.

"Must be her," Nora said.

Sheila O'Malley Parker, in her thirties, carrying fifteen or twenty unneeded pounds, eyes closed, wore a cheap wig of black braids with a single-feather headdress over the wig. The wig didn't fit properly, and a few strands of red hair poked out from underneath. She slowly twisted around a stripper pole to Garth's song. Naked except for a G-string, she wore a buckskin bracelet tied around her wrist. A handwritten placard propped up on a chair read: "Comanche Princess."

Nora fumed. "She's no more Comanche than the Queen of England."

Sheila must've heard Nora because her eyes flew open. Belle had no interest in wasting time with niceties. She charged the stage with every intention of ripping the damn bracelet from her arm. Someone in the audience yelled, "Hey!" apparently not appreciating the interruption. A leg jutted out, tripping her to the floor.

Sheila hopped off the stage and ran through the tables toward a back door, ignoring a few slaps on her bare ass. When Belle scrambled to her feet, some bozo found it appropriate to reach out and grab her boob. Normally she would've immediately demonstrated to him that doing so was highly inappropriate, but all she cared about was catching the Comanche Princess, so the bozo copped a free feel. With Alonzo behind her, they chased after Sheila.

The back door flew open, and Sheila popped out into the sunlight. Belle reached the door first. A big man with pale, tattoo-covered skin, shaved head, and biceps straining his black t-shirt stepped in front of them, blocking their path. Belle noticed the man glance over to the bartender on the far side of the room and nod slightly. The bartender hurried around the bar and out the front door.

The man in the black t-shirt crossed his arms and smirked. "I'm the owner here, sweetheart."

"Whoop-de-shit. *Move!*"

Alonzo lowered his voice and growled. "The lady said, get out of our way."

The owner held his position and actually flexed his biceps. "Ms. O'Malley is a valued employee, and I have a right to—"

Belle drove her shoulder into his chest, slamming the man against the wall. His head snapped back hard against the door jam, momentarily stunning him. "You don't have a right to dog shit." Out of the corner of her eye she noticed the bartender return and take his place behind the bar.

Mr. Clean tried to shake the cobwebs from his brain and flailed a few punches her way, but they were easy to dodge. She tripped him, and he stumbled against a table, then crashed to the floor sputtering some bullshit about all the things he was going to do to her. By the time he climbed to his feet, Alonzo and Belle were out the door in time to see Sheila toss her black wig into an old blue pickup, climb into the driver's seat, and take off.

They ran around the building to the front where the Tahoe was parked. Belle wasn't surprised to see that both rear tires had been slashed.

"Had to be the bartender," Belle said. "He scooted out the front door while we were chatting with the muscle-head." She turned to Nora. "Don't think Alonzo and I are welcome in the Bar bar. See if you can find out where she might be headed, while I deal with the tires." Nora returned to the bar.

Time was running out. They needed to get lucky.

They did. The previous owner had left a tire sealant compressor kit in the spare tire well under the cargo area. The bartender hadn't been smart enough to slash the sidewalls, only puncturing the tread, so it took just a few minutes to fix the tires.

Nora emerged from the bar with the waitress wearing the sparkled shirt in tow. "Tell them."

"Sheila and me, we both dance. All the waitresses dance and share tips. Sheila cheats, and we complain. But Alvie, he don't do nothin' 'cause she takes care of him out in her truck whenever he wants. The rest of us, we don't do that crap. Don't shit where you eat, am I right?"

"You're definitely right," Belle responded. "So where can we find her?"

"She lives with a guy in the bayou on Doll Island. They can give you directions at the Lodge."

Belle couldn't hide her excitement. "Thanks."

"One more thing," the waitress whispered. "You better be careful, 'cause her man? He's fuckin' crazy."

CHAPTER 34

Nora returned to the car from the Lodge lodge with five catfish sandwiches—two for the dog—and a local map showing directions to an outfitter on the edge of the swamp, maybe six miles away.

"They'll set us up with a boat and a guide to Doll Island," she said.

The directions were simple, and it didn't take long to reach Bayou Outfitters. A dingy double-wide rested on cinder blocks twenty or thirty yards from murky water disappearing into a swamp. Belle pulled into the thinly graveled lot, stepped out of the Tahoe, and was immediately besieged by mosquitoes the size of quarters. "I didn't realize Texas had a swamp."

"Same bayou as Louisiana," Alonzo replied. "We're entering from the west instead of the east."

Along one side of the lot a dozen dirty aluminum canoes lay half-buried in tall grass, pointing in all directions like they'd been tossed in a game of pick-up sticks. She spotted Cord's stolen blue truck parked in the far corner of the lot next to a tilted porta-potty nestled down in waist-high weeds.

A screen door slapped shut, and a short, fat man with a motley-colored beard shuffled toward them. He wore a broad-brimmed straw hat, dirty jeans, and a dirtier shirt. Red suspenders rolled over his belly to keep his pants up. Mosquitoes swarmed his blotchy skin, but he ignored them.

"Can I help you?" The man's voice sounded like he was gargling gravel from his own parking lot.

Belle pointed to the truck. "Looking for Sheila."

"What's she gone and done now?"

Same question asked by the waitress at the bar. Seems Sheila has a reputation.

"She's a witness to a robbery, and we need to talk to her," Alonzo responded.

"She was here a little bit ago," the big man said warily.

"So, you do know her?" Nora asked.

"Lives out on Doll Island with Vernon Hardaway. Every day she commutes here in their airboat and uses the truck to drive to work. End of the day, she reverses it. Sometimes Vernon comes along when they have business to attend to."

"What kind of business?" Nora asked.

His eyes narrowed, and he held Nora's gaze. "Not for me to say. We stick to our knittin' out here. Good for your health."

Belle shook her head impatiently. *They're selling drugs. Fine. I don't care.* She pressed the fat man. "We need to go to Doll Island. I understand you can outfit us and provide a guide."

"Only me here today. Y'all come back tomorrow, I can maybe find you a guide."

"We need to go now." She gestured toward the canoes. "How about a couple of canoes and a map?"

The man responded with a sleazy grin. "I can do that, if you got enough cash on you."

"How much do we need?"

"For two canoes, let's say two hundred apiece. So that's—"

"Four hundred bucks. Sounds a little pricey."

The fat man's grin widened, revealing several missing teeth. "You go into the bayou, some chance you might not come back, and I'm out a canoe."

They pooled their cash and came up with the four hundred. Because

Scout needed to ride with Belle, Nora and Alonzo took the second canoe.

The fat man pointed to Scout. "Sure you want to take that big fella in a canoe with you?

He tips it over, you might both end up gator bait."

Scout and Belle often canoed together on Provo River fishing trips. He knew how to stay centered. "Yeah, we're good. So how long will it take us?"

"Airboat, twenty minutes. Canoe, probably twice that."

"You haven't by any chance seen a couple of Chinese guys out here, have you?" Alonzo asked.

"Chinese?" He said the word the same way he might say "Martian." "Ain't sure I ever seen a Chinese in all of Uncertain."

"All of Uncertain" wasn't exactly a thriving metropolis, but Belle took some comfort in his response. Jin had made it clear he and his pals wouldn't let up. Did that include following them into the bayou? Probably not. She checked her pocket, dug out her last fifty, and handed the money to the fat man. "If by any chance a bald Chinese guy shows up, why don't you tell the unfortunate fellow you're closed for the day?"

He jammed the money into his pocket. "I can do that."

"So why do they call it Doll Island?" Nora asked.

He offered a greasy chuckle. "You'll see."

Alonzo followed the fat man across the lot to the canoe pile looking for two canoes in the least bad shape. Belle was about to follow when she heard Nora's phone ping. She ignored it, but the phone pinged again, and Nora pulled it out of her pocket. Her eyes widened, and she nearly dropped the phone.

"What is it?"

Nora rapidly scrolled through what must've been several photos. Unable to speak, she handed the phone to Belle. On the screen a photo showed a large man lying on a bloody carpet in his t-shirt and boxer shorts. Virtually every inch of his exposed skin was sliced through. His underwear was also cut—neatly, not torn—as if diced by a master chef. In fact his whole body resembled an old kitchen cutting board with a hundred cuts scarring the wood in all directions.

The next photo showed a close-up of his face, or more accurately what used to be his face. His throat had been severed but not by a single deep slice; instead blood poured from multiple cuts crisscrossing his neck. He was missing his ear, and one of his eyes had been neatly scooped out like a melon ball from a cantaloupe. The third picture showed a little girl, her face wracked with tears, kneeling over the body. A caption at the bottom of the last photo read: "Solve the code or she dies like her daddy. Go to the police and she dies like her daddy."

Belle opened her mouth to speak, but it took a moment for the hushed words to come out. "Jesus, Oh my God."

Nora reacted with a lethal mix of fear and unrestrained rage. "They have her. Oh my God, they have Sadie. Fen, she did this." She reached out her hand. "Gimme Jenny's phone number. Now!"

Belle softened her voice. "We tried it before. They won't answer."

"Text, I'll text them."

Belle watched over her shoulder as Nora began her message. *Listen to me you mother—* She stopped abruptly and mumbled to herself. "No, I can't make them mad." She erased the first message and tried again. *I will solve the code, just please don't hurt her. Please . . .!!!* She sent the text.

"Let me see those photos again." She handed Belle the phone and scrolled through the images, finding them even more horrifying the second time. "I need to show these to Alonzo."

Nora snatched the phone out of Belle's hand and spoke in a harsh whisper. "No. He might feel compelled to report Buck's murder to the Lubbock police. If he does that, Bai will find out, and they'll kill Sadie." The tears came, and Belle pulled her close. Steve Kelly had warned them about Fen. A psychopathic, unfeeling, killing machine.

Alonzo's voice interrupted. "We found a couple canoes that don't look too bad. Something wrong?"

Nora wiped her eyes and forced a smile. "Just, you know, thinking about poor Jenny."

"Let's get moving," Belle said. "Now."

They dragged two canoes to the swamp bank, slid them into the water, and stepped in. The fat man pushed them off with a warning. "Be careful of Vernon Hardaway. He's crazier than a shithouse rat and mean as a snake."

Earlier Nora and Belle both had decided to arm themselves, and after two warnings now about Sheila's new guy, it appeared they'd made a smart decision.

They followed the fat man's map, and with the twists and turns in the river the double-wide disappeared behind them in a matter of minutes. Actually, calling the water a river was too kind. More like a thread of green murk winding through thick patches of cypress and hanging gray moss. Forty minutes to reach the island. That assumed they didn't get lost. Belle put their chances at fifty-fifty.

Nora held the map and directed Alonzo, who paddled from the front bench of their canoe. Following behind, Belle couldn't see their faces, but she knew Nora was struggling to hold herself together. Scout nestled into the bottom of the canoe in front of her, his head snapping back and forth, alert to the sounds and unseen creatures on each side of the water.

They moved deeper into the swamp, and the moss-covered cypress trees thickened, nearly blocking out all light. The air smelled like sweet decay, a rich dessert left out in the sun too long, and engulfed them like a damp, sugar-coated shroud. Belle felt as if she were breathing dirty water.

"Knees ahead on the left." Belle pointed to a field of cypress knees, woody black cones growing up from the underwater cypress roots like stalagmites, a regiment of stubby black soldiers ready to topple their canoes. Alonzo guided his canoe around the knees, and she followed.

The river split into two forks, and each fork split into two or three more. After about twenty minutes of weaving through the dark green maze, Belle was certain she'd seen the same landmark earlier. Were they going around in circles?

Up ahead, Belle saw Nora struggling with the map.

"Are you sure this is right?" Nora said in angry frustration. "Gimme a break. This map's a piece of crap."

They paddled around another bend. The overhanging moss on one side of the water seemed to knit together with the moss on the other side to create a dim green tunnel. She noticed that a strand of moss hanging over the canoe ahead seemed really low. Except it wasn't moss.

"Snake!"

She struggled to tamp down her ophidiophobia. That's what the shrinks had called her fear of snakes. Another disorder to add to her pot. She pulled the Stealth from her holster. Seated in a canoe was hardly the most optimal location for sighting and firing a pistol, but during Recon training they'd learned to fire with one hand from a boat rolling in choppy waters at night. She squared her shoulders, gripped the weapon in her right hand, and slipped her right thumb across the grip high on the left side of the pistol. She rested her left palm on the grip and wrapped her fingers around her right hand, positioning her left thumb on top of her right thumb. Testing at Pendleton revealed her left eye to be dominant, so she raised the pistol to her left eye.

"Belle, don't!" Alonzo shouted.

She ignored him and gently squeezed the trigger three times in less than a half second. The damp thickness of the swamp air dampened the sound of both the shots and Nora's scream as the snake dropped dead into her canoe. Belle pulled close.

Alonzo held up the long clump of moss for Belle to see. Moss, not a snake.

Shit. "Sorry," she mumbled. "Thought it might've been a Cottonmouth."

"Cottonmouths stay in the water," Alonzo said. "Sometimes brown water snakes hang from trees, but very rarely do they drop into canoes. Snakes are much more fearful of us than we are of them."

'Don't be too sure about that. I hate snakes."

"I remember," Alonzo said, suppressing a grin. He paddled ahead, and they wound their way through the bayou maze for another twenty minutes. The light had dimmed further, and even bigger mosquitoes emerged to feast on fresh meat. They should've bought repellant at the outfitters. The fat man should've suggested it, maybe even thrown it in for free given the amount he was making on the canoe rental. Fortunately, none of them were wearing shorts or short-sleeved shirts, so the only exposed areas were their faces, necks, and hands.

In minutes the bayou's heavy quiet was punctuated with the dulled cracking sound of three tasty humans slapping the backs of their necks. She wondered how Sheila O'Malley Parker decided to leave civilization and a good man like Cord Parker to live in a snake-filled, mosquito-infested swamp. Cord had mentioned she'd fallen prey to drugs which might explain it, but do drug addicts like being bitten by big, fat, blood-sucking mosquitoes? If Belle had a chance, she might ask her.

"Up ahead." Nora pointed to a flickering light in the distance and paddled faster.

Belle followed, and as they approached a small island, Alonzo had to dodge a huge log floating next to his canoe. Then he pulled his gun and aimed it at the log. Then the log opened its eyes. Belle had seen her share of gators during swamp training in Florida and South Carolina, but this fellow was the biggest she'd ever come across, maybe fifteen feet. Scout was wise enough not to bark. Just passing by, have a nice evening. Say hello to Mrs. Gator. When she glided past, his eye followed her. Looking for dinner? She paddled faster and glanced over her shoulder. Was the gator following them? Alonzo's voice pulled her attention away.

"God, look at that."

Doll Island.

Belle pulled alongside the other canoe and took in the view. The island was very small, barely large enough for a rundown shack with three cypress trees in front and some kind of shed in the back. Enough light still remained to see children's broken dolls hanging from the branches of the trees. Some missed an arm, some a leg, some an eye. Few had hair. There must've been a couple hundred of them spread among the three trees. She'd never seen anything like it before, and it creeped her out big time.

The light coming from inside the shack reflected off the dolls, and the light breeze animated their arms and legs, adding to the impression that they were alive, guarding the shack and its inhabitants. The blue plastic eyes of a pasty white doll hanging from a low limb seemed to lock on Belle, moving back and forth, tracking her every action. A chill raced down her spine. *Holy shit.*

Then the lights inside the shack went dark.

She heard the crack of a rifle and a bullet slapped hard into the side of her canoe, easily penetrating the aluminum skin, and exited through the other wall, barely missing Scout. He jumped up, and the sudden weight shift rolled the canoe.

"Scout!"

Both of them tumbled into the slimy black water.

CHAPTER 35

Belle's feet sank deep into the mushy bottom.

She rose upright and found the putrid water reached about chest high. Scout swam easily toward shore, but when she attempted to follow, her feet felt like they were locked in quicksand.

"Belle!" Nora's voice.

Two more shots sailed overhead. She looked over her shoulder and saw Alonzo and Nora run their canoe aground. With guns drawn, they scrambled behind one of the cypress trees.

After taking a deep breath, Belle bent down, locked her arms under her knees, and yanked up, breaking the suction and momentarily freeing her feet. She thrust her legs back in the water, so they wouldn't touch the bottom again, and swam as fast as she could for shore, where Scout welcomed her. She crawled out and crouched low as they made their way to the protection of one of the cypress trees.

Alonzo shouted toward the cabin. "We need to see Sheila!"

Silence for a few moments. Belle gazed up and saw a hundred dolls staring down at her, the closest one directly overhead with no hair, one brown eye, and a mouth frozen in a perpetual smile. The arms moved slowly back and forth in a beckoning motion. Another spine shiver.

A ragged male voice from inside the shack. "You cops?"

"Government," Alonzo responded.

"Unless you got a warrant I have me a right to shoot you just like any other trespasser."

Vernon Hardaway was living up to his reputation.

Staying low, Scout and Belle scurried over to Alonzo and Nora behind the relative safety of the larger cypress. "You guys okay?"

Nora nodded, but she was obviously lying.

"Those walls are thin," Alonzo said. "If we fire into the shack, we could hit Sheila."

"I don't give a shit," Nora snapped. "The bracelet's inside that shack. I need the bracelet. I'm not waiting around."

She stood up, ready to shoot. Belle jerked her down just as she pulled the trigger, throwing off her aim, and the bullet shot harmlessly into the air.

She pulled away, her eyes ablaze. "I need that fucking bracelet now!"

Vernon fired three more shots into the tree.

"You think he'd really kill us?" Belle asked Alonzo.

"Apparently, he's a dealer. Who knows what kind of shit he has warehoused in that back shed. Yeah, I think he'd put a bullet in each of our brains without a second thought and dump us deep in the bayou. Anybody comes looking, he'll deny he ever saw us, and everyone will assume we got lost and ended up gator bait."

No response. They waited.

Suddenly, Scout's ears perked up, and he took off around to the back of the structure.

"There has to be a back entrance," Nora said. Before anyone could protest, she followed Scout, doing her best to remain in a crouched position.

"Shit!" Belle hissed. "She's going to get herself killed. Wait here."

Alonzo put a restraining hand on her arm. "Belle, no. Hardaway will—"

She jerked away and followed Nora around to the back of the shack. When she turned the corner, she immediately faced the shed, maybe half the size of the main shack. She didn't know for certain what was stored inside, but strongly suspected it wasn't a power mower.

She banged into a small generator—the cozy couple needed power to fire up the flat-screen—and off to the right an airboat tied to a dilapidated dock floated on the edge of the shore. She spotted Scout, crouching, baring his teeth, and emitting a low growl, his eyes focused on the back of the shack.

"Freeze, bitch."

Belle turned to see a scrawny man with a scraggly salt and pepper beard in bare feet wearing filthy overalls over a bare chest. One hand wrapped tight around Nora, and the other pointed a semi-automatic at her temple.

"Drop your gun."

Belle complied. "Look, we don't want any trouble."

"Call off your dog, or I'll shoot him."

Belle didn't hesitate. "*Stai li!*"

"Now shout to your pal and tell him to come back. No funny business, or I shoot both you bitches."

Belle nodded. "No problem." She shouted, "Alonzo!"

A moment later he came running around the corner, then stopped when he saw the scene in front of him. "Look, Hardaway, I'm a Federal agent, but I have no interest in arresting you."

"Bullshit. Drop your gun."

Alonzo complied.

Belle said, "We don't care what you have stored up inside your shed. Sheila stole some stuff from Cord Parker. She can work that out with him. But Sheila also took a bracelet, a Comanche bracelet. We don't even want the bracelet. We just want to take some pictures of it. That's all. She comes out with the bracelet, we snap a few photos, then we'll leave you and your amazing doll collection for good."

"But see, easiest thing for me to do, is shoot the three of you and throw you in the swamp."

A voice behind them. "We can't do that, Vernon."

Belle looked back to see the redheaded Comanche Princess standing in the doorway. At least this time she was wearing pants.

"Shut the fuck up." Hardaway, still with his arm around Nora, walked sideways toward the boat.

"Where you goin'?" Sheila asked.

"Soon as I get on the boat, I'm gonna shoot those two and keep this one here as a hostage. But first . . ." Vernon took aim at Scout.

Sheila took aim at Vernon.

She fired first.

The bullet hit him in the shoulder, and the force of the impact knocked the man backward into the water.

"Jesus Christ, Sheila! What the fuck you shoot me for?"

"Shoulder shot. No big deal. Vernon, we can't be killin' folk. Especially feds. You seen TV. They find any body parts and them forensics guys in the white coats? You can't hide nothin' from them."

Vernon floundered, half swimming with one arm, half standing. The water seemed deeper back here. Belle didn't know where his weapon had ended up, so she approached carefully, her gun still pointed at him. "Where's your gun?"

He responded in a voice close to a cackle. "In the water."

Her short exposure to Vernon Hardaway hadn't left her with the impression of a particularly trustworthy man. She scooped up her gun and aimed it at his head.

Alonzo jumped onto the airboat, found a coil of line, and tossed it out to Vernon.

Suddenly Vernon dropped fast below the surface of the water.

The long black log surfaced with Vernon's legs firmly clamped in his jaw.

Vernon struggled unsuccessfully to gain his footing. Even in the low light, Belle could see the whites of his eyes. "Help! *Hel—!*"

The gator yanked him under again. Both Sheila and Belle fired at the dark underwater shape. She knew at this close range at least a few bullets must've found their mark, but the gator seemed unaffected. He swished his tail along the surface, spraying them with fetid swamp water, then turned and disappeared into the black river with his prey.

Sheila whimpered, "Vernon?"

The inside of the shack looked worse than the outside. Two rooms—a kitchen and a bedroom. A web of extension cords ran from the TV, two lamps, a small fridge and a microwave to a mother cord, which in turn snaked through a back window presumably extending to the generator. Belle doubted if the county building inspector had stopped by recently.

The flat-screen rested on an uneven pile of magazines at the foot of the bed—she could only see the cover of one but the title, *Hollywood Big Titties,* gave a hint of the couples' current reading list. On top of a thin sagging mattress with stains of unknown and un-want-to-know substances, a worn blanket with a faded Star Wars image entwined in a twisted swirl with a sheet that might've been washed last year. The whole room smelled of mold and pot. When Nora asked to use the bathroom, at first Sheila didn't respond. Belle could tell by her eyes she was high on something. Which might explain her lack of emotion after witnessing her guy turning into the main dish for the gator family dinner.

She dug a roll of toilet paper out from under the bed, handed it to Nora, and gestured to the backyard. If you live in the swamp, the whole neighborhood is your toilet.

"Sorry about Vernon," Belle said.

"I saved your lives, you know. So ain't gonna be no charges against me, right?"

"Right. Thanks."

Sheila sighed deeply, then shrugged, showing no emotion. "Guess the house is mine now."

Belle stifled a smile. *House? Okay, if you say so.*

Two chairs in the tiny kitchen snugged up against a round, battered table. Alonzo brought the chairs into the bedroom and sat on the bed next to Sheila. She remained topless and unfazed, hardly surprising given her chosen profession. Belle took one chair, and when Nora returned, she sat in the other. Scout curled up between them.

Nora didn't waste time. "Where's the bracelet?"

Sheila leaned back, trying to create a little more distance between her and this very angry woman. "What's the big deal with the bracelet?" Her eyes narrowed. "Wait, maybe this is worth—"

Nora leaped across the bed, shoved Sheila hard to the floor, and snapped the bracelet from her wrist.

"Hey," Sheila snarled woozily. "What the hell you think you're doin', bitch?"

"Since we haven't actually seen any evidence of illegal drug activity," Alonzo said, "how about we take the bracelet, and we don't look inside your shed?"

"We also need you to put off reporting Vernon's death for twenty-four hours," Belle added. "We're in a hurry."

Sheil gaped. "So, you're not gonna arrest me?"

"In return for the bracelet," Alonzo said.

"Deal," Sheila responded instantly. "And don't worry about Vernon. I'll report he was high and fell in the water and the gators grabbed him. And if you want, I'll take you back in the airboat. A lot faster."

Nora eagerly examined the bracelet. After a few moments she lifted her head, her face shining with excitement.

"I think this is it."

CHAPTER 36

Riding full speed through a treacherous swamp at night on an airboat driven by a crazy woman high on drugs was not the option Belle would've chosen, but she and Alonzo were overruled by Nora who made plain she would brook no argument. They'd survived, so maybe their luck was changing.

While hanging on for dear life, Belle tried to take her mind off the likelihood that at any moment the airboat would crash into a cypress root, flip her into the filthy water, and she'd become a tasty evening snack for the gator clan. So, she'd asked Sheila about the dolls. Apparently, a number of years ago, Vernon had found a doll washed up on the island and hung it on a tree for good luck. His drug business began to improve, and he attributed his renewed fortune to the lucky doll. After that, when he left the swamp, he'd stop by the Salvation Army in Marshall and look for toy dolls to hang on his trees. Belle figured the lucky dolls didn't keep Vernon from becoming gator bait, but kept her thoughts to herself. Sheila confirmed she would continue Vernon's business as a tribute to him. Touching.

Nora had tried to examine the bracelet during the ride back, but the bucking movement of the airboat made doing so impossible. But the moment they entered the Tahoe and Belle aimed the vehicle west, Nora dug in using both bracelets to attempt the decipher.

Belle stopped outside Mount Pleasant to gas up, grab a sandwich to. go, and use the restrooms, but Nora never left the car, asking only that Belle bring her back a good number 2 pencil with an eraser and a few sheets of blank paper. She insisted that the interior light remain on while they drove, and with photos of the lance symbols spread across her lap, she went back and forth, comparing the symbols on the two bracelets to the photos. Using the edge of her cell phone as a ruler, she painstakingly reproduced various combinations of symbols. on the paper.

Finally, about a half-hour east of Gracie they heard a tiny squeal

from the back seat."I think I've got it." Nora leaned forward with a sheet of paper containing her rough sketch showing three rows of symbols. She didn't try to hide her excitement. "Look here."

"I can't see," Belle said, as she struggled to see the sketch while keeping her eye on the road.

Nora handed the sketch to Alonzo who held it up under the rearview mirror.

"Better," Belle said, as she checked out the sketch. Fortunately, at that time of night, the traffic was very light.

"The first row is the string of symbols from the lance," Nora explained. "In the second row I combined the symbols from the two bracelets. It took me a while to realize that the bah-has-tkih was not a typical code breaker, like E is K and R is T. Rather, the symbols on the two bracelets are partials, but when combined with those on the lance form a string of completed symbols conveying the real message."

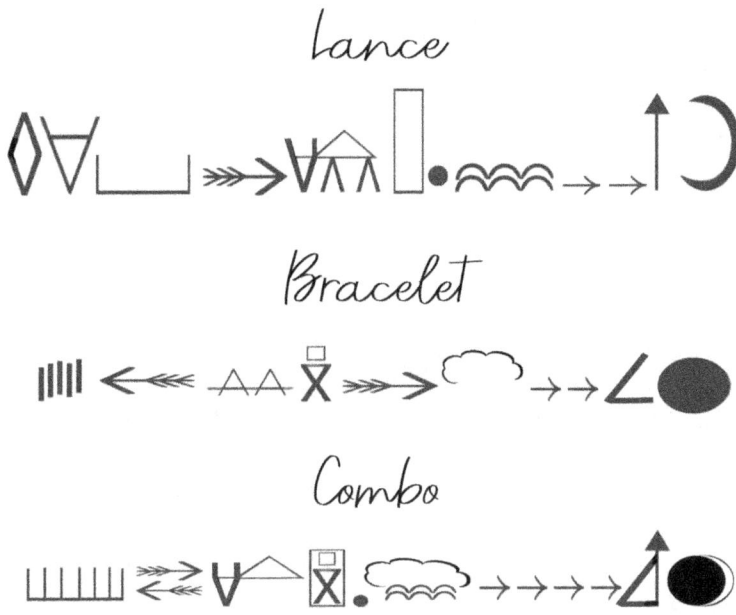

Lance

Bracelet

Combo

Nora eagerly continued. "We already know what the white feather and the antelope mean—Roosevelt and Quanah; they were the two parties. So, then you combine the rest of the symbols, and you get the third line. Look at the first one. You combine the squatty U with the short vertical lines, and you've created the symbol for spring. The two arrows pointing in different directions, that's the symbol for war. The next one threw me, as I'd never seen the symbol on the bracelet before, but when you look at it in comparison with the buffalo symbol, I realized it's a buffalo with no legs. A dead buffalo."

Belle broke in. "A war in the spring against buffalo hunters."

"Correct."

"But there were many times Quanah attacked buffalo hunters in all seasons of the year," Alonzo said.

"Correct again. So, let's continue. The next symbol is a rectangle. We thought it referred to the jade box, but I'm sure now it's the symbol for an enclosure with a dot next to the lower right corner. We combine that with the symbol for a white soldier and another arrow—this one a single arrow representing direction—and we put the soldier inside the enclosure."

"Okay, so in the spring Quanah attacked soldiers or buffalo hunters inside a fort or a settlement," Alonzo said. "Still doesn't narrow it down."

"But the next combination does," Nora's excitement grew. "We add the symbol for water from the lance and the symbol for fire from the bracelets, and you have—"

"Firewater. Whiskey." Belle half-expected a gong to sound and an audience to applaud from somewhere.

"Bingo. Quanah attacks white buffalo hunters in a saloon."

"Did he ever do that?' Alonzo asked.

"Yes!" Nora shouted. "Adobe Walls! One of the last battles of the Indian Wars. June 27, 1874."

Belle had heard of the Battle of Adobe Walls but knew nothing about it. "Where's Adobe Walls?"

"Couple hours northeast of Amarillo in the middle of nowhere. The remaining symbols tell us where to dig. The two horizontal lances from Quanah's lance combine with the two from the bracelet—that's the distance of four lance lengths from the corner of the saloon. Where the dot is."

Alonzo asked, "So we have to dig at all four corners?"

"No. Check out the last two symbols, the vertical lance combines with the backward point, and the red banana-shaped sliver from the lance combines with the black circle. The combination black circle with the red sliver represents the rising sun, dawn.

The sun rises from the east so we're looking at the southeastern corner of the saloon."

Belle got it. "And the vertical lance points to the spot eight lance lengths from the corner; that's where the Hudie Box is buried."

"I don't think so. This backward point threw me, but I think when you combine the backward point and the vertical lance it refers to the shadow from the lance."

Now Belle was the excited one. "So, we stick the lance in the ground eight lance lengths from the southeast corner of the saloon at dawn and dig where the lance shadow ends!"

"Yes. Turns out the lance itself *is* critical to locating the jade box. You were right, Belle, about Quanah burying the box at the site of one of his battles."

"Wonder why Quanah chose Adobe Walls."

"Roosevelt talked to Quanah about the battle. It's in his journal notes. Listen." She tapped a few keys on her phone. "June 22, 1905. Notes from Quanah Parker on Adobe Walls." She read Roosevelt's words aloud:

I of course was interested in Quanah's recollections concerning the battle of Adobe Walls. He explained that the winter of 1873-74 had been particularly hard on the Comanche. Most of the buffalo had been killed by the white hunters, and the majority of his tribe lived on reservations dependent on government rations. White horse thieves stole from the Indians without consequence. Whiskey peddlers traded bad whiskey for valuable buffalo robes. Alcoholism spread like wildfire. Reservation Indians sold anything and everything for whiskey. The few remaining Indians still living outside the reservations subsisted on little food and had to continually avoid squads of soldiers. When skirmishes were unavoidable, the soldiers almost always prevailed, costing the Indians men and horses. Only a few Comanche remained; all the rest had given up.

Quanah admitted to me he'd been looking for retribution. White men had stripped him and his people of their way of life. He also held them responsible for the death of his father and the abduction of his mother and sister.

Quanah's path crossed with a young medicine man called Isa-tai. Isa-tai convinced the Comanches that his medicine would protect them against the white man's bullets. Isa-tai's mysticism and Quanah's leadership formed a strong draw to those wondering if they should give up and join those on the reservation. They willingly followed Quanah on his quest for retribution, emboldened by the promise that Isa-tai's magic would protect them. The band decided their first target would be the buffalo hunters who gathered at Adobe Walls.

On the north side of the Canadian River, about ninety miles north-

east of present-day Amarillo, The Adobe Walls trading post served the 200–300 buffalo hunters in the area. According to Quanah, the site consisted of a couple of hide yards, a blacksmith shop, two stores, and a saloon.

In the early morning hours of June 27, 1874, a force of 250 warriors under Quanah's leadership, Comanche and Cheyenne along with a few Kiowa and Arapaho, gathered atop a bluff along the Canadian River overlooking the trading post. Isa-tai, both his naked body and his horse covered in yellow war paint, mingled among the men. He promised the warriors that the yellow paint meant they were protected from the white man's guns.

Quanah said they fully expected to swoop down on the unsuspecting trading post and slaughter the inhabitants in their sleep—twenty-eight men and one woman.

But as luck would have it, a government scout who lived with the Cheyenne had told the saloon owner, a man named Hanrahan, of the impending raid. He purposely didn't warn the others because he didn't want them to scatter and cost him business. That night, he fired a shot in the air waking the inhabitants. He told them the roof ridgepole on the saloon cracked and was about to collapse endangering those inside. The ridgepole was fine, but with everyone now awake Hanrahan knew they could be ready for the Indian raid if it materialized.

Just as dawn was breaking, Quanah led his braves at full gallop down into the valley toward the trading post. A few Indians didn't make that first charge, when their horses tripped in prairie-dog holes, sending their riders flying in the air.

Inside the buildings, the whites were protected by two-feet thick sod walls that wouldn't burn. The first attack was almost successful as the Indians swarmed the buildings with the terrified inhabitants inside. Given the close quarters both sides resorted to pistols. Quanah and his men fired through cracks and holes in the wall. Inside, the whites could hardly see due to the thick smoke and huddled against the sod walls trying not to get hit by the flying bullets.

Quanah himself tried to crash his horse against the door to break it in, but somehow the door held, and he had to retreat. Later he jumped on top of the saloon and fired down through the roof. But each attack was repelled by the hunters.

Two of the men inside would later become well-known. William "Bat" Masterson, a gambler and gunman, would become sheriff of Dodge City, and Billy Dixon, a reputed sharpshooter, would later receive the Congressional Medal of Honor for his heroism fighting Indians at the battle of Buffalo Wallow.

Eventually the Indians were driven back. While many of Quanah's men were armed with lever-action repeater rifles, the men inside the sod-protected buildings were hardened hunters with unlimited ammunition and a full arsenal including the "Big Fifties"— single-shot rifles with octagonal 34-inch barrels shooting .50-caliber cartridges.

Quanah remembers having his horse shot out from under him. He rolled behind a stack of buffalo hides in the hide yard with nothing but his war lance. The shot had come from one of the hunters who had snuck out of the blacksmith shop and circled around to the hide yard planning to catch the Indians in a crossfire. The hunter spotted Quanah and fired, but the bullet struck a powder horn he carried around his neck and rico-cheted into his upper shoulder, an inconsequential wound. Believing Quanah dead, the hunter focused his fire on the other warriors. Quanah snuck up behind the man, the roar of battle camouflaging the sound of his approach. He told me, word-for-word, "This man represented the end of my way of life, the end of Comanche way of life. A white man, like the white man who had killed my father and stolen my mother and sister. I waited until he felt my spirit behind him. He turned, and I took great pleasure in seeing the fear in his eyes. He tried to raise his rifle but even he knew he could not do so in time. I plunged my father's war lance into his heart with such fury the blade penetrated clean through his body."

But the white men and their guns and their sod barricade proved too much, and the Indians retreated. Demoralized by their failure, Quanah's wounding made things worse. Isa-tai's medicine was not magic. After a few more skirmishes over the next couple of days, the Indians left for good.

Quanah was angry over the loss, and after Adobe Walls he broke his men into smaller war parties. Their raids on settlements in Texas and Kansas over the summer of 1874 resulted in some 200 whites being killed and, in some cases, tortured. I asked Quanah about the torturing. His expression clouded, and his only response was, "That is how Comanche did war." As a result of Quanah's raids in retaliation for his defeat at Adobe Walls, the army mounted a major offensive against him. For a time, he was able to hide in the maze of side canyons in Palo Duro Canyon, but by the following spring, June 2, 1875, almost a year after the Adobe Walls raid, Quanah's band was starving, and he surrendered at Fort Sill.

"I can see now why Quanah would pick the site to hide the Hudie Box entrusted to him by Roosevelt," Alonzo said. "The Adobe Walls battle had been the beginning of the end of Quanah Parker's former life, and it clearly had a profound effect on him.

"Belle, the time," Nora said, pointing to the dashboard clock. Blood drained from her face. "We're not going to make it." She didn't try to hide the anxiety in her voice.

Belle's heart raced. The deadline would pass before they arrived at the battle site. "I need to contact the kidnappers."

"If you give them the location, you have no way of guaranteeing they will release your sister," Alonzo said.

I glanced back at Nora, who nodded her approval. "They also have Nora's daughter, Sadie."

"What? And you're just telling me this now?"

"The important thing is, we have the information Bai needs," Nora said, clearly trying to convince herself. "Hurting Sadie and Jenny does nothing for him. We exchange the information for the two girls. After that, I don't care."

"I can make a call," Alonzo said. "You pass on the information to the kidnappers, and the FBI would have the site surrounded without being seen."

"No." Nora's tone left no room for argument. "There's no place to hide out there. The museum's in the process of re-creating the site, but all we've finished is Hanrahan's Saloon and one hide yard. The structure's located in the middle of nowhere, nothing but prairie grass, a few small stands of trees, rattlesnakes, and prairie-dog holes. The bluff near the river where the Indians gathered is a possibility, but it might be too far away. If the kidnappers see the FBI, they might feel compelled to kill my daughter. I will not permit any chance of that happening."

"She's right," Belle added. She dialed Jenny's number, and as expected after a few rings the call switched to voicemail. "We've discovered the location of the jade box. At dawn tomorrow, bring Jenny and Sadie to Adobe Walls along with the lance." She terminated the call, then texted the same message. "By the way, I'll be going in there alone," she announced to Nora and Alonzo.

"How do you say 'bullshit' in Comanche?" Alonzo said.

"Sadie's my daughter," Nora said. "Do you really think I'm going to let you push me to the sidelines?"

Belle tried to calm her voice, with only modest success. "Okay, Alonzo and I will go. We'll bring back both girls, I promise."

"No," Nora said forcefully. "Number one, she's my daughter. Number two, I'm a big girl who can take care of herself. Number three, I'm the one who can read the code if you run into a problem."

Belle realized she was right. Her phone buzzed. The kidnappers? She checked the screen. A text from Sal. Helen was okay. They'd just landed in New York and would be in Amarillo by ten tomorrow morning. She texted back that she'd call him later and fill him in.

One way or the other, by ten o'clock tomorrow it'll be all over.

CHAPTER 37

Bai Sun poured himself some tea. From the tiny kitchen he could easily see Fen Lao sitting on the edge of the living room sofa, frozen in place, staring at the door to the girls' bedroom like a dog ready to pounce on an intruder once the door opened. He felt a rising concern about his associate.

She'd been humiliated by her superiors, although in fairness he couldn't argue with their decision. Fen was unstable—he'd been aware of that from the beginning. But he needed an assistant. Selling her on the idea of betraying the organization had been easier than he'd thought. The enticement hadn't been money, although she was fully aware her newfound wealth would allow her to find a quiet spot someplace in the world to comfortably live out her life, pursuing whatever "unusual" proclivities she desired. The main draw was the excitement of being back in the game.

Fen had shown an unexpected interest in the young woman's baby. First, she'd insisted that she be the one to kill the hostages when the time came. Then she'd asked if she could have the baby. She would slice open Jenny Bannon's womb, scoop out the child, then slit the mother's throat. The pregnant girl's escape attempt had almost worked. Fen had repeatedly reminded him that there needed to be consequences. Now, as the deadline was about to expire, he needed Fen. Easy decision. He'd told her she could kill the girls and keep the baby.

Jenny Bannon's phone rang.

Jenny knew the deadline was about to expire. The dinner tray remained on the bed untouched. She'd been sitting on the floor for hours, holding Sadie in her lap, leaning up against the crack between the door and the jamb waiting, hoping Belle would call. As the minutes dwindled down to the deadline, she could hear Bai pacing back and forth. If Belle didn't call, would they kill her and Sadie? She didn't know why she'd even asked the question. After the failed escape attempt, of course they'd be killed.

The sound of Bai pacing suddenly stopped. She scrunched down, lying almost prone on the floor, where the crack was wide enough for her to see into the living room. Bai crossed her narrow field of vision, staring at her cell phone. A message from Belle? Had to be. Bai and the Fenbot talked in rapid-fire Chinese. She could tell by the excitement in their voices that something had happened. Bai used another phone to place a call. He spoke in English—must be talking to the one called Mao. She couldn't hear most of what Bai said, but she did catch the words, "Adobe Walls." Then right before he ended the call he said, "When we find the box, we'll take care of Bannon and Yates." Bai paused, presumably while Mao spoke on the other end of the line. Bai replied, "Don't worry, there will be no loose ends."

Bai finished the call. A moment later she heard footsteps approaching her door. She stood up. *Oh my God, Sadie and I are the loose—*

The door swung open, and Fen stepped into the room. Jenny felt but never saw the foot sweep her legs out from under her, and in an instant, she was on her back. Sadie screamed. Fen straddled Jenny's knees, a dagger suddenly in her hand. Sadie scrambled off the bed and huddled in a corner of the room, screaming. Fen yanked up Jenny's shirt and pulled down the elastic, exposing her bare belly.

Fen slowly drew the dagger in an arc under Jenny's rib cage, barely piercing the skin, creating a half-moon trail of blood. Jenny wriggled and squirmed and bucked her hips trying to free herself, to no avail. She balled up her fist and swung it as hard as she could at Fen's face, but the tiny woman easily darted her head to one side so all Jenny punched was air.

"*Wo de baobei.*" My baby.

"Please, please don't. I beg you—"

"*Tingzhi!*" Stop! Bai leaped across the threshold and grabbed Fen's wrist.

For a moment Jenny thought Fen would resist, and she harbored no doubt that the Fenbot would prevail if a battle occurred between her two captors.

Sadie's wails had morphed into heaving sobs.

Then Bai said, "*Hěn kuài.*" Soon.

Jenny didn't understand Chinese, but whatever Bai said did the trick, and Fen crawled off of her. She realized she was shaking and couldn't stop. Suddenly she felt a sharp pain, like someone was squeezing her abdomen in a hot vise. She gasped. Her first contraction. Fen stood over her, the dagger now slack in her hand, staring at Jenny's bloody belly.

"*Wo de baobei.*"

Jenny Bannon began to pray.

Belle couldn't remember for certain when she'd slept last, and she knew Nora felt the same. Since Alonzo qualified as the least drowsy, he'd assumed the wheel. They passed through the town of Stinnet, northeast of Amarillo, and drove north on Route 207 toward Adobe Walls.

Belle tried to doze off, but her spinning mind, along with a few drops of leftover adrenaline, barred her from doing so. Finally, she gave up, and when the Tahoe approached a truck stop up ahead both she and Nora voted to stop for some coffee and food. Being jacked up on caffeine was marginally better than the half-awake, half-asleep mode they'd been experiencing. Belle had to settle for cream and sugar—she guessed truckers weren't into almond coconut or marshmallow mocha.

Truth was, she would've ingested it black; the coffee was stay-awake medicine, nothing more.

When they returned to the parking lot, Belle noticed a Chinese man on his knees behind the Tahoe, but when she approached he rose with a smile and held up a child's toy that had apparently dropped and rolled under the car. He passed the toy to a young boy through the window of a car parked in the next space. Cute. He entered the car and drove away. In an abundance of caution, Belle carefully checked the car for a tracer, but found none, and she felt a touch of guilt for suspecting a man just because of his race.

They'd stopped at a big box store in Stinnett where Alonzo bought a shovel and extra ammo. Belle called Sal and brought him up to date. She did her best to project optimism. They'd successfully decoded the lance and would soon exchange the jade box for Jenny and Sadie. Helen insisted on talking to her, and she could hear the anguish in her aunt's voice. The woman sobbed quietly as she spoke, and Belle could barely understand her words. She asked Belle to guarantee she'd bring Jenny and her baby back safe and unharmed. Belle knew she should've responded, "We'll do our best, but we're dealing with ruthless people, and anything can happen." Instead, she told Helen not to worry, to concentrate on getting better and guaranteed she would save Jenny.

After another twenty miles, they followed a narrow dirt road wandering back and forth in a southeasterly direction. An overcast night posed a problem as they needed to see the sun in the morning for the lance to cast its shadow. Nora tried to check the weather app on her phone, but found no service.

Belle felt as if she'd stepped back in time. No evidence of civilization in sight—nothing but waist-high prairie grass in every direction. From Quanah's account in Roosevelt's journal, she knew a bluff rose to the east beside the meandering Canadian River, but she couldn't see it in the dark. They entered the property of what was once the Adobe Walls Trading Post, in the middle of nowhere. A bomb could go off, and no one would know it.

She wondered where Jin Choi was right now. He hadn't appeared during their adventures in Uncertain, but she knew he would never give up. His country was counting on him to assure the Liaodong Agreement remained buried, and she suspected the consequences for failure would not be pleasant. She needed to keep a sharp lookout.

Nora pointed through the windshield. "There."

Belle could make out the low shadowy outline of an oblong structure up ahead. Hanrahan's Saloon. The long side of the building faced northeast. Alonzo pulled the Tahoe next to a door on the short, northwest side of the saloon.

"So that's what it looked like back then?" Belle asked.

"I was involved in overseeing the re-creation for the museum," Nora responded. She spoke in a near monotone. Her mind was obviously consumed with concerns for her daughter. "Twenty-three feet wide, thirty-nine feet long. Two doors at each end. The sod walls are three feet thick at the base and taper up to the roof. A timber post on each side of each door supports a cottonwood ridgepole running the length of the building. When we go inside, you'll see carve-outs in the sod for firearm use when defending against attack. The research was unclear about windows, but we think at least one glazed window had been installed on the south side. Sawed timber planks supported the sod roof."

"Impressive. What's next?"

Nora waved her hand absently into the gloom. "We're scheduled to build the blacksmith shop as soon as we raise the funds."

Belle opened the car door and Scout jumped out, then immediately ran off chasing something in the dark, probably a prairie dog. They retrieved the shovel as well as their weapons and ammo from the cargo area. She grabbed a blanket, a couple of bottles of water, and her bow with six arrows. Nora twisted the numbered dial back and forth on a simple coded padlock. They heard the *click,* and she opened the lock, then the door. Belle called Scout, and they entered.

"Don't suppose you installed electric lighting," Alonzo said.

Nora shook her head. "When we're finished with the whole site, we'll probably install a generator to make the tours more comfortable for visitors. Might want to stand still until I light the kerosene lamp, or you'll probably knock into something."

Scout, Alonzo, and Belle did as instructed. Nora found the lamp, and in a few moments the single lantern offered low light and long shadows. From what Belle could see, the museum's recreation of the saloon included a bar consisting of sawn planks on top of two giant barrels running most of the way across the room. A Sharps .50-caliber buffalo rifle and an Indian hunting knife in a beaded scabbard rested on one corner of the bar.

"That's Quanah's knife," Nora explained. "We brought it here from the museum."

Two tables, each surrounded by four chairs, separated them from the bar. A line of dusty whiskey bottles with names like Tanglefoot, Taos Lightning, and Red-Eye rested on a long table behind the bar.

"That whiskey authentic?" Alonzo asked.

"Yep. But you wouldn't offer that stuff to your worst enemy. Some consisted of raw alcohol, burnt sugar, and tobacco. Others mixed in turpentine or gunpowder."

"Think I would've become a teetotaler real fast," Alonzo said.

Belle checked her watch. Little over four hours until dawn. "We're going to need to be as sharp as possible when the kidnappers arrive. I suggest we try to grab a few hours' sleep. We'll set our phone alarms. Scout will wake us if they arrive early."

"Sounds good to me," Nora said. Belle handed her the blanket and she spread it out on the floor next to a couple of grain sacks leaning up against the wall.

"You take the blanket,' Belle said. "Alonzo and I can stretch out on the floorboards. We're used to sleeping on hard surfaces."

Nora cracked a half-smile. "Thanks." She stretched out on the blanket. "Doubt if I'll be able to sleep. Sadie's not just the most important thing in my life, she *is* my life. If anything were to happen to her—"

"Nothing's going to happen to Sadie or Jenny," Belle assured her with a level of confidence she neither felt nor could rationally support.

"I don't know,' Nora said, her voice trembling. "Maybe Bai will decide he doesn't want witnesses."

"Bai's interested in one thing," Alonzo said, his tone low and soothing. "Money. Dead bodies, including two young children, would create a lot of heat that he's not going to want to deal with."

"I hope you're right."

Belle chose not to remind her that Fen had murdered her ex-husband. "One other thing," Belle added. "When you see the people who kidnapped Sadie and killed Buck, you're going to have to keep your cool."

"Belle's right," Alonzo added.

"I will," Nora assured them. She paused, then said carefully. "By the way, Belle, I had a thought about your IED. Have you ever considered a Native American chant?"

"No."

"Tribal members used to gather around a campfire, and the shaman would lead them in various chants. This one is supposed to bring inner peace. *Hey ya hey yo, Ya hey e. Hey ya hey yo, Ya hey e.* I used it to keep from lapsing into total unhinged mode inside the caves. You might want to try it next time your lizard door cracks open."

"Thanks."

A couple of minutes passed, and Belle thought Nora was asleep. Then she heard a sniffle.

Nora's voice cracked. "Belle, if anything happens to Sadie . . ."

"Nothing's going to happen to Sadie."

"Promise?"

"Promise." Belle tried to project a level of confidence she didn't feel. *Including my promise to Aunt Helen, that's two commitments I'm not sure I can keep.* She drifted off.

The moon bathed the room with a soft gray light. The sky had cleared, good news for tomorrow's treasure hunt. They needed a shadow. She looked down at the beautiful woman sleeping on the floor. The moonlight enhanced her strong features, and Belle could easily see her as the proud daughter of a warrior chief.

She thought of her little sister—pregnant, afraid—and Sadie, bewildered, thrust into a world of scary adults she'd never experienced in her short life. Their lives would depend on the decisions Belle would make in a few hours. The stunning weight of her responsibility froze her in place. Alonzo came up behind her and slipped her hand in his. With a light tug he led her to the far end of the room where they reclined together on the old plank floor. He removed his jacket, rolled it up, and made a pillow for her. Nothing like a guy who's handy around the house.

He spooned behind her and wrapped his arm around her body. For a few moments she allowed herself the luxury of feeling safe and protected, even though deep down she knew the serious risks they were about to face. If they were alone, would they have made love? She was of two minds: Probably not, because they were too occupied with what the morning held, and probably yes, because both of them might not make it to lunchtime alive. As she drifted toward sleep, she leaned toward a solid yes.

She'd left the tavern door slightly ajar to make it easier for Scout to detect someone approaching. The sounds of the night filtered in: the clicking of crickets and the soft brush of prairie grass blowing in the night breeze. A coyote wailing in the distance.

The music of the prairie. No different than 150 years ago. Strangely comforting as she closed her eyes.

Hey ya hey yo, Ya hey e. Hey ya hey yo, Ya hey e...

CHAPTER 38

A nuzzling wet nose woke Belle from a dreamless sleep.

She scratched her alarm clock behind the ears. Through eyes still focusing, she observed Nora and Alonzo framing the single window, and through that window she witnessed the first rays of sunlight nudging up over the black outline of the distant river bluff.

"Headlights," Nora said.

Belle rolled to her feet, found her firearm, then joined the other two at the window watching a white cargo van approach. She had no idea what Bai planned but figured the more space separating them the better. She stepped outside the door and fired a shot into the air. The van stopped maybe eighty or ninety yards from the saloon. The driver's door opened, and Bai climbed down to the deep prairie grass. She identified him by the bandage around his arm.

"Bring the two girls and the lance," she ordered in a steely voice. "And keep your other hand where I can see it."

"Good morning, Ms. Bannon. Sorry, but I'm afraid that's not how it's going to work. I will enter with the lance. You turn over the jade box, we let your sister and Ms. Yates's sweet little girl walk free."

Belle knew a lousy deal when she saw one, and Bai's offer was a lousy deal. "Let me see them."

MIKE PACE

Bai turned and spoke to somebody inside the van. A thin slice of sun now appeared above the horizon, and except for the silhouette of a thick stand of trees off toward the southwest, nothing but an endless sea of prairie grass extended toward the saloon from the river bluff to the south. She pictured for a moment the image seen by the occupants of the saloon on that morning of June 27, 1874. Two hundred and fifty screaming Indians in full war paint rising out of the fiery sun, led by Quanah Parker in his magnificent war bonnet, galloping full speed toward them through the tall grass backlit red by the sun's rays. They must've felt Satan himself had unleashed the demons from hell.

The silence from the van swelled. She heard the saloon door open behind her. Nora appeared at her side.

"Where is she?"

Finally, a small Asian woman whom Belle assumed was Fen stepped out of the van. She slid the cargo side-door open and helped Jenny and Sadie to the ground. Fen immediately pointed a gun at Jenny's head. The crotch of Jenny's jeans looked wet. Was that blood on her shirt? The little girl clung tight to Jenny's leg, trying to keep away from Fen.

Nora squeezed Belle's hand in a death grip. "Oh, my God, she's scared to death."

Belle could feel Nora's hand tighten even further; she knew Nora wanted to run out to her daughter. Belle needed her to remain controlled, but now could see that was going to be a problem. She pivoted and put both hands on Nora's shoulders, holding her at arm's length. "Listen to me. Sadie's fine, but we're dealing with dynamite here. Any sudden move could put her, could put all of us in danger."

Nora's shoulders tensed, then slumped. She looked away and nodded. "I know. I'm okay." Suddenly her eyes widened. "Jenny!" She turned to see Jenny bent over, holding her belly. "I think she's in labor."

Bai spoke. "Her water's broke. She's about to give birth. She needs to be taken to a hospital. The longer we stand her talking, the longer it will take to help your sister."

Shit. Bai had the leverage, and he knew it. The quicker they found the Hudie Box, the better. "Come in unarmed with the lance." Belle wanted to add something like, "If any harm comes to her, I'll blow your

288

head off," but figured doing so wouldn't help. They needed to find the damn box.

Bai pulled the lance from the back of the van then walked quickly to them and stopped. Belle kept the Stealth trained on his head but he didn't seem bothered. The only other time she'd seen him had been in the museum, and that was a blur. Bigger than she expected, maybe five-ten, early forties, muscular frame, black hair combed straight back.

Bai's sneer blended with a smirk. "Ms. Bannon. And the real Ms. Yates. We finally meet."

Bai's expression tested Belle's resolve, but she controlled her desire to pound his face to a purple pulp. Nora's eyes burned a hole into Bai's forehead, but she also kept herself in check.

"Turn around and lean against the wall," Belle ordered. Bai complied, and she frisked him, making a point to give him a particularly vigorous pat on his bandaged arm.

Bai yelped.

"Oh, sorry. How's the arm, asshole?"

"I suggest we proceed with dispatch if you want to assist your sister."

"Was that blood I saw on her shirt?"

"The girl had an accident. Just a scratch. We dressed the wound. She's fine."

The lizard door opened a tiny crack. *No! Not now.* She closed her eyes, concentrating as hard as she could, and the door closed. She shoved Bai between the shoulder blades, and he almost tripped.

"Follow her."

Nora led him to the southeast corner of the saloon. Belle followed with the Stealth aimed at the back of his head. She removed Quanah's lance from Bai and laid it on the ground with the butt end positioned at the corner, then flipped it end over end three times to achieve the four lance lengths.

Bai asked, "How do you know which direction?"

Nora pointed to the symbols on the lance. "See that rectangle? That's the saloon. And from the rising sun symbol we know the red dot is east on a line extending from the south side of the building."

Belle stuck the lance blade through the grass into the hard earth.

Immediately they saw the shadow, but the deeper she jammed the lance point into the soil, the shorter the shadow. She asked Nora, "How deep?"

Nora checked her sketch. "The lance is pointed up."

Belle flipped the lance around and rested the butt end on the ground. The rays from the rising sun cast a long shadow maybe halfway back toward the saloon. She used her heel to scratch an X in the soil at the tip of the lance point's shadow. "X marks the spot."

Finally, they'd found the location of the Hudie Box.

Nothing.

After twenty minutes of furious digging, Alonzo had excavated a three-foot hole five or six feet square as Belle, Nora, and Bai watched. He found nothing.

Belle caught her breath and glanced across the field to the white van, imagining Jenny lying in the filthy cargo hold suffering labor pains, scared to death. She grabbed the shovel from Alonzo, stepped into the hole, and dug another foot down.

Nora spoke. "Belle. . .?"

"Another foot."

"Belle."

She stopped.

Bai didn't hide his anger. "It is not here. You made a huge mistake. You are both pathetic."

Nora ignored him. "Quanah and Chony would not have made it this difficult. We should've found the box by now." She turned to Bai, struggling to hold back her tears. "I'm so sorry, we tried our best. You have to let them go."

Belle crawled out of the hole, pulse pounding, pulled her gun and jammed it into Bai's ear. "Your life or theirs. Tell your lady friend to bring both girls in unharmed, or you're going to have to figure out how to function with a bullet in your brain. Do it. Now."

Bai's maddening smirk returned, and he didn't move. "Ms. Bannon, my associate is now watching you with high-powered binoculars. She has strict instructions that if I am harmed in any way, she is to kill the girls. Fen is an unusual individual—near robotic, without emotion or typical human feelings. She will follow my instructions without hesitation."

Bai could've been bluffing, but Belle didn't think so. Something in his voice when he was describing his psychopathic partner convinced her he was telling the truth. Besides, she'd seen what Fen had done to Buck Yates.

Nora, eyes brimming with tears of both anger and fear, paced back and forth, studying her notes. "What am I missing?"

Bai pulled out his cell phone, tapped it a few times then spoke in rapid-fire Chinese. Must be a sat phone.

The sun now bathed the grassy plain in morning light giving Belle an idea. "When did Quanah die?"

Nora answered, "1911, why?"

"Not the year, the month."

"February 23."

In the second week of survival training, she'd learned how to determine direction by factoring the month of the year with the position of the sun. "If we assume Chony buried the box within days of Quanah's death, that means sometime in the first week of March. The Vernal equinox occurs March 19th, 20th, or 21st. That's one of only two days a year when the sun rises exactly due east. After that the sun moves south. Chony buried the box a couple weeks before the equinox, so a little north. We're now in early May, so the sun would be rising south of due east and a little farther south from the time Chony buried the box."

Nora checked out the sunrise. "So, if I understand you correctly, we need to dig farther north."

"I think so, yes."

Alonzo walked north of the excavation. "How much?"

"I don't know for sure. Maybe three or four feet." She glanced at the sun; it had almost completely exposed itself. "Doesn't make sense to re-measure now because the sun is higher and the shadow shorter, so we stick with the same distance from the saloon, but move north." She started on the edge of the excavation and took a long stride toward

Alonzo. "That's three feet. I suggest we start here and dig three feet north, maybe another three feet wide."

Bai grabbed the shovel from her hand and plunged it deep through the grassy root layer into the prairie soil.

Ten minutes later, maybe eighteen inches deep, the shovel clunked on something. Belle jumped into the hole and brushed away the soil with her hands to reveal the corner of a box wrapped in watertight oilskin. She continued hand digging until the box was fully exposed, then lifted it up and stepped out of the excavation. The box was lighter than she expected.

"Everyone inside," she instructed.

Bai eyed the box, and for a moment she thought he might snatch it and run. Instead, he turned toward the saloon. Smart move. Once inside, she set the chest on the bar.

Scout seemed agitated, his attention focused outside, not on Bai. Belle checked out the window but, other than the van, saw nothing except prairie grass extending all the way to the river bluff. Probably a prairie dog. She roughed the fur on Scout's head. "Nothing out there."

She turned her attention back to the chest. Maybe two feet square, six or eight inches high. She carefully unwrapped the oilcloth to reveal an old ammo box. The oilcloth had done its job. Except for some rotting at two of the corners, the wooden box remained in good condition. Black stencil markings had all but faded away, but she could make out the word "Sill," and the word "carbine." An old ammo box from Fort Sill.

The box was secured with a large padlock that had not suffered the passage of time well. A jab with the blade of the shovel popped it open. The box's hinges creaked as Belle carefully lifted the lid. Inside was a smaller object covered in oilskin. She lifted it out and unwrapped the oilskin. Nora gasped.

The Hudie Box.

The translucent green jade appeared to glow from its own self-contained light. Chony's preservation efforts had left the box untouched by the ravages of time. Belle never claimed to know much about art, but the image of Empress Dowager Tzu-Hsi surrounded by *hudie*, butterflies, was amazing. The jade box almost seemed alive.

Bai couldn't contain his impatience. He didn't care about the jade box; to him the contents were worth maybe a billion dollars. "Open it."

The box was sealed with wax. Belle used her pocketknife to carefully slice around the lid, then lifted the top. Inside was a yellowing envelope. She removed the envelope and opened it, again using the knife, and pulled out a legal-looking document, maybe eight or ten pages, folded in half. The first page was simply titled, "Lease Agreement" and was written in both English and Chinese. She checked the back page and saw Roosevelt's signature along with someone named Ling Chen on behalf of China. She thought of Jin's warning. *Could these few pages really trigger a war?* She showed the document to Bai and his eyes lit up, probably thinking of all the stuff he could buy with his millions.

Belle replaced the agreement inside the envelope, and the envelope inside the jade box. "Okay, we've done what you asked. Bring the girls in, and you can have the box."

Bai reached for his sat phone. Belle pulled her gun. "Tell her to come unarmed." Bai spoke a few words into the phone, then closed it. Belle watched through the window as Fen stepped out of the passenger side of the van, leaving the door open, and helped Jenny and Sadie to the ground from the cargo section. Jenny appeared in even worse shape, bent over, having to stop and catch her breath every few steps. Without a word, Nora ran out the door to Jenny and her daughter. Belle watched as Sadie flew into her mother's arms. Holding Sadie tight with one arm, Nora wrapped her other arm around Jenny and, with Fen trailing, they moved toward the saloon.

Then the window exploded, showering glass shards across the room.

CHAPTER 39

Everyone dove to the floor.

Bai hissed one word. "Jin."

A fusillade of bullets smacked into the sod wall. Those that made it through the window stitched across the back of the room.

Belle spotted Scout moving toward the window. "*Tu stai gui!*" Stay down! He hesitated, then curled up against the east sod wall.

Alonzo pointed to the bar. "The lamp!"

If a bullet hit the lamp, the kerosene would likely explode, and while the sod walls wouldn't burn, the timber posts and furniture could turn the interior into a furnace. He rolled under a sheet of fire to the bar, reached up, pulled the lamp down to relative safety, and doused the flame.

Belle pressed herself against the wall and peeked out the window. About a dozen men in camo clothing rose up from the grasses like green beetles. Looked like they carried Qs—QBZ-95 Chinese assault rifles with thirty-round mag boxes. Only a few of them were Asian, the rest Caucasian. Where the hell did they come from? *The stand of trees.* In the light she now could barely make out what looked like two black SUVs mostly hidden in the foliage. Jin's men, not prairie dogs. Scout had tried to warn her. She should've listened to her dog.

Outside, Jenny, Sadie, Nora, and Fen crouched low in the grass. Nora was armed. For the first time she hoped Bai had planned to double-cross her and had told Fen to bring a gun.

One of Jin's men moved toward them. Belle recognized him—the young guy with the family who'd parked next to her at the truck stop outside Stinnet. *Shit.* He'd likely been removing Jin's tracer when she spotted him near the Tahoe. From there, all they had to do was follow the Tahoe to Adobe Walls. When Belle found Tyler's tracer, she hadn't thought to check the rest of the car. She dropped to her knees and aimed her Stealth out one of the gun holes in the sod, firing two shots. She was pretty sure she hit him. If the cute kids were really his, Daddy wouldn't be coming home for supper tonight.

Alonzo turned to Bai. "Don't suppose you hid a gun up your ass."

"Unfortunately, no."

She needed Bai's help. If left up to Jin, Bai, and Fen would not leave Adobe Walls alive. Bai needed them. They needed him. Strange bedfellows and all that. She had to go out there and bring Jenny, Sadie, and Nora back to the relative safety of the saloon. And that required laying down as much suppression fire as possible. And that required giving Bai her gun. *Shit.*

She sighed deeply. "Okay, looks like we're both on the same side for the moment." Belle tossed Bai her handgun. "I'm going out there to bring the women back. I need you and Alonzo to keep them down in the weeds." She pointed to the box of ammo on the table nearest him. "Extra shells there. Keep up the fire until we're back."

She didn't wait for his agreement, hoping Alonzo's presence might keep her from receiving a bullet in the back of her head.

She opened the door a crack and immediately heard Bai and Alonzo spraying the attackers with cover fire. Nora, Fen, and the two girls crawled through the grass toward the saloon, then Jenny stopped, unable to move. Sadie disappeared, hiding low in the grass. Nora hovered over the girls like a protective mama bear while Fen accelerated toward Belle in a practiced military crawl.

Nora held her gun in a two-hand grip, panning 360 degrees, daring anyone to approach.

Alonzo and Bai were doing a good job forcing Jin's men to stay put, and Belle reached Jenny, Sadie, and Nora quickly. She could tell Jenny was about to scream out in pain and quickly covered her sister's mouth with her hand.

Jenny panted, sweat pouring off her brow. "Belle . . .?"

Belle held Nora's gaze. "Can you carry Sadie in one arm?" Nora nodded. "Okay, I'm going to carry Jenny, and I need you to lay out suppression."

"Got it."

Because of Jenny's condition, Belle couldn't toss her over her shoulder in a traditional fireman's carry; she'd have to cradle Jenny in her arms. "Now!"

She lifted Jenny in both arms, hardly feeling the weight, and ran, bent over, toward the saloon. Nora followed with Sadie, firing rapidly in the direction of the attackers. With Bai and Alonzo shooting from the saloon, Jin's men were caught in the crossfire and stayed down.

For the most part.

Shooting from a prone position in the grass, several attackers close by tried to pick them off. Belle heard bullets whiz overhead and once heard Jenny yelp. Belle prayed she'd suffered a labor pain and not a bullet wound. Nora's gun emptied just as they reached the saloon and stumbled inside. A moment later, a hail of bullets slammed into the thick oak door.

Nora set Sadie down then flipped over one of the tables and dragged it against the sod wall for added protection. "I want you to crouch down behind this table, no matter what happens."

The little girl shook with fear; tears ran freely down her cheeks. "Why do the men in the grass want to hurt us?"

"Because they're meanies," Nora said, her voice shaking. "But we're going to be fine if you do exactly what Mommy tells you, okay?"

Sadie clutched Nora's shirt. "Mommy, Daddy's hurt. We have to help Daddy."

Nora bit her lip and took a deep breath. "I know, sweetie, we will, but first we have to deal with the bad men outside, so promise me you won't move, okay?" Sadie nodded and hunkered down behind the table.

Belle gestured for Scout to move behind the upturned table, and he complied, curling up next to Sadie. His ears stiffened, and while down, the dog's body trembled with muscle tension, ready to spring up in an instant. Belle pulled the blanket and a grain sack tight against the east wall, then lowered Jenny down so her head rested on the grain sack. The others pressed up against the east wall as the gunfire from outside continued.

"Shrimp, were you hit?"

Jenny grimaced. "Don't think so."

A quick check of Jenny's body revealed no sign of a bullet wound. Belle did spot a superficial cut, held together by a series of butterfly bandages, tracking around the top of her belly. She wanted to ask her sister how this happened, but at the moment there were more pressing matters to address. Jenny's brow was wet with sweat. She breathed heavily.

Alonzo stood behind Bai. "Give her back the gun."

With a slight bow he dropped the Stealth into Belle's hand. Alonzo, Nora, and Belle quickly reloaded.

Jenny screamed, then panted rapidly. "Baby . . ."

Nora handed Belle her gun. "I'll tend to her."

More fire ripped through the window. Belle peeked out the gun hole and saw movement. "They're trying to surround us." Not surprising. But to move they had to rise up. She tossed Nora's gun to Bai. The three of them fired, and two hit a target. By her count Jin was down to eight or nine men.

Scout barked up at the ceiling. A moment later bullets showered down. "On the roof!" Nora cried.

The bullets continued, peppering a path in the floor running the length of the saloon, coming inches from Jenny's head.

Alonzo, Bai, and Belle fired up into the ceiling where they thought the shooter hovered. At that range Belle thought the 240-gram PMC ammo in her .44 mag Stealth packed enough power to penetrate the roof slats, but she wasn't certain.

More shots fired down. Jenny screamed.

Oh my God. "Jenny—!"

Nora shouted, "She's not hit, baby's coming!" Belle glanced toward her sister and spotted the crown of a bloody head emerging. Nora encouraged Jenny. "Push, push sweetie. You're doing fine."

Alonzo jumped up on a table, keeping his knees bent to avoid hitting his head on the ceiling. They heard a scrape, faint but definitely there. The shooter was right above them. Alonzo thrust the barrel of his gun into a crack where two roof slats met and fired four shots. They all heard the shooter scream then saw his body drop past the window. He had red hair. *Maybe the same guy who'd tagged Nora's phone in the grocery store?*

Jin's crew had now been reduced to seven or eight. The shooting suddenly stopped, and for the next couple of minutes the only sounds were Jenny's sharp outbursts, and Nora's soft words of encouragement as the girl strained to give birth.

Jin's voice called from outside. "Ms. Bannon, can you hear me?"

Then the baby was out, covered in the protective, creamy white, vernix biofilm. Nora cleared the infant's throat and gave him a little pat on the butt. The kid squealed in short bursts. She held him up for Jenny to see. "A boy." She turned to Sadie, who'd risen up to see the baby, and failed to hide the panic in her voice. "Sadie, I said stay down!"

Jenny, wide-eyed, tears streaming down her cheeks, pulled her baby tight to her chest. "Oh, my God, they want to kill my baby!"

Jin's voice grew louder. "Ms. Bannon?"

Belle slid along the wall to the window. Jin stood eighty or ninety yards away behind the opened passenger-side door of Bai's white van. What did he want? Stupid question.

Belle didn't quell the anger in her voice. "I hear you."

"We have no quarrel with you, Mr. Longabaugh, or Ms. Yates. You are victims of the traitor Bai Sun." Jin spoke in the smooth voice of a diplomat. "I have seen your excavation and assume you have the agreement in your possession. Give us the agreement, and we will permit you to leave unharmed."

Jin then shouted a few sentences in Chinese.

Belle turned to Bai. "What did he say?"

Bai smirked. "He said his offer did not extend to Fen or me."

She called out to Jin. "We used Bai's sat phone to call for help. Federal agents and local police will be swarming all over you very soon." Even from a distance Belle could see the confident smile spread on Jin's face.

"You do not lie well, Ms. Bannon. An admirable quality. The last thing the traitor Bai wants is to face federal authorities. I will give you five minutes to decide. After that, no matter what you might say or do, I'm afraid you all will die. Non-negotiable."

"*Nooo!*" Jenny wailed as Alonzo covered the baby with his jacket.

Belle could see Nora struggling to remain calm so as not to increase Sadie's fear even higher.

"I need a knife," Nora said, the tone of her voice forced unnaturally low.

Belle had a small penknife in her pocket, and Quanah's knife still rested on top of the bar. A thin dagger appeared in Fen's hand. Where had it been hidden? A sleeve? She took one step toward the child with the knife raised. Belle was about to tackle her when she slashed the dagger through the air and slit the umbilical cord. Nora quickly knotted the cord and laid the child on his mother's breast. Fen slipped the dagger into her belt, no longer hidden.

Belle walked over to the bar, opened the jade box, and removed the envelope.

Bai was alarmed. "What are you doing?"

Nora asked, "Can we trust Jin?"

"Jin is acting on behalf of his government," Alonzo said. "His mission is simple—keep the agreement hidden, or, if it surfaces, destroy it. He will not hesitate to kill us if necessary, but only if necessary."

Scout had made his way to Jenny's side and lain down next to her, protective. The new mother held her child close to her breast, scared out of her mind. Belle didn't give a shit about the agreement and couldn't care less whether her country owned a port in China. She needed to do anything and everything possible to save Jenny, Nora, Sadie, and the baby. Besides, if Jin took custody of the agreement there could be no chance of triggering a war with China.

Without a word, Bai, with Nora's gun in hand, stepped to the edge of the window.

Belle saw what he was about to do. "No, stop—" She lunged for him. Too late. He fired three shots from Nora's gun toward Jin as she crashed him to the floor. Almost instantly a blanket of bullets slammed into the saloon. Jenny and Sadie screamed.

Belle's first impulse was to fire a bullet into the back of Bai's head, but he was watching her out of the corner of his eye, and the last thing she wanted was a shoot-out in close quarters. Could she count on Jin renewing his offer?

Belle yelled out the window. "Jin . . .!"

Another fusillade of fire stitched across the saloon wall.

Non-negotiable. *Shit.*

They returned fire. One more of Jin's men fell. Both Alonzo and Belle were out of ammo.

Belle reached for the ammo box. Empty. The ammo box for Nora's gun was also empty.

She turned to Bai, struggling to keep from strangling the son of a bitch. *Bedfellows.* "How many rounds left, asshole?"

He checked the weapon. "One."

CHAPTER 40

Bai easily read Belle's mind. He moved next to Jenny and aimed the gun at her head. "Just in case you have any more ideas about surrendering to Jin."

One bullet. Belle felt confident she, Alonzo, and Nora, could overpower him, but Jenny would be dead. And the lethal Fen stood erect in the corner, seemingly oblivious to the gun battle surrounding her.

So, now what? Belle remembered how the wounding of Quanah Parker had demoralized Quanah's men and marked the beginning of the end during the Adobe Walls battle. She peeked out the window. Jin still remained crouched behind the opened car door. Even given the long distance she could make out a few black dots on the door where it had stopped their bullets from reaching Jin.

"Our only hope is to kill Jin," Belle said. "Give me the gun, or you take the shot." He paused for a moment, obviously weighing the odds, then shook his head. He figured that single bullet pointed at Jenny was the only thing preventing them from giving him and Fen up to Jin. "Great. Then what's your plan?"

He glanced at Fen; they both appeared uncertain.

More fire from outside. Belle's eyes fell on her bow. Was it possible? An eighty-yard shot was beyond a stretch, but Bai was leaving her with no choice. She reached for the bow. Her quiver contained five two-blades and a specialty Trocar arrow. Unique because its razor-sharp blades did not run from the tip, the Trocar's blades, multi-faced like a pyramid, began below the tip and hugged the shaft. Once the blades pierced the target they flared out like an umbrella. The arrow could penetrate bone, then when the blades flared out, cause significant damage. Would the Trocar penetrate glass? She had no idea.

Belle couldn't shoot through the wall holes and would have to use the window. She peeked out to see Jin still crouched behind the van door peering at them through the glass. Little more than his head and the top of his shoulders were visible. A near impossible shot even if the Trocar did penetrate the glass. And if it did and the umbrella blades opened, would the blades so configured still penetrate a human body? She thought so but wasn't certain. If Jin were seated in the driver's seat behind the windshield the arrow couldn't penetrate. A shot from a crossbow, maybe, but not from the Hoyt. Still, the side window glass wasn't as thick. Possible. Not likely, but possible.

Another problem. The moment she stepped into the window to fire there was an excellent chance she'd be killed before she could pull back the bowstring.

She had an idea and turned o the others. "I need a diversion."

A long moment of silence, then Nora half crouched, half crawled over to the bar and pulled the three bottles of whiskey off the shelf. She uncorked the bottles, and a foul odor immediately filled the room.

Belle understood what she was doing. "Find a wick."

Fen's dagger flashed into her hand and she cut into a grain sack leaning against the wall. In a moment she handed three strips of burlap to Nora, who stuffed them into the bottles' necks.

Nora maneuvered to the north door, as far away from the window as possible. Bai turned over the gun to Fen who kept it loosely aimed now at Sadie while Bai followed Nora. He pulled a lighter from his pocket and lit the wicks. Nora lifted the heavy cross-timber securing that door and pushed it open just enough for Bai to have room. One after another he threw the bottles as far away from the saloon as he could.

Belle watched from the corner of the window as the first one dropped into the grass. Nothing happened. Then the second and third bottle exploded. Gunfire from Jin's men stopped, their attention diverted to the explosions. She only had a couple of seconds.

She nocked the arrow, stepped in front of the window and pulled back on the bowstring until the eccentrics engaged, then pulled back farther than she ever had before. She needed eighty yards, maybe even more. The bow was only sighted for fifty, and she would have to estimate how high to aim. She watched Jin's head through the glass turn toward the fire. She aimed, took a deep breath, then slowly let it out.

She released the bowstring.

The arrow sailed high through the air, and she lost sight of it.

Then it pierced the van's window glass.

Then it pierced Jin Choi's head.

They heard Jin's men shouting back and forth, some in Chinese, some in English. "What are they saying?" she asked Bai.

"They're confused, don't know what to do. Great shot, by the way."

The sound of more gunfire, but these were coming from the north. Belle risked another peek out the window. A shiny black SUV sped toward them with the driver the only occupant. He used one hand to spray bullets from an automatic rifle across the heads of Jin's men while steering the truck with the other. A few seconds later Belle identified the driver Steve Kelly.

Bai fired the last bullet. Jin's men didn't know they were out of ammo; they'd watched their leader die and had to assume they were about to be caught in a crossfire. Kelly stopped firing. Bai came to the window and shouted out at Jin's men in Chinese.

"What did you say?" Belle asked.

"I told them if they gathered up their fallen and left immediately, they would not be harmed."

And that's precisely what they did. They watched what was left of Jin's men lift their dead and wounded comrades onto their shoulders and hurry off to the SUVs parked in the stand of trees.

"Mommy . . . ?" Sadie ran to her mother's arms.

Kelly drove close to the saloon, parked, and Nora let him in the north door.

He stepped inside and pointed his M-16 at Bai's head.

Belle would've shaken Kelly's hand, but he had both hands on the gun pointed at Bai and Fen. "Again, the cavalry arrives in the nick of time to save the day. Thank you."

Kelly glanced down at Jenny lying on the bloody blanket, her son resting on her chest. "I see we have a new member of the team. Congratulations."

Jenny smiled up at him. "Thanks."

Alonzo asked, "Where's Stella?"

"Right behind me with reinforcements, but looks like they're unnecessary."

Belle yanked Bai's sat phone from his pocket. "I better call Ben, make sure he knows we're safe." Kelly seemed like he was about to object, but she quickly placed the call and put the phone in speaker mode. When Ben answered, she could hear the hesitation in his voice, probably because he didn't recognize the number.

Belle felt almost giddy with relief. "It's me. Just want to let you know we found Jenny and Sadie and everyone's safe, thanks in large part to your State Department friend, Steve Kelly. I have you on speaker. He's right here."

Ben paused, and when he spoke the confusion was evident in his tone. "My friend's name is Steve Jankowitz. Who the hell is Steve Kelly?"

Belle froze and turned to see Kelly now aiming the M-16 at her head.

Kelly whispered, "End the call."

"Have to run, thanks again for your help. See you later." She terminated the connection.

Kelly actually looked apologetic. "Sorry, Belle."

Nora's jaw dropped. "Oh, my God."

Alonzo's jaw clenched, and his eyes shot fire at Kelly. "You son of a bitch."

"I assume Stella isn't on the way with reinforcements," Belle said.

"She doesn't know I'm here."

"Fen has it," Bai said.

Jenny pulled her new son close. "I-I don't understand."

Belle thought she did. "I'm guessing Bai and his sidekick aren't the only ones who went rogue." Belle noticed Nora slipping away from Sadie and inching along the wall while their conversation with Steve continued. She had no idea what Nora was doing but pressed forward to keep the focus away from her friend. "Stevie here came to know Bai as an opponent in the field. Brotherhood of spies and all that. The prospect of the hundreds of millions of dollars they knew China would pay for the agreement was too tempting to pass up."

"What about Mao?" Jenny asked. "I heard Bai talking to someone he called Mao."

Bai grinned. "Mao means cat in Mandarin."

Belle didn't get it. Then she got it. "Kentucky Wildcats. Cats for short."

"I didn't want Bai using my real name on the phone," Kelly explained. "I know, probably a little too cute."

"I can't believe it," Alonzo said. "I looked up to you. I'm new to the organization, but I can tell you that everyone looked up to you. You have to know that all of your former colleagues will leave no stone unturned to hunt you down."

While Alonzo spoke, Belle spotted Nora out of the corner of her eye at the bar. *Quanah's knife!*

Kelly projected an air of confidence that was a bit unnerving. "Not so. No one in the American government knows about the agreement. You're right, Belle. I found out about it through Bai. And the amount China will pay us is a pittance compared to what would happen if America claimed the Liaodong Peninsula and Lüshun, Naval Base. Understandably, the Chinese aren't going to be too happy with Bai and Fen, but several hundred mill will go a long way toward keeping the dogs at bay."

Belle spoke forcefully, making her case with a confidence she didn't feel. "Ben knows an agreement existed, and he now knows someone named Steve Kelly helped rescue the hostages."

"He doesn't know you found the agreement, and he's unaware of its contents. If he asks too many questions, he'll become an unexpected victim of a tragic accident."

Jenny clung tight to her child. "Okay, you have what you want. Now get the hell out of here and leave us alone."

The silence that followed swelled as each second passed. Finally, Belle stated the obvious. "They can't let us live. We know what's in the agreement. And we know Stevie here's a traitor and a thief."

Kelly shrugged. "I'm sorry."

Maybe Belle was getting soft, but part of her actually believed he was sorry. She assumed at one point Kelly probably was a good agent, then his head was turned by money. Old story.

"Let Jenny and the baby go. Sadie, too," Belle said. "They can't do you any harm. Even if she did say something there'd be no evidence, no one would believe her. And you're in the business of covering your tracks." She thought Kelly's expression suggested she might be reaching him.

Then Bai spoke up. "Not the time for sentimentality."

Nora was behind them all now, next to a table.

"*No!*" Jenny screamed and rolled to her side, circling her child with her arms.

Kelly swung the gun barrel toward Jenny. Belle was about to lunge for the gun when a black-and-white blur thankfully disobeyed his master's orders to remain down and sprang through the air. Scout's jaw clamped down hard on Kelly's wrist, and he screamed in pain. A rerun of the scene at the museum that seemed months not days earlier. Kelly released the gun from his grip. Belle scooped it out of the air and in one motion smashed the butt down hard on Kelly's head sending him crumpling to the floor.

Bai rushed her before she had time to fully train the gun on Jenny's kidnapper. With a swift arm under the man's chin, Alonzo clotheslined him, and he dropped like a rock, gagging, clutching his throat.

Belle turned and aimed the gun at Fen. Suddenly like magic the gun was out of her hands, skidding across the floor, and Fen's foot was in her face.

For a split second the magician was off balance.

"*AIEEEEE!*"

Belle turned to see Nora leap from a table, springing high into the air. Her long black hair flew wild, her eyes opened wide, her expression contorted with rage. She gripped Quanah's knife tight in her right hand.

The Comanche warrior.

Fen spun in a flash while at the same time pulling her knife from her belt.

Nora landed on Fen full force, knocking them both to the floor. The fall delayed Fen a micro-second before she could bury her dagger into Nora's back. But that blink of time was all Nora needed to drive Quanah's knife through the assassin's right eye all the way to the hilt.

Fen's shriek immediately cut off. Her arm flopped away, and the dagger fell to the floor. blood gushed from the dead woman's eye socket.

"You steal my child and massacre her father?" Nora's voice lowered to a growl *"Unu tuyaaitu kwasinaboo!* Die, you snake!"

Bai coughed and propped himself up on his elbows. He crawled fast across the room to Kelly's gun where it lay under the bar. Belle landed on top of him just as his fingers wrapped around the barrel.

Bai turned on his back and swung the M-16 at her head. She blocked the blow and ripped the weapon from his grasp. Bai snarled and jammed his thumbs toward her eyes. She expected the move and pressed down on his windpipe. Defense trumps offense, and he dropped his hands to try to peel hers away from his throat.

The lizard door cracked open. This man tried to kill Nora and would have killed Sadie, Jenny, and her infant child without an ounce of remorse. She glanced up first at Nora— not the time for Comanche chants of inner peace; she nodded her approval—then to Alonzo. She was sure part of him wanted Bai alive so he could be questioned. Fortunately, the other part of him prevailed and he stepped back. Belle allowed the lizard door to open wide, and she welcomed the intoxicating flood of white light. She squeezed, then squeezed harder. Then squeezed with every ounce of strength she possessed, even beyond the point where she knew he was dead.

"Belle!" Jenny's voice?

"Belle!"

Belle allowed the white light to retreat. She rolled off Bai's body to see Kelly staggering over Jenny. Belle froze in horror. Kelly was holding the squealing baby.

"Kick the gun over here, or I snap the kid's neck."

Nora and Alonzo were both ready to pounce, but wisely held off.

Belle picked up the M-16 and slowly moved toward Kelly. "You're now a baby killer, Steve?"

Shed of his cool control aura, Kelly shouted, "Shut the fuck up and gimme the gun!"

Belle walked toward him, trying to quickly come up with a plan, but him holding the baby eliminated every play. She gave him the gun. He crouched down and handed the infant to his mother.

"Actually, I owe you all a debt of thanks," Kelly said. "Now I won't have to split the money three ways."

"And how are you going to explain six dead bodies including a newborn?" Alonzo asked.

A cold grin. "Easy. I'll blame it all on Bai. This M-16 is untraceable to me. I wipe it down. When I arrived, everyone was—"

"No!" Jenny lashed out a kick to the back of Kelly's knee. He stumbled forward and tripped to the floor, landing on his back. But he still maintained his grip on the gun. Belle had no weapon.

Yes, she did.

She snatched Quanah's lance from the floor. Just as Kelly's finger tightened on the trigger she thrust the blade deep into his chest, easily penetrated the breastbone, and sliced his heart in half.

Belle barely heard the sounds around her . . .

Sadie screaming.

Nora trying to comfort her.

Scout barking.

Jenny trying to soothe her new son.

Alonzo's comforting arm around her shoulder.

She only knew that the third battle of Adobe Walls was over. Jenny, her baby, and Sadie were safe.

And they'd won.

EPILOGUE

T he podium looked out of place rising from the prairie grass in front of Hanrahan's Saloon.

Three weeks had passed since the third battle of Adobe Walls. As far as the world was concerned, the kidnappers' sole interest had been the Hudie Box itself, easy to understand given its great monetary value. The box had been returned to the Theodore Roosevelt Association and would be displayed in the president's Sagamore Hill study. The Association was delighted to receive the artifact, and as a token of its appreciation the trustees decided to make a contribution to the Panhandle Plains Museum for use in completing the Adobe Walls reconstruction.

Before returning home to Park City, Belle and Nora had driven to Carlsbad and met with Lizzie Parker. They'd returned the bracelet and were glad to see Lizzie recovering nicely from her wound. Lizzie had been devastated by her dad's violent death, and though she'd been polite and said all the right things, Belle could tell the young woman held her and Nora partly responsible. Belle couldn't blame her in the least. If they hadn't suddenly dropped into the lives of Lizzie and Neville, Lizzie's world would look much different than it did now.

Belle had spent the last weeks leading fly-fishing excursions on the

Provo River. When Nora invited Scout and her down to witness the ceremony, she took a couple days off.

About a hundred people gathered around the podium, including Uncle Sal and Aunt Helen. Her aunt had fully recovered from the cardiac incident and looked the picture of health. Holding Jenny's new son in her arms was the best medicine anyone could prescribe.

The baby—named Thomas Samuel after his maternal grandfather —was wrapped in a new quilt Belle had made for him. Jenny wanted traditional pastel-colored bunnies, balloons, and teddy bear designs, and that's what she got. When the kid was old enough to understand, Belle intended to make him a red and black quilt simulating a traditional Comanche blanket with an image of Quanah's war lance appliquéd in the center. She'd become so familiar with the lance she wouldn't need to reference any photographs when creating the image. The boy needed to be reminded of his mom's courage in bringing him into this world. Jenny and her fiancé, looking quite handsome in his Marine dress uniform, stood next to Helen. Scout found the ceremony boring and ran off chasing critters in the grass. Belle spotted Stella Alvarez, Steve Kelly's old partner, on the other side of the crowd. She waved.

All eyes were on Nora Parker Yates at the podium. A representative from the Roosevelt Association, a man who actually looked like Teddy Roosevelt, presented Nora with a sizable check that would cover half the expenses needed to complete the Adobe Walls restoration. Nora held up Quanah's lance and explained to an enthralled audience how the symbols led them to Adobe Walls.

The last time Belle had seen that lance its blade had been buried deep inside Steve Kelly's chest. When the dust settled, she'd immediately used Bai's sat phone to call the EMT's, then Uncle Sal. Next, Alonzo made some calls back to Washington and contacted the Lubbock authorities to report the murder of Buck Yates.

After the ambulance transported Jenny and her new son to the hospital in Stinnet, they'd been questioned by the local police. When Alonzo flashed his creds and pointed out Kelly was an INR agent, the sergeant called the Feds and spoke to Stella. Whatever she told him worked, and they were free to go without further questions.

They'd left Adobe Walls and hurried to the hospital where they met

Uncle Sal and Aunt Helen. The new mother and new child were doing great. Belle, Scout, and Alonzo had accepted Nora's kind offer of dinner and use of her guestroom. With all that had happened, one would think she and Alonzo would be so mentally and physically exhausted that all they did was sleep.

One would be wrong.

The next morning, they weren't surprised when Stella appeared at Nora's front door. She was accompanied by a squirrelly fellow—fifties, slight, balding, wearing an expensive suit, saggy socks, and an air of self-importance. Alvarez introduced him as deputy under assistant something-or-other from the State Department. Belle forgot his name a moment after she said it.

Nora offered coffee, he declined. All business.

The suit came straight to the point. "We'd like to know what was inside the jade box."

Belle, Alonzo, and Nora had remained silent. Alonzo and Belle had previously talked, and he'd concluded that it wouldn't be disloyal to his country were he to keep his mouth shut and leave to her any decisions regarding the Liaodong Agreement. He also planned to say nothing to Stella, so as not to put her on the spot.

The suit looked straight at Alonzo. "Mr. Longabaugh, as an agent of the U.S. government I expect that you will be completely candid in answering my question."

Alonzo said, "My focus was solely on Bai. I didn't pay attention to the box."

Kind of true. True enough. Belle and Nora remained silent.

The fellow waited for a response, and when he realized none would be forthcoming his face turned beet red. He sputtered something about federal warrants and the full weight of the United States, blah blah blah. Belle didn't pay any attention. Alvarez put her hand on his arm, and after a moment he quieted.

"There's a rumor the box contained an agreement signed by Roosevelt," Alvarez said.

The suit jumped in. "Yeah, showing America owns valuable strategic real estate in China." He was fishing. No one bit. He continued. "The president himself would be grateful if you cooperated and might even be willing to thank you personally in the Oval Office."

Belle wasn't really one who enjoyed spending time in any office, no matter the shape, and remained silent.

The suit pressed. "If the rumor happens to be true, the president could demand China's compliance. I don't have to tell you that the image of a strong leader would be very helpful in the upcoming election."

Actually, he didn't have to tell Belle because she didn't give a shit. "What about Kelly?"

The suit cast his eyes down, and for the first time seemed a bit defensive. "We've already announced Kelly died in the line of duty fighting to rescue your sister. We hope you'll abide by this explanation. Kelly left behind a wife and a couple of kids. They need to believe their dad died a hero. Not to mention, any potential for embarrassment to the president would be averted."

Belle could've pointed out that Steve the hero had no reservations about murdering a six-year-old girl, a young mother, and her newborn son. But she didn't. This was their show. She forced all emotion from her voice and expression. "So, you want us to lie?"

The suit offered a cold smile, the kind you expect to reveal pointy teeth dripping in blood. But his teeth were shiny white, perfect. "Small price to pay for your country, Ms. Bannon. You fought for your country. Think of our request as another mission to keep America safe."

In Belle's mind it sounded like the mission was also to keep the president's ass safe. Kelly was dead because she'd sliced his heart in half. The armed forces sometimes glossed over the often messy details of a soldier's death to spare additional heartache for his family. No reason to burden a couple of kids for life with the knowledge that their father was a traitorous, murdering scumbag. She nodded her agreement.

The suit smiled, happy with his small victory. "Good, now, we'll expect to hear from you soon about the agreement. If it exists, it doesn't belong to you, and we'll look forward to you turning it over."

He then spoke directly to Nora. "We appreciate everything you went through, and the president will make sure the Department of Interior makes up the difference in what you need to finish the Adobe Walls reconstruction." He stood to leave and gave Belle one of those double-grip handshakes politicians use only when they want to insincerely impress you with how sincere they are. They'd said their goodbyes, and that had been it. After breakfast, Alonzo left for Washington, then almost immediately to a posting overseas, location unknown.

In the ensuing three weeks, the suit had called repeatedly asking about the agreement.

Belle had remained silent and admitted a certain perverse pleasure in hearing him struggle to contain the urge to scream at her. She finally told him she'd speak to Stella Alvarez after the ceremony.

She now watched Stella wind her way through the crowd to where she was standing. Stella nodded to Nora standing at the podium. "Impressive young woman." They both joined in the applause.

Stella walked away from the crowd, silently indicating that she wanted Belle to follow. So she did.

"It's good to see you again, Belle."

Alonzo trusted Stella, which was good enough for Belle. "You, too."

"I now know a lot more about the obstacles you overcame to save Jenny and Sadie, including taking on three of the most lethal intelligence agents in the world. Amazing you're alive and standing here."

They locked eyes for a long moment, and Belle expected her to ask for the contents of the Hudie Box. She was wrong.

"Belle, we could use a woman like you."

Taken aback, Belle paused a moment before speaking. "Uh, 'we' being the State Department Bureau of Intelligence and Research?"

"INR is one of the sixteen intelligence community agencies overseen by the Director of National Intelligence. He wanted his own elite operations unit, something he can call on in special situations, something that for the most part would remain off-book. He created this special unit and slipped it into the INR budget. Only the DNI, the President, and the Secretary of State are fully aware of its existence." A half-smile. "I believe you know that Alonzo and I work for this group. It's called Raven."

"Seriously? Sounds like a James Bond villain."

"I know. Like Spectre. Everyone hates it, but the head guy's from Baltimore and is a big fan of the football team."

"And Steve Kelly was a member of Raven?"

"I'm embarrassed to say, yes."

"Your offer's beyond crazy." Belle's face reflected her skepticism. "I'm guessing that somehow my cooperation in revealing the contents of the Hudie Box is involved."

"Then your guess would be incorrect. Your decision about the Hudie Box and its contents, if any, that's separate."

"I don't think the fellow you brought down to visit would agree."

"Deputy Assistant Undersecretary Feeney. He's expecting you to honor your promise to give him an answer today, but my offer is independent."

"Well in that case I'm flattered, but I'm no secret agent, I'm a hunting and fishing guide."

"I understand. By the way, we heard from Alonzo a few days ago. I can tell you he's in Europe and is safe."

They heard applause and turned to see that Nora had finished her remarks. Belle whistled for Scout, and a minute later he emerged from the grass with a look like a kid called in from recess. When she turned around, Stella Alvarez had disappeared.

Nora and Sadie joined them. Belle's family stopped to say their goodbyes. She was so proud of Jenny; her little sister would be a fantastic mother. Belle cradled little Tommy in her arms, marveling at the coincidence that the child just happened to be the cutest baby in the world. "Great job, Shrimp."

"Thanks. By the way, love the nails."

"Thanks, I—"

Jenny giggled. Belle wasn't sure why. She thought the periwinkle color was quite becoming.

She returned the child to his mother, and after final hugs, they left. With one more glance at the saloon, Nora, Sadie, Scout, and Belle headed off toward the newly repaired Cherokee.

"Any word on Tyler?" Nora asked.

"The Navy gave him the choice of a dishonorable discharge or treatment at an in-patient rehab facility. Ben persuaded him to take the latter. Is he redeemable? I don't know. I sincerely hope so."

"Given what he was prepared to do to you, your compassionate restraint is admirable."

Compassion? Had the effects of Wayne's Lake lingered? Her voice softened. "I just want him to leave me alone."

"And if he pops up again in the future?"

Belle's expression clouded. "If that happens, I might not be so compassionate."

Nora lowered her voice. "So, what are you going to do with the agreement?"

Before she could respond, her phone buzzed. She checked the screen. Unlisted number. She answered.

"Please hold for the president?"

President? *Which president?* She stepped away and waited for a few moments. Then a flicker, then a FaceTime image of an Asian man in his early seventies filled the screen.

He spoke with a deep voice in near-flawless English.

"Good afternoon, Ms. Bannon. I am Peng Xiao."

Uh, okay. The head dude in China's calling. She doubted if he wanted her opinion on the latest trade deficit. *What the hell do you call the head of China? Mr. President?*

"Good afternoon, sir." Belle had no idea whether it was afternoon in China. Didn't think he cared.

"I would assume you do not hold me in the highest regard since, as you know, I was the one who ordered Jin Choi to eliminate your friend, Ms. Yates."

Belle's tone hardened. "Eliminate. Sounds so much more civilized than 'murder in cold blood.'"

Peng sighed, and Belle could detect a weariness in his voice. *Was that a swimming pool in the background?*

"I do not expect you to believe this, Ms. Bannon, but Jin was a patriot, a man of high character. A man who believed, as I do, that a military conflict between our two countries would be disastrous. Jin died as a warrior for his country. And by the way, he had great respect and admiration for you. Word of your near-impossible archery shot has spread. I join in my respect for a worthy adversary. You are aware of one of my female ancestors, as her image graced the Hudie Box. I have another one, Qin Liangyu. Qin lived in the later years of the Ming dynasty. Her prowess with the bow was legendary, and she is the only woman general listed in the history of Chinese dynasties. Jin did not want to die. But falling at the hands of such an esteemed adversary brings honor to his memory."

Belle knew she was being buttered up one side and down the other. She wished she knew the Chinese word for bullshit. Yet something in Peng's eyes intrigued her. Sincerity?

"I suspect you may have in your possession a certain document. Were that agreement to surface, there is a very real chance our countries would be pushed to the brink of war."

Belle remembered Jin telling them that if the Liaodong Agreement surfaced in China, Peng would be ousted from office. She wasn't sure, but the gravity of the man's appearance and voice that suggested his personal situation wasn't what was motivating him.

She held his gaze and spoke evenly. "The agreement to which I suspect you're referring burned to ashes when a kerosene lamp caught fire during the gun battle at Adobe Walls. So, you should have no concern."

Peng sighed, and his voice weakened. "I understand. Thank you for your time, Ms. Bannon." The call ended.

She returned to Nora who'd been joined by Stella. "That was Peng."

Nora's eyes widened. "The president of China? Are you kidding?"

"Yeah," Belle responded absently, her mind whirring. "I mean, no, I'm not kidding."

"So, what are you going to do?"

Peng's call had not changed her mind. She turned to Stella. "Please tell Mr. Feeney that during the gun battle a bullet hit a kerosene lamp which caused the agreement to catch fire. Unfortunately, it completely burned to ashes."

Stella held her gaze. "I will convey your message."

Worried, Nora said, "If Feeney doesn't believe Belle, would she be in any danger?"

Stella offered a calm smile. "No, because I'll back it up with my personal judgment that you're telling the truth." She shook their hands. "Belle, remember my offer still stands." She turned and headed off.

Nora said, "Was it tough to lie?"

Belle did a horrible job of imitating Feeney's grating voice. "Small price to pay for your country."

Nora responded with only a slight smile.

"Stella knows I wasn't telling the truth. She agrees with the decision."

"So, what are you going to do with this agreement that burned to ashes?"

"It currently rests in the back of my sock drawer, which, I suppose, is as good a place as any for it to remain." She shrugged. "Who knows? Maybe someday, if the political landscape becomes a lot less poisonous, I'll pull it out again."

"What offer was Alvarez talking about?"

"She wants me to work for her. Turn me into a secret agent."

"You'd be great. And you'd be working with Alonzo."

She laughed easily. "Not my thing."

They headed for the field where the cars were parked. Tonight, she and Scout were staying with Nora. Might even grab a bite at the Maroon Buffalo. And tomorrow they'd drive back home to Utah.

Her phone pinged. A single tap, and the screen filled with the smiling image of the Sundance Kid's descendant. Her face brightened.

"You missed a great ceremony," she said.

"Sorry I couldn't make it. But I'm going to be in DC at the end of the week for a few days. Any interest in visiting your nation's capital? Love to see you. And, no pressure, but I wanted to talk to you again about joining our group."

"You mean Raven?"

"Yeah. Hokey name, I know."

The last time she'd been in Washington she'd thrown a man down the Exorcist Steps to his death and been assaulted by an ex-boyfriend. No warm fuzzies about DC at the moment. And she wasn't particularly interested in revisiting the ridiculous subject of becoming a clandestine government agent.

On the other hand, she really missed the man with the gas-blue eyes grinning at her from the screen.

"Maybe."

AUTHOR'S ACKNOWLEDGEMENTS
AND NOTES

Many thanks to Laura Ranger, S. J. Pierce, and all of the amazing folks at Foundations Books, especially ace editor, Samuel Carroll. Their motto "Where the Author Comes First" isn't just an empty slogan—they live it in every decision they make.

Thanks to Steve Keithley for teaching me about bow hunting and for allowing me to tour his house full of hunting trophies. I felt like I was visiting the Museum of Natural History.

Thanks to outside editors John Paine and Carol Rosenberg for their outstanding contributions in helping to bring Belle Bannon and her adventures to life. And to my official first editor, Anne Pace.

And finally, special thanks to my friend, Jim Lightlizer, for gifting me S.C. Gwynne's amazing book about Quanah Parker, *Empire of the Summer Moon*. Reading this Pulitzer finalist is what started the idea train hurtling down the tracks.

Now a few words about what's real and what's fiction.

The Panhandle Plains Museum is real and was very helpful in providing a photo of Quanah Parker's authentic war lance. The code contained in the bead design is fiction. To the best of my knowledge, the symbols I used to make up the code are authentic Comanche symbols.

Quanah himself, of course, was real, as is most of his history described in the book. He indeed marched in Teddy Roosevelt's inaugural parade and went wolf hunting with the President. The other meetings described in the book—Quanah's visit to Sagamore Hill and the Oklahoma meeting between Quanah and Roosevelt attended by James Amos—are fiction, to the best of my knowledge.

James Amos was Roosevelt's loyal valet and by all accounts was the last person to see Roosevelt alive. Amos's book, *Theodore Roosevelt: Hero to his Valet* was published in 1927. In 1921, he became one of the first Black FBI agents, and his career lasted over thirty years. Vera Amos is completely my invention, and any resemblance to any of Amos's descendants is purely coincidental.

To my knowledge, there is no Maroon Buffalo restaurant in Canyon, Texas, but maybe there should be. Gracie, Texas is fiction; Uncertain, Texas is real. Doll Island exists, but it's located in Mexico.

The Russo-Japanese war was real and focused on Port Arthur, now Lüshun, the home of a key Chinese submarine base and naval base. Roosevelt won a Nobel Peace Prize for brokering the Treaty of Portsmouth ending the war.

The Carlsbad Cavern is real, and while the Chandelier Cavern is fiction, it's largely based upon a combination of other New Mexico caves.

Most of the information about the two Adobe Walls Indian battles is accurate. Sadly, the description of the full restoration of the site is fiction but shouldn't be.

Harry Alonzo Longabaugh, a.k.a. the Sundance Kid, was very real. Speculation about his love, Etta Place, abounds, and she seems to have disappeared into the mist of history. Could she have left Bolivia with a baby in her womb? Why not? But Belle's Alonzo is pure fiction.

Finally, of course, any and all mistakes are mine and mine alone.

Mike Pace
Belleair, Florida, 2022

About the Author

Born in Pittsburgh, Mike received a B.F.A. degree in painting from the University of Illinois and a law degree from Georgetown University where he served on the editorial board of the prestigious Georgetown Law Journal. He taught art in a Washington D. C. inner-city public school before being appointed Assistant U.S. Attorney for Washington D.C.. After a stint as a commercial litigator, he served as General Counsel to an environmental services company before resigning to practice law part-time, thereby allowing him to focus on his first love, creative writing.

He's a member of the Women's Fiction Writer's Association, the Mystery Writers of America, and the International Thriller Writers Association where he's served

on numerous panels during its annual New York Thrillerfest conference.

Suspense Magazine said of his stand-alone supernatural thriller, One to Go, "Completely unique; you hold your breath waiting for the next shoe to drop!" The book also received strong endorsements from NYT bestselling authors such as Steve Berry ("terrific"), Douglas Preston ("ripping good"), and Gayle Lynds ("devilishly clever").

Kirkus Reviews said of his supernatural thriller, Dead Light "Compelling characters ... thrilling plot."

Writer's Digest called Mike's women's fiction book, The Chocolate Shop (writing as J.J. Spring) "Exceptional," and selected it as the magazine's 2019 first place award winner for contemporary fiction (spebook.)

Mike lives in Florida and when not writing or practicing his sax loves long beach walks with his parti-standard poodle, "Handsome Jack."

Don't miss news on the next book of the series! Sign up for Mike's Newsletter here: https://mikepacebooks.com/newsletter/

Stalk him here:

Website: https://mikepacebooks.com/
Facebook: facebook.com/Mike-Pace-Books-101164015106597
Twitter: twitter.com/mikepacebooks

Hell for the Company by Dick Denny

What stands between humanity and the battle of Armageddon? A sword.

But not just any sword - the Fiery Sword that guarded the Gates of Eden after humanity was kicked out. Before the flood, it was stolen by the 23rd Demon kicked from heaven, who eventually married and imbued it into her human son. But now she's dead, and it's starting to manifest. Humanity's only hope? Nick Decker, a scotch-swilling PI armed with a .45 and the Wrath of God, his nerdy ninja-stripper girlfriend Gretchen, and his loyal acid-dropping, street-doc, war-buddy Jammer. It's up to them to keep the battle of Armageddon from happening... and find the Devil's lost dog.

Hell for the Company is Book One in the Nick Decker trilogy, a Supernatural Thriller series.

www.ingramcontent.com/pod-product-compliance
Lightning Source LLC
Chambersburg PA
CBHW070831280626
47161CB00015B/433